Take Your Breath Away

ALSO BY LINWOOD BARCLAY

Find You First

Elevator Pitch

A Noise Downstairs

Parting Shot

The Twenty-Three

Far from True

Broken Promise

No Safe House

A Tap on the Window

Never Saw It Coming

Trust Your Eyes

The Accident

Never Look Away

Fear the Worst

Too Close to Home

No Time for Goodbye

Stone Rain

Lone Wolf

Bad Guys

Bad Move

Take Your Breath Away

A Novel

Linwood Barclay

HARPER LARGE PRINT

An Imprint of HarperCollinsPublishers

TAKE YOUR BREATH AWAY. Copyright © 2022 by NJSB Entertainment Inc. All rights reserved. Printed in the United States of America. No part of this book may be used or reproduced in any manner whatsoever without written permission except in the case of brief quotations embodied in critical articles and reviews. For information, address HarperCollins Publishers, 195 Broadway, New York, NY 10007.

HarperCollins books may be purchased for educational, business, or sales promotional use. For information, please e-mail the Special Markets Department at SPsales@harpercollins.com.

FIRST HARPER LARGE PRINT EDITION

ISBN: 978-0-06-324181-7

Library of Congress Cataloging-in-Publication Data is available upon request.

22 23 24 25 26 LSC 10 9 8 7 6 5 4 3 2 1

For Neetha

Take Your Breath Away

Prologue

"We can simply kill them, but there are alternatives you might want to consider."

"If we even have any," Brie Mason said. "Maybe it's just one."

"Oh," said the man with the name CHARLIE stitched to the front of his gray coveralls, "you never have just one."

Brie felt her heart sink. "You're joking."

Charlie was on his knees in front of the kitchen sink, the lower cupboard doors open, waving a flashlight around in there.

"Well, mice aren't exactly loners, if you know what I mean. They're social little creatures and they like hanging out with other little mousies." Charlie squinted.

"I'm seeing what could be a couple turds back there under the trap."

"I haven't put out any traps," Brie said.

"Not that kind of trap," Charlie said. "The drain, under the sink."

"Oh, of course," Brie said, thinking she should know better, what with her husband being a contractor and all. She leaned back on the kitchen island, arms folded across her chest in a mock-supervisory pose. "So, by *turds*, you mean droppings."

"Looks like it," he said. "You had mice before?"

"Not that I know of. We haven't been here all that long. Can you, I mean, can you tell how old those droppings might be?"

Charlie chuckled. "Well, I don't exactly know how to do carbon dating on them or anything. If you're not sure you have them, what prompted you to call?"

"I thought I heard something last night," she said. "Some rustling. I was sitting here in the kitchen and it was very quiet. My husband's away, and—"

She stopped herself. Brie hadn't meant to say that. You don't let on that your husband is away when you have a strange man in the house. Not that Charlie was *strange*. He was a state-licensed exterminator, wasn't he? Although, she had to admit, he was a bit of an oddball. Huge, graying handlebar mustache with waxed, upturned peaks like he'd just come off the set of some Wild West flick. Put a top hat on him and he'd look like the guy who ties the girl to the tracks. Before he'd come into the house he'd stood on the front step finishing a cigarette right down to the filter, drawing in hard on those last couple of puffs as if he needed them to sustain him through whatever was to come.

Once he entered the house, Brie nearly passed out from the smell of tobacco, which seemed to waft off his entire body. Those coveralls, she figured, hadn't seen a dry cleaner's since Will Smith had a sitcom.

Aroma aside, he seemed professional enough, but still, you didn't blurt out that you were on your own. She blamed her carelessness on the fact that she was already on edge. Bigger things on her mind than a few mice finding their way into the house.

"Out of town on business, is he?" Charlie asked, turning off the flashlight, putting one hand on the counter's edge to help pull himself up. "Knees not what they used to be," he said.

"I expect him back anytime now," Brie said, nervously twisting the silver choker necklace at the base of her throat. The truth was, Andrew wasn't due home from their place on the lake until sometime tomorrow, probably late Sunday afternoon. Of course, that could change, if things went the way Brie thought they might. His friend and business partner, Greg Raymus, was up there with him, at his own lake house, a stone's throw away. They'd both gone up Friday, and Brie had a feeling their guys' weekend might not go as smoothly as planned.

"What sort of work does he do?" Charlie asked.

"A contractor," Brie said. "Small- to medium-sized projects. Strip malls, town houses, fast-food joints, that kind of thing."

Charlie made a face, his eyes darting about the kitchen for half a second, as though making a judgment. "Okay," he said.

Brie laughed nervously. "Let me guess. You're thinking this isn't much of a house for a contractor."

"Didn't say that."

"What you see here is the *before* picture. The place needs a lot of work. We're at that point where we have to decide whether the place can be renovated, then maybe flip it, or whether it makes more sense to tear the entire house down and rebuild. We're one of the oldest houses on Mulberry." She shrugged. "In the meantime, I'd rather not be sharing the place with little furry rodents."

He smiled, showing off two rows of brown, tobacco-stained teeth. "Well, I don't blame you there. There's a couple things I can do." He sniffed, ran his index finger across the bottom of his nose, careful not to disrupt the perfect symmetry of his mustache. "I can put some traps around, like glue traps and the conventional spring-loaded ones, bait 'em with peanut butter. Put them in the cupboard here, under the stove, out in the garage. Or I can put some poison around in all the same places. Strong stuff. You got pets?"

"No."

"That's good. You wouldn't want them nibbling away on that stuff and getting sick. Downside of the poison is the mice'll crawl away somewhere inside your walls and die and stink for a few days until they dry out pretty much to dust. You ever start opening up the walls you might find some tiny, furry little mouse skeletons."

That gave Brie a shiver.

Charlie paused, appeared thoughtful, and then said, "And there is one other way you could go."

Brie waited while Charlie opened up a large tool kit that looked like something her husband took with him when he went fishing, to hold everything from lures to a first-aid kit. But Charlie's box was bigger. He took out a gray plastic rectangular container, no more than five inches long, about the same shape and size as a stick of butter.

"You see there's a little door at the end," he said. "You put some bait inside, leave the door open, and when the mouse goes in it triggers the door to close."

He demonstrated.

"So when you see the door has dropped, you know you've got him. Then you can take him outside, open the door, and set him free."

"Oh," Brie said. "A humane trap."

Charlie nodded.

"But won't he come back inside again?" she asked.

"So, you go around the house and look for ways he and his friends might be coming in. Fill in the cracks, plug holes. Check dryer and stove vents, in case they're getting in that way. I know it's not as effective as killin' them dead, but it's something to consider."

Charlie's expression turned solemn. "What people forget is, animals have souls, too. Whether it's us, a dog, a cat, even some lowly mouse, we're all God's creatures, you know."

Brie said, "That's . . . an interesting philosophy from someone in your line of work."

He shrugged. "You know, sometimes I'll find something in someone's house and remove it, but I won't kill it. And I won't set it free, either, in the woods or whatever. I'll keep it and take care of it."

"What, in a cage?"

Charlie nodded. "I got lots of little critters I look after. Feed 'em, nurture them."

"Well," Brie said, not sure what to make of that.

"Anyway, back to business. I don't know for sure whether you've got an infestation or not, so let me ask you this: Do you bake?"

"I'm sorry?"

"Muffins? Cupcakes? You make those?"

"Um, not that much. I'm not exactly the world's greatest chef. Andrew, he cooks some." She grinned. "We do a lot of takeout."

Charlie looked disappointed. "Do you have any flour?"

"Flour? Like, for cooking?"

"Yup."

She went over to one of the cupboards, opened it, and pointed to a tin on the first shelf. She brought it down and pried off the lid.

"This?"

"Before you go to bed tonight," Charlie said, "sprinkle that on the floor in front of the sink here. You got mice, you'll see their tiny little footprints in the morning. You don't see anything, chances are you don't have them."

Brie nodded, impressed. "And just vacuum it up after."

"There you go." He put two of the humane traps atop the counter. "Why don't I leave you these, and I'll pop by tomorrow, see if you spotted any tracks, and you can decide how you want to handle this."

She asked what she owed him, and he said they could settle up the following day, once they determined whether she actually had any mice. At that point she could decide on more humane traps, the glue ones, or poisoned bait.

She followed him out to his van and realized she'd stopped noticing the tobacco stench coming off of him. Your nose could get used to just about anything, she concluded.

As he was backing out of the driveway, Brie spotted a familiar vehicle parked on the other side of the street, about three houses down from hers. A blue Chrysler minivan. There was a man sitting behind the wheel, looking her way.

God, she thought. *What the hell is Norman doing there?*

If and when he came to the door, she would politely

tell him to leave, that he had made his apologies and that she had accepted them, and that he should go home.

Sitting in the kitchen that evening, eating dinner alone, she listened for any rustling from under the cupboards or under the walls. Nothing.

Shortly before ten, she picked up her cell, brought up her husband's number from her contact list, and tapped on FaceTime. Seconds later, her husband's face appeared. He smiled warmly.

"Hey," Andrew said cheerily. "How's it going?"

He looks happy, she thought.

"Okay. I interrupt anything?"

"No. Greg's already gone back to his place. Early night. We were out on the water for the better part of four hours. Got a lot of sun. Kind of drained the life out of us."

"You look beat. Catch anything?"

"Other than a burn on the back of my neck, no."

"How's his leg?"

"Limping a little, but pretty much healed. Stumbled once getting in the boat. Idiot. Thinking he could jump down that far. Twenty years ago, maybe, but he's too old for that kind of shit. We both are."

"So, what'd you guys talk about, all that time?"

"I dunno. Usual." Andrew shrugged.

"Work stuff?"

"Some. But mostly just reminiscing, reliving our glory years. Not exactly happy to talk about work, way things have been going." He paused. "And I told him I was done putting you through one renovation after another. If you like where you are now, we're staying. If you want to find your dream home, that's what we'll do."

Brie smiled, as though he might actually mean it this time. "I had someone here today, a pest control guy, checking for mice. Thought I heard something in the walls. He was a bit of an oddball. Doesn't like to kill them if he doesn't have to. A humane exterminator."

"Not surprising we'd have mice. Old house, they've probably got a hundred ways to get inside."

She briefly angled the phone so he could see the floor. "Can you see that?"

"You spill something?"

"It's flour. Exterminator's idea. If I see footprints in the morning, I know I've got company."

"Hey," Andrew said, touching his neck. "Nice to see you wearing that."

She touched the necklace and smiled. "I love it. I'm never taking it off."

"Anything else going on?"

Should she tell him about Norman coming to the door? No, not a good idea.

"Nothing," Brie said. "Listen, I'll let you go. What time you getting back? Should I have a lunch ready?"

"Don't worry about me. Probably midafternoon sometime."

"Okay."

"Love you," he said.

"'Bye," Brie said, and ended the call.

She turned off the kitchen lights and headed upstairs. When Andrew was gone overnight, whether for work or pleasure, she couldn't drop off to sleep right away. She'd read, or watch Kimmel or Colbert, or bring a laptop to bed and watch some rom-com flick Andrew would never sit through.

It was Saturday, so there was no Kimmel or Colbert or Fallon. She picked up the book on her bedside table. It was the latest James Lee Burke, and as was often the case, Robicheaux was having a hard time trying to stop his friend Cletus from ripping someone's head off. Shortly after midnight, having read only two pages, she felt her eyelids slamming shut.

She hit the light and went to sleep.

Brie woke shortly before five and couldn't get back to sleep, wondering whether there were any tiny footprints in the flour in front of the sink. Her curiosity won out over her desire to go back to sleep, so she got out of bed, turned on some lights, as it was still dark outside, and descended the stairs.

As she reached the first floor, she felt a tingle of excitement mixed with dread. There was an atmosphere of suspense in the moments leading up to finding out whether there had been any creatures in the kitchen, but at the same time, she was worried about the consequences. Once any infestation was confirmed, she knew she'd go into a cleaning frenzy, emptying the cupboards and drawers of every pot, pan, knife, fork, and spatula a mouse might have touched and running them all through the dishwasher.

Brie held her breath as she entered the kitchen, flicked on the light, and gazed down at the floor.

There were definitely footprints. But they weren't from mice. Not unless mice wore size-twelve boots.

Brie gasped.

At that moment, she thought she heard something behind her. She whirled around.

There wasn't even time to scream.

Six Years Later

Saturday

One

It felt surreal.

Which was kind of crazy. It was the most commonplace of activities, shopping in a grocery store. Pushing her cart up and down the aisles. Pausing to look at all the fresh produce. Checking out a head of cauliflower. Looking for bananas that were still green. Glancing at the dozens of different boxed cereals. Sugary and delicious and bad for you, or full of fiber and yucky and good for you. About a hundred different kinds of coffee. Had she ever noticed before today how many brands there were? Maybe this was why an activity so mundane suddenly felt strange and unfamiliar. It was as though she were doing it for the first time.

Or at least the first time in ages.

She had grocery-shopped a thousand times—and

that was in no way an exaggeration. A thousand, easily. Say you went out for provisions twice a week. That was more than a hundred times a year. And given that she was in her mid-thirties, and had been doing her own shopping since moving out of her parents' home at age twenty, well, there you go. Do the math.

That's a lot of trips to the local Stop & Shop or Whole Foods or Walmart.

But today was different because she really didn't know what to buy. Did it even matter what she tossed into the cart? She'd entered the store without a list. The basics seemed like a safe way to go. Milk, eggs, fruit. A six-pack of beer. She wondered if a list would have been a good idea. It would have helped her pick up things Andrew liked.

Maybe what made this trip feel so strange was that she didn't want to be spotted. Didn't want to run into anyone who knew her. Not at this point. So she kept her head down as she went up and down the aisles. Tried to withdraw into herself. She was thinking that the next time she went out for groceries, she'd pick a place she didn't usually frequent.

At one point, she thought maybe she'd been spotted, recognized, despite the steps she had taken. As she was passing by the meat counter, a man, shopping alone, attempted to engage her in conversation. He was probably fifty, gray hair, tweed sport jacket, white shirt with a button-down collar. Handsome and, she was betting, divorced or widowed, because he was clearly hitting on her.

They were almost shoulder to shoulder when he picked up a roast wrapped in cellophane and said, "How long would you cook something like this?"

Trying to strike up a conversation.

"I've no idea," she said. "I don't eat meat."

Not the best comeback, considering she had already dropped a small package of ground beef into her cart. The man noticed, and said, "Well, you might want to put that back, then."

She ignored him and quickly pushed the cart farther up the aisle, pretty sure she heard him mutter, "Bitch," under his breath.

As she went down the aisle stocked with multiple varieties of potato chips and other snacks, she thought one woman had given her a second look, but then convinced herself that she was being paranoid. It wasn't like anyone had stopped her and said, "Hey, is that you?"

She was starting to wonder whether this shopping excursion had been such a good idea, but she'd really believed it necessary. Anyway, by this point she thought she had enough in the cart, and headed for the row of checkouts. She'd bought half a dozen too many items to qualify for the express line, and wondered whether to put a few things back. But in the time it would take to return them, she might as well go to one of the regular checkouts.

"You need bags?" the hefty woman at the register asked.

She nodded.

"You got one of our points cards?"

"I'm sorry?"

"A points card."

"No, no, I don't have one of those."

When the groceries were bagged and in her cart, the cashier said the total was fifty-five dollars and twenty-nine cents.

"How you paying?"

The woman reached into her purse and brought out three twenties. "Cash," she said.

"Okey dokey," the cashier said.

The woman had her hands on the cart and was turning it around to point it toward the exit when the cashier said, "Lady, your change?"

She'd been so distracted, she hadn't thought to wait for it. She held out her hand, took the money, and dumped it into her purse.

She wheeled the cart out into the parking lot and

opened the tailgate on a black, mid-2000s Volvo station wagon. She put the bags in, closed the tailgate. Affixed to it was a license plate with letter and numbers smeared with enough dirt and grime as to be illegible.

She got behind the wheel and waited the better part of a minute for other cars to pass before she backed out. Given that it was a Saturday morning, when a lot of people did their week's shopping, the parking lot was busy.

"Don't have a fender bender," she said to herself. That was the last thing she needed.

Once she was out of the lot, she headed across town into one of Milford's west end neighborhoods.

She put on her blinker when she saw the Mulberry Street sign and turned down it. There was a lot of activity in the neighborhood today. Being the second of April—one day too late for April Fools', she thought grimly—many homeowners were engaged in yard cleanup. Raking leftover debris from the fall before, jamming it into paper recycling bags. Men wielding leaf blowers that made as much racket as a low-flying jet. A woman ran alongside a girl, no more than five years old, as she learned to ride a bicycle. Two other women stood at the end of a driveway, one of them still in pajamas and a housecoat, each holding a mug and chatting.

What a nice neighborhood, the woman in the Volvo thought. Like something out of one of those 1950s TV shows. Not that she was old enough to have seen them when they first ran, but hey, was that June Cleaver over there, bringing a tall glass of lemonade out to Ward? Was that young Opie running past with a slingshot sticking out of his back pocket?

To think that something so horrible could happen on a street such as this.

Oh, there it was. Her destination was just up ahead.

She put her blinker on again, waited for a kid on one of those motorized skateboards to whiz past, then steered the Volvo into a driveway. She noticed that at the house next door, a man was sweeping the steps of his front porch. She put the car into park, got out, and went around back to raise the tailgate. She grabbed two bags, came around the side of the car, leaving the tailgate open, and it was at this point that she actually gazed upon the house.

It was, clearly, a new build, judging by the architectural style. Sharp angles, huge panes of glass. Solar panels built into the roof. A modern, contemporary design.

The woman stopped, as though she'd bumped into an invisible wall.

"What . . ."

The man sweeping his porch glanced over in her direction.

The woman turned her head to look at the house to the left, then the house to the right, as though confirming to herself that she was in the right place. Finally she focused on the number affixed to the door of the house she stood before.

36.

"Where . . ."

She dropped her groceries to the ground. A carton of eggs toppled from one, the lid popping open and a single egg shattering onto the driveway.

"Where is my house?" she said aloud. "Where the hell is my house?"

The front door opened and a teenage girl with pink highlights in her hair and wearing workout sweats poked her head out. "Can I help you?" she said.

"Where's my house?" she cried, a frightened edge in her voice. "An old house. Red brick. A porch, a railing. Where the hell is it?"

The man next door took several steps in her direction.

The girl said, "Uh, I think maybe you've got the wrong place?"

"Thirty-six," the woman said.

"Yeah, that's right. But maybe you've got the wrong *street*?"

"Thirty-six Mulberry," the woman said. "This *is* thirty-six Mulberry."

"Yeah," the girl said slowly.

"This is all wrong. *This house doesn't belong here.* There's supposed to be an old house here. With—with red brick and a porch, that kind of sagged. *My* house. It was right here. *Right here!* How does a house just disappear?"

"Yeah, well, that house you're talking about? They tore that down like three years ago and my parents built this one. Did you say *your* house?"

"This is not right," the woman said.

The girl shrugged and went back inside, leaving the woman standing there, staring open-mouthed at the three-year-old home.

"This is not happening," she said.

The man with the broom was standing at the property line now. He studied the woman, narrowing his eyes as if trying to improve his focus, like maybe he didn't believe what he was seeing and needed to be sure.

"Brie?" he asked.

The woman glanced in his direction, her face blank.

"Jesus, Brie, is it you?" he said.

Suddenly the woman got back into her car, keyed the ignition, and backed out of the drive, crushing the remaining eggs with the front wheels as she turned, the tailgate still in the raised position. The car's transmission whirred noisily as the car bounced into the street, narrowly missing the kid on the motorized skateboard making a return trip.

The Volvo's brakes squealed as the car came to an abrupt halt. It sat there for half a second while the woman put it into drive, then took off down the street, the man with the broom watching it speed away.

Two
Andrew

I rolled over onto my side, opened my eyes, and looked at the clock on the bedside table. Nearly eight. Jesus. I almost never slept that late. There was some momentary panic as I thought about being late to an appointment with a potential client, then realized that not only was it Saturday, but that my appointment was on Friday and had already happened.

I turned back over again to see whether Jayne was awake and found her staring at me with one eye, half her head buried into the pillow, her brown hair splayed across it. She flashed half a smile at me.

"Morning, Andrew," she said with mock formality.

"It's almost eight," I said. "How long you been awake?"

"Five minutes, maybe," she said. "I was watching you. Woke you up with my mind."

I grinned and slipped one arm around her under the covers and pulled her closer to me. "You have great powers."

"Indeed," she said, and gave me a kiss so light it was as if she'd brushed a feather across my lips. "I can *read* minds, too."

"Okay," I said. "What am I thinking?"

I guess she rolled both her eyes, but I only saw one. "Too easy. Give me something hard."

I smiled. "Amazing. Got it on the first guess."

It took her a second, and then she grinned. "I was actually going to guess French toast. Your usual Saturday morning demand."

"Okay, maybe that, too. In a bit."

Jayne shifted in closer to me, pressing her body up against mine. I caught a glimpse of the open bedroom door.

"Might want to close that," I said.

She whirled around, saw the door, threw back the covers, and got out of bed. Her oversized T hung down almost to her knees. As she padded toward the door, she stopped halfway, turned, and said, "Did you hear him come in last night?"

I tried to recollect. "No," I said. The truth was, I

didn't really listen for Tyler Keeling the way she did. He was her brother, after all, not mine, and while that didn't mean I didn't care about his welfare, he was biologically more her worry.

"I don't think I did, either," Jayne said.

Tyler had texted around ten thirty, promising his sister he'd be home before eleven, or soon after, that he was just about to leave his friend's place. Jayne had offered to go pick him up, wherever he was, but he'd said no problem, one of his other buddies, who was old enough to drive and had his mom's Hyundai, would drop him off. He'd left his bike at home, not wanting to take it out at night in case someone swiped it when he left it outside his friend's house. Locks weren't much of a deterrent when the thief was determined enough.

Jayne had texted, OK, and felt she could go to bed, confident that he'd be home soon after she was asleep.

But now, as she stood between the bed and the door, I could see doubt cross her face.

"I'm just gonna check," she said, and slipped out of the room and down the hall. I sat up in bed and waited. She was back in under ten seconds.

"His bed hasn't been slept in," she said.

"Maybe he's already up." But even as I said it, I knew how unlikely that was. It was Saturday morning. Tyler would not be up early, and even if he were an early riser, he wasn't one to make his bed without being reminded.

"I don't think so," Jayne said.

"Shit," I said, and threw back the covers. I was in a pair of boxers, decent enough to mount a search of the house.

I slipped past Jayne in the hallway and shot a look into Tyler's room myself. The bed was made.

"You don't believe me?" Jayne said.

I went down the stairs and into the kitchen. No sign of him there, either. No bowl in the sink, no half-eaten banana left on the table. Jayne had her phone in her hand and was getting ready to text him or maybe phone him, when I happened to look out the kitchen's sliding glass doors that opened on the backyard deck.

"Jayne," I said.

She was already tapping. "What?"

"Outside."

She came up alongside me and took in the view. Tyler was sprawled out on one of the recliners, arms circled around himself to keep warm, the blue hoodie not quite up to the job. I noticed what appeared to be a smudge of vomit on his sleeve, an observation that was confirmed by the puddle of puke on the deck about four feet away.

"Jesus," Jayne said, unlocking the door and sliding

it back on its track. She stepped out onto the deck, and I was one step behind her, the planking cold under my feet and damp with dew the morning sun had yet to burn off. I let Jayne take the lead here.

"Tyler," she said, standing over him. Then, more sharply, "Tyler!"

He stirred slightly and opened one eye. "Oh," he said. "Hey."

"When did you come home?" his sister asked.

"Um, not exactly sure," he said, struggling to sit up.

"Go in and clean yourself up," she said, waiting as he managed to get to his feet.

As he passed me, I could smell the booze, and the vomit, on him. I held him back gently by the arm and pointed to the mess he'd left on the deck. "Hose is over there, pal."

"I'm not your pal," he muttered without looking me in the eye.

To his credit, he did clean up his mess before coming into the house, but rather than coil the hose back up again and hang it by the tap, he left it in a mess on the grass. He trudged past us as we stood in the kitchen, but not before Jayne reminded him that his shift at Whistler's Market, one of west end Milford's independent grocery stores, started at noon.

Jayne and I went back upstairs, took turns in the shower, and met back in the kitchen about half an hour later, neither of us saying anything. I knew Jayne was embarrassed by her brother's behavior, and maybe waiting for me to say something, but I didn't want to wade into it, at least not yet.

I got the coffee going, and Jayne still made French toast, but didn't bother setting a place for Tyler, who we knew wouldn't surface until the last possible moment. He didn't have a driver's license yet, but he could ride that ten-speed like nobody's business, so the chances of him getting to work late were remote. One thing about Tyler: he didn't seem to give a shit about a lot, but he got to work on time. He liked his money, and it about killed him to pass over twenty bucks a week to his sister in a token gesture of contributing to the household. It wasn't me who asked for the money. It was all Jayne.

When we sat down opposite each other, Jayne picked at her toast, then finally said, "I'm sorry."

I shook my head. "Don't worry about it. I was seventeen once, and—"

"Sixteen," she reminded me. "He'll be seventeen in another month."

"Okay, sixteen. Lots of kids get drunk earlier than that. Doesn't make him an alcoholic. He'll feel like shit today. Maybe it'll teach him a lesson."

"I don't know."

"When I was his age, I'd done far worse," I said. "It's a rough period, and he's been through a lot. He'll be a handful for a while."

"He shouldn't have to be your handful, Andy," she said.

We'd been over this before. No matter how many times I told her I did not mind having her brother live with us, she could not be persuaded.

Tyler had been here nearly two months. He had been living with his dad, Bertrand Keeling, at the family home in Providence. Jayne and Tyler's mom, Alice, had died about five years earlier. Jayne, now twenty-nine, hadn't lived at home since Tyler was ten. He'd been one of those "surprise babies." Jayne's parents figured they were done with kids—Bertrand had always said Jayne was enough of a handful all on her own—but then Alice found herself pregnant when she was forty. The thirteen-year age difference might as well have been a century. Hard to be a "big sister," and all that that entails, when you're already in high school and your brother's in diapers.

Bert dropped dead of a heart attack back in January, shoveling the driveway after a heavy snowfall. Bad enough for Tyler that he'd lost his dad. He was also carrying a lot of guilt. It was his job to clear the driveway, but he'd slept in and his dad had decided not to wake him. If Tyler had gotten his ass out of bed, his father might still be alive.

He went to live with his never-married aunt—his mom's sister—in town, but she soon found that looking after a teenager was something she was not up to. That was when Jayne started wondering what she should do. She felt she'd never really been there for Tyler, and maybe now was the time.

She was going to end our living arrangement and move back to Providence. She and Tyler would live in the family home, which had not yet been sold. She drove up there to explore the idea, see if she could get the house off the market.

"I'm sorry," she'd said to me on the phone one night. "I love you, but . . . he's my brother."

After we had finished talking, I spent an hour or two thinking about her situation, then finally picked up my phone and sent her a text:

Tyler can live with us.

The phone rang in my hand almost immediately. Jayne said, "No, I would never ask that of you."

"It's okay. Honestly. He can move in. There's an extra room. We have the space."

"It's not my house," Jayne protested. "I don't have the right to ask that of you."

"It is your house. It's our home. And you're not asking. I'm offering. You forget what I went through." I reminded her how my own parents had both died within a year of each other. When my father died of lung cancer, I had just turned twelve. Ten months later, as though God himself wanted to show he had a cosmically dark sense of humor, my mother was killed when a drunk driver ran a red light in Stamford and T-boned her Toyota. With no extended family to take me in, I bounced around from foster home to foster home until the age of eighteen, when I struck out on my own.

"I know what it's like to have nowhere to go," I'd said. "I can only imagine how great it would have been to have extended family step up and take me in."

So it was done. But Tyler was less thrilled about it than I thought I might have been in similar circumstances. He had to leave behind his school, his social circle. Leaving Providence and coming to Stratford meant starting all over again. And he wasn't crazy about his sister taking on a pseudo-parental role. The kid was adrift, and Jayne and I believed we were doing the best we could to provide a stable environment for him.

Some days, we felt we were failing.

Later that morning, I was in the garage, trying to

make some sense of the mess in there. The Keeling home had finally sold, and while much of the furniture had gone into storage or been donated, there were several dozen boxes in the garage of family keepsakes and mementos that Jayne wanted to go through. "Photos" and "tax records" and "Tyler stuff" were scribbled in marker on the boxes. I thought I could at least sort them into neater stacks along the garage walls so that we could get both Jayne's small car and my aging Ford Explorer in here.

Seconds after I powered open the double-wide door, I heard the door that enters into the house squeak on its hinges. Jayne had a beer in each hand, and held out the bottle of Sam Adams in her left.

"A little early for this?" I said, taking the beer anyway.

"What the fuck," she said, pushing out her lower lip and blowing a lock of hair out of her eyes. "It's Saturday." We clinked bottles. She was drinking something different, the label on her bottle mostly obscured by her hand.

She watched me take a swig, and frowned. "Maybe we're not setting a good example. Drinking before noon."

I smiled. "At least we don't puke on the deck."

Jayne shrugged. "Got stuff to do," she said, and went back into the house.

I was about to take another sip when the cell phone tucked into my back pocket rang. I dug it out, saw MAX on the screen. I was surprised to see the name of my former next-door neighbor. It had been a long time since we'd spoken.

"Hello," I said.

"Andy?"

"Hey, Max. Long time."

"Yeah, well. It was lucky I still had your number in my phone. Not sure I would have found you otherwise, because, well, I'd heard you changed your last name and I didn't know what it was. You're still in Milford?"

"No," I said. I wasn't comfortable talking about changing my name, and didn't volunteer my new one. "In Stratford now. You cross the Housatonic, it feels like you're in another state."

"So, this is going to sound crazy, and I didn't know whether I should call or not, but I figured this is something you'd want to know about."

"What is it, Max?"

"So I was out front, this morning, and this car pulls in to your place. Well, your old driveway. Not your old house, since they rebuilt on the lot, but—"

"I'm aware, Max."

"Anyway, this car pulls in, and this woman gets out, and she looks at the house and she goes kind of crazy, asking what happened to her house, where did it go?"

I felt the hairs on the back of my neck start to stand up.

"You there?" Max asked.

"I'm here."

"The girl next door, the one who lives in the house where yours used to be, she came out, told this lady it was a new house, the old one was torn down, and this woman looks kind of freaked out, gets back in the car, takes off. Didn't even close the tailgate. Like she'd seen a ghost. Or, I don't know. As if maybe *she* was the ghost."

Max paused, as though steeling himself.

"The thing is, Andy, I mean, I know Brie's been missing six years now, and everyone figures something bad happened, and I don't want to get your hopes up and all, but . . ."

Another pause, and then:

"But I think it was her."

I needed to be sure I understood what Max was telling me. "Say again?" I said.

"Brie," he said. "I think it was Brie."

Three

Statement of Charles Underwood,
June 7, 2016, 12:30 p.m.,
interviewed by Detective Marissa Hardy.

DETECTIVE HARDY: Mr. Underwood, what is the name of the company you work for?

CHARLES: Triple-A Pest Control. We're in the book under AAA Pest Control, so we're the first ones you're going to find if you've got a problem.

DETECTIVE HARDY: And you received a call from Brie Mason when?

CHARLES: Saturday morning. She said she thought she'd heard something in the walls the night before and she was kind of freaked out and she left a message on the voice mail since we don't usually take calls on the weekend. But I checked the message and she sounded pretty upset, so I said I could come over that afternoon.

DETECTIVE HARDY: And when did you arrive at her residence, at, let me just check . . . thirty-six Mulberry?

CHARLES: I guess it was around two, two-thirty. Yeah.

DETECTIVE HARDY: She met you at the door?

CHARLES: That's right.

DETECTIVE HARDY: There was no one else at home?

CHARLES: Just her. She said her husband was out of town, but coming back any minute.

DETECTIVE HARDY: Did he come back?

CHARLES: Not while I was there, no. I had the feeling . . . sometimes, when you're in a house with a woman who's on her own, they get a little nervous. So she might have been saying he was going to be back soon even if he wasn't so I wouldn't try anything.

DETECTIVE HARDY: Try anything?

CHARLES: You know. Make a pass or something.

DETECTIVE HARDY: Is that something you sometimes do? Make a pass at customers?

CHARLES: Shit, no. Sometimes, well, sometimes it's the customers that end up coming on to you.

DETECTIVE HARDY: Really.

CHARLES: Been known to happen. I've had calls, over the years, a woman didn't have so much as a spider in her house, but she calls me to check the place out. Some people are lonely, you know. I'm no prize, I get that, but some ladies, they can be on the desperate side, if you know what I mean.

DETECTIVE HARDY: How long were you there?

CHARLES: 'Bout an hour. Didn't see much evidence of any kind of infestation, although an old house like that, you wouldn't be surprised to find something. If not mice, termites. Who knows? Lots of ways for the little rodents to find their way inside with an old place. You know mice can actually climb walls? Had them come into one house through the outside vent for the fan over the stove. Mice would have had to climb up an eight-foot brick wall to get to the vent. They're a very interesting species. Did you know—

DETECTIVE HARDY: And when did you return to the house?

CHARLES: The next morning.

DETECTIVE HARDY: What time?

CHARLES: Just before eleven, guess it was.

DETECTIVE HARDY: She had asked you to come back? She called you?

CHARLES: No, but I think I'd said something about coming back the next day to see if she'd caught anything. I gave her a couple of traps. The kind that don't kill the mouse, just catch him, so you can take him outside and set him free.

DETECTIVE HARDY: Is that the kind you recommend?

CHARLES: We're all God's creatures. I don't always feel good about what I do, to be honest. Trapping and poisoning things. But we've all got to pay the bills, am I right?

DETECTIVE HARDY: How did Ms. Mason seem to you?

CHARLES: You mean on the Sunday? Because she wasn't there on the Sunday. Neither was her husband.

DETECTIVE HARDY: I mean on the Saturday. How was her mood? Anxious? Apprehensive?

CHARLES: She seemed a little antsy, to be honest with you. But like I said, having a man in the house, that might have made her a titch uneasy. Although I don't think I come across as threatening. Do you think I do?

DETECTIVE HARDY: You seem perfectly charming, Mr. Underwood. Did she talk about her husband? Other than that he was coming home soon?

CHARLES: That was about it.

DETECTIVE HARDY: So, back to the Sunday, the following day. What happened when you returned?

CHARLES: I knocked on the door, but I got no answer. I figured she was home because the car was in the driveway.

DETECTIVE HARDY: Just the one. The one that was there the afternoon before?

CHARLES: Yeah. A little Volkswagen. A Golf.

DETECTIVE HARDY: And the husband, he wasn't around, you said.

CHARLES: Yeah. Whether he was there between the time I left the day before and when I came back the next morning, that I couldn't tell you.

DETECTIVE HARDY: Okay, go on.

CHARLES: I thought maybe she was in the bathroom or went for a walk or was out back. So I knocked again, and waited, then walked down the side of the house and into the backyard, but she wasn't there, either.

DETECTIVE HARDY: And that's when you left?

CHARLES: No, no. I went up to the door there. You go in that way and you're in the kitchen, which is at the back. I called in, instead of knocking. Said, "Hey, Ms. Mason, you there?" And I didn't hear nothin' back. That's when I noticed the door wasn't quite latched.

DETECTIVE HARDY: The door was open?

CHARLES: Not open, just like when you let a door swing shut on its own, and it needs that little push to lock it into place. It hadn't had that push. Am I going to get in trouble here?

DETECTIVE HARDY: Why would you be in trouble?

CHARLES: Well, did I, like, break-and-enter or something?

DETECTIVE HARDY: Don't worry about that. Go on.

CHARLES: The thing was, I wanted to check what happened with the flour.

DETECTIVE HARDY: Flower? You saying you brought Brie Mason some flowers the day before? Or were these flowers from her husband?

CHARLES: Not a flower, flower. But flour, like you bake with.

DETECTIVE HARDY: I'm not following.

CHARLES: Okay, so, if you want to know if you've got mice scurrying around in the night, you sprinkle some flour on the floor so you can see their footprints.

DETECTIVE HARDY: You did that?

CHARLES: No, but I told her she should do that before she went to bed. Sounded to me like she was going to do it. I wanted to take a peek and see if there were any tracks. If there were, then we could get a little more aggressive, dealing with the infestation.

DETECTIVE HARDY: Where was she to sprinkle the flour?

CHARLES: On the floor in front of the sink. I thought I'd seen some turds—you know, mouse droppings—

DETECTIVE HARDY: I get it.

CHARLES: —under the sink area. So I thought, if they were running around, that was a good place to spread some flour.

DETECTIVE HARDY: And you had the impression she was definitely going to do that? Sprinkle the flour?

CHARLES: Pretty much.

DETECTIVE HARDY: We didn't notice any flour on the floor when we went through the house.

CHARLES: Huh. Well, maybe she didn't do it, or . . .

DETECTIVE HARDY: Or what?

CHARLES: Or she saw the tracks in the morning, and then vacuumed it up.

DETECTIVE HARDY: Her, or somebody else.

Four
Andrew

I told Jayne I was making a run to Home Depot for some bags of weed and feed. The scraggly front lawn was clearly in need of some springtime TLC.

Once I was behind the wheel of the Explorer I drove out of my Stratford neighborhood, across the bridge that spanned the Housatonic and headed for the east end of Milford, where I used to live, with my wife, Brie. I avoided not just this part of Milford, but all of it, as much as I could. Not so much because familiar sights triggered unpleasant memories. I didn't need familiar sights for that.

I just didn't want to run into people I knew.

There was still a risk of that, of course, living in nearby Stratford. But at least the risk was reduced, going to different stores, frequenting different restaurants. Had I never moved, still been a fixture on Mulberry, I'd have had to deal with the inevitable questions and comments, even six years after Brie disappeared.

"Have you heard anything, anything at all?"

"The not-knowing must be the worst of it, right?"

"I can only imagine how much you must need some sense of closure."

You could guess the questions on the minds of those who chose to say nothing.

"Did you do it?"

"You feel pretty smug, thinking you got away with it?"

Or just:

"Why?"

I'd stayed in the Mulberry house for the better part of a year after it happened, and would have moved away sooner had I been able to sell the house more quickly. But the place was tainted. Prospective buyers, one way or another, had heard the stories about the current owners, or, more accurately, owner. There was no actual evidence anything grisly had actually happened on the property. It wasn't as if someone had been buried in the basement or tucked a body away in the attic. But that didn't do much to tamp down some potential purchasers' anxieties. At least I was *allowed* to sell it. I'd registered the house in the name of my company. If it had been jointly owned with Brie, and I'd needed her signature to complete any sales deal, the house would still be there, and in all likelihood I'd still be living in it.

The plan had always been to do major renovations on the place, knock out some walls, blow out the attic to make a more usable third floor, redo the kitchen. Maybe live there, maybe sell it. Buying an older house, renovating it while we lived in it, and then selling it, was something we'd done three times before, and Brie was more than fed up with living that way. It was a major source of tension that nearly ruined our marriage. That, and a couple of other things. This house on Mulberry was one we were debating whether to settle in permanently.

The basic structure of the house—the *bones*, I called it—had been good. There was something to work with there, but everything about the place was out-of-date. It needed to be rewired, the plumbing was a catastrophe waiting to happen. I'd ripped away the drywall on some of the exterior walls and found insulation black with mold. The previous owner had been there for nearly fifty years, since the late seventies, and hadn't done much beyond replacing the roof shingles. Those avocado appliances in the kitchen were but one item on a very long list of things that had to go. And that pink toilet in the upstairs bathroom?

"Don't get me started," Brie used to say.

But once everything went to shit, and my life became a public spectacle, fodder for true crime shows and social media speculation, I needed a fresh start. The house finally sold for about ten percent under what I was asking, and I felt lucky to get that. I found my current residence across the river in Stratford, but I hadn't actually bought the place. I found it difficult to make decisions that involved permanence, so I was leasing with an option to buy.

I was, for a very long time, a mess. Having your wife disappear, and hearing the whispers behind your back that you're responsible, will do that to you.

I lost my friends, except for one, and for a long stretch lost work. Nobody was keen to hire the guy who might have killed his wife and gotten rid of her body. I drank. A lot. I found alcohol helpful because when I was sober, I couldn't sleep. At least drinking would put me out for a while.

If I had any real goal in the first three years or so after Brie vanished, it was to achieve a total state of numbness. I wanted to feel nothing. Happiness and contentment were off the table, but I didn't want the flip side, either. The booze helped block the depression and the guilt and the grieving.

At least, up to a point.

One day, waking up fully clothed in an empty bath-tub with no memory of how I got there, I decided that it was time to make a choice. Kill yourself, or get your shit together. I chose the latter. That one good friend helped me get through it.

And I got better, but I never fully pulled out of that dark place. Not until I met Jayne Keeling one day when her car stalled in the drive-through line at McDonald's, blocking half a dozen vehicles behind her, including mine. I came to her rescue, got her car moving, and something just clicked between us.

That was when I forced the door shut on all that had happened to me in the preceding six years. I didn't want Jayne to have even a peek into that room. I was afraid if she knew what I had been through, what some suspected me of having done, she'd walk away. Brie was gone and the world would have to carry on without ever knowing what had happened to her.

And then came the call from Max.

I did not know what to make of it.

"I think it was Brie."

My wife, missing for six years and presumed, by many, to be dead, had shown up at my old address?

Impossible.

I figured, if I went over there in person, I might be able to extract more detail from him. He'd also said a girl living in the house that had been built on the site of my former home had seen this woman. Maybe I could talk to her, too.

I had the sense that my universe, such as it was, was on the verge of some kind of . . . unraveling.

There was so much I had not told Jayne.

Max had been expecting me, and was sitting on his porch when I pulled up in front of his house, parking the Explorer at the curb. He came down to greet me, extended a hand.

"Andy," he said. "Nice . . . to see you."

Nice and awkward was more like it. Max and I had been good neighbors to each other, chatting on trash pickup day when we would find ourselves bringing garbage and recycling to the street at the same time. If he needed a special drill attachment, he could borrow one from me. If I ran short of ice on a Saturday night, Max could provide. Brie and I occasionally socialized with him and his wife, Ruth. A backyard barbecue once or twice a year. But we weren't what you would call close.

Max told me basically the same story he'd related over the phone. The black Volvo pulling into the driveway, the woman getting out and looking at the house, distressed that it was not the one she expected to find. His description of the woman was imprecise. She kind of *looked* like Brie, but he couldn't swear to it. The closest he got to her was probably forty feet.

"But who *else* would be shocked to find the house gone?" he asked. "I heard that the McGuires, who you bought the original house from, have all passed, so, who else would come back here expecting to find a house that got torn down a long time ago?"

I had no idea how to respond to that.

As we stood in his driveway, I looked at the home that now stood where mine had been. It was a dramatic-looking building. Angular, modern, lots of glass. It didn't fit in with the other, older houses on the street, but the neighborhood was slowly evolving, and in another ten years, as more homes came down and new ones went up, no one would give this place a second look.

I noticed, mounted discreetly under the eaves, a small glass bubble. A security camera with a wide-angle view.

I left Max standing there as I crossed the property line, went up to the front door, and rang the bell. It was one of those camera doorbells you see advertised all the time on television. It had the ability to capture a decent image of someone on the front step, but that camera below the eaves would have a broader field of vision.

The door was opened by a tall, portly man in his forties. I wracked my brain, trying to remember the name of the buyer on the property transaction from several years ago, but it wouldn't come.

"Yes?" he said.

"Sorry to bother you," I said. "My name's Andrew. I used to live here. Well, not in this house. But the house that was torn down to build this one."

The man's eyes narrowed. "Andrew Mason?"

I didn't see the point in correcting him. That was my name at the time, and was the name on all the real estate documents. The fact that my name was now Andrew Carville didn't seem important right now.

"Yes," I said. "I know I should know your name but I can't pull it up."

"Brian," he said. "Brian Feehan."

"Right," I said, now remembering that there were two names on the documents. "And your wife is Sonia."

"Yes."

"Your neighbor, Max? He gave me a call a short while ago to tell me about something he witnessed. Here." I waved my hand toward the driveway. "Something that your, I'm guessing, daughter, something she saw as well?"

Brian slowly nodded. "Yes," he said. "It was very strange. A woman. She caused quite a scene. There were groceries spilled all over the place. Is that what you've come for? Because we did save them. We gathered them up in a bag. It's in the kitchen."

"Very kind of you, but no, that's not what I was wondering about." I pointed a finger skyward. "You've got a security system."

"Yes."

"I'm hoping you'd let me have a look at the incident. I'm guessing your system records video, saves it for a period of time. And this would be just a short while ago."

Brian eyed me warily. "Why's this a concern of yours?"

"Mr. Feehan, I'm sure you knew what I'd been going through when I sold this property to you. The personal tragedy I was dealing with."

He nodded. "I . . . was aware."

"Of course you were. It's one of the reasons you were able to get the property for ten percent under what I was asking. It had a history." I didn't know, when I sold, that my house would be torn down and replaced with another. I wondered if the house's notorious past was a factor for the Feehans, or if they'd planned to rip down the house regardless. Had Brie not disappeared, we might very well have taken the same path, and replaced it with something as nice as what the Feehans had built.

I continued: "Without getting into the specifics, Max believes what he saw might have some bearing on my situation. That's why I'd be grateful if you'd let me see what he saw."

The look I saw in Brian Feehan's eyes was one I'd seen before many times in the last six years. *What's your game?* he was wondering. *What are you hiding? Why should I help someone like you?*

"Please," I said. "It's probably nothing, but then again, it might be important."

He studied me for another second, then said, "Wait here."

He went back into the house and closed the door. He returned a minute later with a touch-screen tablet. He'd already opened an app that accessed his household security system. On the screen were four video boxes, like we were about to have a Zoom chat with a few friends who'd not yet stepped into the frames. In each box was a different view of the property. One showed the backyard, two others offered views down the side of the house, and one was fixed on the driveway and the street beyond.

"I'm scrolling back to early this morning," he said. "It's motion-activated, so when something moves into any camera's field of vision, it begins to record."

I knew all that.

He had tapped on the tablet to enlarge the feed that scanned the front yard. He dragged his index finger across the bottom of the image, fast-forwarding through the morning. I'd moved to stand next to him so I could watch.

"There," I said.

The Volvo wagon slowed, turned into the driveway. The car came to a stop, and after a few seconds, the driver's door opened and a woman got out. Immediately she turned her back to the camera as she went to the rear of the car, and by the time she turned to face the house, she was obscured by the open tailgate.

But then she came out from behind the car and took a few steps toward the house.

And stopped. And dropped her grocery bags.

While there was no audio, she could be seen mouthing some words. At this point, she was looking directly at the camera.

The image, however, was not crisp.

"Can you pause that?" I asked.

Brian did so.

I reached out a hand. "You mind?"

After a moment's hesitation, he handed the tablet to me. I stared at the screen for a few seconds, then placed my thumb and index finger on the screen to expand the image and enlarge the woman's face.

It was still a soft image, just bigger. And yet . . .

"Jesus," I said under my breath.

Five

Statement of Andrew Mason,
June 7, 2016, 4:13 p.m.,
interviewed by Detective Marissa Hardy.

DETECTIVE HARDY: Mr. Mason, thank you for coming in again. How are you managing?

ANDREW: How do you think I'm managing? How would you be managing if your spouse had been missing for two days? Not well.

DETECTIVE HARDY: I understand. What you're going through, it's, uh . . . it's a nightmare.

ANDREW: No kidding. Tell me you've found Brie, or some lead as to where she might be.

DETECTIVE HARDY: Rest assured this is a number one priority for us and we are doing everything we can to find your wife, Mr. Mason.

ANDREW: (*mumbles*)

DETECTIVE HARDY: And just to make sure I have all my notes correct, Brie's maiden name is McBain?

ANDREW: That's correct.

DETECTIVE HARDY: But she took your name when you married.

ANDREW: Yes.

DETECTIVE HARDY: A bit of a traditionalist, is she? Most women these days, seems they keep their own name when they get married.

ANDREW: Is this somehow relevant?

DETECTIVE HARDY: Maybe, maybe not. It's possible your wife, wherever she might be, is not using her married name. It's just good to know.

ANDREW: Why would she be out there using another name?

DETECTIVE HARDY: I don't know that she is, Mr. Mason. I only want to know as much as I can about her, and that includes her name before she married you. I think we should move on. Now, I have some questions, and I know some of them are going to seem repetitive, like it's ground we've already covered, but maybe, going through this again, you'll recall something you hadn't thought of before.

ANDREW: You're spinning your wheels here.

DETECTIVE HARDY: I know you may feel that way.

And as I said, I understand, but there are things I'd like to go over with you.

ANDREW: Fine.

DETECTIVE HARDY: Let's go back to Friday night. You left around six? To head up to Sorrow Bay? Where you have a cabin?

ANDREW: That's right. *Cabin* makes it sound pretty rustic, but it's nicer than that. It's got all the so-called modern conveniences. A new kitchen, Wi-Fi. But yeah, it's on the water and it's our getaway place.

DETECTIVE HARDY: And why didn't Brie accompany you on this trip?

ANDREW: It was a guys' weekend.

DETECTIVE HARDY: Just one other guy, yes? Gregoire Raymus?

ANDREW: That's right.

DETECTIVE HARDY: He's your friend and business partner.

ANDREW: Yes. He goes by Greg.

DETECTIVE HARDY: And what is this business again?

ANDREW: We build stuff. Small plazas, businesses, low-rises, that kind of thing.

DETECTIVE HARDY: And you've known Mr. Raymus for how long?

ANDREW: Fifteen years, I guess? We met in college.

Engineering. Been good friends since, formed a partnership.

DETECTIVE HARDY: And you went up together?

ANDREW: No, I told you this. We took separate cars because he couldn't get away as early. His cabin is about a hundred feet down from mine.

DETECTIVE HARDY: How long a drive is it?

ANDREW: Couple of hours. Sometimes a little longer, if there's traffic getting out of the Milford area. Can do it in under two if there's nobody else on the road.

DETECTIVE HARDY: Hmm.

ANDREW: What?

DETECTIVE HARDY: Nothing. So you didn't actually share quarters.

ANDREW: Not for sleeping. We had a late dinner at my place Friday night, dinner over at his on Saturday.

DETECTIVE HARDY: What time did you leave his cabin Saturday night?

ANDREW: Before nine. We're not exactly night owls anymore. There was a time, we might have sat up drinking till midnight. His leg was sore and I think he took a couple of painkillers.

DETECTIVE HARDY: What's wrong with his leg?

ANDREW: He was at a job site, up on a wall that was under construction, and he thought he could make the jump down instead of using the ladder. Broke his left leg below the knee. But it's pretty much mended.

DETECTIVE HARDY: And Sunday morning? What happened then?

ANDREW: I made my own breakfast but went over to his place for coffee around nine, I think it was.

DETECTIVE HARDY: So you didn't see Mr. Raymus between nine o'clock the night before and when you went over for coffee in the morning.

ANDREW: That's right. We did some more fishing and then in the afternoon we both headed back.

DETECTIVE HARDY: Catch anything?

ANDREW: No.

DETECTIVE HARDY: When did you get home?

ANDREW: Just after three.

DETECTIVE HARDY: And Brie, she wasn't home.

ANDREW: *(sighing)* No. How many times have we been over—

DETECTIVE HARDY: But the car was there? And the house was unlocked?

ANDREW: That's right. When I couldn't find her I thought maybe she'd gone for a walk.

DETECTIVE HARDY: So what did you do then?

ANDREW: I called her cell. And heard it ringing in the house. Upstairs. It was plugged in to the charger, next to her bed. That didn't make any sense. That was when

I started to get worried. I searched the entire house. Wondered if she might have fallen down the stairs to the basement.

DETECTIVE HARDY: Why would you think that? Did she have a habit of tripping or something?

ANDREW: No. But things can happen. I was looking everywhere.

DETECTIVE HARDY: When had you last spoken to her?

ANDREW: The night before. She called me. We did a FaceTime thing so we could see each other. She told me about having some weird pest control guy there because she thought we might have mice.

DETECTIVE HARDY: She said he was weird?

ANDREW: Yeah. I mean, nothing really crazy. That he was an exterminator who didn't like to exterminate things. That struck her as kind of odd. Me, too. Have you talked to him?

DETECTIVE HARDY: Yes.

ANDREW: You need to take a close look at him. He was the last person to see her alive.

DETECTIVE HARDY: Well, not technically. You saw her during your FaceTime chat.

ANDREW: Okay, yeah, but he was the last person to actually be with her.

DETECTIVE HARDY: You said he'd have been the last one to see her alive. You think she's dead?

ANDREW: I didn't mean it like that. I have no idea. I'm praying to God she's okay, that there's got to be some kind of explanation for this.

DETECTIVE HARDY: And what about the flour?

ANDREW: The what?

DETECTIVE HARDY: Did you notice any flour, baking flour, on the floor in the kitchen?

ANDREW: She told me she'd done that, to see if there were mouse tracks in the morning.

DETECTIVE HARDY: Did you see the flour on the floor when you got home?

ANDREW: No.

DETECTIVE HARDY: You didn't vacuum it up?

ANDREW: No.

DETECTIVE HARDY: And you had no further chats with your wife after that Saturday night call?

ANDREW: No. That . . . that was the last time . . . I talked to Brie.

DETECTIVE HARDY: Do you need a minute, Mr. Mason?

ANDREW: (*unintelligible*)

DETECTIVE HARDY: Mr. Mason?

ANDREW: I'm okay.

DETECTIVE HARDY: Do you want a glass of water?

ANDREW: No. Yes. Thank you.

DETECTIVE HARDY: So, you called her cell, searched the house. What did you do after that?

ANDREW: I drove around the neighborhood, hoping I might spot her. I called one of her friends, Rosie Holcomb. Didn't want to panic her, just asked if Brie was there, and she said no. Not long after that I called you. Well, the police. I called the police, I think, around five.

DETECTIVE HARDY: That's right. The call came in at five-oh-three. You look very tired, Mr. Mason.

ANDREW: I haven't slept for two days.

DETECTIVE HARDY: Do you think it's possible your wife might have decided to just up and leave?

ANDREW: No. That makes no sense.

DETECTIVE HARDY: Even though you'd been having some troubles in your marriage?

ANDREW: I'm sorry, what?

DETECTIVE HARDY: Some troubles. Thinking about a separation? A possible divorce?

ANDREW: Where the hell are you getting that from?

DETECTIVE HARDY: So you're saying no problems on that front.

ANDREW: We'd been through a rough patch, but we'd moved on from that. Did somebody tell you something?

DETECTIVE HARDY: A rough patch?

ANDREW: Look, Brie had this very brief . . . I don't know what you'd call it. It wasn't an affair or anything.

DETECTIVE HARDY: What's that person's name?

ANDREW: I don't think there's any point in making his life any more miserable than it already is. And anyway, I'd been kind of an idiot myself in that area.

DETECTIVE HARDY: Would that be with Natalie Simmons?

ANDREW: Jesus.

DETECTIVE HARDY: She's the woman you had an affair with, correct?

ANDREW: (*unintelligible*)

DETECTIVE HARDY: I'm sorry, what was that?

ANDREW: His name. The one Brie had that thing with.

Six

Albert McBain pushed tentatively on the hospital room door and stepped in quietly. He didn't want to wake his mother if she was sleeping. He would settle into the vinyl-covered chair across from her bed and play some Reversi on his phone, or take the spiral notebook from his pocket and make some notes for the play he had written and was currently directing, and wait until Elizabeth McBain woke up on her own.

He needn't have worried. As he approached the bed, he saw her eyes were fixed on the television that hung on a swing arm from the ceiling. The headset tucked into her ears was barely visible under her stringy gray hair. Her jaw was moving back and forth, suggesting to Albert that she was grinding her teeth, something she did when she was angry.

Before Elizabeth realized her son was in the room, she said, "Idiots!" under her breath. "Morons," she added.

But then she caught sight of her son standing there. Her grim expression morphed into a smile and, awkwardly with her spindly arms, pulled off the headset.

"Albert," she said, trying to shift herself into more of a sitting position.

"Let me help you," he said.

He got an arm around her back and helped her up, taking a second to glance at the television to see what had gotten her thin blood boiling. It was one of the cable news networks, a panel of talking heads debating the latest scandal out of Washington.

"Hey, Mom," he said. "How we doing today?"

Elizabeth pointed a bony finger at the screen. "You wouldn't believe what that pinhead just said. They just spread lies, without any regard whatsoever for the facts. They know they're lying, but it gets their base riled up and they make money off it. Assholes, the lot of them."

"I know, I know," he said, trying to calm her.

"What happened to facts? What happened to evidence?" Her speech became breathy.

"Take it easy," Albert said. "You get a little winded when you're upset."

She sighed and closed her eyes briefly, composing

herself. "I'm fine." She raised a finger again. "It's just that these lying—"

"Mom, let's talk about something else. How was your night? You get a good sleep?"

Another sigh. "They never let you rest around here. Waking you at the crack of dawn."

Albert nodded sympathetically. "They kind of get going around six a.m. in the morning here."

His mother shot him a look. He knew instantly he'd stepped into it, wished he could claw back his words.

"Albert, you can say it's six in the morning, or you can say it's six a.m., but there's no need to say six a.m. in the morning. It's redundant. It's like saying it's six o'clock in the morning in the morning."

He cracked a smile. "Maybe I was just testing you."

His mother rolled her eyes. Elizabeth had never been able to resist correcting him, or his sisters, when they misspoke. She might have retired nearly two decades ago, but she hadn't forgotten what she'd learned from a career in newspapers. She'd bounced around several Connecticut dailies, starting in Hartford, then back and forth between New Haven and Bridgeport, almost all of that time on copy desks, turning reporters' error-riddled accounts into something that was not only readable, but unlikely to necessitate a correction in the next day's edition. Elizabeth McBain had waged a lifelong war against vagueness, woolly thinking, accusations without evidence. It was a battle she fought on the home front as well. If Elizabeth asked one of her kids how school had gone that day, and heard, "Okay," in return, she wanted specifics. What made it just okay, instead of great? What was the source of disappointment? Was it a friends issue? A bad mark on a test? A forgotten assignment?

Albert fussed with his mother's pillow until she waved him off. He looked hurt, briefly, but he was used to his mother's brusqueness. If anything, her hard-edged nature was one of the things he loved about her most. And he was strangely grateful that, if these were to be his mother's final days, at least they were happening now, and not when that virus was raging. Back then, he probably wouldn't have been allowed in to visit her at all.

"Is your sister here?" Elizabeth asked.

"No. I think Izzy's going to visit later this afternoon."

His mother nodded wearily. "She came last night with Norman." Elizabeth sighed. "What a production."

"What are you talking about?" Albert asked, although he had a pretty good idea.

"She got up here first while Norman parked the car,

and when he arrived she quizzed him about where he parked it. In the lot, he says. They charge too much for parking, she tells him. He should have found a free spot on a nearby street, she says. I looked, he says, and couldn't find one. You must not have looked very hard, she says. I can *always* find a spot. It went on forever."

"I guess you can get a replay if she comes in this afternoon."

Another sigh. "How's the new play coming?" she asked.

Albert's face fell. "We're so far behind. Opening night's less than two weeks away and no one's got their lines nailed down and the set construction is behind and the ticket sales are slow."

"You'll be okay," she said, reaching out a withered hand and patting his. "Things always come together at the last minute. That's community theater for you. They're not professionals. Everyone's got regular jobs, their own lives, just like you do at the bank, you know? They're all volunteers. The important thing is everyone loves what they're doing. And ticket buyers, lots of them wait till the last minute. There'll be lots of walk-ins, you just wait."

"I hope you're right, Mother," Albert said, sounding more like a little boy than a grown man. He almost always called her *Mother* instead of *Mom*. Sounded more respectful, more formal. More devotional. "I don't even know anymore if the play's any good."

"It is, it is," she assured him. "I read it and liked it very much. It's very funny in places."

"It's supposed to be funny all the way through."

"Oh, it is. You know what the word for it is? *Madcap*. It's very madcap."

Albert smiled gratefully, letting his mother's opinion rule. "Thank you."

"How . . . are Dierdre and the children?"

"Okay," he said, somewhat glumly. "Dierdre and I are talking now about a trial separation."

Sorrow overtook Elizabeth's face. "It's a terrible thing to go out of this world knowing there's this to be sad about, too."

"Maybe . . . maybe we can work it out," he said.

"Oh please. I may be on my last legs but I'm still pretty hard to fool."

"Yeah," Albert said. "I know." He paused, collecting his thoughts. "She's a good woman, Dierdre. She's a wonderful mom to the kids. But there's just . . . the spark is gone. And she . . . she doesn't understand that I have dreams, you know? She resents all the theater stuff. It's not my fault she doesn't have something of her own that gives her joy. I've tried to get her involved. With costumes, or handling ticket sales. Anyway. But

I'm there for Randy. I take him to practice. Same with Lyla, anything she needs. She's on the soccer team now." He paused, looked away. "Is it wrong that I have a dream?"

Elizabeth could think of nothing helpful to say.

"One day, some theater person, some producer from New York, will see my work and I'll be on my way. It could happen. What I'd give to walk out of the bank and never go back, never have to approve another mortgage."

"You have a dream," Elizabeth said, almost dismissively. "And so do I."

Albert smiled pityingly. "I know."

Elizabeth broke eye contact.

"The important thing," Albert said, "is you have to get better so you can get out of here, come home."

"Albert, don't," she said. "The cancer's eating me up. If it weren't for all the damn painkillers they give me I wouldn't be able to have this conversation."

"You never know," Albert said. "It could go into remission. You'd have more time. More time to be with all of us."

"Not *all* of you," Elizabeth said.

She closed her eyes for several seconds, as though the conversation, barely under way, had already exhausted her.

"I know," Albert said.

"Dying isn't the worst of it. It's dying without knowing."

"Mother, we all feel the same way." He paused, then, "What about that letter? Last December?"

Elizabeth did a feeble raspberry with her lips. "That nut who wrote a letter claiming to be her? Please. Police get stupid things like that all the time. Bogus psychics, someone saying they saw her beamed up into a spaceship."

She closed her eyes briefly, pinching out a tear on each side. "Even to know, for sure, that she was gone, that'd be something, I suppose. If I believed in heaven, that might be some comfort. The idea that we'd be reunited." Elizabeth shook her head. "But all there is, is this. When you're done, you're done."

"I don't know what to say," Albert said. "We'd all give anything to know where Brie is. If she's alive . . . or not."

Elizabeth's gaze had turned back briefly to the television. "Facts," she said. "The world no longer has any interest in them."

She looked back at Albert, smiled weakly, and patted his hand. "I'm sorry. I don't mean to be difficult. I know you, and Izzy, you're both trying to say and do the right thing. There is no right thing. I'm very proud of you. I'm proud of all three of my children. You and Izzy. And Brie. There's never been a moment when I haven't wondered where she is."

"I know."

"Izzy's never moved on, either," she said. "I'm not saying you have, understand, but it's different with her. It's the hate, her wanting to get even, that's consumed her. It's devouring her. She hates Andrew so much, she's so convinced he did it, that he did something to Brie. I say to her, where's your proof? Give me something, other than a feeling. I think, sometimes, not about whether he really might have done it, but about what if he *didn't*? What if Izzy's wrong? And if Andrew didn't do it, think how horribly we've treated him all this time. He's suffered, too, you know. He lost his wife. He lost the love of his life."

Albert gave his mother's hand another squeeze. As the cancer spread and the end grew near, she spoke of little else but Brie. Would knowing what happened to Brie really bring Elizabeth any comfort if it turned out her daughter was dead?

Albert had his doubts.

"I think," he said tentatively, "if Brie were alive, and knew what condition you're in, she'd find a way to get here, to see you."

The door opened and a male nurse walked in.

"Hey," he said with false cheer. "How are we doing today, Mrs. McBain?"

She looked at her son, rolled her eyes, and said, "Just peachy."

"Just wanted to see if you'd like to get wheeled down to the atrium for a change of scenery?"

Elizabeth shook her head. "No, thank you."

"I'll check in on you again later in case you change your mind." The nurse spun on his heel and left.

Albert leaned over his mom and gave her a kiss on the forehead. "I'll come back and see you this afternoon. Is there anything you want? Anything I can bring you?"

"You know what I want," she said, and her eyelids slowly descended.

Seven
Andrew

I'll admit, looking at that image of the woman standing in the driveway did give me something of a jolt, prompting me to involuntarily let the son of God's name slip from my lips.

But the image was by no means conclusive.

Did this woman—this blurry woman, at that—bear a passing resemblance to my wife, Brie? Yes. She was about the right height. She had dark hair and wore it roughly the same way. Above the shoulders, and curled around her face. The way she moved from the driver's door to the tailgate, I couldn't really say whether her gait was similar to Brie's. It was only a few steps. Not enough to really tell.

The clearest shot was when she stood looking directly

at the house, when she dropped her groceries, seemingly stunned by what she was looking at.

The house that was supposed to be there was gone.

If Brie were to miraculously return after six years, and if those six years for the rest of us had somehow seemed to be no more than a day to her, well, for sure, stepping out of some kind of time machine, finding your house gone and another one in its place, would certainly throw you for a loop.

But the very idea seemed preposterous.

Impossible.

Whoever this woman who'd shown up here this morning was, it could not be Brie.

How could it be? Unless . . .

"You done?" asked Brian Feehan, holding out his hand.

"I want to email myself this image."

Brian seemed to be trying to think of any reason he should say no, and, not coming up with one, slowly said, "Fine, go ahead."

It took me a second to figure out how to export the photo, but once I had, I typed in my own email address and hit send. A couple of seconds later, I heard the ding of an incoming message in my front pocket.

I gave him back the tablet. "Thanks."

"Well?" he said. "Who is that?"

"No idea," I said.

"But you want the picture anyway," he said.

"Sorry to trouble you."

As I started heading back to my ride I got out my phone to check that the pic had arrived intact. And it had, from Brian Feehan's email address. I opened the email, made sure the picture was at least as good as the image from Feehan's tablet—which was not saying a lot—and then closed it.

And wondered what the hell I should do with it. What I was supposed to *feel* about it.

Shocked? Bewildered? Hopeful? Worried?

Bewildered, certainly. I hardly knew how else to react to the picture without knowing what it really meant. Was I meant to believe that Brie was back, after six years?

I had questions, but wasn't sure what they were or to whom they should be directed. But I needed to talk to somebody. I got out my phone, opened my contacts, and scrolled down to the *R*'s. I tapped on a name, put the phone to my ear, and waited for the pickup.

"Hey," he said. "What's happening?"

"Greg," I said. "It's me. How's it going?"

"Been worse. Still buying lottery tickets, though, so I can become a man of leisure. What's up?"

"Need to talk."

"Yeah, sure." His voice went low. "You in a bad place again, man?"

"No, it's not that."

"'Cause you sound sober."

"I am."

"Good, good, that's good. I never want to see you like you were that time. So what's happening?"

"I got something I need to show you. Where are you?"

"You know the old TrumbullGate Mall? The one they mothballed?"

I had to think. Maybe fifteen to twenty minutes north and west of Milford. "Yeah, and I can GPS it if I have to. What are you doing up there?"

"Picking over the bones. One of the owners, an old friend, is letting me go through it, recovering all kinds of stuff I can use before they hold a proper auction. From pipe to shelving to railings and fire extinguishers. All kinds of shit."

"Since when did you do salvage?"

"It's a buck. Anyway, I'm here. Come to the south service door. That's about the only way in. Look for my truck. You might see Julie."

"Julie?"

"She's great. You'll like her. She's easy to spot. Turquoise hair. She's kind of edgy."

"I'll be there," I said, and pocketed the phone.

I had my hand on the door when I realized Max was heading toward me.

"Andy, wait up," he said. "Could you see her on Brian's security camera? Did you see her?"

"I saw somebody."

"Was it Brie?" he asked almost breathlessly.

"I don't know who it was."

Max bit his lower lip for a second. "I hope I haven't opened up some can of worms. I know this whole thing, it really put you through the meat grinder. And you need to know, I never believed any of the bad things they said about you. I heard the rumors, saw what they did to you. But I think I know you, the kind of person you are."

Max paused, as if waiting for me to thank him for not believing I was a murderer. But I said nothing.

"So when I saw what I saw, I was thinking, oh my God, if that really *is* Brie, I had to let you know. Not just because it'd be amazing news that she was okay, but it would blow away that cloud that's been hanging over your head all this time."

"You don't have to worry about me," I said. "I've learned how to roll with all of it."

Max nodded his understanding. "Sure, sure, I get that."

I opened the door and put one leg up, ready to haul myself into the driver's seat of the Explorer.

"One thing, though," Max said.

I brought my leg back down and put it on the pavement.

"What's that, Max?"

"You have to understand, what I did, I was trying to help."

It was all coming back to me, what I used to find exasperating about Max when I lived next door to him. The man always took a long time to get to the point.

"Spit it out, Max."

"Okay, well, you weren't the only person I called."

I waited.

"I put in a call to Detective Hardy. You remember Detective Hardy?"

I definitely remembered Detective Hardy.

Eight

Statement of Isabel McBain,
June 8, 2016, 3:14 p.m.,
interviewed by Detective Marissa Hardy.

ISABEL: Have you arrested him?

DETECTIVE HARDY: No, Ms. McBain, we have not arrested him.

ISABEL: What are you waiting for?

DETECTIVE HARDY: What you told me when I talked to you the other day is not evidence that Mr. Mason killed your sister, Ms. McBain.

ISABEL: Of course it is. He wanted to go off with this other woman. He needed to get my sister out of the way so he could start a new life with her. Didn't want to have to go through all the trouble of divorce. That seems pretty clear to me. I don't know why you can't see it.

DETECTIVE HARDY: That might, possibly, be a motive, generally speaking, when a spouse goes missing. But there is no evidence that Mr. Mason did any harm to Brie.

ISABEL: Because you haven't found the evidence. And you haven't found her. Isn't that evidence in itself? That you can't find her? He killed her and got rid of her body. You really believe he was at his cabin all that time? I know how long it takes to get up there. He could have come back in the middle of the night and killed her and still had time to get back up there. Have you searched his cabin?

DETECTIVE HARDY: We have people up there, yes. Searching the cabin and the woods. The entire property and beyond. The state police have been up there.

ISABEL: That'll be where be buried her. You just wait.

DETECTIVE HARDY: Ms. McBain, I know you harbor a great deal of animosity against your brother-in-law, but negative feelings aren't evidence. But I want to review some of what you told me about Mr. Mason's relationship with Natalie Simmons.

ISABEL: He was fucking her. That's what I know.

DETECTIVE HARDY: When I asked Mr. Mason about Ms. Simmons—

ISABEL: Whatever he said, it was a lie.

DETECTIVE HARDY: He made no attempt to hide the fact that he had a relationship with Ms. Simmons, but he said it was brief, that it was more than six months ago, and that he and Brie had worked things out.

ISABEL: Yeah, right.

DETECTIVE HARDY: What can you tell me that makes you dismiss that?

ISABEL: Brie was devastated by what he did. I don't care if it was brief. If it had only been a one-night stand, that would have been devastating enough, but it was more than that.

DETECTIVE HARDY: So how long was it?

ISABEL: Well, Brie says it went on for at least a couple of weeks. I really had to pry it out of her. I only found out by accident. I came by to see her and I could tell she'd been crying and I got her to tell me what happened. She tried to make out like it wasn't a big deal but I knew better.

DETECTIVE HARDY: How did Mr. Mason meet this woman?

ISABEL: Not sure. I did some checking on her myself and she went to UConn and that was where Andrew went, so I don't know, maybe she was looking up old boyfriends on Facebook and found him, made a connection.

DETECTIVE HARDY: Mr. Mason isn't on Facebook.

ISABEL: Like I said, I guess she found him some other way. At the coffee shop or at the mall. Why are you asking me for details? Isn't that your job?

DETECTIVE HARDY: So far as you know, were there other occasions when Mr. Mason was unfaithful?

ISABEL: Not that I know of but it wouldn't surprise me.

DETECTIVE HARDY: Did Brie tell you she and her husband had patched things up?

ISABEL: (*unintelligible*)

DETECTIVE HARDY: I'm sorry?

ISABEL: She said they had. But I think she was just putting a good face on things. She knew how angry I was with Andrew and she wanted to put him in a better light. Justifying why she hadn't left him.

DETECTIVE HARDY: Have you ever known Mr. Mason to be abusive? Has he ever struck your sister? Did you notice any injuries? Did she, say, have a bruise and tell you she bumped into a door or something like that?

ISABEL: No.

DETECTIVE HARDY: How about emotionally abusive?

ISABEL: Having an affair is being emotionally abusive. Are you married? If your husband cheated on you, wouldn't you call that abusive?

DETECTIVE HARDY: The relationship I have with my partner is not what we're here to discuss today. Can you cite any specific examples where Andrew Mason was

emotionally abusive to Brie? When you saw them together, did he speak disrespectfully to her, threaten her?
Did Brie appear fearful of him?

ISABEL: Not exactly.

DETECTIVE HARDY: Let's come at this from the other
direction. Mr. Mason told me that Brie had also been unfaithful. Do you know anything about that?

ISABEL: No. Did he say who it was?

DETECTIVE HARDY: Yes.

ISABEL: Who was it?

DETECTIVE HARDY: That's not something I'm going
to share with you, Ms. McBain. I want to check out this
individual's alibi.

ISABEL: My guess is it's not even true. Andrew's
making excuses. Wants to justify what he did by saying
she did it, too. And even if it *is* true, it doesn't matter.
The only reason she might have done something like that
is because Andrew wasn't treating her right. It was horrible living with him. You know what he'd do?

DETECTIVE HARDY: Why don't you tell me.

ISABEL: He renovates houses. So they'd buy one that
needed work, and he'd fix it up while they lived in it.
Total chaos, living in a house while it's being ripped
apart. And then when it was all fixed, when they had a
nice place to live, he'd sell it, make some money, and buy
another fixer-upper, and do it all over again. Imagine

living like that. Never having a place that's really home. Brie couldn't take it anymore.

DETECTIVE HARDY: I'm not so sure what you've described constitutes emotional abuse.

ISABEL: All I'm asking you is to do your job.

DETECTIVE HARDY: And where were you this past weekend?

ISABEL: Excuse me?

DETECTIVE HARDY: I'm just getting a sense of where everybody was. Building a timeline, that kind of thing.

ISABEL: We went away Saturday, overnight, to Boston. To see family.

DETECTIVE HARDY: We?

ISABEL: My husband, Norman, and I. And I feel sick about it. If we'd been in town, maybe there's something we could have done. Brie might have called me if she was in some kind of trouble. You know, instead of talking to me, you should be out there looking for her.

DETECTIVE HARDY: Believe me, we're doing that. Mr. Mason insists that he and Brie both felt guilty and regretful about what they'd done, and that it prompted them to reassess their marriage, that it actually brought them closer together.

ISABEL: And you believe that?

DETECTIVE HARDY: Do you?

ISABEL: What I believe is you need to talk to Natalie

Simmons and see what she has to say. Maybe Andy told her he really was in love with her, that he wanted to make a life with her, and all he had to do was get my sister out of the way first.

DETECTIVE HARDY: We intend to talk to all relevant parties in our investigation.

ISABEL: Have you talked to her already?

DETECTIVE HARDY: No, we have not.

ISABEL: Good God, what kind of detective are you? You should have talked to her the moment I gave you her name.

DETECTIVE HARDY: I will. As soon as we're able to find her.

Nine
Andrew

As I drove away from the scene of whatever it was that had happened on the street where Brie and I used to live, I noticed a car coming the other way that was obviously an unmarked police cruiser. You don't exactly have to be Jack Reacher to spot them. Black or dark gray, unadorned by chrome, the cheapest hubcaps money can buy. You'd think the cops would have figured out by now that even a simple ten-dollar pinstriping kit would make it less obvious who they were.

I initially had an impulse to slide down into the seat, below the window, but that's not an easy thing to do when you're behind the wheel. So I sat up straight, back rigid, and tried my best not to turn for a better look at the driver as we slipped past each other. Being a gawker, I figured, would only draw attention to myself.

But I did get enough of a look to satisfy myself it was Detective Marissa Hardy behind the wheel.

Thanks, Max. Thanks a bunch.

She hadn't changed much since I'd last seen her, which had been maybe a year and a half ago. I saw plenty of her, of course, in the eighteen months or so following Brie's disappearance, and sporadically after that. An occasional encounter, to let me know she hadn't forgotten me. She'd probably have visited me more often if I hadn't hired a lawyer, Nan Sokolow, and threatened Hardy's department with a harassment suit.

Hardy still had the short, almost buzz-cut salt-and-pepper hair, the oversized black-rimmed glasses. I'd always thought she looked more like a stern women's prison librarian than a cop, but maybe that's some unfair typecasting of prison librarians. But Marissa Hardy certainly never endeared herself to me. She was humorless and annoying and, I guess I have to give credit where credit is due, relentless. She was not the kind of person you wanted hounding you if you'd done something wrong.

Now it seemed likely she'd be back in my life again, unless she deemed what Max had to tell her as jumping to conclusions, or considered the surveillance video from the house next door as inconclusive. Except that didn't strike me how Hardy would react. If she saw the slimmest opportunity to make my life hell again, she'd take it.

I headed north out of town on the Milford Parkway, and when I reached the Merritt Parkway I took the long curving ramp to get onto the westbound lanes. I stayed on the parkway until I got to Trumbull, where I took the White Plains Road exit. I made a few rights and lefts until I reached TrumbullGate Mall. Took no more than fifteen minutes.

It had been a few years since this place had been a shopping destination. The massive lot was empty, save for part of the south end that had been cordoned off and was full of new Hyundais. A local dealership was clearly renting some space to store their stock. Even though Greg had told me to come in through the south end service entrance, I did a loop of the mall just to get the lay of the land.

All the windows, including the grand entry points, were boarded up. Most malls, considering that they looked inward instead of to the outside, which explained why so many of them were so goddamn ugly, didn't have that many outward facing windows to begin with. The outer perimeter of a mall was usually a maze of cinder-block corridors that allowed stores to bring in merchandise without traipsing it through the main concourse.

I found the south service entrance partially hidden behind a false front that would have allowed tractor trailers to be unloaded without being seen by the public. Tucked in there was an early 2000s Audi A3 in black parked behind Greg's oversized pickup truck. The cargo bed was loaded with all manner of building materials. Scraps of railing, pipe, several mannequin torsos and limbs, undamaged ceiling panels.

A regular door up on the loading bay was propped open an inch with a chock of wood to keep it from locking. I was reaching for the handle when it opened from the other side.

A woman stepped out and was briefly startled to see me, then smiled broadly.

"You must be Andrew," she said. "I'm Julie."

She stuck out a hand. She was almost as Greg had described her on the phone. Short turquoise hair, yes, but also with streaks of black. Petite and instantly cheerful, with a smile that took over half her face.

"Hi," I said.

"Oh hell," she said, and threw her arms around me for a quick hug. "Greggy has told me so much about you I feel I know you."

"Well," I said, a bit caught off guard, "it's nice to meet you."

"I'm just heading off," she said. "Back in a while with more donuts."

I didn't remember Greg being much of a junk food addict. She must have caught my puzzled expression.

"Not for him," she said. "You'll see. Just head in and follow the buzzing and hammering. You'll find him. Gotta run."

She headed for the Audi as I entered the facility. I found my way through the service area that shoppers never see until I reached a door that took me to the mall proper. There's something about a now-abandoned but once-public space that raises the goose bumps on one's arms. The mall consisted of two levels, open through the center so you could look down from the upper concourse to the one below. I'd come in on the lower level, near one of the abandoned anchor stores that at one time had been a thriving Sears, JCPenney, or Kohl's.

Countless roof panels from the upper shopping level that hung over the first floor had come free and were arranged as though set up for some psychotic hopscotch game. Trees planted in interior gardens that had, at one time, brought a hint of nature to the concourse were now dead and leafless. Tentacles of ivy from those same gardens snaked out beyond their enclosure across the debris-strewn floor like some-thing from an alien movie. Water dripped down from a cracked skylight overhead, no doubt from an overnight shower. An immobile, rusted escalator was just ahead, its rubber handrails missing, several steps absent, making the stairwell look like a gap-toothed, vertical mouth.

I saw no people, but that didn't mean I was the only living thing here. A squirrel went bounding up the dead escalator. A couple of pigeons flew overhead. A rat was slinking into what used to be, judging by the cracked sign overhead, a Cinnabon.

Over by the entrance to one abandoned store I saw a grungy sleeping bag balled up against the wall. Not surprising that this place might have a few squatters, homeless people using it for shelter until this entire complex came tumbling down.

I was briefly startled by the shadow of something flying over me. I glanced up and saw not a pigeon, but what looked like a hawk, judging by the wingspan. It was a mini-postapocalyptic world in here.

And if it seemed foreboding now, I imagined what it would be like at night. The power would most cer-tainly have been cut off to the facility, and had it not been for that windowed ceiling that ran from one end of the mall to the other, I'd have had a hard time find-ing my way without a flashlight.

Given that the place was not bustling with shoppers, noises carried, and somewhere on the floor above I could hear the sound of a power drill. I made my way carefully up the escalator, stepping over the gaps, and when I was on the upper level, I paused, waiting for another blast of the drill.

When one didn't come immediately, I decided to make some noise.

"Greg!" I shouted, my call echoing throughout the abandoned space.

Some ten stores away, a goggled man stepped out of one of the stores, looked in my direction, and waved.

"Down here!" Greg shouted.

It didn't surprise me that he'd be working on a Saturday. He'd always been something of a workaholic, as well as a hustler.

Greg and I'd had our ups and downs over the years, but we never stopped being friends. I didn't have anyone from my high school days that I kept in touch with, having moved from school to school depending on which foster home I was billeted with at the time. But I saved up my money to attend UConn, the University of Connecticut, and it was there I connected with Greg.

Back then he mostly went by the name his parents had given him: Gregoire. He figured college might be a good time to trade on his French name—his mother, from Lyon, had fallen in love with his father, an Albany native, when she'd come to America in her late teens as an exchange student. As a kid, he'd always gone by Greg because his classmates made fun of his real name, mispronouncing it on purpose, calling him "Greg-Wire." But once he got to UConn, he went back to it, thinking it gave him something of an international flair. "Sounds sexy," he told me back then.

"Yeah, well, not to me," I said, and always called him Greg.

We'd met in some engineering classes we shared, and I soon saw in Greg the characteristics I lacked in myself. I was cautious where he was adventurous. I gave careful deliberations to the consequences of my actions while Greg was impulsive. I remember once, signing up for courses, picking ones that would complement my engineering classes. Math, physics, stuff like that. Greg was on the same track as me, but seconds before making his final selections he learned some hot student from Sweden he was desperate to bed was taking a poli-sci class, so he signed up for it. Didn't give a rat's ass about politics, but oh, how he wanted to sit next to that girl in the lecture hall. The joke was on him. At the last minute, she dropped the politics course for one in environmental science.

Greg wasn't just adventurous. I saw him as fearless. He was the one who'd sneak into the college pool after hours for a midnight swim, who'd drive his dad's car, when he had it for the weekend, at high speed over a small hill in the hopes of catching air, who'd take a running leap off a cliff's edge into a quarry reservoir, who once kept a VCR that had literally fallen off the back of a truck that had been making a delivery to an electronics store. He had, in a word, balls.

While his impulsive nature ebbed some as he got older, there remained a youthful spirit. And there was also, I believed, beneath the bravado and playfulness, a good soul. Greg had been the one who kept an eye on me after Brie vanished. He was the one who had found me passed out, fully clothed, in that bathtub.

"Man," he said to me at the time, "you have got to get your shit together. I am not going to let you do this to yourself."

It was a wonder, in many ways, that we had remained friends.

We had once been business partners. We ran a contracting company together, but in the months before Brie's disappearance we'd lost out on several jobs that could have turned around our fortunes. We decided, in the wake of those failures, to dissolve the company and go our separate ways.

Greg had kept himself afloat, in the years since, jumping from one contracting gig to another, usually offering discounts to clients who were willing to pay in cash. And if things got slow, he'd try something totally different, like spending a month working on a fishing boat, or joining a road construction crew. ("College prepared me well for flipping a sign from STOP to SLOW," he told me over a beer one night.)

Greg had the edge over me on impulsiveness, but it was that very trait that sometimes got him in over his head. And I was the one, he was willing to concede, who could think fast enough to rescue him. Like the time, a couple of years out of college, we were bar-hopping in Hartford and Greg, with about ten beers in him, took an unprovoked swing at some guy and knocked him out cold just as a police car was pulling into the parking lot. There wasn't time to organize an escape, so I took a swing at Greg, bloodied his nose, and told him to drop.

When the cops wandered over and took in the scene, I laid it all out for them. The other guy swung first, broke my buddy's nose, and Greg had but a second to land a punch of his own.

I got him out of there before the other guy came to. Good thing we'd settled our tab in cash, so there were no credit card receipts for the cops to use to follow up.

To this day, Greg's nose had a slight tilt to it, thanks to me.

Now, as I closed the distance between us, I saw Greg had one of his trademark cigarettes between his lips. As part of his image back in school, he started buying imported French tobacco and rolling paper to make his own smokes. The elaborate ritual of it became part of who he was, and it was a habit he had never lost.

Hanging from his arm was a cordless reciprocating saw, one of those Uzi-looking gadgets with a powerful cutting blade that stuck straight out the end of it like a tiny bayonet that moved back and forth at the speed of light.

"Good to see you, man," he said, setting down the saw and tossing away that last millimeter of his cigarette so he could throw his arms around me.

"Same," I said.

Greg looked a little thinner since I'd last seen him a month or two ago. His face and neck—with about two days' worth of whiskers on them, as always—seemed more drawn, the skin hanging somewhat under his chin. His gray hair was thinner, too, but he was still a handsome guy, even if he did look closer to fifty when I knew he had only just turned forty.

"Sorry you missed Julie," he said. "She really wanted to meet you."

"We connected as I was coming in," I said. "She new on the scene?"

Greg shrugged. "Five, six weeks, I guess. She's great, heart of gold. She's working on making me a better person." He grinned. "Who knew I needed improving?"

"So what the hell are you doing here?" I asked.

"I'm the hyena feeding on the carcass," he said with no small measure of pride. "They're going to rip this whole place down soon, and I worked a deal with the company that's going to do it to have a few days in here to get some very usable shit. There's hundreds of dying malls across the country. Victims of online shopping, the loss of anchor stores that've gone tits up, and then you throw in a fucking pandemic on top of that. Malls can't cut it."

I shook my head, marveling that these were this huge structure's final days. I went over to grasp the railing that overlooked the lower level, taking in the view.

"I wouldn't lean against that, if I was you," Greg said. "I've already started taking out some of the bolts securing it to the floor. I can repurpose those a hundred ways. On a balcony, around a deck."

I stepped back. "I saw your truck. Looks like you've got a pretty full load already. Mannequins?"

He laughed. "All kinds of places will buy those. Last trip, scored some store signs. Like, a McDonald's, a Baskin-Robbins. People snap those up, hang them in their rec rooms. You know the huge shed I've got behind my place? Gonna cram as much into that as possible." He was digging into his pocket for papers and a small pouch of tobacco to make himself another cigarette. "How's things going with Jayne?"

They had met a couple of times since Jayne had moved in with me.

"Good. And we've got her brother living with us now. Tyler. Sixteen. His dad passed, and he's kind of messed up. Adrift, you know? Reminds me of myself at that age, when I was being shunted from home to home."

I became aware of someone approaching. Thinking Julie had returned, I turned to say hello, but it was a young guy, mid-twenties, shuffling toward us. His clothes were worn and filthy, and he didn't appear to have shaved in at least a week.

"Hey, Neil," Greg said. He pointed his thumb into the store he'd stepped out of. "Box of donuts in there. Help yourself, but leave some for the others."

Neil smiled. "Thanks, man. Sorry to interrupt." He shuffled on into the store as I gave Greg a questioning look.

In a low voice, he said, "A few homeless living in here till they tear it all down. Me and Julie bring in a few treats for them. Best to have them on your side if you're gonna be sharing space with them. Give some of them odd jobs, twenty bucks to haul stuff to my truck. So, what's up?"

I got out my phone and brought up the picture I'd sent myself off Brian's tablet. I handed it to Greg without comment. He studied the picture, then enlarged it with his thumb and index finger.

"What am I looking at here?" he asked.

"That was taken a couple of hours ago, off a security cam. Where my house used to stand. That's the driveway."

"Okay. And?"

I told him what Max had told me. And what the woman in the picture allegedly said. Asking what had happened to her house.

Greg kept staring at the picture. "What are you getting at here? What are you suggesting?"

"I'm not suggesting anything. I'm showing you that and waiting for your reaction."

He gave the picture another five seconds and then handed the phone back to me. He finished making his cigarette, stuck it between his lips, and lit it with a lighter that he'd tucked into his shirt pocket.

"I don't know, man. What are you thinking?"

"It's not a very good picture."

"Seriously, you know what it is? It's just some woman took a wrong turn. Got her directions mixed up. Maybe it's one of those grocery delivery services. Lot more of those since COVID. She made a mistake. Last week I got an Uber Eats at the door that I never ordered. Was for someone else. People are careless."

"Maybe. Doesn't explain why she got so spooked she dropped everything and took off."

Greg took a drag off his cigarette, held the smoke in his lungs for a moment, and then exhaled. I'd snuck plenty of smokes when I was in foster homes, but it hadn't turned into a lifelong habit. So I was no expert on tobacco, but this brand Greg favored had its own distinctive aroma.

He looked me in the eye.

"Whatever this is, Andy, and honestly, I have no *idea* what's going on here, but you can't let it get your hopes up. That can't be Brie. I mean, okay, at a glance, whoever that is could pass for her from a distance, but it doesn't make any sense. What are we supposed to take from this? That she suddenly reappeared as if five years—"

"Six."

"What?"

"Six. It's been six years."

"Jesus, has it really been that long?"

"Yeah."

"Anyway, are we supposed to think Brie's actually okay and that she went through some *Star Trek*–like space-time continuum and thought it was six years ago and expected to find the house she used to live in?"

"I don't know what we're supposed to think."

At this point, Neil came back out of the shop, chewing on a donut in one hand and carrying a second in his other. He raised it and said to Greg, "This one's for Karen, okay?"

"No problem," he said, then turned back to me and whispered, "He's here with his girlfriend. Can you imagine, living here with someone?"

I shook my head.

"Anyway," Greg said, "there was one of those stories on the news the other day, about some sick pervert who kept a couple of women prisoner in his house for years, and one of them escaped. Well, I'll tell you this, she didn't escape and get herself all dressed up nice and head to the supermarket with her station wagon. I mean, if Brie were back, or had, you know, escaped or something, she'd go to the police."

"Sure," I said.

"I mean, come on," he said. "Look, I know it's

hard to move on, that it's hard to put this behind you. I was thinking, back when I found you in the tub, passed out, that was kind of a turning point. You pulled yourself together after that, despite the odds. You've got this new lady in your life. And you've got a new name, which is like starting over, right?"

"Yeah."

"And you're bringing in some money? Paying the bills?"

"Yeah," I said. "Like you. A job here, a job there. About to start on finishing off someone's basement. Did a couple of decks last month. Moderately steady."

"Good, good, that's all good. Don't let whatever's going on in that picture fuck with your head. You've got a good life now."

"You're saying I should ignore this. Pretend I never saw it."

Greg sighed. "If that was Brie, if it really fuckin' was her somehow, appearing out of thin air, you think the first thing she'd do is go pick up some eggs and some Tater Tots? No. She'd *call* you. If we're supposed to believe that's her in that picture, then what the hell has she been doing for six years? She go to the store and get lost? She been wandering a Walmart since the last time you saw her?"

Greg put a hand on my shoulder. "Sorry, man. That was . . . insensitive. I know how hard this has been on you. All this time, the not knowing, the wondering. But there's no rational answer to this. It can't be her. Can't be."

He seemed to be trying to convince himself as much as he was trying to convince me.

"Did your neighbor—what's his name?"

"Max."

"This Max, did he see any camera crews around or anything?"

"Camera crews?"

"Yeah. Maybe it's one of those crime reenactment shows. You know. 'Whatever happened to . . .' kind of thing. Or some type of stunt." His face lit up and he snapped his fingers. "I've got it."

"What?"

"So this guy, the one who built that new house on your lot? It's a nice house, right?"

"Yeah. Very."

"Yeah, I drove by one day. Very sharp. So, someone out there wants to buy that house. But first they need to freak him out. Like, make him think a spirit that used to live on the property is coming back to haunt him and his family."

"That's beyond nuts."

"They scare the guy into unloading the place at below market value."

I sighed. "You're insane."

He smiled smugly. "Okay, I'm sure your explanation makes more sense."

"I should go," I said.

"Let me ask you something, and don't take offense, okay?" he said.

"Go ahead."

"What's got you worried the most? That this lady making an appearance, it'll get your hopes up and then they'll get dashed, because it was a trick or a stunt? Or . . ."

"Or what?"

"Or . . . that it really *is* Brie? And if she's back, it's gonna turn your world upside down?"

Ten

Jayne was starting to wonder whether Andrew had run into a problem. A trip to Home Depot shouldn't take this long. It wasn't like him not to check in with her if he'd been delayed.

Maybe he'd run into someone he knew, she thought. Or maybe he couldn't find what he was looking for at the Home Depot and decided to try another store. Although it struck her as unlikely that Home Depot would be out of weed and feed.

Jayne considered phoning him, but didn't want him to feel hounded, like she was checking up on him, expecting a full accounting of his activities. She trusted him, didn't need to keep him under surveillance. He'd been so good to her and her brother that she didn't want him questioning whether he'd made the wrong decision, bringing the two of them into his home.

Jayne loved this man. He wasn't perfect. She knew that. Maybe, one of these days, they'd even get married, but marriage was definitely a topic Andrew tended to steer away from. The worst was when he went into a deep, emotional funk, like something invisible was weighing him down. She worried about these moods and tried to draw him out, to get him to talk about what was on his mind, but he always told her it was nothing. He'd been forthcoming about his teenage years, after both his parents had died, and that horrible period when he was bounced from foster home to foster home.

Andrew had even told her he'd been married for a while, but it hadn't worked out, and she didn't press him on that subject when he declined to provide details. There were emotional wounds from that relationship that hadn't healed, she supposed. And the last five or six years of Andrew's life remained something of a mystery. A trauma of some kind. One of these days, she figured, he'd tell her.

When the phone finally rang at one point, she thought it would be him, but it turned out to be Tyler's phone, which he had left sitting on the kitchen counter. Jayne looked at the screen, saw that it was Mr. Whistler, from the grocery store.

She answered. Tyler, Mr. Whistler said, could take the day off if he wanted because they were well staffed, but could he work Sunday instead?

"Hang on," Jayne said, and took the phone with her up to Tyler's room, where she found him sound asleep, stripped down to his boxers, facedown on top of the covers. If it weren't for the gentle rising and falling of his back, someone might have taken him for dead.

Holding her finger over the speaker, she said, "Wake up. It's Mr. Whistler."

Tyler stirred, rolled onto his side. "What?"

Jayne handed him the phone. "You sort it out."

Tyler said, "Hello?" Then: "Okay, sure, that's good. Okay, see you tomorrow."

He put the phone onto the bedside table, dropped his head back onto the pillow, and closed his eyes. Sensing that his sister was still in the room, he opened one eye and saw her standing there by the door, arms folded across her chest.

"What?" he said.

"We need to talk," she said.

"I'll be down in a while," he said, closing his eye.

Jayne, not about to be dismissed, sat on the edge of the bed and put a hand on his shoulder. "Not in a while," she said. "Now."

Tyler rolled onto his back, opened both eyes this

time, and said, "Okay, I'm sorry, I fucked up. Sorry about barfing on Andy's precious deck. I sprayed it off."

"What happened last night?"

He sighed. "I was at Cam's. We kinda had some vodka, I guess. I might've had a couple shots too many."

"Where'd this happen?"

"At his place. His parents were out."

"That's the only place you were. Just between Cam's place and here?"

"Yeah, pretty much," Tyler said.

"When we talked you said you were on your way home."

Tyler managed a shrug while on his back. "You're not my mom, you know. Or my dad. Never much of a sister, either."

That might have cut deeper if it had been the first time he'd said it. She'd made her apologies, and excuses, before. It wasn't her fault their parents had two kids thirteen years apart.

"I know," Jayne said. "But let me lay it out for you. You're right. I'm not your mom, and Andy's not your dad. So maybe you're thinking, you don't owe us anything. But that works both ways. We don't owe *you* anything. Andy sure doesn't. But we've made a choice. We've stepped up. You're my brother and I may not have been there for you in the past but I want to be there for you now. And Andy knows a lot about what it's like not to have a home. He wants to make one for you here."

Tyler moved his legs around Jayne so he could sit on the edge of the bed next to her. His head hung low. "I guess," he said.

"It didn't work out with Aunt Clara," Jayne said. "She tried, gave it her best shot, but after what you—"

"It was an accident. I didn't mean for it to happen."

"If it had been anyone else, you probably would have been charged. But she wouldn't do that, because she loves you and understands you've been through a lot."

"I didn't know the glass would break like that. I kind of lost it for one second. Jesus, no one's ever going to let me forget it."

"I don't want to debate that all over again now, Tyler. But you blew it with Aunt Clara. Andy letting you live here, this is your second chance."

"You haven't told him," he said.

"No," Jayne said. "And as long as you keep on the straight and narrow, there really isn't any need to. But we've both got your best interests at heart. And there's another thing."

She paused, took a breath, let it out slowly. Tyler waited.

"I love him," Jayne said. "I love this man, and I want to make it work. There's things going on I haven't even told you, or Andy, but it's really crucial that we all have some, you know, structure in our lives right now. It's important."

"What haven't you told me?" Tyler asked.

Jayne bit her lip, making a decision. She leaned in, put her lips close to his ear.

"You don't have to whisper," he said. "There's nobody here."

But whisper she did. Tyler's eyes went wide as she moved her head away.

"So, I need you to help me make this work," she said.

Tyler saw the tears forming in his sister's eyes and slipped an arm around her. "I'll try," he said.

"That's all I'm asking," Jayne said.

When Jayne came back downstairs, she thought about what Tyler had said, wondered why he'd lied to her.

She knew he'd been places other than Cam's house. Her little brother wasn't the only one with some tech skills. Jayne had secretly put an app on his phone that would let her know where he was at any given time, and when she had looked at it earlier this morning she'd noticed he'd been hanging out in a nearby cemetery. Maybe that was where he and Cam had gone to get drunk.

But she'd decided not to call him on it. Once he knew what she'd done, he'd delete the app. The good thing was, unlike most kids his age, Tyler was not all that tech-savvy. It wasn't that he couldn't figure stuff out. It simply didn't interest him that much. Anyway, Jayne tried not to overdo it when it came to snooping on her brother, but she believed it was a prudent move to be aware of his comings and goings.

She sent Andrew a text.

Everything okay?

And hit send.

She watched the screen for a few seconds, waiting for the dancing dots that would indicate a reply was in the works.

Nothing.

And then she heard the car pull into the driveway.

Before she opened the door, she peeked outside. There was a black, nondescript sedan sitting there with a woman behind the wheel. Jayne wouldn't have called herself an expert in these things, but she thought the car was some kind of police vehicle, given how plain it looked.

The woman behind the wheel got out and started walking toward the front door. Stocky, short hair, big glasses. Jayne opened the front door and stepped out.

"Can I help you?" Jayne said.

The woman smiled and said, "Hi. I'm Detective Marissa Hardy. Milford police."

"Yes?"

Oh God, no. There's been an accident.

This was why she hadn't heard from Andrew. Someone running a red light had broadsided him. Something had fallen off a high shelf at Home Depot and crushed him. Maybe some crazy, random event with a shooter. There was always one of those somewhere in America on any given day.

"Is it Andrew?" she said. "Was he in an accident?"

"No, ma'am, not to my knowledge."

Her second thought was that this had something to do with Tyler. Maybe when he got drunk with his friend last night they'd gotten into something they shouldn't have. Broken a window, tipped over a mailbox, spray-painted the side of someone's house.

"How are you today?" Hardy asked.

"Just fine," she said, coming off the step and getting within whispering range. "Is this about Tyler?"

"Tyler?"

"My brother. He lives with us."

"No," the detective said. "I'm looking for Andrew."

"Andrew?"

"Andrew Mason."

Jayne blinked. "Who?"

Hardy paused, the corner of her mouth going up a tenth of an inch. "I'm sorry," she said. "Force of habit. I'd forgotten he goes by Andrew Carville now. Took me a little longer to find this place because of that. Is he here?"

Jayne suddenly felt dizzy.

Andrew Mason?

Andrew had changed his name? He'd never told her anything about that. Who changed their name? Movie stars, maybe. But not regular people.

"What's your name, ma'am?" Detective Hardy asked.

"Jayne Keeling."

"You live here?"

"Yes."

"With Andrew Carville?"

She swallowed. "Yes."

"And is he here?"

Jayne shook her head slowly, her mouth suddenly very dry.

"Well, that's too bad, but now that I'm here, I wouldn't mind talking to you," the detective said. She smiled innocently. "Maybe we could go inside and talk? Truth is, I could really use a coffee. If that's not being too huge a bother."

Jayne looked at the detective as though she were a talking giraffe.

"Coffee," Jayne said.

"That'd be great," she said.

Jayne's phone, still in her hand, buzzed with the sound of an incoming text. She glanced down and saw the message from Andrew.

Everything fine. Back in a bit.

"Is that him?" Hardy asked.

"Yes. He's out running some errands. I don't know when he'll be back."

"That's okay. We can talk before he gets here."

Jayne turned and gestured for the detective to follow her into the house. She led her to the kitchen and pointed to a chair. Hardy sat down, placing her own phone facedown on the table.

"Decaf, if you have it," she said. "But it's okay if you don't."

"I . . . yes, I have that."

Jayne opened the cupboard, brought down a tin of coffee, put a filter into the machine. As she spooned in some ground coffee, some of it spilled across the counter.

"Damn it," she said.

She cleaned up the mess, and as she ran water into the carafe to pour into the coffee machine, she asked, "Why did you ask for Andrew *Mason*?"

"Are you married to Andrew?" Hardy asked.

"No."

"But you've been together awhile?"

"Yes."

"How long?"

"Since the latter part of last year. And I moved in here with him a few months ago."

"Oh," Hardy said. "Are you from Stratford?"

"No," Jayne said. "I moved here a couple of years ago. From Providence."

"What made you move down to this neck of the woods?"

"I assess properties for insurance companies. The one I worked for in Rhode Island was winding down, the owner retiring, and an insurance firm in Stratford was looking for someone, so I made the move."

"Just you?"

"I'm not—I wasn't in a relationship. My family—my father and my brother—were there, but they didn't move with me, of course."

"And Tyler is . . ."

"That's my brother. He joined me here later. After our father died. You haven't answered my question."

"Which one was that?"

The coffee machine was starting to make a gurgling sound.

"Why you called Andrew . . . Andrew Mason. That's not his name."

"That *was* his name. He had it legally changed four years ago. I can't say as I blame him, considering."

"Considering what?" Jayne asked. "A financial failure? A bankruptcy? He had a building company, with someone else, but that got dissolved some time ago. Did it have something to do with that?"

"No," the detective said. "Since you're relatively new to the area, I guess you wouldn't have been exposed much to the news around here six years ago."

That corner of Hardy's mouth was still curled up a notch, as though she might actually be enjoying this.

"A splash of milk," Hardy said.

"I'm sorry?"

"My coffee. That's how I take it. I figured you'd get around to asking sooner or later."

Jayne took two mugs down from the cupboard and a carton of milk from the refrigerator. The coffee continued to drip down into the carafe. When there was enough for one serving, Jayne filled one mug, added some milk, and put it on the table in front of Hardy.

"Thank you," she said.

Jayne said nothing.

"Has Andrew ever mentioned anything to you about his wife?" Hardy asked.

Jayne blinked. "His ex-wife, you mean."

Hardy shrugged. "Sure."

"He told me he used to be married. That it didn't work out. He doesn't like to talk about her very much and honestly I don't think it's any of my business."

"He tell you her name?"

"Brandy, I think," she said.

That brought a smile to the detective's face. She picked up her phone. "Let me show you something."

She held up the device for Jayne, who took a couple of steps closer. A picture filled the screen. It was a soft image of a woman standing by a black car. It was parked in a driveway, the tailgate in the raised position, and there were what appeared to be a couple of bags of groceries spilled on the driveway.

"Okay," Jayne said. "Who's that?"

"*That* is the question," the detective said. "The image could be crisper, I know. I got this nifty little app on my phone you can run photos through, the idea being that it sharpens them up some. Admittedly with varying degrees of success. So I used the app on this shot and enlarged it and it's not a lot better, but there is some improvement. Here, have a look."

She was about to pass the phone to Jayne when Tyler strolled into the kitchen. He'd pulled some jeans on over his boxers but was naked from the waist up, and shoeless.

"Oh," he said, seeing Hardy. "I didn't know someone was here."

"Hi," Detective Hardy said, putting the phone down and extending a hand. Tyler took it. "I'm Detective Hardy with the Milford police."

Tyler looked as though he'd received a minor electrical shock. "Uh, what?"

"The police," Jayne said. "Detective Hardy just had some questions about a neighborhood thing."

Tyler saw the detective's phone and picked it up. "Who's this?" he asked, looking at the picture.

"That's why I'm here," Hardy said. "Wondering the same thing."

"Nice ride," Tyler said.

"I'm sorry?" the detective said.

"The Volvo wagon. I like those."

"Is there something I can do for you, Tyler?" Jayne asked.

"Was just gonna get some breakfast or something."

"Sleep in, did you?" Hardy asked.

He looked at her, not sure whether to answer. Jayne said, "Could you give us a couple minutes?"

"Fine," he said, handing the phone back to Hardy and padding out of the room in his bare feet.

"Sorry about that," Jayne said.

"No problem." She tried again to hand her phone to Jayne, and this time Jayne took it and looked at the image.

"Why are you showing me this?" she asked.

"Do you recognize her?"

"No."

Hardy took back the phone. "Okay. Let me ask you this. Where—"

"No," Jayne said abruptly. "I'm not answering any more questions until you answer mine. Why did Andrew change his name, and why are you asking me about the woman in that picture?"

"Okay," Detective Hardy said. "Why don't you have a seat and I'll fill you in."

Eleven

Statement of Greg Raymus,
June 8, 2016, 6:42 p.m.,
interviewed by Detective Marissa Hardy.

DETECTIVE HARDY: Thanks for coming in, Mr. Raymus.

GREG: No problem. Anything to help. This is just an awful thing that's happened.

DETECTIVE HARDY: Let me just get this right for the record. Your name is Gregoire Franklin Raymus.

GREG: Right, but I just go by Greg.

DETECTIVE HARDY: I want to ask you about the Saturday night when you and Mr. Mason were up at your respective cabins at Sorrow Bay, but first I'd like to ask you about how things have been between Mr. Mason and his wife, Brie.

GREG: Um, okay.

DETECTIVE HARDY: How would—I'm sorry, but you can't smoke in here.

GREG: Oh, sorry. It's not a joint or anything, but I do roll my own.

DETECTIVE HARDY: You just can't smoke in here. How would you describe the relationship between your friend and his wife.

GREG: You know. It's a good marriage, I guess. I mean, is there any marriage out there that's perfect?

DETECTIVE HARDY: Are you married yourself, Mr. Raymus?

GREG: Me? No.

DETECTIVE HARDY: But you'd say that your friend and his wife were getting along okay.

GREG: You know, ups and downs.

DETECTIVE HARDY: By ups and downs, are you referring to the affair that Mr. Mason had?

GREG: Oh, you know about that.

DETECTIVE HARDY: Yes, I do.

GREG: It wasn't that big a deal. Didn't last long, and it ended some time ago. Months, in fact.

DETECTIVE HARDY: And you know this woman Mr. Mason was seeing?

GREG: No. I never met her. I mean, Andy told me about seeing her, about how he felt he'd made a big mistake, but I never knew her at all.

DETECTIVE HARDY: Do you know what prompted Mr. Mason to cheat on his wife?

GREG: I think they were in a bad place. I got the impression maybe Brie had kind of strayed, too.

DETECTIVE HARDY: Do you know with who?

GREG: Nope. Andy didn't say and I didn't ask. Thing is, they really love each other, but there was some friction about how they've been living. Getting a house, fixing it up, selling it, moving to another, doing it all over again. The lack of a permanent home base was getting to her. She talked about it in the office sometimes.

DETECTIVE HARDY: The office?

GREG: Our construction office. A trailer, actually. Brie comes in sometimes to help with the books and stuff. But I think Andy was saying this was the last time, that they'd probably stay in this house, the one on Mulberry.

DETECTIVE HARDY: You've known Mr. Mason a long time?

GREG: Since UConn. College. And then we eventually went into business together. Which we are now.

DETECTIVE HARDY: How's that going?

GREG: A bit like a marriage. Ups and downs.

DETECTIVE HARDY: Your friendship, or the business?

GREG: Business is a little shaky right now. I guess you'd call it cash flow issues. Lost some jobs we thought we'd get. To be honest, I think we may be going our separate ways before long. I'm gonna do my thing, Andy's gonna do his.

DETECTIVE HARDY: Do you know whether there's an insurance policy on Brie Mason's life?

GREG: Huh? Beats me. Christ, what are you suggesting? You think Andy did something to Brie to collect some insurance to help with the company? That's totally insane. And if that was his plan, well, you'd want to know she was dead so they'd pay up, right? I mean, where is she?

DETECTIVE HARDY: That's the million-dollar question, isn't it? What did you do to your leg?

GREG: It's fine, hardly giving me any trouble at all now.

DETECTIVE HARDY: You're using a cane.

GREG: Probably going to retire it this week. I'll be limping for a while, but that's okay.

DETECTIVE HARDY: What happened?

GREG: I was on a job site, working alone, and the ladder somehow fell over and I was up about ten feet on some scaffolding and figured I could make the jump. Could have done it, too, but there was a short length of angle iron I hadn't noticed and I hit that and broke a bone. Stupid, you know. I shoulda known better.

DETECTIVE HARDY: Glad you're on the mend. Do

you have any idea where Brie might be? Would she have run away? Disappeared without saying anything to anyone?

GREG: You know, I suppose it could be something like that. That she just needed to get away and think things through. But she'll probably show up anytime now.

DETECTIVE HARDY: If that's what she did, you'd think she'd have taken her purse and credit cards and her car wouldn't still be in the driveway.

GREG: Yeah, well, there's that. But she still might have gone someplace to clear her head.

DETECTIVE HARDY: About what? You said two seconds ago you think their marriage is fine.

GREG: I don't know. Maybe I'm not ready to think something bad has happened to her. I don't want my mind to go there. I love Brie. She's terrific. And if something's happened to her, it'll destroy Andy.

DETECTIVE HARDY: Your cabin, and Mr. Mason's, are they pretty close together?

GREG: About a minute's walk. If that.

DETECTIVE HARDY: Can you see his place from yours? And vice versa?

GREG: There's a line of trees between the two cabins. At night you can see some light through the leaves. If it's the fall, when the leaves are all gone, there's a pretty clear sightline through, but not now.

DETECTIVE HARDY: Did you notice any lights on at Mr. Mason's through the night?

GREG: I didn't look.

DETECTIVE HARDY: You can make the drive from Milford to Sorrow Bay in, what, ninety minutes or so?

GREG: If there's no traffic.

DETECTIVE HARDY: So, if you'd decided, say, for the sake of argument, at ten that night to drive back, you'd be in Milford by midnight. And if you wanted, you could turn around and come back in time for breakfast.

GREG: Yeah, well, I didn't do that. I stayed. We went back Sunday, like I said.

DETECTIVE HARDY: So let's talk about Saturday night.

GREG: We had some dinner at my place. I did some burgers on the barbecue. Didn't catch any fish, so it was a good thing we brought food. Had some drinks. And around nine or so he went back to his place. We were pretty bushed. And my leg was throbbing some. Took some Advils for it.

DETECTIVE HARDY: And you saw Mr. Mason in the morning.

GREG: He came over for coffee around nine, ten, I guess it was.

DETECTIVE HARDY: You didn't see Mr. Mason between nine the night before, and the following morning.

GREG: Um, no.

DETECTIVE HARDY: Did you hear his car start up after he left?

GREG: No.

DETECTIVE HARDY: You're sure? Nothing at all?

GREG: Well, even if a car did start I'm not sure I'd hear it from my place. And anyway, I slept like I was in a coma. And I hadn't even had that much to drink. I didn't even get up in the night to take a piss, which, you know, sometimes I have to do.

DETECTIVE HARDY: You normally sleep that soundly?

GREG: Now that you mention it, no, not usually. Maybe it was all the fresh air, being out on the water, the booze, and the painkillers. Or maybe Andy slipped me some knockout drops.

DETECTIVE HARDY: Are you suggesting—

GREG: That's just a joke. Sorry. I guess there's not much about this that's funny.

Twelve
Andrew

I had to know this day would come.

Now that it seemed to be upon me, I needed time to think. So I drove around town, doing just that.

Thinking.

Honestly, it was amazing things hadn't started to unravel before now. The fact that Jayne had been with me for this long and still did not know my history was nothing short of a minor miracle. It helped, of course, that she hadn't lived in this part of Connecticut when it all happened. While Brie's disappearance occasionally attracted national interest, it was, for the most part, a local story. By the time Jayne had come from Providence to Stratford, next door to Milford where it all happened, my notoriety had diminished.

And I couldn't have been more grateful.

But I feared this morning's call from Max—even if it might not, ultimately, turn out to mean anything—was going to have the effect of a concussive blast, knocking us all off our feet in an ever-expanding radius.

If it hadn't been this latest development, any day the truth could have come out in a thousand other ways. Running into someone at the mall when Jayne was with me. Maybe someone would stop to say hello, offer condolences, ask if I'd ever learned what had happened to Brie, or was it one of those cold cases by now. Or maybe someone would pass by and say nothing at all, but shoot a scornful look my way. A look I'd have to explain to Jayne.

I'd always been mindful of the risks of an awkward encounter in public. So I made a point, whenever we were together, of avoiding Milford. We dined out in Stratford, or places to the west, like Bridgeport or Norwalk or Stamford. We rarely went to the movies. I had a big-screen TV and subscribed to several streaming services. Why go out, I'd say, when we have access to so much entertainment at home?

I was masquerading as a homebody when I was anything but.

When there were errands to run, especially if they

took me anywhere near where I used to live, I tended to do them alone. "I've got this," I'd say to Jayne. "I won't be long." If I ran into people who knew or recognized me when I was out solo, well, that was fine. I could deal with that. And it wasn't as though Jayne were waiting around to accompany me. She had her own career, and it kept her busy.

As I drove around town, I went over in my head how I would tell her the things I'd kept from her. And why. The second part was a little easier. I loved her and had worried that telling her everything about myself would scare her off. You don't bring up in conversation on a first date that your wife is missing and the police consider you a prime suspect.

But I might very well scare Jayne off now.

"It's time I told you more about myself," I would say. "It's true that I was married. But what I failed to tell you is how that marriage ended. Six years ago my wife, Brie, vanished."

I was trying to picture the look on her face when I told her. And that was only the beginning.

Brie was never found, I would have to tell her. The police, after all this time, still did not know what had happened to her. They'd had to consider whether she had disappeared of her own accord, or if she'd been abducted. Maybe there had been an accident. Brie went for a walk and tumbled down a hill, her body hidden among the foliage.

Some of the theories were more preposterous than others. But one of them had to be true, right?

Jayne would probably ask whether Brie had been depressed. Was there a chance she'd committed suicide? Left the house in the middle of the night, walked to the middle of the Washington Bridge in the west end of town, and jumped into the Housatonic?

I would have to be honest and tell her Brie had not seemed depressed. Not in any clinical kind of way. I would have to tell Jayne that the police had considered that as a possibility, but no body had been found.

I would have to tell her that very quickly the investigation focused on me. That Milford Police Detective Marissa Hardy believed I had killed my wife because I was interested in taking up with a woman named Natalie Simmons. I would tell her it was a brief affair and meant nothing, but that Brie's sister, Isabel McBain, had been convinced from the very beginning that I'd had a hand in her disappearance, and death.

If Jayne asked why I'd been unfaithful, I would tell her I'd been an idiot. That Brie and I had been going through a bad patch, that we both had made decisions we'd deeply regretted. If Jayne asked whether I knew who Brie had cheated on me with, I would have to say yes, but I would have to add that I had never revealed this person's identity to anyone except Detective Hardy—after some prodding—and that she had looked into this person and concluded he had nothing to do with Brie's disappearance.

I would have to tell her Detective Hardy believed I'd used a weekend fishing trip with my friend Greg as a cover story—an alibi—and that in the night I'd actually driven back to Milford, killed Brie and disposed of her body, then returned before dawn and joined Greg for coffee later that morning. She further believed it was possible I'd drugged Greg so that he slept through the night, thereby making it nearly impossible that he'd notice my absence.

I would have to tell her that, while I was never charged in connection with Brie's disappearance, the media was well aware that I was a suspect. (I blame Hardy for that, she no doubt leaked it in order to put more pressure on me.) For a while there, I had TV news trucks sitting at the end of my drive every morning, trying to get some kind of comment from me.

I would have to tell Jayne that despite the lack of any concrete evidence that I'd done anything wrong, Isabel continued to campaign for my arrest, even though Brie's mother, Elizabeth, and her brother, Albert, and his wife, Dierdre, seemed willing to give me the benefit of the doubt. But Isabel's stridency scared the other members of the family, including her own husband, Norman, from ever speaking up on my behalf.

Isabel's harassment took several forms. She wrote letters to newspapers, filled with wild accusations, about what it was she believed I had done. The papers, thankfully, did not print them because they were deemed libelous, but that didn't mean that they didn't do occasional updates headlined "Where Is Brie?" or "Brie's Fate Still a Mystery."

Isabel hired a lawyer to sue me in civil court, where the bar is set a little lower than in criminal court when it comes to holding someone, at least financially, responsible. She didn't win—Nan Sokolow's firm helped me with that, too—but the legal bills wiped out most of my savings.

Isabel's quest to get justice for her sister had always struck me as somewhat ironic, given that she'd always seemed to resent Brie and been jealous of her since they were much younger. It was a one-sided rivalry, so far as I could tell. Brie had always been happy for Isabel when something good came her way, but it was rarely the other way around. I believed it went back to their teens. Only a year apart in age, they competed in such fields as parents' attention, academics, and boys.

Anyway, Isabel's vindictiveness couldn't have come at a worse time, considering that my business partnership with Greg was dissolving, and my prospects were not good.

I would have to tell Jayne that things deteriorated to the point that I decided to legally change my last name. At least that way, on paper people did not recognize me. There was no longer a need for an unlisted number. (Still a bit old-school, I was and am one of the last people on earth to have a landline.) When anyone did a Google search on my new name, the allegations against me did not come up. I mean, who wanted to hire someone to work on their house who many believed had killed his wife and disposed of the body?

It was a lot to tell.

But I felt I was going to have to spill all of it to Jayne. It was better coming from me than someone else.

She'd have questions, I knew that. I'd have at least one for her, too. And it wasn't to ask her whether she would forgive me. I couldn't see any reason why she would, or even should. If the positions were reversed, could I forgive her for keeping something this big a secret?

No, my question for her would be more like, "Do

you want to stay here and I'll move out, or can I help you find a place?"

I would be willing to do either.

Of all the things she might choose to ask me, I imagined the number one question would be short and to the point.

"*Did* you kill your wife?"

And I would look her in the eye and I would say, "No, I did not."

I was imagining that exchange as I sat in a bar, sitting alone in a booth, working on my second or third or fourth Sam Adams. I didn't remember driving here after seeing Greg and Julie, or even coming inside. I felt as though I had always been here, that this booth was my past, my present, and my future. I existed entirely in this moment in time.

As I sat there, I engaged in one of my nervous habits, which was to tear off bits of a paper napkin, roll them up into balls the size of a pea, then flick them off my upturned thumb with my middle finger. Sometimes the ball would fall off my thumb before I could launch it, other times I could shoot one across the room.

When the waitress, a heavyset woman in her fifties, came over to see whether I wanted another beer, she glanced down at the half dozen paper pellets I'd fired off.

"Nice range," she said. "Another?"

I was about to say yes, but any more to drink and I wasn't going to be able to drive myself home. I was probably already in the danger zone.

"No, I'm good," I said.

The waitress stood there a minute, looking at me.

"You been in here before?" she asked.

"Not sure," I said, which was true. "Not in a while, anyway."

"Because you look familiar to me. Pretty sure I've seen you somewhere. Although not lately."

"Maybe I just have that kind of face," I said.

"What's your name?"

"Carville," I said. "Andrew Carville."

"Oh, okay," she said, nodding. "I had you pegged as somebody else, but his last name was Mason."

"Well, there you go," I said, and slapped some bills on the table as she waltzed away.

I couldn't put it off any longer. I went out, got in the Explorer, and headed for home.

I was almost there, not even a block away, when I saw that car again, the one I'd seen heading down the street to Max's house.

Detective Hardy.

Coming from the direction of my place.

I watched her unmarked car disappear in my rear-view, then hit the blinker to turn down my street.

When I got to my house, Jayne was sitting on the front step, waiting.

Looked like I wouldn't have to tell Jayne much of anything, after all. I was guessing the detective had already filled her in.

Thirteen

"I brought flowers," Isabel McBain said. "This room needs some color."

Her mother, Elizabeth, turned her head wearily on the pillow to see what Isabel was up to. She was arranging a small bouquet in a foot-tall metal vase on the movable dining table that had been wheeled away from the bed. Isabel's husband, Norman, tall, thin, and balding, stood back, watching his wife fuss about.

"What do you think of that?" she asked. "Don't they look nice?"

"They look wonderful, Izzy," Elizabeth whispered. "How are you today, Norman?"

"Fine, Elizabeth," he said flatly while Isabel continued to arrange the bouquet. She took a step back, studied her handiwork, concluded they were not quite right, then repositioned several of them. "Norman, what do you think?"

"That one in the front seems a bit droopy."

Isabel shot him a look. "It's supposed to be that way."

"Whatever you say."

"Stop fussing with it, Izzy," Elizabeth said. "I like it just the way it is."

Isabel glanced at the television, saw that it was tuned, as usual, to a cable news show. "Oh, you have to stop watching this all the time," Isabel said, looking for the remote half-hidden under the covers near Elizabeth's hand. She grabbed it, aimed it at the screen, and powered it off. "It just gets your blood boiling, and you hardly need that right now."

Done with the flowers and the television, Isabel turned her attention to her mother. "Look at you. You're all wrinkled."

She could have been talking about the woman's face, but she was referring to Elizabeth's nightgown, which had bunched up around her upper thighs. Isabel tugged the hem down toward her calves and admired her handiwork. "That's much better."

Elizabeth sighed. Norman, still standing, had taken out his phone and was reading some online news.

Isabel glanced over at the window, which was

shielded by a blind in the down position. "You need some light in here," she said. "It's a beautiful, sunny day out there. Norman, open the blind."

"I'd asked them to lower them," Elizabeth said, "because of the glare. Made it hard to watch the TV."

"Well, the TV is off now," Isabel said, and waved a hand at Norman to get busy doing what she had asked him to do. He found the drawstrings and raised the blinds to the halfway point.

"All the way," Isabel ordered.

Norman brought the blinds up until sunshine filled the room. Elizabeth, squinting like someone enduring a police interrogation, used her hand to shield her eyes.

"Isn't that better?" Isabel said enthusiastically. "It makes the room cheerier, if you ask me."

"Whatever you say," Elizabeth said wearily, turning onto her side so her back was to the window.

"So what have you been up to?" Isabel asked with relentless cheeriness.

"Well," Elizabeth said, "last night I went bowling, and this morning I went into the city to do a walk around Bloomingdale's but didn't end up buying anything."

Isabel frowned. "Come on, now. That was a serious question. Are you comfortable?"

"Not really much different than yesterday or the day before that or the day before that," her mother said.

Isabel looked down at her mother for several seconds and looked as though she might start crying.

"Don't," her mother said.

"Don't what?"

"Don't get all emotional and weepy around me. I can't bear it."

"I just love you, that's all."

Elizabeth nodded. "I know."

"I want to do anything I can for you, is all. If you don't like the flowers, I can take them away."

"They're fine."

"You want some magazines? I could go to the gift shop and get you a *New Yorker* or something."

"Reading is hard," Elizabeth said. "I need stronger glasses and I don't see any point in getting them now. The TV is all the entertainment I need."

Elizabeth's eyes fluttered, signaling to Isabel that she was going to fall asleep. At that moment the door opened and Albert walked in. Isabel immediately put her finger to her lips, shushing him in advance of any sound he might make. Norman looked up from his phone, took a step toward his brother-in-law, and extended a hand.

"Hey, Albert," he said quietly.

"Norman."

They stood there for a moment, shoulder to shoulder, as though Norman had found an ally, someone who understood what it was like to be in a room with Isabel.

Albert took a step toward the bed and whispered to his sister, "How is she?"

Isabel stood and motioned for Albert to follow her out into the hall. Norman wasn't included in the gesture, so he opted to stay in the room while the siblings excused themselves.

In the hallway, Isabel allowed the tears she had been holding back to flow. She pulled a tissue from inside her sleeve and dabbed at her cheek.

"What is it?" Albert asked. "Has something happened? Is she worse?"

"She's so . . . tired. And kind of irritable. Her glasses aren't strong enough for reading but she says there's no point in getting new ones now."

Albert offered a resigned shrug, acknowledging their mother was probably right. "So long as we're able to make her comfortable, we're doing the right thing," he said.

"I want to be able to do more," she said.

"We're doing all we can, honestly."

"Every day she looks thinner. Have you seen her arms? They're like toothpicks."

"Mom's a fighter, Izzy. She's always been a fighter."

Isabel tucked the tissue away. "Oh for God's sake,

you say that like she's suddenly going to get better." She sighed. "I'm running on empty. I come every day, sometimes twice. Everything's gone to shit at home."

"We should go back in, see how she's doing."

"Norman can keep her entertained," she said, and rolled her eyes. "He can tell her some gripping story about radial tires."

"Come on, let's go in."

She sniffed, nodded, and followed him back into the room.

Norman was stepping away from the window and taking a seat close to Elizabeth, gazing mournfully at her while she slept. Isabel stood behind him, evidently waiting for him to get up and surrender the chair to her. Albert strolled over to the window, felt the sun on his face. He stood there looking out onto the parking lot below.

Norman got the unspoken message and vacated the chair. Isabel was lowering herself into it as Albert became fixated on something outside.

"Izzy," he whispered.

Her butt had just landed and she was studying her mother's face, her closed eyes, waiting on the chance that they might open. She either did not hear her brother, or had chosen to ignore him.

"Izzy," he whispered again, more urgently.

Isabel turned her head. "What?"

He waved her to come over. When she was slow to rise out of the chair, he waved again, urgently.

She came to his side and whispered, "What?" The two, standing together, had crowded out Norman, who stood behind them, peering over their shoulders.

"Look," he said, pointing.

Isabel took in the view of the parking lot and the roofs of buildings beyond. "Look at what?"

"Right there. Down there. See the red car? The Corvette?"

"I don't know cars."

"Who doesn't know a Corvette?" Norman quipped.

"Do you see the red car?" Albert said. "The sports car?"

"Yes, okay."

"Okay, count over two to the left. That woman."

Isabel squinted. Slowly, she said, "I see her."

Very slowly, Albert said, "Don't you think she looks . . ."

Neither of them said anything for several seconds. They both seemed to have stopped breathing. Isabel placed her palm on the glass.

The woman, dark-haired, slender, was leaning up against a black Volvo station wagon, arms crossed, as though waiting for someone.

"It's just . . . it's just someone who *looks* like her," Isabel said.

"Her hair, the way she's holding herself . . ."

"Let me see," said Norman, squeezing in between them so he could look for himself. "Where?"

"There," Albert said.

Norman squinted.

"Sometimes . . . I feel like I see her all the time," Isabel said softly. "I'll see someone walking ahead of me in the mall, something about the way the woman is walking, it reminds me of her, and I'll run and catch up, just to make sure . . ."

"I know, I know. I do the same."

Isabel and Albert were now talking to each other, less focused on the woman in the parking lot.

"Guys, look," said Norman.

The woman, as though she could sense she was being observed from afar, turned and gazed up in their direction.

Looked directly at their window.

And waved.

Fourteen

Jayne Keeling, listening to Detective Hardy, had felt her world falling apart.

She'd sat across the table from her, hearing details about Andrew that she could hardly bring herself to believe.

"Why do you suppose Andrew hasn't told you any of this?" Hardy asked.

Jayne did not know what to say.

"He was lucky, finding someone like you, someone from out of town who wouldn't have been following the news at the time."

"What do you want?" Jayne asked. "Why are you telling me all this?"

The detective smiled, leaned in. "I guess, if I were

you, I'd want to know. I would feel I had a *right* to know."

"But why now?"

Hardy offhandedly pointed at her phone, still on the table. A reference to the picture she had shown her moments earlier. "A development."

"*Is* it a development? I mean, what do you make of this?"

Hardy shrugged. "I don't know yet. But I have to check it out."

"But if . . . if that's Brie, then everything you've believed about Andrew is wrong. She's alive, and he had nothing to do with it."

"The first part might be true. That she's alive. But I don't know that that means he had nothing to do with her disappearance. All the more reason for me to talk to him. Why don't you text him and see when he's coming back."

"I did. Just before you got here."

Hardy shook her head. "You know what? I'll catch him another time." She picked up her phone, scrolled through some contacts. "I still have a number in here from six years back, unless he changed that along with his name." She read it out to Jayne. "Is that still it?"

"Yes."

The detective pushed back her chair, stood, dropped

the phone into the small purse that hung over her shoulder. She pulled a business card from it and placed it on the table.

"If you want to call," she said.

Jayne glanced at the card but did not pick it up.

"And if you need someplace to go," Hardy said, "I can help you with that. Someplace for yourself, and for your brother."

"What are you talking about? Are you talking about a *shelter*?"

Hardy nodded.

"We don't need to go to any shelter. I'm not being abused. Tyler's not being abused."

"Okay. But there's my number, should you change your mind."

Jayne followed Hardy out of the house and watched her get into her car, start it up, and drive off.

She was numb.

So this is what it's like, she thought, *to be in free fall, to be plunging through the air with a parachute that won't open.*

She was about to go back into the house, then decided to wait out here for his return. She sat on the front step, placed her palms on the cool concrete. As soon as he came around the corner in his Explorer, she would see him. And then she had a thought.

Maybe he isn't coming back.

He knew all about what had happened that morning. The detective had told Jayne that when she went to talk to that Max person, he'd told her his first call had been to Andrew, that he had already been there, listened to Max's eyewitness account, then seen what was on the next-door neighbor's security camera.

So much for going to Home Depot for weed and feed.

Jayne wondered if what he'd seen in that surveillance camera image had somehow frightened him. Made him want to run.

She knew the truth, knew about the secrets he had kept from her, and now he was heading for the hills.

She thought of all the stories she'd read over the years of women who'd been duped. Women who had met the man of their dreams, only to learn he was a con artist intent on swindling them out of their fortune. Or a bigamist with another wife, and family, on the other side of the country.

Well, Jayne had no fortune, so there went that motive. And if Andrew had another family somewhere, he certainly hadn't been spending any time with them.

But was he a murderer?

No, no, not possible.

Then she heard the car. There, coming down the street, was Andrew.

The sight of his SUV prompted both relief and a wave of dread. Relief that he'd not run, and dread over the discussion that lay ahead.

Why had he not told her about Brie? How did you go through something like that and not feel the need to talk about it?

She began to make excuses for him. As they'd grown closer, as they'd fallen in love—and she had no doubt, at least not until now, that she loved him and believed in her heart he loved her—he might have wanted to tell her everything, but was afraid that if he did, she'd break things off.

And she had to ask herself, had he been honest with her, would she have stayed in the relationship? Would she have moved in with him? Would she have brought her brother into this home?

That had to have been his reasoning. He didn't want to lose her. He was afraid to tell her.

Of course that was it.

And let's face it, she thought. *It's not like I've told him everything, either. About Tyler, or about myself.*

Fifteen
Andrew

I pulled into the driveway, killed the engine, opened the door, and got out slowly. I was feeling a little woozy from my visit to the bar, or maybe it was stress that had thrown me off balance. Either way, I was glad I'd made it home without getting stopped.

I had a feeling my luck was about to run out.

Jayne remained sitting on the front step. Didn't get up. I could see in her face she knew. I walked over slowly, stood a couple of feet away.

"So," she asked, deadpan, "how'd it go at Home Depot? You get the weed and feed?"

"No."

"A trip back to the old neighborhood instead?"

"Yeah," I said. "And then I kind of drove around

for a while." Didn't mention my trip up to Trumbull to talk to Greg.

Jayne nodded solemnly.

"Detective Hardy was here," I said.

"Yes."

"And she filled you in."

"Yes."

I drew in a long breath, let it out slowly. "I'm sorry. I'll pack up my things right now and get out. You can stay here. Whatever you want, that's what I'll do. Or I can just leave right now and you can throw my shit out here onto the lawn. I'll come back later."

She put one hand down on the cement to help push herself off the step. I extended a hand to help her up but she didn't take it.

"I have one question," she said, a slight tremble in her voice.

Here it was, I thought. I was ready with my answer. *No, I did not kill my wife.*

"Okay," I said.

"If it's her, if she's back, what happens to us?"

I blinked. Before I could think of what to say, she had a second question.

"Do you still love her?"

I didn't know how to answer that question any better than the first one.

"Can we go inside and talk?" I asked.

She considered the suggestion, finally nodded, and said, "Okay."

I followed her into the house.

Jayne already had a pot of coffee going, so she poured me some, refilled her own cup, and we sat down at the kitchen table. She looked particularly fragile. Her chin trembled ever so slightly, the mug shaking as she set it in front of me.

"I should have told you," I said.

Jayne's eyes were moist, and it was a safe bet she'd been crying.

"When we started going out, I kept thinking, I should tell you everything, and the more time that went by, the more difficult it was for me. Because the closer we got to each other, the more there was to lose."

I wasn't lying about that.

"I figured, if I told you everything, about Brie's disappearance, about the police investigation, how Detective Hardy considered me the prime suspect for a long time, I'd lose you. And I wouldn't have blamed you for bailing. If things had been reversed, I don't know what I would have done. I know I'd have felt the way you do right now. Duped. Betrayed. Lied to. And this isn't much of a defense, but I don't think I ever lied to you.

Not outright. But by omission, yeah, I plead guilty to that."

Jayne had said nothing through all this.

"The thing is, you're the one who saved me," I said. "I was lost. I was coming out of a pretty low point, but I was still struggling up that hill. If I could have had some answers, if what had happened to Brie had been resolved, I might have been able to put my life together. I'd been drinking a lot. Unable to focus on work. Greg, you know, my friend, was with me the night Brie went missing. We'd gone up to our places on Sorrow Bay. I told you about that cabin I had, the one I ended up selling a few years ago because I needed the money when I wasn't getting much work. I was spending too much time in my own head. Drinking. A lot. I was pretty depressed there for a while. Spent a lot of time just sitting on my ass, trying to find the energy to get back on my feet again."

I took a breath, and a sip of the coffee. I picked up a paper napkin on the table and tore off a tiny corner of it, started balling it up with my fingers.

"Took me about four years to start coming out of it, to get my life back into some kind of order. I changed my name, legally. In this part of Connecticut, people remembered. If I said I was Andrew Mason, people would wrinkle their foreheads and say, hey, aren't you the guy who killed his wife? What do you say to something like that? So I became Andrew Carville. Carville was my mother's last name, so at least I was hanging on to something from the family, you know?"

My mouth was dry. I thought maybe if I paused Jayne would have something to say, but she showed no signs of ending the silence. So I had more coffee and kept on going.

"And going back a bit," I said, "there was the matter of the house. When Brie and I bought it, the idea was that we'd fix it up. It needed a lot of work, but the basic structure was sound. I was going to redo pretty much everything. Knock out some walls, make the kitchen bigger, modernize the bathrooms. It would have taken a lot of time, but we got the house for a good price and whatever I didn't know how to do myself, which wasn't much, I knew the best people to do it. But after Brie vanished, I didn't have any enthusiasm for anything, let alone fixing up that house, maybe flipping it for a profit. And then there was the fact that everyone knew where I lived. For a long time, I'd have reporters waiting to talk to me when I came out the front door. Gawkers, driving by, pointing, you know, hey, that's the house that lady disappeared from."

I set the pea-sized paper ball on my thumb and flicked it. It flew across the table and sailed across the room, landing just in front of the fridge. Jayne snatched the rest of the shredded napkin away from me and wadded it up into her fist. She did not look amused.

I went on with my story.

"So I put the house on the market, got what I could for it. And the new owners, they decided it made more sense to rip it down and start over, which, to be honest, was probably the smartest thing to do. And there was a part of me that was relieved, you know? If I happened to drive down that street, which I went to great pains not to do, at least I wouldn't see the place where Brie and I had lived."

I sighed. "And I guess Detective Hardy told you about Natalie Simmons."

Jayne's eyebrows popped up, as good a clue as any that Hardy had not, in fact, brought up the subject of Natalie Simmons.

Shit.

"Oh," I said. "I'm that guy digging a hole and thinks the best way to get out is to keep on digging." I tried a weak laugh, but if I thought Jayne was going to respond with a chuckle I was reading the room wrong.

I continued: "I need to back up a bit. Brie and I had gone through a bad patch. You know they say finances are the biggest cause of problems in a marriage. Anyway, it was how I made a living that was a source of stress for us. Fixing up homes, flipping them, never settling in one place. Brie was done with it, and I was too dumb at the time to appreciate why. We were hardly talking to each other, and that was around the time I met Natalie. It wasn't a big thing, and it didn't last long. A little after that, Brie kind of cheated on me, too. Once. I don't know how, exactly, but we came to our senses, talked it through, forgave each other, and tried to move on. And I said that last house, if she wanted to stay there when it was fixed up, we would. If she didn't, the next house would be permanent. We came through it, but we hurt each other along the way."

I had a sip of cold coffee before continuing.

"No matter what Detective Hardy might have thought at the time, my lapse had nothing to do with Brie's disappearance. The detective tried to turn it into a big deal. This Natalie woman, it wasn't serious. At least, not for me. Maybe it meant more to her, but I broke it off and that was that."

Jayne remained mute.

I pushed the chair back, stood up, paced the kitchen. I wanted Jayne to react. I wanted her to get angry. I wanted her to start screaming at me, throw something. She had every right. But she just sat there, watching me.

"Look, I should have told you. There's nothing I can

do about that. I fucked up. You deserved to know. I'll understand if you can't excuse that. I'm not going to ask for forgiveness. I don't deserve it. All I can tell you is that you're the best thing that's happened to me in the last six years. You brought me back from the edge. Maybe that sounds like bullshit, like I'm laying it on thick so you won't walk out that door and take Tyler with you. But it's the truth."

I put a hand to my forehead, stopped my pacing, and leaned my back up against the fridge, knocking a couple of magnets to the floor.

"I've got nuthin' else," I said. "Christ, say something."

Maybe now, I thought. Maybe she'd ask me now.

If she didn't ask whether I'd done something to Brie, it meant one of two things. It could mean she had faith in me, that she believed I wasn't the kind of man who'd murder his wife. Or it might mean she was fearful I'd provide an answer she didn't want to hear.

Anyway, she was looking like she was ready to break her silence.

She took a sip of her coffee, set the mug down, then linked her fingers together so tightly they looked like they might snap. She rested her hands on the table and looked right at me.

"I'm pregnant," Jayne said.

Sixteen

By the time Isabel McBain emerged from the hospital and ran out to the parking lot, the woman was gone.

That moment when the woman had looked up at Isabel and her brother and her husband, grouped together in the window of their mother's hospital room, and waved, changed everything.

A stranger wouldn't have waved. A stranger wouldn't have recognized them. A stranger would have assumed they were looking at something else and not her.

But Brie would have spotted them for who they were.

Brie would have waved.

"Oh my God!" Isabel had shouted, no longer thinking to whisper as her mother lay sleeping. "Oh my God!" she'd said a second time.

And then she had started running, pushing Norman and Albert out of her way. She raced from the room and down the hospital corridor to the elevator. She pressed the down button, but after five seconds she no longer had the patience to wait. She spotted the sign for the stairwell and dashed off in that direction, with her husband and brother right behind her.

She scurried down the stairs, not quite coordinated enough to jump every other step, but she made good time just the same. When she emerged from the stairwell and into the hospital lobby it took a moment to get her bearings, having zigged and zagged her way down to the ground floor, not sure which way to go to exit the building and reach the lot.

"This way," said Albert, who'd reached the lobby half a second behind her.

The three of them emerged from the building and circled around to the parking lot, but there was no one there.

At least, not the woman they had seen waving to them.

"Are you sure this is the right lot?" a breathless Isabel asked.

"This is it," Norman said. "There's the red Corvette."

"Where is she?" she asked. "She couldn't just disappear into thin air!"

Albert looked back, and up, at the building. "There's Mom's room right there. This is the spot. This is where she was."

Isabel nodded. Norman appeared miffed, as if she needed assurance from her brother over him.

She spun around, scanning. "This is insane. Where did she go?"

"It did take us a couple of minutes to get down here," Albert said, leaning over and putting his hands on his knees as he struggled to get his wind back. "That's enough time to run away or get in a car or God knows what."

"Let's split up," Norman said urgently. "I'll go that way, you guys head down the sidewalk in different directions, meet back here in a couple of minutes."

Isabel didn't need a second opinion from Albert. "Okay."

They fanned out. And, as Norman had suggested, they regrouped a few minutes later. No one had spotted the woman.

"I didn't believe . . . I didn't believe it was her,"

Isabel said. "I didn't think it was possible, not until . . . not until she waved."

"I know," Albert said. "I mean, it could have been her, but it could have been a lot of people who *looked* a bit like her. But when she spotted us . . . Christ. It was like she knew who we were. Like she recognized us."

Isabel was starting to look unsteady on her feet. Norman and Albert flanked her, each taking an arm, in case she suddenly fainted.

Crying, she said, "Oh God, could she really be alive?"

"I don't know," Albert and Norman said almost at the same time.

"If she is, why do this? Why torture us this way? How does she know Mom's in the hospital? Is Brie watching us? Is she keeping tabs on us?"

"Izzy, Izzy, calm down," Albert said. "We need to . . . we need to . . ."

"Need to what?"

"I don't—maybe we should call her."

"Call her? Call Brie? How the hell are we supposed to do that?"

"No, not Brie. The detective. What was her—"

"Hardy. Marissa Hardy. Yes, yes. Call her. Call her now."

Albert got out his phone. "I don't know if I still have her in my contacts . . ." Before he'd found a number, he stopped himself. "She'll think we're crazy. She'll think we're seeing things. And you . . . you were always on her case."

Isabel looked defensive. "I was not."

"You were, demanding that she arrest Andrew."

"I had reason, and you know it. She never went after him hard enough. She should have charged him! That man should have been put on trial and—"

She stopped herself.

"Unless," Albert said.

Isabel needed a moment to put it together. "If it *is* Brie, then . . ."

"Maybe we should be calling *him*."

Isabel considered that for a second. "No, no, not him. We don't know that was Brie. He's not getting off the hook for this yet. Call that detective."

Albert went back to scrolling through contacts on his phone. "Hang on, I think I still have . . . Here she is."

Norman watched as Albert took the lead, tapping the screen and putting the phone to his ear, listening for the rings.

"It can't be," Norman whispered to Isabel. "There's just no way."

Isabel, ignoring him, said to Albert, "Is she answering?"

"Jesus, just hang on. Not yet— Hello? Is this Detective Hardy?"

Isabel sidled up close to him so she could hear both sides of the conversation.

"Yes, this is Hardy," the detective said.

"You might not remember me, Detective, but my name is Albert McBain. Six years ago, my sister—"

"*Our* sister!" Isabel shouted loud enough to be heard at the other end of the call.

"*Our* sister, Brie, disappeared and you were the lead detective, and—"

"I remember. What can I do for you, Mr. McBain?"

"We weren't even sure whether we should call you. Our mother, she's in the hospital. We've been visiting. And we were looking out the window, and in the parking lot—I know this is going to sound pretty out there, but we think we might have seen Brie."

Detective Hardy was silent.

"Hello?" Albert said. "Are you there?"

"I'm here," Hardy said slowly. "When did this happen?"

"Just now. Like, ten minutes ago. We're in the parking lot. We saw her, this woman, and rushed down, but by the time we got here she was gone. I mean, maybe it was someone who looked like her, but when she saw us in the window, she waved. It was like she recognized us."

"That's . . . interesting," the detective said.

Isabel snatched the phone from her brother's hand. "Detective Hardy? It's Isabel."

"Hello, Isabel." Hardy's voice suddenly sounded wearier.

"What do you mean, interesting?"

Another pause from the detective. "There was another . . . possible sighting of your sister this morning."

"*What?* Where? Where was this? Why didn't you call?"

"I don't want anyone jumping to conclusions, but it was at her last known address, on Mulberry. The neighbor said a woman pulled into the driveway and seemed stunned that the house that was there several years ago was no longer standing."

"He said it was Brie?"

"He said she looked something *like* your sister, but the identification was far from conclusive. Look, Ms. McBain, give me some time to look into this."

"Do you think it's even possible? Could Brie be—"

Hardy cut her off. "I said I'll look into it. If you see whoever this was again, call me. Anytime, day or night. Goodbye."

Isabel was ready with another question, but the detective had ended the call. Isabel, visibly annoyed, handed the phone back to her brother.

"She *says* she'll look into it."

"Do you believe her?" Albert asked.

Isabel shrugged. "I don't know."

Norman spoke up. "My guess is she's just shining you on. It's crazy. She's not going to do anything about it. If I were her, I wouldn't take this seriously. I mean, come on."

Albert was shaking his head. "If she says she's going to look into it, I think she will. I've never known her to bullshit anyone."

Isabel sighed, then slowly looked back up to the window of her mother's hospital room.

"Oh God," she said quietly.

Albert followed her gaze and guessed what she was thinking.

"What do we tell Mom?" Isabel asked.

Seventeen

Statement of Natalie Simmons,
June 11, 2016, 11:04 a.m.,
interviewed by Detective Marissa Hardy.

DETECTIVE HARDY: Took us a little while to track you down, Ms. Simmons. Thank you for coming in.

NATALIE: I'm sorry, I've been out of town.

DETECTIVE HARDY: Where were you?

NATALIE: I was visiting an aunt in Nova Scotia. In Halifax.

DETECTIVE HARDY: Oh. Nice vacation?

NATALIE: Not exactly a vacation. She's been ill. She's almost eighty and she's having trouble moving around, so I had to organize visits from local support groups and that kind of thing. I'm pretty much her only living relative, so there you go. I went up about a week ago. Took the car. It's about a thirteen-hour drive, so I broke it up into two days.

DETECTIVE HARDY: You went alone?

NATALIE: Yes. Can you tell me why I'm here? No one's told me anything. There was a note on my door when I got home.

DETECTIVE HARDY: We tried to reach you on your cell.

NATALIE: I don't have a cell phone.

DETECTIVE HARDY: Really? You're a rare breed.

NATALIE: They're bad for you. The radio waves can affect your brain. But the media doesn't report it because they're getting paid off by the cell phone companies. If everybody finds out, they'll stop using them and Verizon and all the others will lose a ton of money. Plus, they can track you, you know. They always know where you are.

DETECTIVE HARDY: They?

NATALIE: The government. Whoever. It's all over social media. I follow sites that investigate this kind of thing. Like, they have cures for major diseases but hold them back to keep the drug companies rich.

DETECTIVE HARDY: Would the government be having some reason to track your movements, Ms. Simmons?

NATALIE: I think they'd be pretty bored if they bothered, but you never know. Right?

DETECTIVE HARDY: I suppose. Anyway, I wonder if we could get started.

NATALIE: Okay.

DETECTIVE HARDY: First, I want to confirm some information. This address we have for you, that's current?

NATALIE: Yes.

DETECTIVE HARDY: And what do you do for a living?

NATALIE: I work in an art gallery in Stratford. Maybe you know it? The Decca Gallery? Anyway, they're pretty good there, and were totally understanding when I had to go up to Halifax.

DETECTIVE HARDY: I believe you know an Andrew Mason?

NATALIE: Uh, yes.

DETECTIVE HARDY: Have you known him very long?

NATALIE: Uh, I guess I met him a year ago? Something like that? But I sort of knew him from a long time ago. College. More like acquaintances back then.

DETECTIVE HARDY: So, more than an acquaintance now.

NATALIE: Well . . .

DETECTIVE HARDY: Things will move along more quickly here if you'll just answer the questions honestly and directly.

NATALIE: I know him a bit better now, yeah. What exactly is this about?

DETECTIVE HARDY: When did you start going out with Mr. Mason?

NATALIE: It was, I don't know, a few months ago.

DETECTIVE HARDY: How would you describe the nature of your relationship with him, then?

NATALIE: We, you know, we sort of were seeing each other.

DETECTIVE HARDY: Seeing each other?

NATALIE: Seriously, what's this about? Has something happened to Andy? Is he okay? Is he in some kind of trouble?

DETECTIVE HARDY: Were you and Mr. Mason in an intimate relationship?

NATALIE: What do you mean, exactly, by intimate?

DETECTIVE HARDY: Was it a sexual relationship?

NATALIE: Yeah, I guess that was a part of it.

DETECTIVE HARDY: Is there some doubt? I think that's the kind of thing you'd know one way or another.

NATALIE: Yeah, okay. It was what you said.

DETECTIVE HARDY: And when did this relationship begin?

NATALIE: I guess around four months ago? It only went on for like a month.

DETECTIVE HARDY: Why was that?

NATALIE: Well, he's married.

DETECTIVE HARDY: Did you know that when you started seeing him?

NATALIE: Sort of. I mean, he had a ring and all.

DETECTIVE HARDY: So is that when you broke it off?

NATALIE: No, I didn't break it off. Andy did.

DETECTIVE HARDY: Oh. Were you upset about that?

NATALIE: (*unintelligible*)

DETECTIVE HARDY: Ms. Simmons? Are you okay?

NATALIE: It's just . . . I really liked him, you know? I mean, yeah, I knew he was married, but there must have been something missing there if he wanted to spend time with me. I started thinking, sure, this could get messy, but maybe there was more to it than just, you know, sex.

DETECTIVE HARDY: Have you been married, Ms. Simmons?

NATALIE: Once. Lasted only two years. His name was, well, his name is Conroy Hill. He moved out to L.A. about ten years ago. He's in the music business.

DETECTIVE HARDY: Did you ever entertain the idea, the hope, that Mr. Mason might leave his wife for you?

NATALIE: I don't know. I hoped. The thing is, he was so different than my usual type.

DETECTIVE HARDY: How do you mean?

NATALIE: Well, you work in a gallery, you meet a

lot of creative, artsy types. Head in the clouds, eccentric, pseudo-intellectuals. And, of course, half of those are gay. But Andrew, I mean, he's like a carpenter, you know? Okay, more than that. A contractor. Works with his hands. Not my usual type. But he still appreciates stuff like movies and art. And he's kind of . . . how do I put this? *Manly.* You know? Like, a more rugged type, and I liked that about him. But a bit stressed. But that could have been because he had business problems, and there was the whole thing with his marriage, of course.

DETECTIVE HARDY: Did you ever meet Brie?

NATALIE: Once, and it was totally awkward. I was in the food court at the Post Mall and turned and there he was, and I was like, hey, how are you? And then I see this woman standing next to him. So his face is all flushed and he quickly introduces me to his wife, said I was someone he met through work, pretended like he couldn't remember my last name. I could tell, though, looking at her, she knew he was lying. Look, I'm not answering any more questions until you tell me why you brought me in here.

DETECTIVE HARDY: Brie Mason is missing, Ms. Simmons.

NATALIE: She's what?

DETECTIVE HARDY: She's been missing since this past weekend.

NATALIE: Oh my God. No one's heard from her?

DETECTIVE HARDY: No.

NATALIE: And you—Jesus—and you think I had something to do with it?

DETECTIVE HARDY: No, I—

NATALIE: Because whatever my ex told you, it's bullshit.

DETECTIVE HARDY: Okay. Tell me about that.

NATALIE: And it was a long time ago, too. What did Conroy tell you, anyway?

DETECTIVE HARDY: Maybe you should give me your side of it.

NATALIE: It was a onetime thing. And it was after we'd split up. I saw him with Charlotte, and—

DETECTIVE HARDY: Charlotte?

NATALIE: The first one he went out with after we separated. I saw them at the Stamford Mall, in the parking garage. I was heading for my car and I saw them getting into his, and yeah, okay, I walked right past the car, but there's no way he could prove it was me that keyed his Jag.

DETECTIVE HARDY: You keyed his car?

NATALIE: The security video didn't show anything.

DETECTIVE HARDY: So it wasn't exactly an amicable split with him.

NATALIE: All I'm saying is, I've got nothing to do with this woman going missing.

DETECTIVE HARDY: What I was about to ask you was, did Mr. Mason ever say anything about his wife that would lead you to believe he might want to harm her in any way?

NATALIE: Oh, okay. Wow, I'm such an idiot. I thought—

DETECTIVE HARDY: Did he complain about her? Make disparaging remarks?

NATALIE: No. He was pretty depressed a lot of the time, feeling guilty, you know? About seeing me. I mean, okay, there was the one time he said he could just kill her, but—

DETECTIVE HARDY: He said what?

NATALIE: Andy said . . . I'm trying to remember now . . . but he said something like, "I could just kill her."

DETECTIVE HARDY: He said that.

NATALIE: He did. But it was more in a kidding way. Like, a figure of speech.

DETECTIVE HARDY: What was the context?

NATALIE: I think they'd a fight about something. A disagreement. They're renovating that house, right? And I think it was about picking out things for the kitchen. Brie couldn't make up her mind about colors or taps or countertops or something. I don't really remember, but Andy was annoyed because it was slowing the project down.

DETECTIVE HARDY: Okay. That does sound like an offhand comment. My partner wanted to kill me when we were trying to pick a paint color for our bedroom.

NATALIE: I know, I'm making too much of it.

DETECTIVE HARDY: So there was nothing else along those lines.

NATALIE: Not really. In fact, he said one time, about Brie, he said, and this got me thinking that maybe it wasn't going to work out with him, and these were his exact words: "I love her to death."

Eighteen
Andrew

I have to admit, I hadn't seen that coming.

If I had, maybe I would have known how to react, could have prepared myself, said something that gave the impression I was thrilled with Jayne's news. Because when someone tells you she's pregnant, you want to look delighted. And I'm not saying I wasn't. I believe, given a moment to get my head around what Jayne had told me, I would have been more than delighted. I would have been downright fucking thrilled. Having a child was not something we'd really talked about, but we would have gotten there eventually, and when that time had come I know I would have been on board with the idea.

But considering the kind of morning it had been—

the appearance of that woman, Detective Hardy coming to the house, my relationship with Jayne seemingly on the verge of unraveling as my past came to light—I wasn't quite in a mood to jump up and down. I should have said something along the lines of, "That's wonderful!" or, "Oh my God, that's great!" A simple "Wow!" might have done the trick.

What I said was, "What?"

And I imagine I looked pretty stunned when I said it.

"I'm pregnant," Jayne said again.

I was frozen for about two seconds, then bolted forward, and, given that she was still in the chair, went down to my knees and put my arms around her for a hug. She returned the embrace, but it didn't feel as though she was putting as much into it as I was.

I pulled away and said, "When did you find out?"

"Yesterday," she said. "I'd done the test last weekend, peed on the stick, you know? And it was positive, but I wanted to go to the doctor first, get her two cents' worth, before I told you. I saw her yesterday."

"That beer," I said. "When you came out with those two bottles, yours looked different."

"Non-alcoholic," she said. "I picked up a six-pack yesterday, tucked them into the back of the fridge where you wouldn't find them." Jayne motioned for me to stand up, which I did, then sat back in the chair across from her. "You didn't exactly look thrilled a moment ago."

"You caught me by surprise," I said. "It's been a day full of them." I ran my hand over the top of my head and sighed. "Man. How far along?"

"About seven weeks, the doctor figures," she said. "I think it happened the weekend we went to Mystic. Couple of days before Tyler joined us."

My mind immediately went back to that mini-vacation. I behaved like someone released from prison. Jayne was no less insatiable.

I couldn't help but grin. "Yeah, it could have been then. We were going to do a charter, check out the museum, but I don't remember our leaving that B&B much."

"I'd had this plan," she said. "That we'd go out to dinner tonight, that I would tell you the news, but now . . ."

"Jayne."

"This can't be happening," she said. "Not now."

"Wait, what do you mean? You don't want to have the baby? I thought—"

"That's not what I mean," she said. "This, whatever this is, what's happened *today*. That can't be happening."

"Jayne, I swear, I don't know what the hell is going on."

"What if she's back?"

"We don't know that it's Brie," I said. "It doesn't make any *sense* that it's Brie."

"Why do you say that?" she asked. "How do you know it *couldn't* be?"

That was the closest she'd come to asking the question. I took a moment to consider my answer.

"Because, if that was Brie, how do we explain it? Where's she been for six years? Why would she just pop up out of nowhere? I mean, what's she been doing all this time? If it was really her, why'd she decide that *this*, of all the times she could have come back, was the right time? Did someone keep her prisoner and she finally escaped? And if that was what happened, why didn't she go straight to the police? How does she end up showing up at our old house? There's no rational explanation for it."

"But it happened."

"*Something* happened. Someone showed up at the house."

"Let's say, for the sake of argument, it *is* your wife," Jayne said. "She . . . she was abducted by aliens and they just brought her back, for Christ's sake. I don't know. But if it is, don't you *want* it to be her?"

Jesus, how to answer that.

Slowly, I said, "Yes."

Jayne's face looked ready to crumple.

"Yes," I repeated. "Because if it's her, it means no harm has come to her. That she's *alive*. Who knows, maybe some harm *had* come to her, but it would mean that whatever it was, she'd survived it. She'd still be with us, and that would be a good thing. Never, not for a minute, have I hoped that she was dead. I admit, plenty of times I wished I knew one way or the other what had happened to her, but that doesn't mean I actually hoped she was dead. So, yeah, I'd want it to be her."

Jayne swallowed hard as she listened.

"And, you know, there's been this cloud hanging over me for a long time. There are people out there who still think I killed my wife. I'm sure this latest development's ruined Detective Hardy's day, because I know she's always thought I did it. She *wants* to believe I did it. If—and I think it's a big if—but if this woman is Brie, then there you go. I'm not a murderer." I managed a weak smile. "It'll ruin Izzy's day, too, although that might be offset by getting her sister back."

I was almost finished.

"But if by some miracle it is Brie, it doesn't mean it's the end of *us*. We'll find a way through this. We will."

"It's like *Cast Away*," Jayne said.

"Like what?"

"The movie. With Tom Hanks, and what's her name, the one from *Mad About You*. Helen Hunt. The one where his jet crashes on an island and he's there for, like, I don't know, a few years, and everyone thinks he's dead. His only friend in the world is Wilson, a volleyball. And Helen Hunt, eventually she has to get on with her life, and she finds another man and falls in love with him and moves in with him, and then it turns out Tom's not dead, and he comes back."

I remembered the movie.

"I'm Helen Hunt," I said.

That almost made Jayne smile when she nodded. "What's she supposed to do? She loved Tom, but now she has this new man in her life, and she loves him, too. It's devastating, for everyone involved. She's in an impossible situation."

"But she stays with the new guy," I said.

"It doesn't mean it will work out that way with us," Jayne said. "We're not in a movie." She looked into my eyes. "Think back to the last day you saw her."

"Okay."

"On that day, before she went missing, did you love her?"

I reached across the table and took her hand in mine. "I love *you*," I said.

"But that's not my question. The last time you saw her, talked to her." She took a breath. "Slept with her. Did you love her?"

"Yes," I said.

"So doesn't it stand to reason that if she walked through that door right now you'd still love her?"

"Jayne, I—"

"I mean, if you suddenly went missing, and six years went by, and you walked in here, I'd still love you, no matter how I'd gone on with my life."

"These . . . these questions, I feel like there's no right way to answer them."

"I'm the one who's going to have your baby."

"I know."

"You and Brie didn't have children."

"We . . . she said she didn't want to raise a child if we didn't have a home. A real home. Not one fixer-upper after another. Something stable. It was one of the issues we were working on."

"Well, what we have here, I think this is a home, and it looks like I'm going to have a baby in it. That's why this can't be happening. I need to know you're with me. Totally. All these things I learned about you today, they're . . . God, they're pretty fucking unsettling, is what they are. But even though you've kept so much from me, I believe, in my heart, that I know you. That I know the kind of man you are. I'm willing . . . I was going to say forgive. I don't know that I'm there yet and I don't know when I will be. But I want to move past this, so long as you're totally honest with me going forward."

"I will be," I said.

"I feel like I'm walking along the edge of a cliff," she said. "Any second now, I'm going to fall."

I dragged my chair around the table until it was butted up next to hers, put my arm around her, and held her close.

"I'm telling you, we're going to be okay."

"You're a good man," she said. "I'm sure of it. I see how you are with Tyler. How patient you are. You're not pushing things with him. He needs time."

"I know."

"He's never going to see you like you're his father. But a big brother, maybe. A mentor."

"I'm giving it my best shot," I said.

"Tyler's not perfect."

"Maybe that's something he and I have in common."

"Please tell me this is just a blip. That this, whatever this is, that it's going to pass."

"It will," I assured her, putting my arm around her. I felt her softening in my arms, accepting my comfort.

I added, "Look, if it really was Brie, she'd call me, wouldn't she? She'd get to a phone and she'd call me and say, hey, guess who's back in town."

That was when the phone in my pocket started to ring.

Nineteen

Albert and Isabel entered their mother's hospital room quietly. They had brought someone with them. And it wasn't Isabel's husband, Norman.

Elizabeth had been taking a break from watching the news, her endless flipping through CNN and MSNBC and Fox, thinking that the world she was leaving was in a much bigger mess than the one she came into. She thought back to when she worked in newspapers, tried to remember if the country was ever in as bad a shape as it was now. Sure, she edited and slapped headlines on countless stories involving unimaginable heartache. But at least back then it seemed as though they were spaced out some. You didn't have a mass shooting every day. There weren't kids in cages. A pandemic hadn't brought the nation's hospitals to the breaking point. You didn't have political parties making excuses for domestic terrorists.

Maybe Isabel had been right the last time she was here, making her turn off the damn TV.

But now she was back, with her brother and this other man. Her eyebrows went up a notch at the sight of the stranger.

"Hey, Mom," Isabel said. "This is someone we'd like you to meet. This is Max. Max, this is our mother, Elizabeth."

Max stepped forward and, tentatively, extended a hand. Elizabeth placed her bony fingers into his palm and he gave them the gentlest of squeezes.

"Hello," she said. "Are you a doctor?"

"Um, no," Max said.

It had been nearly two hours since Albert, Isabel, and Norman had stood in the parking lot, wondering whether to go back to their mother's room and tell her that they had seen a woman they thought could be Brie.

Albert, initially, thought it was a good idea to head straight up there and break the news. But Isabel was worried about giving their mother any false hope that their sister might still be alive.

Norman agreed. "You can't go raising her spirits on something as flimsy as this. We saw that woman from several floors away. It could have been anybody."

"Maybe a false hope is better than none," Albert said.

But then he made the point that their mother might not even believe them. She was, after all, a hardened skeptic. She'd think they'd made it all up, that it was some cheap ploy to make her feel better, to boost her spirits in the time that she had left.

"But what if it was somebody other than us?" Albert had said. "Not a relative."

"The neighbor," Isabel had said. "Someone without a personal reason for wanting to give Mom some good news." The detective, without getting into details, had said a former neighbor of Brie's had reported seeing someone who looked like her.

"We have to find that person," Albert said.

So Albert and Isabel had driven to Mulberry Street and found Max, who confirmed he was the one who'd called Detective Hardy about what he'd witnessed. (Norman had felt that they could handle this mission without him, and went home to check on their son and daughter, both in their mid-teens.)

Albert had asked Max whether he'd be willing to accompany them to the hospital and tell their mother what he'd seen. He'd be a more credible witness, Albert and Isabel argued. Not only would he have no reason to lie to Elizabeth, he'd gotten a much closer look at this woman than Albert and Isabel had from the hospital window.

With some reluctance, he agreed.

And now he was standing next to Elizabeth's bed, but it was Albert who set the stage for the story he was about to tell.

"Mother," said Albert, "there's been something of a development today with regard to Brie."

Elizabeth sat up in bed, surprisingly quickly, considering her health. Her face was a plane crash, every fold in her aging skin diving in anticipation of bad news.

"Oh God," she said. "They found her." And by her expression, it was obvious Elizabeth feared it was her daughter's body that had been found.

Isabel jumped in. "No, Mom, it's not like that. Just wait. Listen to what Max has to say, and then . . . then Albert and I have something to tell you as well."

Albert turned to Max. "Over to you."

Max told his tale. Elizabeth listened carefully and without interruption. When Max was done, she nodded thoughtfully.

"I see," she said. "I have a few questions."

"Of course," Max said.

"How much distance was there between you and this woman?"

"I would guess maybe thirty, forty feet."

"Do you drink?"

"Excuse me?"

"Do you drink, Max? Had you been drinking the night before?"

"A couple of beers, maybe."

"If, hypothetically, my daughter were to call you on the phone, out of the blue, would you recognize her voice?"

"Uh, well—"

Albert felt a need to step in. "You'll have to excuse my mother, Max. Her background's in journalism and fact-checking and always getting it right."

Elizabeth shot her son a look. "Don't apologize on my behalf." She focused on Max again. "Would you know her voice?"

"I don't suppose I would. But this woman didn't *not* sound like Brie, if you know what I mean."

Elizabeth's expression turned sour. "Did you get a look at the license plate on the car?"

"No."

"Did she call you by name, like she knew you?"

"No."

Elizabeth found the strength to lift her hands six inches off the bed and wave them dismissively. "Thank you, Max."

"There's more," Albert said.

He told her what he and Isabel and Norman had witnessed from the window, and how they had then raced down there to try to find the woman who had waved to them.

"But you didn't find her," Elizabeth said.

"We didn't," Isabel said.

"And you saw her from this window, which would have been a lot farther away than Max here was from her, if it was the same person."

"True," Albert said. "But—"

"Stop," Elizabeth said. She appeared exhausted. "I don't know what you expect me to think. It's just . . . I don't know. If only one of you had managed to get a picture."

"Oh," said Max. "I have a picture."

The room went quiet as Elizabeth looked at him. "You have a picture?"

He got out his phone. "Our neighbor, Brian, the one who built the new house on the lot, has a security camera. Before I came over here I went over to see him and he gave me a screen capture—"

"A what?"

"A photo of what the security camera picked up," Max said.

He brought the image up onto the phone's screen and handed it to Elizabeth. She fumbled about under her covers for a pair of glasses, found them, and slipped them on.

"These don't work that well for me anymore," she said. "But let me have a look." She still sounded skeptical as she touched the screen.

"What happened?" she asked, flustered. "What did I do?"

"It's okay," Max said. "You probably touched something you shouldn't have." He took the phone, found the image again, and held it out to her.

Elizabeth took a moment to focus. "It's hard to see."

Max took the phone back from her once again, this time using his thumb and index finger to enlarge the image. This time, he held it in front of Elizabeth so she wouldn't have to touch the image and possibly disrupt it somehow.

"What do you think, Mom?" Albert asked.

His mother was silent for several seconds. She put her hand to her lips and held them there, as though trying to stop herself from saying what she wanted to say.

"Mom?" said Isabel.

Elizabeth took her hand away. When she spoke, her voice was no more than a whisper.

"Oh my God," she said. "It's Brie."

Twenty
Andrew

The ringing of my phone had startled both of us, considering I'd just told Jayne that if Brie were still alive, she'd call. We both must have looked as though we'd heard an ominous sound in the basement. I felt my heart skip a beat.

I got out my phone and looked, first, at the screen. Nothing. The caller ID was blocked. Jayne had raised her head, trying to see who the caller was, so I turned the phone so she could see for herself. By this point, it had rung four times.

"Are you going to answer it?" she asked.

I nodded, tapped the screen, and put the phone to my ear.

"Hello?" I said.

Nothing.

"Hello?" I said again.

"Is it her?" Jayne asked. "Is it Brie?"

I wasn't going to ask that question, but I allowed whoever was on the other end another five seconds to say something, anything. When no one spoke, I finally ended the call.

"Who was it?" Jayne asked.

"Nobody."

"How do you know?"

"Well, they didn't say anything. It was probably a nuisance call, like, from a telemarketer or something. Or someone threatening to come arrest me because I haven't paid my taxes. I hear that half the time, when you answer, these scammers are still busy annoying someone else and never get to you. I'm sure that's all it was."

Jayne did not look convinced.

"Honestly," I said, "I'm sure it was—"

The phone, still in my hand, rang again, causing us both to jump for a second time.

"Jesus," I said. This time, however, there was a name on the screen. GREG. I answered. "Hey."

"Hi," Greg said. "Thought I'd check in, see if you knew anything more than you did a few hours ago."

"No," I said, looking at Jayne.

Jayne mouthed the words "Who is it?" and I mouthed my friend's name.

She whispered back, "What does he want?"

"Hang on," I said to Greg, then put my hand over the bottom half of the phone. "I went to talk to him. About this morning."

"You talked to him before you talked to me?" she asked.

"I wanted his take, to—"

"Hello?" Greg said. "You there?"

"Yeah, I'm here," I said.

Jayne was visibly pissed, no doubt because I had talked to Greg before I'd come clean with her. She pushed back her chair, stood, and walked out of the kitchen.

"Shit," I said under my breath.

"What?" Greg said.

"Nothing. Just . . . not a good time." I heard the front door open and close.

"Sorry, but I had a thought and wanted to pass it along."

"Fine," I said. "Go ahead."

"I don't want you to take this the wrong way," he said. "Because you're my friend, no matter what, and I've got your back regardless, you know? I mean, I've always been straight with you, haven't I?"

"What are you getting at?"

"I think you need to be careful."

"What do you mean?"

"Have the cops been around to visit you?"

"That detective, the one that gave me such a hard time back when it happened, came by when I was out. Remember her?"

"Yeah, I remember her. So if she's coming to see you, have your guard up."

"I'm not reading you, Greg."

There was a pause. "It could be a trap."

"A trap?"

"Yeah."

I stood and walked out of the kitchen and to the living room window, wondering if Jayne was out front. "What do you mean, a trap?"

"Look, the odds that it was really Brie are like a million-to-one, right? But I'm thinking, you're *supposed* to think it's her."

"And who would want to make me think that?"

"The police. Let's say, for the sake of argument, that you did it. That you did something to Brie."

"For fuck's sake, Gre—"

"Hear me out, man. But that's what this detective has always believed. So, if Brie suddenly shows up, that's designed to put you on edge. Throw you off your game."

"Greg, you can't—"

"I'm almost done. If you're the killer, suddenly you start doubting yourself. You go check and see if the body is where you left it. Like, say, in some concrete foundation or in the wall of a building. And when you do, *bam!* Hardy's waiting for you like Columbo."

I sighed. "That's not going to happen."

"Agreed. But I bet they're watching you. Probably got a tracker on your car. And they're clever, letting it be your old neighbor who sees her. Knowing he'll call you. Maybe he's even in on it."

I said nothing.

"You still there?"

"I'm still here."

"The thing is, Andy, I've got your back. Always have, always will. No matter what you've done."

"What's that supposed to mean?"

There was silence at the other end.

"Greg?"

"You don't remember," he said.

"Don't remember what?"

"I mean, it's not a surprise that you wouldn't. You were so shit-faced at the time."

I remained at the window, wondering if Jayne was still on the property, or whether she'd gone for a walk.

"What are you talking about?" I was starting to lose patience with my friend.

"That night I came over, found you sitting in the tub, taking a bath in your piss and vomit. The night you finally decided you had to get it together."

"I haven't forgotten that."

"But I guess you forgot what you said to me."

"What did I say, Greg?"

Another pause. "You said, 'It's all my fault.' You said, 'I fucked up.' I asked you, I said, 'What are you talking about?' And you said, 'Brie.' But I never told a soul you said that. Never told that detective."

An unmarked car came to stop out front of the house. Detective Marissa Hardy had returned.

"I'm gonna have to get back to you, Greg," I said, and ended the call.

Twenty-One

When Tyler had wandered into the kitchen and found that police detective there, he thought, *Holy shit.*

His first assumption had been that she was there because of what he and Cam had been up to the night before. They'd done a little more than get ripped on some vodka. They'd wandered into one of the local cemeteries and, putting their combined weight behind the effort, managed to knock over half a dozen gravestones.

They'd gone to the cemetery only intending to get drunk, but then Cam had begun speculating on how hard it would be to knock over one of those marble slabs, and one thing led to another and whaddya know, it wasn't that hard at all. At least, not with some of the smaller ones. After they'd dropped the sixth one, they saw some headlights at the entrance and, figuring it might be the police, beat it the hell out of there.

Even before that lady cop showed up at the house, he'd been worrying that he was going to get caught. Maybe there were surveillance cameras at the cemetery. Or, if not actually on the property, they might have been caught on some security video from a nearby business.

So when it turned out the detective wasn't there about that, Tyler was mostly relieved, although he wondered if it was possible that she was there about his aunt Clara. But that had all been sorted out. The police got called but she didn't press charges and that was the end of it. Tyler left the kitchen reasonably sure that the cop being in the kitchen had nothing to do with him.

But that didn't mean he wasn't curious.

So he went back upstairs to his bedroom, which was located directly over the kitchen, and if you put your ear close to the radiator grille on the floor, you could hear conversations down there pretty clearly.

When Andrew and his sister were down there, he'd hear the soft murmuring of their voices when he was sitting at the desk in his room, but what they had to say didn't usually interest Tyler. Just boring shit, like who was going to pick up what at the store or how work was going, or what they might watch that night on Netflix. Stuff Tyler couldn't give a rat's ass about.

But this was different. It wasn't every day you had a police detective in the house.

So Tyler closed his bedroom door and stretched out on the floor, on his back, his right ear near the floor heating vent, and looked at the ceiling.

What a fucking eye-opener.

Andrew Carville was actually Andrew Mason, and he was married to a woman named Brie, and this Brie chick had gone missing six years ago.

After the cop left, Tyler grabbed his laptop and entered several key words into the browser's search field. Words like *missing* and *Brie* and *Andrew Mason*.

All sorts of stories came up, and not just newspaper accounts, but video from various TV stations. Most of the results were from more than five years ago. There were only a few more recent stories, whatever-happened-to kinds of pieces.

Tyler couldn't find any story to suggest Andrew had been charged with anything. Brie's disappearance remained a mystery. A cold case.

Whoa.

He was still reading stories when he heard Andrew come home from wherever he had been. Tyler got back into position, listening to the conversation between Andrew and Jayne.

Man oh man oh man.

He told her everything. Well, at least it sounded like he'd told her everything. Tyler kept trying to send his sister a telepathic message: "Ask him if he killed her!"

But Jayne never asked him a direct question like that and Tyler figured that was because it never even occurred to her that he might be guilty. Either that, or she was scared shitless about what he might say.

Tyler wasn't sure how he felt. If the police had the goods on the guy, they'd have arrested him, right? Then again, if they couldn't find a body, maybe they couldn't prove it.

But all that went out the window if Brie had actually returned. Tyler had seen plenty of photos of Brie while he did his research, and he had to admit there was more than a passing resemblance between her and the woman he had seen in the photo on the detective's phone. So if she was back, then Andrew wasn't some bad guy, right? And that would be a good thing, because you didn't want your knocked-up sister falling in love with some dude who'd killed his wife.

Speaking of which, Jayne had told Andrew what she had whispered into Tyler's ear a couple of hours earlier. The news that she was pregnant.

Man, what a shit show.

Tyler could only begin to imagine how fucked up his sister must be feeling. It was one bombshell after another. And Tyler was wondering just how *he* should feel. What, if anything, should *he* be doing about this?

The thing was, he'd never had much problem making his sister feel guilty about never really being there for him when he was growing up. But he also knew, in his heart, that it really wasn't her fault. She was already starting high school when he was born. By the time he reached that level of education, she was already out of college and had a job. Jayne couldn't help it that their parents made something of a miscalculation the night he was conceived, probably thinking pregnancy was no longer in the offing for them, maybe getting a bit careless about taking precautions.

Tyler really did love his sister, had always looked up to her. From afar much of the time. And he knew she'd taken a chance, bringing him into this home, running the risk of ruining this good thing she had going with Andrew. Well, until today, that is. Everything was looking a little shaky today.

And Tyler had to admit that Andrew didn't seem like that bad a guy. Tyler knew he'd been kind of a dick in his dealings with his sister's boyfriend. It was almost like he didn't want to be friends with him. Tyler was pretty good at pushing people away these days, even before his dad died shoveling snow.

That was supposed to be my job.

No sense getting close to people, Tyler reasoned, because it was inevitable that you were going to disappoint them.

Tyler acknowledged, to himself, that he might need to work on his attitude. Jayne wasn't kidding when she said this place was his second chance.

He'd fucked things up big-time when he went to live with Aunt Clara after his father's death. All that anger he was feeling, all that guilt, it was only a matter of time before he lost it. Clara, always trying to get him to talk about his *feelings.* Always asking how he was. Did he want to talk about losing his father? How are you *today*? Any better than *yesterday*? You know I'm here for you if there's anything you want to talk about? They say that time heals all wounds. Did you know that? Things that hurt us only make us stronger.

He was listening to what he thought of as "Claratherapy" when he just couldn't take it anymore. "Shut up! Just shut up and leave me alone!" he'd shouted at her. And then he took the drinking glass in his hand and slammed it down so hard on the table that it shattered. Right in his fucking hand. Got a nasty cut on his palm.

But that wasn't the worst of it.

One tiny little shard went flying. Right into Aunt Clara's left eye.

She threw a hand over her eye and screamed.

"Oh shit!" Tyler said, and, wrapping a dish towel around his palm to stanch the blood flow, got his aunt to open her eye so that he could have a look. Thinking maybe he could get the glass out himself.

"Don't touch it!" she shouted.

So Tyler ordered up an Uber and rushed her to the hospital. The staff in the emergency room wouldn't stop asking questions about how Clara had been injured. The fact that she wouldn't say led them to think the worst, and they called the police.

"I never threw it at her," Tyler told the investigating officer. "I wasn't aiming for her. It was a fluke."

Clara didn't lose her sight, but she had a bandage over that eye for the better part of three weeks. Clara, bless her, didn't want her nephew hauled off to juvenile court or anything, but the authorities pressured Tyler to go for a period of counseling, some anger management shit, and he was pretty sure there remained a file on him back in Providence.

If he screwed up again, someone would dig up that file. If he screwed up again, even his sister might decide he was too much of a handful for her, the way Aunt Clara had.

And then where would he end up?

There'd be no Jayne. There'd be no Andrew. He'd end up spending the rest of his teen years the way his sister's boyfriend had, living with strangers who really didn't give a shit about him.

Tyler didn't know how this was going to play out, but he knew how he wanted things to go. He wanted this mystery woman to be the real Brie. Tyler didn't have a clue how that could possibly be, but if it did turn out that way, then the police, and everyone else, would know Andrew wasn't a killer.

But he also wanted this Brie to decide she no longer wanted to make a life with Andrew. That'd mean Andrew would stay with his sister.

And when the baby came, Andrew would be there for her.

Me, too, Tyler thought. It'd be cool to become an uncle.

But if this woman was Brie, and she did want to go back to being Andrew's wife, well, shit, what the hell was going to happen then?

Twenty-Two
Andrew

Detective Hardy backed her car up a few feet so that it blocked the end of the driveway. I guess she thought I was going to jump into my Explorer and make a run for it, which seemed kind of ridiculous, given that I'd never tried to escape from her in the past when things were looking pretty goddamn grim.

She got out of the car and smiled. "Caught you this time."

"Sorry you missed me before," I said. "But I gather you had lots to talk about with Jayne."

Hardy closed her door and approached. "We had a good chat."

"You never get tired of trying to ruin my life. My old one, and now my new one."

"You make it sound like it's personal, Mr. Mason. Oh, sorry, Mr. Carville." She smiled. "It's hard to get used to that."

"Am I going to have to change it again?" I asked. "Have you already leaked a few juicy tidbits to the media? Am I going to have CNN on my doorstep by tomorrow?"

Hardy feigned hurt feelings. "I can't control what the press chooses to cover. It's a free country, you know."

"I get this sense you'd like to make it a little less free for me."

"There are matters still unresolved," she acknowledged. "Brie's still missing."

"And I wish you would find her, or find out what happened to her. There's nothing I want more in the world than that."

Hardy nodded slowly. "Of course. I guess that's why you hired your own private investigator to look for Brie, or started some big media campaign to get the public's help to find her."

I had done neither of those things, which of course was her point.

"You have no idea what I did trying to find Brie," I said. "Maybe it didn't include hiring my own detective, or mounting some social media blitz, but you know why? Because I was stupid enough, naïve enough, to believe you would do it because that was *your* job."

Hardy winced, as though maybe I'd landed a glancing blow.

"It was *your* job—it's *always* been your job—to find Brie, bring some kind of resolution for those who love her. And maybe if you hadn't zeroed in on me as your number one suspect from the very first day, you'd have opened your eyes to what else might have happened to her. But no, you make up for your ineptitude by accusing me of not being an amateur detective."

I shook my head in disgust. "You have no idea what I did or didn't do, no idea of the sleepless nights, no idea how many times I drove the streets at all hours, night and day, and wandered the malls and walked along creeks and searched everywhere I could think of. You have no idea how much I've tortured myself over this. I've wondered, could she be dead, and if so, how did it happen? Who killed her? But then I'd think, maybe she isn't dead, maybe there's hope, but then, if she's alive, why hasn't she been in touch? Why did she leave me? Why has she put me through this? What did I do that would make her want to hurt me this much? I mean, which would be worse? To find out she's dead, or that she's left me without so much as a goodbye. Answer me that."

I was out of breath.

The silence between us lasted several seconds.

"Which brings us to today," the detective said.

"I don't know what to make of it," I said, knowing what she had to be referring to.

"I've been doing a little digging," she said. "You know, like, doing my job. The groceries she dropped were from the Stop & Shop in Milford's east end. You ever shop there?"

"No."

"Did you and Brie ever shop there?"

"Maybe occasionally."

"Anyway, talked to the employees there, the folks working the checkouts, and no one remembered seeing her this morning. Of course, it's pretty busy on a Saturday, and what with all that scanning and beeping, maybe no one noticed her."

"Can't you check the credit card receipt?" I asked.

"Saw the receipt from the bags she dropped. She paid cash. And then there's the matter of the car."

"It was a Volvo," I said. "A station wagon."

She smiled. "You know your cars. A wagon. A 2012 model, we think. Black. With what looked like a dimple in the hood, a little dent. Like if, you know, a baseball landed on it or something."

I listened.

"The car didn't look all that dirty, but you know what was? The license plate. Had some muck or something on it. Doesn't that seem odd to you?"

I shrugged. "Sometimes plates get dirty."

"Yeah, but if the rest of the car was more or less clean, why would the plate be the only thing that was dirty? Like this lady, whoever she was, or whoever owned that car if it wasn't her, didn't want anyone to make out that plate."

"Sometimes people do that. To avoid tolls or tickets."

"True," she said. "Something deliberate."

"I don't know what you're getting at."

"Anyway, the make of the car, the model, its color, and that ding in the hood, that'll help. We put the word out, folks out on patrol, they see a car like that they can do a check on it."

"I would imagine there are a lot of black Volvo wagons in this part of Connecticut," I said.

"Yup, no question. But you never know. We find that car, maybe we find that woman who was driving it." She gave me a wry smile. "Whoever it happens to be."

"You don't think it's Brie," I said.

"I like to keep an open mind," Hardy said. "But if it is, well, that opens up a whole lot of questions."

"And if it isn't, I'd say just as many."

She nodded. "No argument there." She pondered a

moment. "But I ask myself, who would benefit if your wife were to be spotted around town?"

"I would imagine everyone who cares about her," I said. "And, of course, Brie, because we'd rally around her, help her get through whatever happened."

"Yes, but who would benefit most?"

I didn't want to help her with this.

"No?" she said. "I think that would be you. If it began to look as though your wife was still among us, making mysterious cameo appearances here and there—"

"Here and there? Has she been seen someplace else?"

Detective Hardy waved away the question. "Anyway, if there are sightings of her, then you couldn't very well have killed her, could you?"

"What are you saying? I've somehow *staged* this? Hired some woman to pretend to be Brie?"

"There has to be some explanation."

"Yeah, well, that's not it. I mean, why the hell would I do that? And why would I do it *now*? When Brie's disappearance, I'm sorry to say, has clearly no longer been a priority for you? When most people, other than me and her family, have pretty much forgotten about her. Why now?"

"Good question," Hardy said. "Maybe to convince

your new girlfriend that you're not a killer. Maybe she already knows more about your past than she's let on. Maybe you need to put her mind at ease."

"It's been nice talking to you," I said, and turned to head back to the house.

"One of these days," she said, turning to walk back to her car.

"What did you say?"

Hardy stopped and turned. "One of these days, I'm going to get you. Maybe you've been thinking I've given up, but I haven't. I'm just waiting for the right piccc of evidence to come along, the one thing that will nail you to the wall. Maybe this is it. Maybe you've overplayed your hand, gotten a little too cocky. I guess we'll see how this plays out."

She walked off, got into her car, and drove away.

I didn't go back into the house. I went into the garage, thinking about Greg's theory, that the police were running a game on me, that Brie's reappearance was designed to unnerve me, second-guess myself, go back to where I'd supposedly left Brie's body.

With the cops following me all the way.

But to listen to Detective Marissa Hardy, I was the one behind this entire charade. I had someone out there pretending to be Brie to persuade Hardy, once and for all, that I had done nothing to harm my wife.

I was more confused now than I'd been all day. I was starting to wonder whether Brie really had returned, and was running a game on all of us.

And maybe that's why my frustration level soared right up into the red, clouding my eyes with a bloody mist, but not so much that I couldn't see the hammer atop my worktable. I grabbed it and swung it like a madman, over and over again, into the wood surface, leaving shallow, quarter-sized dents. The table shook so badly that a couple glass jars of nails slipped off the edge and hit the cement floor with a crash, nails and bits of glass scattering all over the place.

I thought I had my life together.

Yeah, well, not so fast, pal.

Twenty-Three

Truth be told, Matt Beekman was already feeling anxious and unsettled about this current assignment before he got the call, out of nowhere, concerning a problem with a previous job.

This latest gig had taken him all the way up to Hartford. Not that he hadn't gone out of town before. About a year ago, there was a job that took him a few hundred miles away to Buffalo. In fact, that had been the last one he'd done before this. It wasn't that Matt liked to space them out. It was more that this type of work didn't come to him as often as he would have liked. He figured he only got the call when the A-list guys were busy. Pissed him off, but what could you do?

So when someone did have work for him, he jumped

on it. He could always use the extra cash. Running the laundromat was keeping him and Tricia afloat, barely, but something unexpected was always coming up. Like when their fifteen-year-old fridge conked out last month. Beekman was pretty handy—he did most of the servicing of the washers and dryers at his business—but the old Frigidaire was toast. And Tricia was making noises about the kids needing new shoes. And had he noticed, she'd asked him the other day at breakfast, that their son Curtis's two front teeth were sticking out, like maybe he was going to have buck teeth? They needed to get him to an orthodontist pronto for a consult.

Jesus fucking Christ, he thought. *It's always something*.

So, a cash infusion was certainly welcome. A satisfactory outcome on this job would cover the fridge and maybe even the dental work.

The target's name was Glenn Ford. No shit, just like the actor from years ago, the one who played Superman's adoptive dad, Pa Kent, in the first Christopher Reeve movie. Not that many people today even knew who Glenn Ford was. Anyway, this Glenn Ford guy was a witness in a murder trial that was about to get under way. There'd been a little war between rival biker gangs around New Haven, and this Ford guy was some poor schlub who happened to be in the wrong place at the wrong time, and saw Wilson "Banger" Smith, from gang number one, shoot Delbert "Snooker" Bundy, from gang number two, right in the head.

Happened out front of a KFC, in the parking lot. Ford had just picked up a bucket of chicken and a side of slaw and was sitting behind the wheel of his Nissan Pathfinder. The windows were tinted dark enough that Wilson had taken no notice of him, but when the police showed up, Ford, a civic-minded individual—the dumbass—told them everything he had seen, providing not only a detailed description of Wilson, but the license plate number from his getaway car, which happened to be his wife's Toyota Prius, she being more environmentally conscious than your average biker's spouse.

Anyway, the state's entire case rested on the testimony of Mr. Glenn Ford, so Wilson, through some of his associates, had put in a call to Matt to take care of things for him. Ordinarily he might have asked one of his biker buddies to do it, but the police were watching all of them pretty closely.

There was ten grand in it for Matt, so he said,

"Okay." Shit, if he'd been offered three he'd have done it.

The police hadn't exactly hidden Ford away, although they'd taken some precautions. The first was the aforementioned surveillance of Wilson's associates, the ones the cops believed were the most likely to do him harm. But the cops had also suggested Ford get the heck out of New Haven until the trial was over.

Ford was a writer who didn't have to clock in to some factory or office every day from nine to five, so he could pretty much do his job from anyplace. Easy for him, but harder for his wife, who worked in a chiropractor's office. But she opted to take a break from work and the two of them went to live with her sister, who had a nanny's apartment in her basement and, as luck would have it, no longer any need for a nanny.

Ford and his wife had been pretty circumspect about their new living arrangement, but the bikers had gotten a tip from someone—didn't much matter to Matt who it might have been—and were able to supply Matt with an address.

Matt had driven up to Hartford a couple of times to scope out the situation, get a sense of Ford's routine. He felt there was a lot riding on this one. Do the job right, maybe more work would be coming his way.

The wife left the house around eight every morning to go for a run that usually took about an hour, which was more than enough time to slip inside and kill Ford, but there was always the risk she might come back early, and then Matt would have to do her, as well. Then there was the issue of Ford's sister-in-law, who lived in another part of the house. This whole thing could go south in a hurry if he wasn't careful.

Ford and the missus left the house together mid-morning to go to a local coffee shop. Weather permitting, they'd grab a table outside and chat while they sipped lattes and dipped biscotti. Again, not terribly helpful.

But in the evening, Ford liked to take a solitary contemplative walk, probably figuring out what he would write the next day. Matt didn't know a lot about writers, but he figured they had to do a lot of thinking. Ford's walk took him through a wooded area of a nearby park. And on the other side of the woods was a road where Matt could park his car.

Perfect.

So on his third trip to Hartford, Matt was ready. He dressed himself as a jogger—sneakers, track pants, T-shirt, iPod strapped to his arm with a wire running up to buds tucked into his ears—and timed it so he was running down the path through the wooded area as Ford was strolling along in the other direction.

No one else on the path.

When they were about thirty feet apart, Matt pretended to stumble, as though he had tripped on a lace, and went down.

"Shit!" he said.

And as he'd expected, Ford closed the distance, knelt down, and asked, "You okay?"

Which was when Matt took a mini-can of mace and sprayed it into Ford's face. Ford let out a yelp as the mist blinded him, but he didn't make noise for long. Matt made a fist and drove it into the man's temple hard enough to render him unconscious. Then all he had to do was drag him into the bushes and finish him off, which he accomplished by straddling Ford and holding one hand over the man's mouth while pinching his nose shut with the other.

Matt didn't know quite how to explain it, but he liked this part. Was fascinated by it.

He'd be the first to admit he didn't spend a lot of time pondering the mysteries of the universe, but he was intrigued by that moment when a living thing stopped being a living thing, and the power one felt at making that moment happen.

He tried to think of the word for it. A *rush*. That

was it. It was all over so quickly. He wished he could make the feeling last a little longer.

A vibration from his muted phone brought him out of his reverie.

When Matt looked at the phone—one of two he had on him—he was surprised to see the name that came up. Not just because of *who* it was, but because the person wasn't using a burner phone, or blocking the caller ID. There was the name, right fucking there. How would this person even have his cell number? And then Matt remembered that a few years ago he hadn't been quite as careful as he was now, didn't always have a burner as a backup. He'd learned a lot since then.

Matt took the call.

"Hey," he said.

"We need to talk."

"About what?"

"You fucked up," the caller said.

"What're you talking about?"

"Six years ago. You messed—"

"Shut up. Hang up. I'll text you a number. Call it. A woman will give you my *other* number, and then you call *that* number, and not from your own phone. Think you can do that?"

A pause at the other end. "Yeah, okay, okay, sorry, I got it."

Matt ended the call and shook his head. He called up his wife's number and wrote:

SOMEONE WILL CALL. GIVE THE NUMBER.

Matt got out his second phone. The burner. The one he would get rid of on the way home. He waited. And with each passing second, his anxiety grew. What the hell was this person talking about? Fucked up what? It had been six goddamn years, and—

The burner buzzed.

"What?" Matt said.

"Something went wrong on that job. Did you even do it? Did I pay you for nothing?"

"I don't know what you're talking about."

"She's back."

"Who's back?"

"The one you were supposed to . . . you know, is back."

Matt's brow furrowed. "Back?"

"Brie. I'm talking about Brie. She's been seen."

"Bullshit."

"I'm telling you, it's true. There are witnesses."

"*You've* seen her?"

"I've seen enough to know this could be bad. Really bad. For both of us. If she's back, if she's alive, you think she'll have forgotten *you*?"

Matt went quiet. His skin felt like a hundred spiders were crawling all over it. He hadn't disguised himself, worn a mask, anything like that on that job. Just like tonight. What was the point? This wasn't exactly a catch-and-release thing.

"It can't be," he said. "She was . . . she was dead. I felt . . . the moment."

"The what?"

"I'm telling you, she was dead." He paused. "She had to be."

"You sound like you're not sure."

"Look, I didn't do it in the house. Didn't want to leave a mess. Chloroformed her, got her out of there, drove to the location, buried her. She was dead."

"How long did you stay there?"

"I didn't stay there."

"Why didn't you stay?"

"Why the fuck would I stay?"

"Could she have been, like, just unconscious when you put her in the ground?"

"Fuck, no. And even if she was, the dirt would have smothered her."

"What if the second you walked away, somehow she dug herself out? Held her breath for a while. Like, an air pocket or something."

"No way," Matt insisted. "And even if, somehow, she got out, then what? She crawls out of a hole and goes on a six-year vacation? She go on a cruise?"

"Look, I don't have all the answers. First step is confirming whether she's alive. Second step is to find out where she's been."

Matt was thinking this was not good. This was not good at all.

"Maybe . . ." And now Matt was really grasping, trying to come up with any possible explanation. "Maybe someone saw me bury her. Rescued her, gave her mouth-to-mouth or something. And, you know, nursed her back to health."

"You think someone else was out there?"

"If there had been, you think I wouldn't have done something about it? This is insane. Maybe she had amnesia or something and just realized who she is."

"You better hope she *did* get amnesia and still has it. She gets her memory back, she'll remember the last person she saw before everything went dark."

Matt looked at the dead writer. The day had been going so well.

"Where's she been seen?"

"Milford."

"Maybe she's a fucking ghost," he said. "My work doesn't guarantee against spirits."

"You better—"

But Matt had heard enough, and ended the call. He took a few deep breaths and let them out slowly.

He was so sure.

He remembered the moment so clearly. When her essence left her body. Like he had inhaled it. Before he put her in the ground.

Had Matt been mistaken? Had he imagined the moment? It was one of his earlier jobs.

"Shit," he said under his breath.

Looking down at the writer, Matt felt a wave of doubt wash over him. He was sure he'd suffocated the man, but what if he hadn't?

So he scanned the ground for a rock that was equal to the task, picked it up with two hands, held it over Glenn Ford's head, and made sure.

Twenty-Four
Andrew

I didn't come up to bed right away.

Jayne and I barely spoke through dinner. Tyler was uncharacteristically agreeable, asking if he could get anybody anything when he got up to refill his glass with water, even clearing the table when we were done.

I almost responded sarcastically, wanting to ask him who he was and what had he done with the real Tyler. But instead, I placed my hand lightly on his back at one point and said, "Thanks, man."

"No problem," he said.

The miracles didn't end there. As we were heading to the living room, Tyler said he was going upstairs to do some homework, some assignment that was due on

Monday. This time it was Jayne who thought of making a quip, but she didn't stop herself.

She looked at me and whispered, "Homework? On a Saturday night?" And then, as Tyler mounted the stairs, she called out, "Who are you?"

But Tyler was taking the steps two at a time and didn't bother to reply. Jayne quietly told me she believed he was on his best behavior because she'd told him earlier in the day that she was pregnant.

"I don't expect him to tiptoe around me for long," she said. "But even a couple of days would be nice."

We started watching one of the movies from the Bourne trilogy—I don't even know which one, but they were the kind of movies you could drop into at any point and just let your brain go—but before it finished, Jayne said she was heading up to bed. We hadn't spoken through the movie, and I knew she was not only trying to get her head around all that she'd learned about me today, she was annoyed I'd spoken to Greg about the supposed reappearance of Brie before I'd talked to her about it.

When I made motions to follow her upstairs, she held up a hand.

"It's okay, finish the movie."

I got the message.

Over the next hour, I puttered about, finally finding myself in the kitchen, staring into the fridge at a bottle of red. I wanted to pour myself a large glass, and then another, and another after that, but as much as I needed to deaden my senses, to round the edges of the day, I also needed a good sleep, and alcohol was not the way to go about it.

I finally went upstairs and entered our room quietly, figuring Jayne would be asleep. Her bedside light was off, and she was under the covers. But she was awake, eyes wide open.

"Hey," I said.

"Hey," she replied, the light from my side of the bed casting half her face in shadow. "Did I hear you on the phone earlier?"

"Nope," I said. "Must have been the TV."

"I thought maybe you were talking to Greg. Because clearly you talk things out with him first."

"I'm sorry. He's my friend. We made shitty business partners, but on a personal level, he's always been there for me."

I started to unbutton my shirt.

"I'm worried about Tyler," Jayne said.

Of all the things she might have said, I wasn't expecting that. "Okay."

"He lied to me. He and his friend were hanging out in a cemetery last night, and there was a story online about some vandalism there. Graves knocked over."

I didn't have to ask her how she knew her brother had been there. She had told me about how she kept tabs on him.

"But tonight at dinner, I thought, maybe he's trying to turn things around. He's finally starting to settle in here, willing to give it a chance, but now . . ."

"What?"

"I asked you if he could come live with us because, first of all, I believed you'd be a good influence on him and that we could provide some stability. But now, well, this feels like a house of cards. Like it's all going to come crashing down at any moment."

"Because of me," I said. "So this is about more than Tyler. It's about you and Tyler."

"It's about all of us. You, me, him, and this baby that's suddenly complicated everything."

"It's not a complication," I said. "It's wonderful news."

"You didn't look like you thought it was wonderful when I first told you."

"I was surprised. But I'm not unhappy about it."

Jayne did not look convinced.

I came around to her side of the bed, perched myself on the edge. I put my hand to her cheek and said, "I love you."

Jayne said nothing for a few seconds. Then, "What if you have to make a choice? What if you love both of us?"

"Jayne, it's not . . . it's never going to come to that."

"How can you know?"

I couldn't come up with a reply.

Jayne said, "There's no way this ends well, is there? I mean, if it's Brie, then our life's in total chaos. If it isn't her, this detective never stops trying to prove you killed her. Either way, I could end up losing you."

"No," I said.

She turned her head away.

"We just have to see what happens," I said.

"That's your plan?"

"I don't know what else to say. We can't worry about things we're powerless to change. Our priorities, as of this moment, are to make sure you and this baby you're carrying are okay. And that we can make things work here for Tyler."

I leaned in and hugged her. She put her arms around me but didn't squeeze.

"Maybe I should . . . maybe this is the wrong time to bring a child . . ."

"No," I said. "Don't think that way."

I stood, gave her the most comforting smile I could muster, and went into the bathroom to brush my teeth. As I stood there, looking into the mirror, I had to concede that maybe Jayne was right.

There's no way this ends well.

The last thing I did before I turned off the light was mute my phone and plug it into the charging cord I left sitting on the bedside table. A second after I hit the light, my phone lit up silently with an incoming call.

On the screen, the word NORMAN.

I couldn't think of anyone I wanted to talk to less than Isabel's husband. So I flipped the phone over and got under the covers.

Twenty-Five

Norman was sitting in one of the two family room recliners, in darkness except for a dull glow from the phone he held in his palm, when Isabel tracked him down.

"What the hell are you doing down here?" she asked, flicking on a light.

"Nothing," he said, tucking the phone under his thigh. He was in his pajamas, wrapped in a housecoat, his legs propped up, his upper body tilted back.

"I woke up, you weren't in the bed. I thought maybe you were sick. Are you sick?"

"I'm fine," he said.

"Is it your stomach?" she asked, almost accusingly. "You buried your potato in sour cream. You *know* that can upset your stomach. I knew when you did it that you were going to have problems. Did you take some Pepto?"

"I told you, I'm fine," he said.

"Maybe you should have some Pepto anyway, just to be sure," Isabel told him.

He turned and looked at her. "Why can't you ever just leave me alone?"

"I show some concern, and that's what you say?"

"You're never concerned," he said. "You just look for opportunities to pick at me." In a mocking voice, he said, "You had too much sour cream. Why'd you have that extra beer? Why didn't you find a free parking space?"

"You're being ridiculous," Isabel said. "And maybe, if you'd been through what I've been through, you'd understand if I'm a little on edge."

"Six years of being a little on edge is about six years more than I can take."

Isabel found herself momentarily speechless.

"I keep wondering what it is that drives you," he continued. "At first I thought it was an honest desire to get justice for Brie. That you were hounding Andrew because you believed it was the right thing to do. But I've decided it's more than that. I'm not even sure you think he did something to Brie, that he killed her. I think you just need to shift the guilt you feel onto someone else."

"How dare you," Isabel said.

"At first I thought you felt guilty because you weren't here for her, that we weren't part of the search for the first couple of days. That if we hadn't gone to Boston that Saturday night, if you hadn't canceled plans to see your sister, maybe none of this would have happened. I still think it's guilt that drives you, but not about us being away."

"Jesus, Norman, you're embarrassing yourself. You think you're Dr. Phil."

"You wish you could take it all back. All the things you said."

"I have no idea what you're—"

"Oh please, this is me you're talking to. It was always a competition to you. Who was the smarter sister, the prettier sister. The way you talked about her behind her back, putting her down. Kind of like you do with me. It's how you make yourself feel superior. But then when Brie vanished, you felt badly about all those things you'd said, all those—"

"I'm not listening to any more of this," Isabel said, and started to walk out of the room.

But Norman wasn't finished. "You know what I

think? I think you're hoping it wasn't Brie that we saw today. That'd be the last thing you'd want. So then you can go on blaming Andrew. If it's really her, you'd have to face her, come to terms with the contempt you've felt for her."

Isabel kept on walking, flicking off lights along the way.

When he heard the upstairs bedroom door close, Norman took his phone back out from under his thigh and brought it to life. Still on the screen was an image he'd been looking at when he'd had to hide the phone from his wife.

A picture of Brie.

Maybe Isabel wasn't the only one burdened with guilt, he thought. And you could mix in a dollop of fear while you're at it. Fear that one day Isabel might learn the whole truth.

Twenty-Six

The nights were long for Elizabeth McBain, especially when she couldn't sleep.

After all, when you were in a hospital bed, and spent your entire day stretched out in it, why should anyone be surprised when you lay awake half the night staring at the ceiling?

It gave her time to think, of course. Way more time than she needed.

So much to think about, when you were eighty-one years old. A lot to reflect on. One tended to spend far too much time on regrets, and contrary to what the song said, not too few to mention.

Starting with her husband, Jackson. Gone eleven years now. A long, drawn-out decline after a diagnosis of lung cancer. A heavy smoker, starting in his teens, he'd maintained the habit right up until his diagnosis. Actually, even after, because his lungs were so riddled with the disease that stopping wasn't going to make much of a difference.

He lived the better part of a year after they'd discovered the cancer, but it had been a long year, the last three months spent in the hospital. At the time, Elizabeth kept thinking that when it was her turn, she wanted to go fast. A massive heart attack, maybe. Something that would kill her before she hit the ground.

And yet, here she was. One miserable day dragging into the next.

Elizabeth had managed to get through the loss of her husband with the help of her kids. Albert and Isabel, and, at least for a while, Brie.

With the kids married and out on their own, and now without a husband, Elizabeth had no need for a big house, and keeping it going on a reduced income was going to present some challenges, although she did make a few extra bucks doing some freelance editing. As newspapers and magazines started cutting back— staff editors getting the cut before reporters, in most cases—Elizabeth found her expertise in occasional demand. She did a lot of work for a glossy real estate magazine that was distributed throughout parts of the state. It didn't pay much, but it was nice to keep her hand in.

Still, she hardly needed a house, so she sold the place and moved into an apartment not far from the Post Mall so she'd be handy to everything she might need.

Her children came to visit when they could. Albert had always been the most attentive, taking her to lunch every week, often popping in unannounced to see her. Izzy and Brie came by less frequently, but tried to make up for that with weekly phone calls. And it was always nice to have a visit with the grandkids. Andrew and Brie had no children, but Albert and his wife, Dierdre, had two—Randy and Lyla—and Izzy and her husband, Norman, had two in their teens, who were a handful but good-hearted.

Too bad about Albert and Dierdre, going through a trial separation. Elizabeth sometimes wondered whether she herself was partly to blame. Allowing Albert to tend to her so dutifully over the years had undoubtedly led to some resentment on Dierdre's part. When Elizabeth's husband died, Albert had insisted on taking her on a trip to Europe—without Dierdre—to help ease her grief. When Elizabeth's cat passed, Albert was there the next day with a kitten.

Elizabeth had always thought it was a mother's role to ease a child's suffering, but with Albert, it was the other way around.

It weighed heavily on her that both Albert and Isabel had troubled marriages. At least Isabel and Norman hadn't separated. God knows she and Jackson had tried to set a good example. They'd been devoted to one another, always faithful. Even when Jackson had been on the road, back when he drove for a shipping company, she was certain he had never strayed.

Some things you just knew.

She'd made it a point not to pry into her children's lives, but that didn't mean you didn't worry about them. What was that phrase? "I'm only as happy as my saddest child." She knew Brie and Andrew had gone through some tough times. And when Dierdre wasn't annoyed by Albert's devotion to his mother, she had to resent the fact that he'd rather spend time on his theatrical projects than with her. Writing and directing plays was his passion. Who could blame him? Elizabeth thought. It had to be so boring, working in a bank.

And as for Izzy and Norman, well, if Elizabeth was honest with herself, it was Norman she felt sorry for. Izzy could be a handful. A complainer, a nitpicker, a proverbial dog with a bone on any number of issues.

Relentlessly critical of her husband. She didn't seem to understand that she had a good man in Norman and ran the risk of losing him if she didn't change her ways. What kind of woman left a Post-it note over the toilet to remind her husband to pee straight?

After losing Jackson, she joined some clubs, attended lectures, took an online course in early American history, occasionally went into New York for an overnighter to see a show or tour a museum. (Albert was always buying her tickets to something.) There was even a man there for a while, a widower dentist who had retired and wanted her to tour New England with him. He had an Airstream trailer that he towed behind a Chevy Suburban big enough to have its own zip code. They went out on a couple of dates, but she took a pass on the New England adventure. She couldn't stop comparing him to Jackson, and he came up short.

Life was more or less okay.

And then Brie disappeared.

As the days turned into weeks and the weeks into months, with no clue as to what had happened to her, Elizabeth came to envy Jackson. She wished she could have gone when he did. Jackson had been spared the anguish of Brie's disappearance, the agony of not knowing.

Heartbreak, she believed, was worse than just about any disease you could think of.

Was there ever a day when she didn't wonder what had become of Brie? Of course not. And who did she blame? Izzy had always been certain Andrew had killed Brie and disposed of her body somewhere. Elizabeth was less sure about that. But she thought it highly unlikely that Brie was still among the living.

Had she been alive, she'd surely have found a way to get in touch.

But then came today's developments. Elizabeth didn't know what to think, but she felt her natural inclination to skepticism being challenged.

That picture on Max's phone.

Admittedly, not a very good image. Not sharp enough to say it was Brie, but not sharp enough to say it wasn't. But it did look like her daughter. It was but a tiny sliver of hope. Nice to have at least that, when there was so little time left.

The cancer had continued its assault, tentacling its way to the far corners of her body. It wouldn't surprise her, she thought, if she had cancer of the big toe. Staring at the ceiling of her darkened room, she chuckled. You found your laughs where you could.

Elizabeth closed her eyes, tried to get back to sleep.

There were mercifully few noises at three in the morning. The occasional nurse walking in on her soft-soled shoes to check that she hadn't fallen out of bed or gotten tangled up in her sheets. Sometimes soft chatter could be heard in the hallway.

She was aware, through her eyelids, of a brief flash of light. Probably the door opening. This was usually followed, within a minute, by a second flash of light, as one of Elizabeth's uniformed nocturnal visitors departed.

But the second flash didn't come. Slowly, Elizabeth began to sense that she was not alone in the room. She opened her eyes, which didn't need time to adjust to the darkness.

There was someone there.

Standing over by the door. A darker figure silhouetted against a darkened wall.

"Who is it?" Elizabeth asked.

The person—Elizabeth was pretty sure it was a woman, given her height and shape—did not move.

She wondered whether she might be dreaming. Or maybe she was awake, but was hallucinating. A side effect from one of the many painkillers they'd given her. God knows they had her on enough meds these days.

She gave her arm a pinch.

I'm awake.

Unless the pinch was part of the dream.

"Who are you?" Elizabeth asked. "What do you want?"

The figure took two steps closer to the bed but remained shrouded in darkness. Elizabeth blinked several times, tried to focus. Definitely a woman, she had little doubt of that. Maybe five-three, five-four. But it wasn't a nurse. The woman was dressed in black, appeared to be wearing a long coat.

The word caught in Elizabeth's throat. "Brie?" she said.

The woman replied in a whisper. "I just wanted you to know I'm okay."

Elizabeth struggled to pull herself up.

"No, no," the woman whispered urgently. "Don't do that. Stay put."

"Where have you been?" Elizabeth asked, her voice breaking.

"Away."

"But why . . . why have . . ."

"It's too hard to explain. But I'm okay. I'm getting a few things in order."

Tears started to run down Elizabeth's cheeks. "I can't believe it's you. I've worried so. I never allowed myself to hope, not until now."

Was there a smile on the woman's face? Impossible to tell in the darkness.

"I love you," the woman said. "Everything's going to be okay."

"Come here," Elizabeth said, reaching out a withered arm. "Come to me."

"I . . . I can't."

Was she a ghost? Elizabeth wondered. If she could put her arms around her, would she dissolve in her arms like smoke? Elizabeth was certain she was awake, that this was not a dream, but that didn't preclude a visit from the supernatural, did it?

"Are you . . . alive?"

A whispered giggle. "I'm standing right here, aren't I?"

"I've missed you so much."

"And I've missed you, Mom," the woman said. "More than you can possibly know." She glanced back toward the closed door. "I'm going to have to go."

"No, please stay. Pull up a chair. Tell me where you've been. Tell me everything."

"None of that matters. That I'm here, let that be enough. Visiting hours are over. If they find me here I'll be in big trouble."

"They'll understand! Please, Brie, don't—"

But she backed away and pulled the door open, allowing light from the hall to flood that corner of the room. The sudden brightness blinded Elizabeth and she instinctively closed her eyes for a second, shielded them with her hand.

When she opened them, and took her hand away, the door had closed, and the woman was gone.

Elizabeth twisted around in the bed, looked frantically for the buzzer that would send a message to the nurses' station that she needed help. She found it, jammed it with her thumb repeatedly until, about thirty seconds later, the door opened and a male nurse ran in.

"Yes, yes, what's the problem, Mrs. McBain?" he said.

"The woman!" Elizabeth said. "Bring her back! Stop her!"

"Woman? What woman?" he asked.

"My daughter! Tell her to come back!"

Calmly, he said, "Visiting hours were over long ago. It's the middle of the night."

"But she was—"

"I've been out there the whole time and I didn't see anyone go by. You must have been having a dream or something. Here, let me get you tucked in."

"But . . ."

"Shhh, now, you need to rest," he said. "Get some sleep before they wake you at the crack of dawn for breakfast."

The nurse gave her a patronizing smile before departing. "You have a good night, now."

Sunday

Twenty-Seven
Andrew

I lay awake much of the night, rolling over and looking at the digital clock on the bedside table: 1:05,
then 2:17, then 3:01, and so on until slivers of sunlight
started piercing through the blinds. I kept thinking
about something Greg had said to me yesterday.

He'd been talking about that time he'd found me
drunk, more down and out than I'd ever been before.

"You said, 'It's all my fault.' You said, 'I fucked up.'
I asked you, I said, 'What are you talking about?' And
you said, 'Brie.' But I never told a soul you said that.
Never told that detective."

It's all my fault.

It was pretty clear what Greg had read into those

comments. I had no memory of making them, but then again, there was a lot from that time, and that day in particular, that I don't remember very well.

I supposed it was possible I might have said those words. But they didn't have to mean what Greg clearly believed they meant.

I might have tried to make that point with him, but that was when Detective Hardy had pulled up in front of the house. I might have told Greg that, yeah, maybe it was my fault. If Brie vanished because I'd betrayed her, I could have argued, then, yeah, that was on me.

But to interpret what I'd said to him in a drunken stupor as a confession was a leap. As I lay in bed I wondered whether I should phone and tell him that.

Then again, maybe I should call and thank him.

"*Never told that detective.*"

I was in debt to him for that. For sure, there was only one way Detective Hardy would have read that comment.

Speaking of her, I was also rolling around in my head something she'd said to me after I'd ended my conversation with Greg. Her assertion that I hadn't done enough nosing about on my own to find Brie, that I never hired some private investigator to accomplish what the police could not, really rankled.

Detective Hardy had no idea how I responded to Brie's

disappearance. I supposed she wanted me to become some sort of amateur detective. The fact was that I was under so much scrutiny at the time, I could hardly go into a Dunkin' Donuts for a coffee without being watched by the police or some local TV news crew.

Well, if that was Hardy's expectation of me, maybe it was better late than never. Now that she was looking into the possibility that Brie was alive, I was ready to start asking a few questions on my own, and not just for appearances' sake. My goal wasn't to make Detective Hardy proud of me. I wanted to find out what the hell was going on.

But I had to be careful how I went about it.

I had a new life with Jayne. A good life. And now we were going to have a child together. I loved her. Jayne might view any steps I took where Brie was concerned as wanting to get back together with her.

If she was actually alive.

I appreciated her concern. She had to be thinking that if Brie was back, presumably our marriage would still be valid. Brie had not been gone long enough to be declared legally dead and I'd made no petitions to have such a declaration made.

Maybe it was time, discreetly, to go back to where this all began. Make the rounds. Talk to people I believed Detective Hardy should have paid more attention to. I'd often wondered why she hadn't had the exterminator higher on her list of suspects.

Charlie Underwood.

After all, he was the last person, so far as Hardy knew, to have seen Brie alive (not counting our FaceTime chat on that Saturday evening). He'd been in the house with her. He knew her husband was away for the weekend on a fishing trip. If he'd returned that night, he'd have had every reason to believe Brie would be alone. And, as I had related to Hardy at the time, Brie had found him to be a pretty odd character.

If I'd been Hardy, I'd have been looking at him very closely.

I was up before Jayne. She mumbled into her pillow that she'd had a terrible night of tossing and turning, so I told her to stay in bed and see if she could go back to sleep. I quickly gathered what clothes I needed, slipped out of the room, and closed the door. I showered, shaved, and dressed, and was down in the kitchen by half-past eight.

I was surprised to see Tyler there.

He was sitting at the kitchen table in a pair of boxers. Tyler wasn't big on bathrobes. He hadn't made coffee, but there was half a glass of orange juice in front of him and a bowl with the dregs of some soggy cereal. He was looking at his phone when I walked in.

"Hey," I said. "You're up early."

He looked up, shrugged. "I guess."

"You working today?"

He nodded. "I start at ten."

"You want a lift or anything?" I asked as I went over to the coffee machine.

"That's okay."

I had my back to him, running some water from the tap into the carafe, when he said, "Need to ask you something."

"Sure."

"Did you kill your wife?"

I froze a moment before slowly turning around to look at him. I supposed I shouldn't have been surprised the secret was out, although I wondered who'd brought Jayne's brother up to speed. Maybe it had been Jayne herself.

"Your sister talked to you," I said.

Tyler shook his head. "Nope. I just listened. Yesterday, when that detective was here. And later, when you came home. You can hear everything from my room." He pointed to the ceiling briefly.

I felt my face flush. The little shit had been eavesdropping.

"Well," I said. "That's a good thing to know, if a bit late."

"So you haven't answered my question. I don't think my sister actually asked you flat-out, unless I missed that part."

I pulled out a chair and sat across from him.

"No," I said.

Tyler poked his tongue into his cheek as he thought about my answer. "But if you did kill your wife, that's what you'd say anyway."

"Then you have to wonder if there's any point in asking," I said.

"I read everything about Brie online," he said. "Six years. Man. That's a long time to go without the police figuring out what happened."

"Long time for me, too," I said.

"I just want what's best for my sister."

"Same here."

"Especially now that you've, you know, got her pregnant and everything."

"I agree."

"I think becoming an uncle will be kind of cool," he said.

"I'm looking forward to being a dad."

"I know I've been kind of an asshole at times," Tyler said, "with puking on your deck and stuff, but I've been thinking things have been working out okay here."

"I think so, too. It's been a big adjustment for all of us. You know my story, what I went through when I was your age. I've been there, having to get used to a new place, and a lot of the time not liking it."

"Yeah," he said, nodding. "But now, with what's happened, it could all go to shit."

"I'm hoping that won't be the case," I said.

"So what if, somehow, it really is her? What if the woman who came to that house is Brie? What then?"

"That seems to be the number one question. I'm gonna try to be honest with you here, Tyler. I don't know. This is all uncharted territory. I'm in the woods without a compass. But the last thing in the world I want to do is hurt Jayne. So I'm taking this a day at a time. Maybe this is a whole lot of fuss about nothing. Maybe that was just some woman who went to the wrong house and for whatever reason flipped out. The thing is, I don't see how it can be Brie. It seems very highly improbable."

My phone rang.

I pulled it out of my pocket and saw a name I was not expecting, and certainly wouldn't have been hoping to see.

ISABEL.

I tapped the screen and put the phone to my ear.

"Hello, Isabel," I said, although as soon as I'd said

her name I wondered whether it might be Norman using her phone. He had, after all, tried to reach me the night before, and I had declined the call.

But it was definitely Isabel who said, "Andrew."

"What can I do for you?"

"My mother wants to talk to you about something."

"About what."

There was a pause, followed by, "Brie came to visit her this morning."

Twenty-Eight

When Hannah Brown opened her eyes and rolled over, she was expecting to find her partner next to her. But the covers were pulled back, the other half of the king-sized mattress empty.

They often slept in on Sunday mornings, but evidently not today. Hannah swung her legs down to the floor, tucked her feet into a pair of furry Ugg slippers, and walked down the hall to the bathroom.

No one there.

She went downstairs to the kitchen, and it was there that she found Marissa Hardy, perched on a stool, reading something on an iPad that she'd propped up on a stand.

"It's Sunday," Hannah said. "What the hell are you doing up so early?"

"Did you know that Agatha Christie once vanished for ten days?" Hardy said, looking up.

"What?"

"The mystery writer. She went missing for ten days, and finally showed up at a health spa, and she would never say where she'd been or what she'd been doing for that period of time."

"Oh."

"Of course, ten days is not six years."

Hannah blinked a couple of times. "No, it certainly isn't. It's shorter."

"And here's an interesting one. Guy named Lawrence Joseph Bader, from Akron, Ohio. Sold kitchen supplies or something. Goes on a fishing trip to Lake Erie and disappears. A boating accident, right? But then, eight years later—eight fucking years—he's found in Omaha, Nebraska, working as a local television announcer or personality or something. And he's got a different name. They never figured out what actually happened, whether he had amnesia or whether he faked his death. What do you make of that?"

"Have you made coffee?"

"And then there was that Ariel Castro guy, in Cleveland? Who kept three women as prisoners in his house for eleven years. Remember that? Back in 2013?"

"What I was thinking," Hannah said, "was that

we should go out for brunch today. I don't even care where. Even IHOP. What do you think?"

Hardy looked up from the iPad. "Hmm?"

"You know. Pancakes, sausage, that kind of thing."

"I guess," Hardy said, eyes going back down. "Might have to work today."

"Today's your day off."

"I know." She paused. "I really, really hate being wrong."

"No kidding."

"What if I am? What if I'm wrong?"

Hannah went over to the coffee maker, pulled out the empty carafe. "Would it have killed you to start a pot?"

"But he looked good for it, you know? I still think he could be good for it."

"I think I'm going to make tea for a change." Hannah put water into a kettle and plugged it into an outlet.

"Where could she have been all this time?" Hardy asked. "If he didn't actually kill her?"

Hannah tore off a banana from a bunch in a bowl and pulled up a stool on the opposite side of the island from the detective.

"Jacksonville, Florida."

"What?"

"I don't know, it's a place. Just trying to help. Let's

talk about bacon. A side order, extra-crispy." She started to peel the banana.

But Hardy wasn't thinking about food. "He had time, you know. To drive down from the cabin, kill her, get rid of her body, and get back up there. He can't prove he was there all night. It's even possible he gave his buddy something to knock him out. But what's the motive? He'd broken it off with that other woman. He didn't have any huge insurance policy on her. If he'd killed her in a fit of rage, that could happen, but making the drive down, intending to kill her, that's premeditation. And for premeditation, you need a motive. There has to be one. I just haven't figured out what it is yet."

Hannah broke off an inch of banana and popped it into her mouth. "I like this part."

Hardy looked up again. "What?"

"It's like seeing the inside of a computer or something. Watching you talk it through, thinking out loud. It's interesting to watch."

The kettle was starting to boil.

"You want some tea?" Hannah asked.

"Nothing for me."

"Okay, then." Hannah slid off the stool and opened a cupboard, where she found a box of tea bags.

"It's usually the husband."

"Say again?"

"When something happens to a wife, it's usually the husband."

Hannah dropped a tea bag into a cup and poured in some water. "But is that how you usually operate? Based on statistics? I thought you went into each case with eyes open, no presuppositions. No tunnel-vision stuff."

Hardy studied her for a moment, then said, "You mentioned something about bacon."

"I did."

"I'll need a shower."

"I'll join you," Hannah said.

Twenty-Nine
Andrew

Isabel wanted to meet for a coffee first, before taking me to the hospital to see Elizabeth. She suggested the Starbucks on the Boston Post Road, just west of the turnpike. When I got there, she was sitting at one of the outside tables, both hands wrapped around a paper cup as if using it to keep herself warm, even though it was about seventy-five degrees out. There was a second cup on the other side of the table.

"I took a chance on a latte," she said. "It's still warm. I just sat down."

Isabel buying me a coffee had me wondering whether I'd entered the Twilight Zone. I didn't know whether this was a peace offering or a trap. Maybe she had a sniper positioned somewhere across the road, ready to take me out.

"A latte is fine, thanks," I said, taking a seat. "How's Norman?" I decided not to mention that he had tried to call me the night before.

She looked downward. "Oh, you know. Norman's Norman."

"So tell me what happened with Elizabeth."

I had always liked Brie's mother. A straight shooter, spoke her mind, but at the same time knew when to hold her tongue. She never stuck her nose into other people's business, kept her opinions about how her children lived their lives to herself. But, not surprisingly, we had become estranged after Brie's disappearance, which I attributed largely to Isabel persuading her that I was the cause of it.

Isabel's chin quivered slightly. "She doesn't have all that much longer. She has cancer. It's all through her."

"I'm sorry," I said, and I meant it. "I didn't know. I've always liked her."

"She wants to talk to you."

"Okay."

Isabel said, "You know about what happened yesterday morning. On Mulberry. Where you used to live."

Word was getting around, but I wasn't surprised to

learn that she'd very likely been talking to Detective Hardy.

"I know."

"After we found out about that, Albert and I went there and talked to the people who live in the new house that got built where yours used to be. And to your old neighbor, Max."

Just to confirm my suspicions, I asked, "I guess it was Detective Hardy who called you."

"Not exactly. Albert and I called her before we'd talked to Max."

I was getting confused by the timeline here. "So Max called you? After he'd been in touch with me and Hardy?"

Isabel shook her head quickly. "No, shit, I'm leaving out the most important thing." She took a moment. "When we were visiting Mom yesterday, from her room, looking down at the parking lot, we thought we saw Brie, or someone who sure looked like her. She waved to us, like she knew who we were."

It was coming into focus now. Hardy had hinted that this woman who looked like Brie had been seen someplace else.

"I don't know who or what we saw," Isabel said. "But then last night—early this morning would be more accurate—Mom saw her again."

"Okay," I said slowly.

"She says Brie came to her hospital room. I think she imagined it. The nurses, no one saw anything. It was the middle of the night. Visiting hours had ended at nine. Mom's on all sorts of medications. I blame myself, well, myself and Albert, for getting her all hyped up. We brought Max in to tell her what he'd seen because, well, you know Mom. She takes some convincing on things. She's not what you'd call a fan of conspiracy theories. I realize now it was a huge mistake. It put the idea into her head that Brie was . . . alive . . . and so then she has this vision in the middle of the night."

"Sounds like that's what it was," I said.

Isabel drank from her cup. A little smidge of foam settled on her upper lip and I licked my own, trying to send her a signal. After a moment, she stuck out her tongue and got rid of it.

"You and I have had a pretty strained relationship since it happened," she said.

"That's putting it mildly."

"I'm not sorry for anything I've done. Any actions I took were to get justice for my sister."

I said nothing.

"But my mother, she thinks some kind of apology is in order. That if who we saw, and who she saw in the night, is really Brie, well, then, you didn't do what we—well, me for sure—thought you did."

"I see."

"Just so you understand, it's not me who's apologizing, because I don't know what the hell is going on. I don't know, for certain, any more than I did a week ago, about whether my sister is alive. Maybe we just saw someone who looked, at a distance, like Brie, and she waved at us because we were looking at her. I don't know. But Mom has come to a more definite conclusion." She took another sip, this time avoiding any foam. "She asked me to get in touch with you, to ask you to come and see her so that she can tell you she's sorry."

I thought about what she was asking of me.

"I don't know," I said.

"What?"

"I don't know whether I should do it. I might be accepting an apology under false pretenses."

Isabel's eyes went wide. "Christ, what are you saying? Are you admitting it? Are you confessing to me that you *did* kill Brie?"

"No, of course not. I'm not confessing to anything. But I don't know who your mother saw, if she even saw anything. It'd be wrong to let her apologize to me based on a delusion."

"Oh, for fuck's sake," Isabel said, looking fed up and

frustrated. "Tell me you didn't do it. Tell me you didn't kill Brie."

"I didn't kill Brie. But I've told you that a hundred times since she disappeared and you've never believed me before."

"Christ, just let her apologize for thinking you did do it."

"Maybe the one who should apologize is you, since you're the one who made her think that."

"Look," Isabel said, composing herself and bringing her voice down. "Albert thinks—we both think—that Mom needs this. Her prognosis is bad. She could go today, tomorrow, maybe a month from now. God, she could pass on before we get to the hospital. She's got some reason to hope her daughter isn't dead, and maybe it's okay if she goes to her grave with that. Even if it turns out not to be the case. And part of that involves making things right with you."

I drank some more of my latte, finishing it.

"Okay," I said.

I followed Isabel's car to the hospital and went up to the room with her. Elizabeth was awake when I walked in.

I hadn't seen her in person in nearly six years. In the early days of Brie's disappearance, I'd been in regular contact with Elizabeth and both of Brie's siblings, comparing notes, sharing what few leads there were, making joint appearances on the local news pleading for information.

But as Detective Hardy narrowed her list of suspects to, well, me, and she let it be known I was her prime suspect, Elizabeth distanced herself from me. She'd take my calls at first, but as Isabel continued her attacks, my mother-in-law stopped having anything to do with me.

I couldn't really blame her. It's hard to be nice to your son-in-law when you've been brainwashed into believing he killed your daughter.

My memory of her was of a strong, vibrant, independent woman, so it was something of a shock for me to see her today, how the disease had ravaged her. She'd lost probably sixty pounds, and she never had a lot of meat on her to begin with. The skin on her arms looked more like crepe paper, and her cheeks appeared to have melted around the bone. But there was still something very Elizabeth about her, and that was her eyes. She'd always had beautiful blue eyes, and they hadn't changed. Still that lovely aqua color, piercing and insightful.

She smiled when she saw me, and that brought back memories, too. Her smile, always genuine, radiated affection. Even now.

"Andrew," she said. "It's so good to see you."

I knelt over her as she lay in her bed, and slipped my arms around her frail, emaciated body.

"Elizabeth," I said. "I'm glad you asked me to come."

She looked over my shoulder and eyed Isabel. "Thank you, Izzy. You can go now."

Isabel blinked. "You don't want me to stay?"

"It's okay," Elizabeth said. "Andrew and I have some catching up to do."

Isabel didn't look pleased about being dismissed, but after a second or two she turned on her heels and exited the room.

"You think she's hiding behind the door, listening?" Elizabeth asked, a hint of mischief in her eye.

"You want me to check?"

She nodded. I went to the door, opened it half an inch. Isabel was not there.

"All clear," I reported.

"Pull up a chair," Elizabeth said. I did and, leaning in, got as close to her as I could. "You look good," she said. "Considering everything."

I smiled. "I suppose."

"Don't even bother to tell me the same. I know how I look. I look like shit."

"You still have that sparkle in your eye."

"You were always my favorite. I mean, of the ones my children married. Favorite in-law. Oh, I don't mean to put down Norman and Dierdre, but I always had a soft spot in my heart for you."

I sighed. "Until."

Elizabeth's eyes closed for a moment. "I know. I allowed Izzy to let me believe the worst about you. But now I realize I misjudged you, wronged you."

She held out her hand and I took it, gave it a gentle squeeze. Her fingers felt like twigs cloaked in old linen.

"I've seen her," Elizabeth said. "So I know you never did her any harm."

"Isabel told me. In the night." I felt obliged to add, "Isabel thinks you imagined it, and she might be right."

"I know what I saw." She returned the squeeze. "I can't explain it. I don't know where she's been, and I don't know why she's been in hiding. The whole thing is a huge mystery, but knowing that she's alive, right now, it's enough for me. I wasn't prepared to believe it at first. It was just too fantastical. But now . . . Anyway, that's why I've brought you here, to tell you I'm sorry. So very, very sorry for doubting you, for thinking you could have done something so horrible."

Accept her apology, or not? I did some quick ethical calculations, the way a math whiz might solve a complicated equation in his head in seconds.

I said, "All is forgiven."

She smiled. "Thank you, Andrew. That means more to me than you could know."

I thought maybe we were done, but when I went to pull my hand away she clung to it.

"Don't go so soon," she said. "This is probably the last time I'm ever going to see you. I want to talk."

"Okay."

"How are you doing these days?"

I shrugged. "You probably know this, but I changed my last name. I'm Andrew Carville now."

"Oh, that has a nice ring to it," Elizabeth said. "You don't have to tell me why. I can guess. Whatever it cost you to have it done, you should send the bill to Izzy. And what about work?"

"I manage," I said.

"And . . . are you . . . did you . . . ."

"Remarry?" I said. "No. But there is someone. Her name is Jayne, and she's moved in with me."

Her face fell. "Oh my. It's going to be so difficult for her. Having to give you up."

I said nothing.

"Do you think Jayne—is that what you said her name is?"

"Yes."

"Do you think Jayne will understand?"

I had no idea how to address that question. Elizabeth wasn't too far gone to notice my hesitation.

"Andrew, promise me something."

"What's that, Elizabeth?"

"You'll forgive Brie. Whatever the reason was that she left, whatever she's done all this time, that you will forgive her."

"Yes, of course."

"And take her back."

I forced a smile and gave her hand a squeeze. "How could I not?"

I was glad Isabel was not in the room to hear me make a promise that I had no idea how to keep.

She looked relieved. "Well, that's good. Now we only have to worry about the IRS wondering why she hasn't filed a tax return in six years."

Amazingly, we both had a chuckle over that. But very quickly, her expression grew serious, and she said, "You know, Jackson and I did our best."

"I'm sure," I said, not certain where this was going but content to wait.

"My three—Brie and Izzy and Albert—I love them all, you know. But I know none of them has ever been perfect. Made mistakes. Things with Albert and Dierdre aren't very good these days."

"I didn't know that. I always thought they were pretty solid."

"I suppose they were at one time, but . . . Anyway, and then there's Izzy and Norman, that poor man. He must be some kind of saint to put up with her. How did she become so judgmental?" Before I could answer, she offered a theory. "I think she always wanted to make more of herself. You know she had dreams of becoming a lawyer."

"I know. Thing is, Elizabeth, we're all wired our own way. You did everything right."

Elizabeth chortled. "That's why I always liked you. You're such a good liar." She still had not let go of my hand. "Maybe it's a generational thing. Maybe young people today—well, younger, I mean, none of you are kids anymore—maybe they don't have the same values. They don't cherish fidelity."

"I plead guilty," I said.

"Oh, not just you," she said. "You know how I know you're a good man, that you could never have done anything to hurt Brie?"

"How?" I replied slowly.

"Because of the secret you kept. The one you could have revealed, but never did. I don't think I'd have been able to behave as honorably if I'd been in your position."

"That's not quite true," I said, reasonably sure what she was referring to. "I told Detective Hardy. But she cleared him. It couldn't have been him. He went to Boston that night. He had an airtight alibi, as they say. Me, not so much."

"Even so, you could have told others what he'd done. One person in particular."

"What would have been the point of that? And I'd have had to dishonor Brie to do it. I wasn't going to do that. None of this matters now, Elizabeth. It's the distant past."

"Brie told me. She told me everything."

I did not know that.

"When?" I asked.

"A month or two before she disappeared. We could always talk, you know." She took a breath. "Can you hand me that glass of water?" I handed her the glass. Her mouth moistened, she continued. "There Isabel was, making your life hell, and still you held your tongue."

"Ruining Isabel's life wouldn't have done anything to make me look any less culpable."

"Norman's never thanked you, has he?" Elizabeth asked. "Never expressed any gratitude that you didn't tell Isabel that her husband had slept with her own sister."

"I've never sought it," I said. "He doesn't owe me a damn thing. It was a long time ago."

"It's never too late to offer regrets," Elizabeth said. "Why do you think I wanted to see you before I'm gone?"

Thirty

More than a few people slept poorly Saturday night to Sunday morning. Matt Beekman was among them.

He didn't get back to New Haven after his Hartford assignment until three in the morning. There was a note on the kitchen counter from his wife, Tricia, that there was a plate of Chinese food in the fridge. He took it out, reheated it in the microwave, but could only pick at it. He'd lost his appetite on the drive home, thinking about what might have gone wrong six years earlier.

Matt went up to bed, slipping carefully under the covers so as not to wake his wife, and stared at the ceiling until almost five, at which point his mind could dwell no longer on events of the past, and he fell asleep.

But he was startled awake by Tricia shortly after seven as she pulled back the covers and put her feet on the floor.

"When'd you get in?" she asked.

"Around three," he mumbled into the pillow.

"Did you get paid?"

"What?"

"Did you get paid? For the job?"

He sighed. "They pay when the job is done."

"I thought you got something up front."

"Well, this time I didn't. I'll see them today or tomorrow, settle up."

"Because I need some money. I thought you'd have some cash. Cheryl needs new runners. I don't want to put anything more on the Visa."

Matt grumbled something into his pillow.

"And what was that call about last night?" Tricia asked.

"I don't want to talk about it."

"Was it about another job? They think you're getting good at this, more work's going to come your way."

"An old job," he said, rolling onto his back, resigned to the idea that he was not going to have a chance to go back to sleep.

"Why would someone call you about an old jo—"

"For fuck's sake," he said, sitting up, "I'm barely awake, and you're like the fucking Gestapo."

Tricia didn't even blink. "I want to be at the mall when they open."

"You do that."

"You promised the kids McDonald's today."

"I gotta go into the shop," he said, referring to the laundromat. "One of the dryers is acting up, needs a new belt or something." Matt had someone run the place on the weekends and didn't usually have to go in.

"So do that after lunch," Tricia said. "Snooze another hour if you want, but you're not getting out of this."

Matt dropped his head back onto the pillow and closed his eyes. He loved this woman, but God, she could be a bitch and a half.

He ended up getting out of bed half an hour later, once Tricia had gone downstairs to the kitchen. Had a long shower, standing there until the hot water ran out, thinking.

Matt and Tricia and their kids, Curtis and Cheryl—one big happy family—were in the mall by eleven, which was when Tricia pulled a fast one on him. She wanted to take Curtis to the music shop. He'd recently shown interest in learning to play the piano, and she wanted to check out one of those little electric ones.

"You take Cheryl to the shoe store and I'll catch up with you," she said.

"The fuck do I know about kids' shoes?"

"Just let her look around. I'll be there in time to decide."

Like he couldn't be trusted. People put their faith in him to go out and kill people, but he couldn't pick out a pair of shoes for a five-year-old.

Little Cheryl knew her way around a shoe store. Walked straight in, grabbed a pair of white runners with pink stripes off the display, and found a saleswoman without any help from her father.

"Would you have these in my size?" she inquired in her tiny voice.

The saleswoman smiled and said, "Let's have a look at those feet of yours and see what you need."

Matt stood near the front of the store and watched the foot traffic go by.

She was buried in dirt, he thought. *She was in a fucking grave. But if by some chance she wasn't dead when I put her there . . .*

And it was true, he hadn't stuck around. Hadn't seen the point. Why would he? When the job was done, the job was done, and it made sense to get the hell out of there as fast as he could.

It would have to have been like a scene in a movie.

A hand coming up out of the dirt. Then another. Then a frantic scramble to get herself aboveground, get some air.

No no no no no.

And yet, she'd been seen. *Supposedly.*

He sensed a presence next to him. Someone very small, walking about awkwardly, trying on shoes to see how they felt.

Matt turned and knelt down and said, "How do they fit? Are your toes all squished—"

It was not Cheryl. It was a different girl, probably the same age, about the same size. The little girl looked at him, eyes wide, then turned and ran back to a woman standing by the cash register. Her mother, evidently.

Cheryl was still sitting in a chair, shoeless, legs swinging back and forth while she waited for the saleswoman to bring her something to try on.

And suddenly Matt had a thought.

I got the wrong girl.

Had the woman he was supposed to kill been seen in recent days because he never got her in the first place? It wasn't like he'd asked to see her driver's license or fill out a questionnaire when she'd come down to the kitchen early that morning. He went to the address he'd been given and left with the woman who lived there. Wasn't a whole lot of chitchat. Could there have been someone else there instead? Someone staying over? A house swap? But even if that were the case, where had the woman he'd been paid to get rid of been the last six years?

"Daddy?"

He looked down, and this time it was, indeed, his little girl. "Yeah, sweetheart."

"Do you like these?"

She held up one foot and then another, displaying a pair of shoes emblazoned with dozens of small, sparkling pink stars.

"Wait for your mother."

He considered the possibilities. If Brie Mason really was alive, she'd either survived and dug herself out, or he'd killed someone else by mistake. There had to be a way to nail this down. He would need to toss a shovel into the truck and go for a drive.

And take someone along with him. Someone who might be able to identify what was in that grave after all these years, if there was even anything there at all.

Maybe the client.

Maybe somebody else.

Matt was feeling something unfamiliar. He was feeling scared. And he would do whatever was necessary to make that feeling go away.

Thirty-One
Andrew

Brie had confessed to me about Norman.

I believed her when she said it had just been one time. I don't think you can call having sex a single time with someone other than your spouse an affair. A mistake, sure. A betrayal, no doubt about it. An error in judgment, without question. But an affair? I wouldn't say that. My transgression with Natalie Simmons fell into that category. And it also qualified as a mistake, a betrayal, and an error in judgment.

I would say, however, that to sleep with your brother-in-law, even once, is kind of fucked up.

What Brie did betrayed not only me but her sister, Isabel, as well. Not that there wasn't plenty of blame to go around. That son of a bitch Norman was at fault here, too.

I didn't take it well.

Amazingly, I didn't have to pry it out of her. But Brie, wracked with guilt, felt the need to unburden herself. Maybe she thought it was going to come out at some point anyway, and wanted to get ahead of it.

"I can only explain it one way," she said. "Pity."

"Pity?" I said.

She told me how it happened. Brie, while no accountant, had a head for figures and was a whiz at doing tax returns. She not only did ours, but she volunteered to do them for Albert and Dierdre, and Isabel and Norman. Brie always refused payment, no matter how much they insisted, but she—and by that, I mean we—were rewarded with numerous bottles of very drinkable, if not terribly expensive, wine.

Brie headed over to Isabel and Norman's one evening to sit down at the kitchen table and, armed with a laptop and the most up-to-date tax software, proceeded to figure out their returns. Isabel was heading out for the evening with the kids to some school function, leaving Brie alone with Norman.

She had several questions for him, and he had gone searching for various forms and receipts that he and

Isabel kept in a shoebox, then sat down at the table next to her, trying to find the information she needed.

Norman asked if Brie would like a beer, and she said yes. He decided to have one, too. There were, I guess, a couple more each after that.

At one point, Brie said she needed a break from staring at the computer, and asked Norman something innocent, along the lines of, "So how's things?"

And Norman said, "How is it you turned out like this?"

"Turned out like what?"

"Nice," he said.

"I like doing people's taxes," she said. "You're actually doing me a favor. I love this stuff."

"I don't mean with the taxes," Norman said. "I mean, how is it you turned out so nice, and your sister didn't?"

Norman, I should point out, was a handsome-enough-looking guy, with a dry wit, and in his youth had hoped to be a filmmaker. But real life has a way of crushing creative ambition, and Norman ended up running a Firestone franchise, where the closest he got to being a filmmaker was when he made short video spots for his website advertising a sale on snow tires. When he and Isabel started dating, Brie had told me, she wasn't quite the person she would later become.

Negative, sure, but she had not yet perfected her gold-medal-worthy nitpicking skills.

Thing is, to cut her some slack, Isabel had abandoned her dreams just as Norman had. She had wanted to become a lawyer—she'd always been a fan of legal dramas; as a kid she'd watch old episodes of *L.A. Law* and *Matlock* and even the old black-and-white *Perry Mason* series—but had neither the resources for law school, nor marks high enough to be admitted. In my more generous moments, I felt this had a lot to do with Isabel's unhappiness. Not that she ever confided in me, confessed her discontent, but I don't think one could be the way she was without being disappointed with herself. However, her skills at working the system to hound me in the years after Brie's disappearance were evidence she might have had the chops to pursue a career in the law.

But back to the night in question.

Brie tried, at first, to apologize to Norman for her sister, to argue that ultimately she meant well. That what Norman saw as haranguing was Isabel trying to make their life better.

And that was when Norman revealed perhaps his darkest secret: that when he'd been dating Isabel, it was Brie he felt himself falling in love with. There was a period before I met Brie when she and her sister were living together, sharing an apartment in Bridge-port, and Norman always wanted to pick Isabel up from there, not meet her someplace, because it might allow him, even for a few minutes, to be in Brie's company.

Isabel, Norman told Brie, was perceptive enough to figure out what he was up to back then, which explained why at every opportunity she told him stories designed to trash Brie's reputation. That Brie was a slut, that she thought she was better than everybody else, that she only cared about how people looked and not what was inside.

Brie had never heard this before. Maybe it was what tipped her over the edge, learning the terrible things her sister had once said about her. That, and the fact that by this time she knew I'd had—and ended—my brief affair with Natalie.

The way Brie told it, that was when she gave him a hug. It was only meant to be consoling, but turned into something else.

"I can't explain it," she told me, weeping. "It just happened."

She begged me not to do anything to Norman. I don't think I'd ever given Brie reason to believe I was the type of guy who'd jump in the car, drive over to his place, haul him out on the front lawn, and beat the shit out of him. But then again, we'd never been in a place like this before. And I won't lie. I did think about it.

But what would beating Norman to a pulp have proved? There was so much guilt to go around.

Still, I had a hard time dealing with it. We didn't speak for several days, aside from the most basic communications. I slept on the couch, ate meals alone. It was Greg who finally talked some sense into me.

"Stop being an asshole," he said. "You're the luckiest guy in the world. Stop this shit. Patch this up. Brie is beautiful and kind and if we pushed the people out of our lives who had made one mistake we'd all be totally fucking alone. If she's willing to take you back after what you've done, you need to let this go."

Interesting advice, coming from Greg. Brie was not his biggest fan, and he knew it. A few years earlier, when Brie and I were engaged, Greg made a pass at her. She made it very clear to him that she was not interested, and when she told me about it later, I made a mistake that I like to think I wouldn't make today, if such a thing were to happen with Jayne.

I made excuses for Greg. You know what he's like, I said. He didn't mean anything by it. He probably had too much to drink. Maybe he thought you were someone else. It was a party and it was crowded. He's a friendly guy. Don't worry about it.

I dismissed Brie's concerns. I didn't take them seriously. I failed to appreciate how uncomfortable my friend had made her feel. Maybe now, in the wake of Me Too and a little more self-reflection on the part of the male gender, I would see things differently.

Anyway, back then, I took his advice. I told Brie I wanted to start over. I would move past what she had done if she would move past what I had done. We went to counseling. I pledged to create a more stable life for us, not moving from fixer-upper to fixer-upper.

The odds might have been against us, but we beat them.

Things played out differently at Norman and Isabel's house. Norman did not confess. Isabel, so far as we knew, remained unaware, and Brie wanted it to remain that way. She made me promise I would never, ever tell Isabel what she had done.

"Even if I were dead," she'd said at the time.

I promised.

She did not make me promise not to tell the police, however, should the circumstances warrant it. When Detective Hardy pressed me for every possible detail about Brie's personal life, I disclosed the information about Norman, without suggesting in any way that he might be responsible. And Hardy concluded he wasn't, given that he was in Boston with Isabel Saturday night and into Sunday, during and after my FaceTime chat with Brie.

Norman had to know that I knew, and anytime we were in the same room, such as a family gathering, I'm sure he saw me as a ticking time bomb. That I would punch his lights out, or, even more frightening, rat him out to Isabel. What she might do to him would be far worse than any punishment I might mete out.

Anyway, I did neither.

Not even when things were at their worst. When Isabel was hounding Detective Hardy to charge me with something, anything, I resisted the urge to retaliate, to tell her that the sister for whom she was seeking justice had betrayed her in the worst way. It would have been so easy to bring her entire world crashing down with the revelation, but I couldn't do it.

I wouldn't do it to Brie. I'd made a promise and I intended to keep it. I would not destroy her extended family to score points, even though I was tempted.

I wasn't the only one to keep the secret. Elizabeth knew, too. I wondered if Norman was aware. I wondered if Elizabeth had quietly taken him aside in recent days and told him he owed me a debt of gratitude. I wondered if that was why Norman had tried to call me the night before.

And going back six years, I wondered whether this

had been weighing heavily on Brie that last day I spent with her. The Friday, before driving up to the cabin that evening. Something was troubling her. She was pensive, thinking about something. Didn't say a word at breakfast. Our mistakes were behind us, but I supposed it was possible she hadn't stopped turning them over in her mind.

"I can tell you're thinking about something," I said. "Talk to me."

"I'm fine," she insisted.

"If you don't want me to go away, I'll cancel. Greg and I can do this another time. He's going to be hobbling around all over the place, anyway. Might do to wait another week or two when his leg's totally healed."

"No, I *want* you to go," she said. "You *have* to go."

"You trying to get rid of me?" I said. I meant it as a joke, but she took the comment seriously, as though I harbored some suspicions about what plans she might have.

"God, tell me we're not slipping back," she said.

"No, no, that's not what I meant. I was kidding. Seriously." I took her into my arms. "We are definitely *not* slipping back."

She buried her head in my chest. Brie didn't want me to see her cry. "I want you and Greg to have this weekend," she said, and sniffed. She wiped her nose against my shirt and I laughed.

"I could get you a tissue," I offered.

"No need," Brie said, and did it again.

She pulled away. "Will you call me? Let me know how things are going up there?"

"I don't imagine there'll be much to report," I said. "We'll fish, we'll drink, we'll sleep. Pretty much in that order. And I'll be back Sunday afternoon. Maybe we should go out." I grinned. "Maybe that seafood place, because odds are I won't be eating much of it at the cabin. The lake's probably fished out."

"Okay," she said, and smiled. "That's what we'll do."

We both went to work. Brie had a job doing payroll for several small local businesses, and I was off to give several estimates before taking off for the weekend. The car was already packed, and I'd be on the road before Brie got home Friday afternoon.

We would talk Saturday night, and she would tell me about her adventures with Charlie the exterminator.

But that Friday morning would be the last time I'd hold her in my arms.

Thirty-Two

No one was very excited about a midday Sunday rehearsal, but Albert felt there was no way around it. His play, *The Casual Librarian*, a comedic farce, was set to open in less than two weeks and they were far from prepared, and as the writer and director, Albert was more responsible than anyone for getting the production ready.

As if he didn't have enough to worry about. But as he liked to say, to the collective eye roll of everyone else in the production company, *The show must go on.* He had asked everyone to arrive by one.

The rehearsal was not being conducted in an actual theater, but in a rented space in an industrial mall in the north end of Milford. It was here where all preparations were made. Not just rehearsals, but set construction and costume design. As opening night approached, the sets would be carefully dismantled and loaded into a cube van, transported to whatever venue they had booked to present their show, and reassembled. There were some proper theater spaces in Milford, and if they were putting on a show that drew a large audience, like the annual Christmas pageant, they'd book one. But productions that didn't have a guaranteed, built-in audience were presented in a local high school gymnasium or community center.

The Casual Librarian, as it turned out, was one of the latter.

Actors in community theater often weren't actors at all, at least not professionally. Acting, for these folks, was a hobby, an extracurricular activity. Everyone had nine-to-five, Monday-to-Friday gigs, like Dick Guthrie, who worked in the Milford city tax office and was playing the librarian's son, or Fiona Fitzsimmons, who was a real estate lawyer and was hamming it up as a Miss Marple–like detective. And there was Albert himself, who was the assistant manager at the Devon Savings and Loan office on Broad Street when he wasn't a playwright and a director.

Not everyone, of course, worked normal hours. Lyall Grove, who was donning heavy makeup to play an aging lothario, worked for Milford's fire department, and his shifts were all over the place. But he'd traded off with a coworker so he could be off much of Sunday. Constance Sandusky, forty, who was totally getting into the title role as an extremely randy librarian, worked as a 911 operator, and like Lyall, had rotating shifts. She had come off one about twelve hours earlier, and as anyone who worked an emergency hotline knew, Saturday nights were often the craziest. More car accidents, more bar fights, more domestic disturbances. She'd arrived with an extra-large coffee from Dunkin' and was leaning up against a wall, sipping quietly.

Arriving late was Rona Hindle, just barely out of her teens, bitten by the acting bug in her high school theater arts class. She had a small role as a waitress. She was certain this was her ticket to Broadway, and Albert didn't have the heart to tell her that was unlikely. Also wandering in twenty minutes after one was Candace DiCarlo, mid-thirties but looked younger, who did work a standard Monday-to-Friday routine at a fitness center in New Haven. She was once a personal trainer, but now worked in the office. In Albert's play, she had the role of the librarian's sister, whose attempts to fix up her sibling with the perfect man would lead to a series of comic misunderstandings.

Right now she was doing more yawning than acting

and was filling a paper cup with foul-looking brown liquid from an aging coffee canister.

It wasn't just the actors who were present. Two carpenters who volunteered their time to build the movable sets had arrived and were hammering away at the same time Albert was trying to guide his actors through a critical scene in the second act.

"Guys?" he called out. "Guys? Can you ease up on the hammering? Just for a couple of minutes?"

They both looked at him like he was an idiot. If they couldn't build the goddamn set, then what the hell were they doing here?

"Okay, everyone," Albert said. "If we could gather round."

"Us, too?" one of the carpenters asked.

"No, not you guys," Albert said.

The half-dozen actors and actresses formed a semicircle around Albert, all standing, arms crossed. Constance took another sip of coffee. Candace yawned. Lyall discreetly tried to reach around and scratch his butt.

"I want to do a read-through of act two before we actually go through the motions. It's the pacing we need to work on. Some of the lines, they're not getting the right punch, you know?"

"Is there any way I could get more lines?" asked Rona. "I've only got, like, eight."

Albert sighed. "I'm afraid those are the only lines your character has."

"Yeah, but it's not like this is a play by Shakespeare or something where you can't mess with it. You're the writer. Couldn't you come up with more for me to say?"

"I'll take a look at it, okay?"

"Well, if you're going to do more lines for her, what about me?" asked Alice. But she was smiling wryly, and Albert was pretty sure she was giving him the gears.

"Why don't I give everyone twice as many lines and we can have a three-hour play instead of ninety minutes?" Albert said, making a joke to disguise the fact that he was getting pissed off with the lot of them. Wasn't there a line in an Elmore Leonard novel, something about how movies would be so much easier to make if you could do them without actors?

"Okay," he said, "let's do this."

He directed everyone to a long folding-leg table, the kind one would find at any flea market. Everyone dropped into some cheap plastic chairs and, armed with copies of the script, prepared for the run-through.

Albert, nodding at Constance, said, "Let's start with your line at the top of page eighteen."

Constance found the page, cleared her throat, and, raising her chin as if getting ready to belt out a tune, said, "Has anyone seen my garter belt?"

Candace said, "I think I might have seen it in the car."

"The car? How on earth could—"

A phone began to ring.

"Oh, for God's sake," Albert said. "Can we all remember to mute our phones, please?"

Everyone pulled out their phones as the ringing continued.

"Not me," said Dick.

"Not me," said Rona.

The ringing was coming from somewhere else in the room. "Oh shit," Albert said. "I think it's mine."

He jumped up and walked over to the table where the coffee machine was sitting, spotted his phone, and picked it up.

"Hello?" he said.

"It's Izzy. You need to get to the hospital as fast as you can."

Thirty-Three
Andrew

My unexpected meeting with Isabel, and the subsequent visit with Elizabeth, had thrown me off my game somewhat. I'd left the house that morning intending to visit Charlie Underwood, the exterminator who'd answered Brie's plea for help when she thought our house might have a mouse infestation.

And, in fact, I later learned that it did. In the midst of having to deal with all the fallout from Brie's disappearance, I began to spot mouse droppings around the house. Under the sink, in the basement where the wall met the floor, even in a kitchen drawer. I had tried to solve the problem on my own, buying traps and commercially available poison, but I wasn't able to get a handle on the problem.

Finally, I had called Charlie Underwood.

But when he realized I was Brie's husband, he passed on the job. He would have known, by that time, that I was Hardy's prime suspect. She would undoubtedly have spoken to him many times in the course of her investigation. Maybe he thought I had some ulterior motive, that I wanted to pump him for details about his meeting with Brie. I supposed it was possible Hardy had warned him I might get in touch.

I just wanted to get rid of the fucking mice.

But now, six years later, I wondered if Charlie's refusal to return to the house had any further significance. And, since I didn't know what else to do at this point, he seemed like a good place to start.

His home was a run-down, vinyl-sided, two-story dwelling up Forest Road, before it turns into Burnt Plains Road north of the turnpike. It was set back a good hundred feet from the blacktop, and behind it sat a square, squat structure made of cinder blocks. I pulled into the driveway and parked next to a seriously rusted panel van, some of the rust eating right through the letters of UNDERWOOD PEST CONTROL painted on the side. The van was sitting on the rims and clearly hadn't been driven anywhere for some time. An old, original Beetle—not one of the new, redesigned versions—was parked farther up the drive. Just as rusted out, but on fully inflated tires.

I got out, and as I approached the house noticed that the second-story windows were all boarded up. I climbed the two steps to the porch and knocked on the front door. When no one showed up after twenty seconds, I tried again. Same result.

I walked around the corner of the house and noticed that the door to the cinder-block structure was ajar. As I approached it I started to get a whiff of something that took me back to when I was a little kid, when I visited my uncle's farm. He kept pigs, and the stench from the indoor pens could literally take your breath away.

The smell got stronger as I reached the door. I rapped on it, but since it was open, I poked my head in at the same time and said, "Mr. Underwood?"

"Back here!" someone shouted, and coughed.

Breathing through my mouth, I stepped inside. The building, maybe thirty feet square, was filled with makeshift tables constructed of sawhorses and four-by-eight sheets of plywood. The tables filled the room, spaced apart to create several aisles.

And atop every table, cages. Dozens and dozens of cages.

The room was a cacophony of chittering noises, scratching noises, scurrying noises. Each cage contained one or more animals. Rats, mice, squirrels, raccoons.

A possum or two.

As I walked down one aisle, tiny eyes fixed on me. A black squirrel gripped the wire caging of its enclosure, stood on its hind legs, and watched me as I passed. My arrival had created a commotion. Word seemed to be spreading among the creatures. Someone new was here. A stranger. An interloper.

It was a fucking zoo of pests and vermin. And they were living in their own filth.

At the end of the aisle, his back to me, was Charlie Underwood in a pair of blue coveralls. He was stooped over, and as I got closer, he went into a coughing fit. When he was done, he made a retching sound that sounded like someone trying to scoop gravel out of the bottom of a well. Then he spit something onto the floor and I felt my own stomach do a slow roll.

He turned, saw me, and said, "Help you?"

"Mr. Underwood?"

"That's me."

"You, uh, did some pest control at my house a few years back."

"Don't do that anymore," he said, then smiled, showing off brown teeth. "Dying," he said, matter-of-factly.

"Sorry to hear that."

"You work with poisonous chemicals your whole

life, it has a way of catching up with you," he said, and laughed, triggering another coughing fit.

"I can imagine." I looked about the room. "What is all this?"

"You're not one of those fucking inspectors from the city, are you?" he asked.

"No."

"Because they'd take a dim view of what I'm doing here if they found out," he said, and coughed again. It echoed all the way down to his shoes. He smiled, waved his hand at the room. "They wouldn't understand that this is a rescue operation. These are the ones I didn't have to kill. Saved them all. Some of them, been looking after them for years."

"These are all . . . pests you got out of people's houses?"

He nodded proudly. "Lot of people, they want 'em dead, but if I can get them out alive, I bring 'em here."

I could think of only one question. "Why?"

He blinked, a little surprised by my question. "Because they're all God's creatures, you know. See this rat over here? That's Susie. Anyway, caught her at a restaurant on the green downtown. I'd tell you which one but then you'd never eat there again and they got good food so I won't tell you. And that raccoon was living in the attic of a couple in Devon. I accidentally broke his paw getting him out, so I keep him here. Figure he wouldn't make it out in the wild. His name is Waldo. You say I came to your place?"

"About six years ago."

"Who are you?"

"Carville. Andrew Carville. But back then, it was Mason."

He blinked again, taking a second to put it together. It was like watching an old computer start up.

"Son of a bitch," he said, and coughed again. "You're the guy. The one who killed his wife."

"I didn't kill my wife."

"Yeah, well, what else would you say? Whaddya want with me?"

I had no answer ready. Now that I was here, I honestly didn't know. "Going over old ground," I said. "Still looking for answers. Still looking for Brie."

"Sure you are," he said.

"I know it was a long time ago, and that you've talked to Detective Hardy probably a dozen times, but is there anything you held back, anything you wish you'd told her?"

He shook his head. "Can't think of anything. I talked to her a lot." He grinned. "I was thinking, at one point, that maybe she thought I did it. They even came out here to my place, searched around, looking for anything, but they didn't find a damn thing. I guess that's when they started zeroing in on you." He shook his head and grinned once more. "Guess you beat them on that one."

"How did Brie seem that day? Was she anxious? Did she seem like she was worried about anything?"

His grin faded. "Well, first of all, when people call me, they're worried they've got mice or rats or God knows what, so it's fair to say they're a little on edge. And your wife was like that."

"You think it could have been something other than mice?"

"All these years later, what makes you ask?"

I didn't want to get into the events of the last two days. "Just asking, is all."

"Well, I'll tell you this much," he said. "She struck me as a woman who was just waiting for something bad to happen. That's not something I ever told the police because it was a little too vague."

"What do you mean?"

He shrugged. "I think she was worried about what you were going to do when you got home."

"She had nothing to worry about from me," I said.

Another shrug, and then a grin. "Now can I ask *you* something?"

"Sure, go ahead."

"Like I said, I'm dying. I'm wondering if you'd be interested in taking any one of these rescue animals home with you? I need to off-load them as soon as possible."

"Sorry," I said. "I can't help you there."

Charlie nodded and smiled. "Never hurts to ask."

On the way back into town, I glanced at the gas gauge and noticed the Explorer was running on fumes. I pulled into a gas station, and used a credit card to get the self-serve pump operating, started to refill the tank. When I was done, I couldn't get the pump to print out a receipt, so I went into the building and got one from the guy sitting at the cash register.

I didn't notice, until I was actually back in the Explorer, that there was someone sitting in the passenger seat who hadn't been there before.

A woman, late thirties. Smiling.

"Surprise," she said. "I *thought* that was you."

"Natalie," I said. "I'll be damned."

Thirty-Four

The four of them were there, at Elizabeth's bedside.
There was Albert and his wife, Dierdre, who had put aside their differences to be here at this difficult time. Isabel and her husband, Norman, were present, too, the four of them ringed around the bed, the siblings near the head, on either side, and the in-laws by the foot.

Isabel was leaning over, rubbing her hand gently across Elizabeth's forehead, stroking her almost as if she were a pet in need of comforting.

"I love you, Mom," she said.

Albert, on the other side, had a tear running down one cheek. He was holding Elizabeth's hand.

Elizabeth's eyes were closed, her breathing so shallow as to be almost undetectable.

A woman in a long white hospital jacket entered the room quietly. Isabel was first to notice her and whispered, "The doctor."

The four moved away from the bed and circled the doctor in the center of the room.

Albert said, "She seemed pretty good yesterday."

Isabel added, "I saw her for a few minutes this morning and she was alert."

The doctor nodded sympathetically. "I know. Things can change very quickly. I've seen patients rally near the end. Within a day of passing, they're more alert, more communicative. It's as though they know what's coming, and want a chance to say goodbye to everyone." The doctor smiled sadly.

Isabel dabbed her eye with a tissue.

"I think she feels it's okay to let go now," she said. "There was someone she'd been hoping to hear from. She wanted to hear from her so badly I think she imagined that it happened." She sniffed.

The doctor's face was questioning, but she simply said, "Anything is possible."

Norman asked, "You don't think it's possible she might still wake up and . . . tell us things?"

Isabel gave him a look. "Like what?"

"Like anything," he said. "Like how much she'll miss us."

"Like I said, anything is possible," the doctor repeated.

Dierdre spoke for the first time. "How much time does she have?"

The doctor sighed heavily. "I think coming here now was wise."

The four of them could think of no further questions. The doctor told them to get in touch if there were any further developments, and quietly left the room.

Isabel and Albert resumed their positions on either side of the bed, while Dierdre said she and Norman were going to get some air. Once they had left the room, Albert whispered to his sister, "What was all that about imagining something?"

"Mom said Brie came to her in the night. She was probably dreaming. We put the idea in her head."

"You didn't tell me about that," Albert said.

"I knew you had rehearsals today. Thought I'd give you a break."

Albert nodded a thank-you. Elizabeth, her eyes closed, showed no sign that she was aware of their conversation. Still, he whispered. "Maybe Mother hasn't been the only one seeing things."

His sister studied him, waiting for him to elaborate.

"When we saw that woman in the parking lot, we were

seeing what we wanted to see. In the night, Mom did the same. If that allows her to slip away with some degree of comfort, thinking Brie is alive, I'm okay with that."

"What about what the neighbor saw?"

"I can't explain that."

"So you don't believe it," Isabel said.

"Believe what?"

"You don't believe Brie's alive."

Albert quickly glanced at his mother and then back to Isabel, worried that even their whispers might be heard. He motioned for her to follow him into the hall-way. Once they were out of the room, he went back to his normal voice.

"Izzy, I'd like to believe," he said. "But . . ."

Isabel's jaw hardened. Her cheeks flushed. "That bastard."

"What?"

"Andrew."

"What about him?"

"Mom wanted to see him, to apologize. I brought him here this morning so she could talk to him. He was coy about it with me, saying he couldn't accept an apol-ogy when we didn't really know what was happening. But he let her do it. I talked to her after. She apologized and he accepted it, the smug bastard."

"Izzy—"

"No, no, something's not right here. I eased up on him. I eased up on him too soon."

"Christ, Izzy, let it go."

"I'm going back in," Isabel said, and with that pushed open the door and returned to Elizabeth's bedside. Albert followed.

As they stood watch over her, Isabel said, "I don't think she's breathing."

Albert leaned over, put his ear to within an inch of his mother's mouth. "I don't hear anything. Not feeling anything."

"Mom?" Isabel said, her voice starting to crack.

Albert glanced at the monitor that hovered over the bedside table, hunted for the line that kept track of heartbeat.

It was flat.

"Mom?" Isabel said again, putting her face close to hers. "Can you hear me?"

Not so much as an eyelid fluttered.

The door opened and Dierdre and Norman stepped in. They read the room quickly, seeing how distressed their respective spouses looked.

"Oh, Mother," Albert said.

As he laid his head on her chest and began to weep,

Dierdre stepped forward and looked ready to place a hand on his shoulder, but held back.

"I'm so sorry," she whispered.

Norman didn't move. He watched from afar as his wife began to sob, and appeared to sigh with relief.

Thirty-Five
Andrew

Seeing Natalie Simmons in the passenger seat put me into a momentary stupor, but the blast of a car horn woke me from it.

I glanced into the rearview mirror and saw another driver waiting to pull up to the self-serve pump I'd finished using a moment earlier. I keyed the ignition and drove out from under the canopy that hung over the pumps, then brought the car to a stop at the edge of the lot.

"Where's your car?" I asked.

Natalie pointed to a low-slung Porsche Boxster pulled into a spot out front of the gas station.

"Just whipped in to buy some smokes," she said.

"Keep trying to quit, but hey, we're all addicted to something and sometimes there's no point fighting it."

"Nice ride," I said, giving a nod toward the car.

"I own the gallery now," she said, and grinned. "Movin' up in the world."

"Congrats."

"So how've you been?" she asked. "I mean, you're not in jail, so that's a good thing, right?" Natalie let loose a nervous laugh, like my possibly doing time for killing Brie was a subject of amusement.

"I suppose so," I said.

Her smile faded. "I kept following the story in the news, you know? Googled it every once in a while and eventually it faded away. They never found her, huh?"

"No," I said.

She nodded, almost with a sense of admiration, as though whoever might have disposed of Brie had done the job well.

"So many times I thought about calling you, seeing how you were, but then thought, that'd be weird, right? I mean, like I was trying to put a move on you now that your wife was no longer in the picture."

She shook her head and smiled slyly. "Although, I won't lie. I was tempted. We had a good thing going. Fun while it lasted, you know?"

"Yeah, I guess," I said.

"But how would that have looked? Not good, right? Especially with the police keeping an eye on you. I'm pretty sure they were keeping an eye on me, too. There were times I'd see some car parked down the street, like someone was watching the place."

If Detective Hardy had ever been conducting a surveillance on Natalie Simmons, I'd known nothing about it. Natalie was the type who'd see a tail where none existed. She was, to put it kindly, a bit of a flake. Natalie was easy prey for spreaders of conspiracy theories. She'd have been among those who thought COVID was a hoax. Back when I'd been seeing her, she didn't even have a cell phone, believing they allowed the government to trace everyone's whereabouts. I had to call the gallery landline if I wanted to get in touch.

But I was also reminded, as Natalie sat there in the front of the Explorer, what had attracted me to her. She was a looker. Well curved in all the right places, long legs, dark hair that fell softly to her shoulders, brown eyes. Some of the same attributes Brie had possessed, I realized at one point.

I met her when I'd been doing some renovation work on the business next door to the gallery. A soon-to-open bagel place. She had popped in during construction, wanting to know when the opening was going to be, and when we got talking, I learned that we had both gone to UConn, even been there at the same time.

"Oh my God," she'd said. "I remember you." She'd watched me studying her, waiting to see whether I remembered her, too.

"That one party, you helped me search through that huge pile of coats in the bedroom, trying to find mine, and things kinda happened?"

And then it all came back to me. A one-night thing.

While these thoughts ran through my head, Natalie was still talking.

". . . wondered if maybe she could even have left the country, but why would she do that? Or got some new identity, you know? I mean, you have to have been asking yourself these questions for years."

"Nice to see you, Natalie, but I really have to get going."

"Oh, sorry," she said. "When I saw you, I just had to say hello." She laughed. "God, you must think I'm stalking you or something. I hope you're doing okay. You with someone now?"

"Yes."

Natalie nodded approvingly. "That's good, that's good. You have to move on, right? But hey, if you're going by the gallery, stop in, okay? We can catch up."

I smiled. "Sounds like a plan."

She flashed me one last smile, opened the passenger door, and got out. She looked back over her shoulder once on the way to her Porsche and gave me a small wave, and a wink.

On the way home I found myself replaying what Charlie Underwood had said about Brie, that she had seemed anxious about what would happen when I returned home from my fishing trip. Clearly, he believed I was the source of Brie's anxiety.

Maybe Underwood was right, that Brie was apprehensive about my return, but not for the reason he assumed. What might have had her concerned? Had something happened between the time I left on Friday and Underwood came to the house on Saturday? Something that she didn't want to have to tell me about, but knew she would have to eventually?

Could it have had something to do with Norman or Isabel? I'd often wondered whether Brie would ever confront her sister about the things Isabel had said to Norman, years ago. Running down her character. At one point, Isabel was going to come over on the Saturday night while I was away, a "sisters night," but her plans had changed and she and Norman had gone to

Boston. Had Brie been planning to have it out with her? When Isabel canceled, did Brie just pick up the phone and give her a blast?

Unlikely.

If I knew Brie, she'd have felt there was nothing to be gained by stirring up old rivalries, revisiting old grievances. Sometimes you had to move on.

So what else, then?

Something financial? Did Brie know something I didn't? Were things in even worse shape than I knew them to be? She kept better track of the books than I did. The company was definitely in a precarious state, having lost more than a couple of major bids for work. But I was trying to be optimistic about the future. You win some jobs, you lose some jobs. Our bids had not been competitive, so we were going to have to find ways to cut our costs.

That could be it.

But I never stumbled upon any evidence—bank statements, budget documents—that would support that theory.

Did she resent my going away for the weekend with Greg? No, that couldn't be it. She'd *pushed* me to make the trip, urged me to go away with him, which was somewhat out of character. Brie was not Greg's biggest fan, for reasons I'd mentioned earlier. But she knew he was my closest friend, and understood that hanging out with him for a couple of days would probably reduce my stress level.

So, I had nothing.

If Brie'd had something on her mind that troubled her, I couldn't guess what it might have been.

That night, we ordered in pizzas. One with the toppings Jayne and I liked, and a second with everything Tyler liked. For a while there, things felt almost normal.

We had dinner together at the kitchen table. There was no talk of the visit the day before from Detective Hardy, no more questions about who I might or might not have murdered. It's always nice to get through a meal without being quizzed about your possible homicidal background.

I got a call while I was on my second slice. It was Albert's wife, Dierdre. I'd always had a pretty good relationship with her before Brie's disappearance, and she'd never quite frozen me out despite Isabel's efforts. If I ran into her when I was out and about in Milford, she would at least speak to me.

I excused myself from the table and took the call on the back deck. "Hey, Dierdre."

"I had a feeling no one else might call," she said, "but we lost Elizabeth today."

"I'm so sorry," I said. "Please pass on my condolences to . . . everyone."

"I heard that you had been to see her this morning," she said.

"Yeah. I'm glad I had that chance."

"Okay, then. You take care."

It was a short conversation.

By the time I returned to the kitchen, the mood had changed.

"Why not?" Tyler said.

"I just think it'd be better if you stayed in tonight," Jayne said.

"Why?"

"Well, for one thing, it's a school night."

Tyler's eyes rolled. "Hello? Can you remember all the way back to last night? How I went upstairs and did homework and shit? And you made a crack about whether I'd been taken over by a pod or something?"

"I never said that."

"You made a crack. You said something."

"What's going on?" I asked.

"I'm a prisoner," Tyler said. "She's treating me like I'm five."

"He wants to go out," Jayne said.

"Out where?" I asked.

"Just *out*," Tyler said. "Would you like me to prepare an itinerary? Where I'll be all night. Like, from eight to eight-fifteen, the 7-Eleven, and from—"

"Stop it," Jayne said.

"Maybe," I said, dipping my toe in, "if Tyler promised to be back by ten, because like you said, it is a school night."

Jayne shot me a look. "This is between me and him."

"Whoa," Tyler said. "Better be careful what you say, sis, or he might kill you."

The room went quiet. Jayne looked as though she'd been slapped across the face. It's possible I looked the same. Even Tyler appeared surprised by what he'd said, realizing he'd crossed a line.

"Get out," Jayne said. "Get out of my sight."

He was happy to oblige. Tyler left the kitchen. Seconds later, the front door slammed.

I didn't know what to say.

It was Jayne who broke the silence. "So he knows."

"He was listening in, yesterday. To Hardy, and then us."

She closed her eyes and slowly lowered her forehead to the table. I rested a hand on her shoulder. She raised her head and asked, "Who called?"

"Brie's mother's been in the hospital. One of the family called to tell me she passed away today."

"Oh," Jayne said. "Did she think the worst of you, too?"

"She came around to my side at the end."

"Well, that's something, I guess."

There was nothing more to be said about it.

We'd just gone upstairs to our bedroom, a few minutes before ten, when we heard someone enter the house. Tyler was back. Jayne and I glanced at one another, decided it was good news that he had returned at a reasonable hour, and there was no need to make a big deal out of it.

I was starting to unbutton my shirt when the sound of an incoming text came from my phone. It was Greg.

Out front. Got a sec?

"What is it?" Jayne asked, and I told her.

I tapped back: 2 mins.

"What's he want?" she asked.

"Why don't you join me and we'll find out."

We came out the front door together and found not just Greg waiting for us, but his turquoise-coiffed girlfriend, Julie. In fact, she was standing ahead of him, Greg half hidden behind her, as though using her as a shield.

Greg, out of respect, stepped out when he saw Jayne. "Hey," he said.

"Hi, Greg," she said.

He introduced Julie, who shook Jayne's hand. "I've heard lots about you," Julie said.

Jayne only smiled, not sure whether that was a good thing or a bad thing.

"What's up?" I asked them.

Julie turned to Greg, priming him. "Go on. Ask him."

Greg took half a step forward, eyes on his own feet. "We shouldn't have come. It's late. This can wait until tomorrow."

"You're here now," I said.

Julie sighed. "He's too proud to ask," she said to me. Then, to him, "Spit it out."

Greg seemed unable to make eye contact. If he owned a brimmed hat, this was where he'd have it in his hands, moving it in a slow circle with his fingers.

"The thing is," he said slowly, "ever since we stopped working together, things haven't, well, they could be—"

"He's lost without you, that's what he wants to say," Julie said.

"Yeah," Greg said sheepishly. "In a nutshell, yeah.

On my own, I'm always scrambling, you know? Have had some pretty long stretches between jobs. When we were a team, we did pretty good."

"Except toward the end there," I reminded him.

"I know, I know, we hit a bad stretch. But the economy was kind of stalled, too, at the time. It was one of those things."

That wasn't quite how I remembered it, but I let that go. I said, "I'd have to give it some thought."

"That's all we're asking," Julie said. "Right, Greg? We can't ask for any more than that."

Greg nodded. "Sorry to have disturbed you so late, man. Jayne, nice to see you. Apologies for the interruption." He turned and headed for the street. Julie's little Audi, not Greg's truck, was parked there.

But Julie didn't follow, and instead closed the distance between us. She kept her voice low.

"He thinks the world of you," she said. "He really wants to give it another go."

"Like I said—"

"I know I'm new here, and sticking my nose in where it doesn't belong, but I can see how worn down he is. He tells me you guys, you had a good thing going at one time."

"We did," I conceded.

"And it's not just about him," Julie said. "He's worried about you, and all the stuff—"

She looked at Jayne, wondering whether she was about to say too much.

"It's okay," I said. "Jayne's up to speed on things. Guess you are, too."

"Yeah. He knows you've got this cloud hanging over you, and he wants to, I don't know, make a statement by going back into business with you. That he believes in you even if there are some out there who still don't."

Greg, who had gotten behind the wheel of Julie's car, lightly tapped the horn.

"Have to go," she said, and ran to the car.

"That was interesting," Jayne said.

We watched them drive off, then went back into the house.

"What do you think?" Jayne asked as we were getting under the covers.

"I don't know."

"You know what I think? You should consider it. With all the shit that's been happening, maybe it's a good sign. An opportunity."

I wasn't convinced that was how Jayne really felt, but maybe after a long and unsettling weekend she wanted to grab on to anything that might allow us some reason for optimism.

So it was just as well I kept my thoughts to myself. I wasn't looking forward to Monday morning. I couldn't think of a single reason to believe we were heading into a good week.

Thirty-Six

The woman behind the wheel of the black Volvo station wagon was driving a circuitous route. A left here, a right there. She could not be sure, but she believed she was being followed. She'd seen enough TV shows to know that when you think someone is following you, you start driving randomly. See whether the vehicle you fear is trailing you makes the same moves.

When she first set out, after the sun had set, she hadn't noticed anything out of the ordinary. She glanced into the rearview mirror occasionally, the way any careful driver would, and around the second or third time she noticed that the car behind her had a couple of amber fog lamps mounted below the bumper, giving it a distinctive look.

She was heading west on Bridgeport Avenue, past

the hospital, when she began to wonder whether the car was actually following her. So she made a quick left down Seemans Lane, gave the Volvo some gas, and checked her mirror again.

Mr. Fog Lamps had made the turn, as well. (She was thinking of him as *Mr.* Fog Lamps, but she had no idea who was behind the wheel or how many people might be in the car.) She tried to get a look at the car as it was making a turn, see what type of vehicle it was. A sports car, she thought. Low to the ground.

She clipped along Seemans, made another left onto Meadowside, then a quick right onto Surf Avenue, heading south toward the beach house area of South Broadway.

The other car stayed with her.

If the car really was following her, who could it be? She thought immediately that it might be the police. There was every reason to think they'd be looking for her. Her appearances had no doubt caused some consternation and been brought to their attention. But wouldn't the police just put on their flashing lights, hit the siren, and pull her over? And did the police have sports cars?

The thought of being stopped by the police filled her with dread. But then, if *not* the police, then who? That possibility made her even more anxious.

She glanced up at the mirror again, just at the moment that the car's amber fog lights went out. The driver must have cottoned on to the fact that the lights were giving him away. If, in fact, it was the same car.

At East Broadway, she hung a right, zipping past the beach houses. Pretty much all of the ones that had been damaged when Hurricane Sandy came ashore back in 2012 had been replaced or repaired. It was one of her favorite stretches in all of Milford, but not something she could appreciate right now.

When East Broadway came to an end she turned right onto the Silver Sands Parkway, a name that made it sound like a major highway but was actually no more than a two-lane road that wound its way through a tract of land known as the Silver Sands State Park. She followed it all the way out of the park and back up to Meadowside, and when she looked in her mirror again, there was no car there.

Gone.

At first she wondered whether the driver had killed his regular headlights, in addition to the fog lights, so as not to be seen, but no. There was no car behind her.

Her heart was pounding. She made a left, then pulled over to the curb to let her pulse rate return to normal, and put the car into park. Her palms were sweaty on the wheel. She wiped her hands on the tops of jean-clad thighs.

Maybe it was nothing. Maybe no one had been following her, at least not deliberately. It was someone else out for an evening drive and by coincidence were taking the same route as her. The only ones who might reasonably have followed her would be the police, and clearly it wasn't them.

Get a grip.

She looked at her phone, sitting down in the center console. Should she call and say she'd been delayed? No, if she went straight there now, she'd only be five to ten minutes late. Not a big deal.

She took a deep breath, put the Volvo back into drive, and headed up Avery Avenue, hit Route 1 for a very short distance before turning left on Schoolhouse, by the Ford dealership.

She could see the sign up ahead.

The Motel 6.

She steered the Volvo wagon into the lot and decided, in the event that someone really had been following her, that she should park where the car wasn't visible from the main road. She drove around to the back of the building and parked beyond the pool, under the cover of some trees.

Another deep breath.

She got out of the car, locked it with the remote, and headed into the building, a bland four-story structure. Her destination was a room on the fourth floor, so she took the lobby elevator up, stepped into the hallway, took a second to figure out which way the room numbers went, and struck off to the left.

When she got to the room she stopped and looked both ways down the hallway, as if checking that no one was watching her. You couldn't be too careful. The hallway was empty. She was without a key, so she rapped lightly on the door. No more than five seconds went by before it opened.

"Sorry I'm late, I—"

Before she could finish apologizing, the man who'd opened the door had his arms around her and his mouth on hers. She responded in kind, pulling him in close, dropping the purse she had been carrying to the floor as the door swung shut.

They began to undress each other, fumbling with shirt and blouse buttons. They quickly decided it was easier to accomplish this task on their own. The woman stripped down, taking slightly longer than the man, who had kicked off his shoes and whipped off his pants in record time before pulling back the covers and getting into the bed.

But she wasn't ready to slip between the sheets with him, not just yet.

"I need to talk to you," she said.

"What?"

"I think . . . I could be wrong about this, but I think someone was following me tonight."

"Following you?" he said.

She nodded.

"Did you get a look at who it was?" he asked.

"No. I thought at first it was the police, because the car had some yellow lights under the bumper. Like fog lamps."

"I don't think the police have those."

"And then he turned the lamps off because he must have known how obvious it made him."

"Or maybe he turned them off because it's not foggy."

"And then the car was gone." She dropped her head, as if in defeat. "Maybe. I guess I'm feeling a little paranoid."

"That's my fault," he said. "Come here."

She crawled into the bed. Instead of having sex, they each propped themselves up on an elbow to face each other.

"It was a lot to ask, I realize that," he said. "But I really believe it was worth it. And it's not like you did anything illegal. I mean, what would they charge you with? I can't thank you enough."

"It's okay. I liked doing it. I really got into it. And that last performance? I think it went really well." She grinned. "Academy! Academy!"

But the man wasn't grinning. He was starting to cry.

"What?" she said. "What's happened?"

"I'm sorry," he said. "Shit, I don't think I can do this. I really *needed* to, just to get my mind . . ."

He got off his elbow and dropped onto his back, stared at the ceiling.

"It's okay," she said, laying a hand on his chest. "Talk to me."

The man swallowed, struggled to compose himself. "It's over," he said.

"Oh no," she said.

"It happened this afternoon."

"Oh no. Oh, I'm so sorry."

The man nodded. "I love you," he said. "I love you so much."

"I love you, too."

The woman with the black Volvo station wagon inched closer, hugged him, brought her face up close to his.

"It's okay to cry," she said. "Just let it go, Albert. Mommy's gone. Just let it go."

Monday

Thirty-Seven
Andrew

It was Monday, and we all had places to be.

I'd had two calls the previous week about possible jobs, so I was going to visit the sites today and provide some estimates. Jayne, who'd briefly considered taking a mental health day, and then an actual sick day when she woke up feeling nauseated from the pregnancy, decided in the end that she was going to go into the insurance office.

Tyler, while not exactly cheery, at least did a reasonably good impression of a human being at breakfast. He was dressed as though going for a shift at Whistler's, in black pants and a white shirt, instead of his usual hoodie and jeans.

"What gives?" Jayne asked.

"Mr. Whistler asked if I could come in today, from like eleven to two, because some people are off sick and stuff. I've got no classes then so I said I could whip over and do them."

Jayne didn't look convinced, but said, "You sure you've got time to get over there and back before your afternoon classes?"

"I'm sure."

"You want me to take a break and drive you over?" Jayne asked.

"Or I could," I said.

Tyler had his bike, but school was in Stratford, and Whistler's was across the bridge in Milford.

"I can do it," he said. "Unless it rains. If it rains, can I call one of you guys?"

We both nodded.

I was, at some point today, going to try to learn what sort of arrangements were being made for Elizabeth McBain. Would I be welcome at any possible service? If not, should I at least send flowers to the funeral home? I was thinking I'd get back to Dierdre later, given that she was the one who'd let me know Elizabeth had died.

Jayne was the first to leave for work. She got in her car at half-past eight, about two minutes before Tyler hopped on his bike and went tearing down the street, headed for school. I was settling in behind the wheel of the Explorer when I noticed, in the mirror, a vehicle stopping at the end of the driveway, blocking my way.

Shit, I figured. *Detective Hardy again.*

Except it wasn't, unless Hardy had traded in her unmarked cruiser for a pickup truck. In my oversized door mirror I could see Greg behind the wheel. I was going to get out, but he bailed from his truck first and came up to my door.

I powered down the window.

"Hey," I said.

"Hey," he said, resting his elbow on the sill, one of his personally rolled French cigarettes dangling between his lips. It was down to about a quarter of an inch and appeared to have gone out.

"Thought I'd swing by on my way to work and apologize for coming by last night," he said, resting his arms on the door sill, his face partway into my car.

"For what?" I said.

He laughed. "I feel a little foolish, is all. I'd been talking for a while with Julie about whether I should ask you about teaming up again, you know. Finally, she says, I'm sick of hearing about this, why don't you go and ask him? No way, I says. It's late. So what, she says, get your ass over there and ask him. So, I did."

"Sounds like Julie might be the best thing that's happened to you in a while."

"Yeah, that's true. I did kind of put you on the spot."

"I said I'd think about it. But for what it's worth, Jayne thinks I should go for it."

Greg looked impressed. "Well, nice to have her on my side."

"Look," I said, "I wanted to talk to you about something you said the other day. About when you came to see me, when I was at my worst. You know."

"Yeah, what?"

"That part about me saying that it was all my fault. About Brie."

"Don't worry, man. I've never said a word about it."

"That's not—no, that's not what I mean. I just wanted to say, that doesn't have to mean what you might have thought."

Greg shook his head. "You don't have to explain."

"No, I think I do. I can believe I might have said something like that. I mean, Brie and I had our troubles, and a lot of them were my fault. I think it's more likely that's what I meant."

Greg nodded confidently. "I hear ya."

"I'm serious. I think that's what it was."

"Then let's consider it case closed," Greg said. "We don't ever have to mention it again."

He smiled, and the butt that had been dangling from his lower lip dropped into my car, landing somewhere on the floor mat. I don't think Greg noticed, and I pretended not to.

"Anyway," he said, "I'm off. Gotta grab some donuts on the way to the mall. Want to keep the squatters on my good side."

He gave me a thumbs-up, took his elbows off the door, and headed back to his truck.

My first stop was a waterfront home, worth a cool two mill easy. The owners wanted to build a large walkout from the back of the house, where they'd have a nice view of New Haven Harbor. I'd brought along an iPad and showed them a few pics of what they might want to consider, then took some measurements so that I could better prepare an estimate. Right off the top of my head, I was thinking twenty-five thousand to do the job, which after materials would allow me to clear a good six or seven grand. Of course, once you got started on a project, the client always started adding things. Hey, what if we put in a firepit over here? What about some overhanging beams we could let vines grow on? You just had to make it clear that there was an upcharge for everything. Once they saw the potential in a project, they usually went along with the extra cost.

I had a second stop planned for the afternoon, up in Orange. A young couple with a six-month-old was considering bumping out the back of the house to make a new baby's room. The husband was the one who'd taken a leave from work to look after the kid, and his wife, a corporate lawyer, had the flow, and wanted to be there when I scoped out the job, so I wasn't due there until five.

So I went home for lunch.

There were the makings for a decent sandwich in the fridge. Sliced ham and oven-roasted turkey from the deli counter at Whistler's. (We figured, if the owner was good enough to hire Tyler, we should buy our groceries there.) I found some sliced cheddar in the fridge and half a loaf of whole wheat in the cupboard. I took three slices of ham, three of turkey, two of cheese, and made the thickest honkin' sandwich this kitchen had ever seen.

Washed it down with a beer.

I was killing off the last of the Sam Adams when I heard a car out front. I went to the window, saw it wasn't a car but one of those huge GM SUVs. A black Chevy Suburban. So far as I knew, the cops didn't use Suburbans, although they were often the vehicle of choice for big-time government law enforcement types.

Maybe the CIA was paying me a visit. I mean, was that any crazier than some of the other shit that had happened lately?

But the guy getting out didn't look like someone who'd been sent from Washington to talk to me. He was about five-eight, pushing two hundred and twenty pounds, judging by the slight paunch hanging over his belt. He was in jeans and a button-down-collar work shirt, and he had a red ball cap on I thought might be a political statement in favor of a former president, but it had no message on the front. Not even a logo for a tractor or a sports team.

I came out the front door as he was walking up the driveway.

"Help you?" I asked.

He smiled. "Would you be Andrew Carville?"

"I would."

"Glad I caught you while you were home. Kinda took a chance on it since I was passing by this way."

"What can I help you with?"

"I hear you do renos, additions, that kind of thing."

"You heard right," I said.

"So, I've got this place up Wheelers Farm Road. You know it?"

"I do."

"Got a house up there. Not the one I live in, but I rent it out. Kind of an investment place. Anyway, had a tenant lived there for a few years and he just moved out and he left the place kind of in a mess. Holes in the drywall, a busted door. Couple of windows need replacing. Bunch of little things, and maybe I made a mistake getting a place like that when I'm not all that handy, but it needs some loving attention before I can even think about renting it to anyone else."

It didn't sound like the kind of job I'd enjoy doing. Of course, money's money. But if the morning project came through, and this other afternoon prospect looked promising, this was something I wouldn't mind giving a wave. Then again, if I got neither of them, I'd be a fool to have turned this down.

"How'd you hear about me?" I asked.

"Someone you did a job for in West Haven gave me your name."

"I built a two-car garage for a guy there last year. Wanted a place to park a couple of old, original Minis. That the guy?"

"I think that was it," he said.

That would make sense. Only more recent customers would know me by my new last name.

"So this house of yours," I said. "I could take a run up there tomorrow, or later in the week."

"You think," he said, looking hopeful, "you could take a look at it any sooner? Like today? The reason I ask is, there's one or two places where the water's getting in, doing damage to one of the interior walls. This asshole I was renting to never bothered to mention it to me and I kind of want to get a jump on at least that before it starts raining later in the week and the damage spreads."

"I don't—"

"If you could do it now, you could follow me," he said.

It wouldn't take that long to drive up to Wheelers Farm Road. I did have time to kill before heading over to do that other estimate in Orange.

"What the hell," I said. "I guess I could have a look."

"Oh, that's great," he said, smiling.

"I don't think I got your name," I said.

"Oh shit, yeah," he said, smiling and extending a hand. "My name's Matt. Matt Beekman."

Thirty-Eight

Tyler had gotten home in time the night before, but that didn't mean that he and his friend Cam hadn't gotten into some trouble.

Cam had brought some weed, and while Tyler wanted to partake, he was too worried that he wouldn't be able to get the stink off him before he got home. His sister was like a fucking sniffer dog, he said. He'd no sooner be in the door than she'd know something was up.

So they'd decided against that and had a couple of beers instead before they wandered over to a town house development and slashed a few tires. Cam had an honest-to-God switchblade that his older brother had given him. Flicked the switch and a five-inch blade popped out.

"Holy shit," Tyler had said. "Aren't those illegal?"

"Yeah, well, so is slashing tires," Cam had said.

They slashed tires on maybe a dozen cars, never more than one tire per vehicle. "Spread the joy," Cam had said.

It was something to do.

When they were done, Tyler felt nothing. No sense of excitement, no thrills. Maybe, just maybe, some regret. He kept hearing the words *second chance* in his head. He was thinking there might be better ways to spend his evening. And he had to admit he probably wouldn't be doing any of this shit if it hadn't been for making friends with Cam. He also worked at Whistler's Market, and it was when their shifts overlapped that Tyler got to know him. Cam showed him how you could swipe the odd six-pack of Budweiser or a package of Twinkies without old man Whistler ever knowing a thing about it. After all, when you were in charge of unpacking the deliveries and stocking the shelves, you had first dibs on the stuff you wanted.

"Doesn't that also mean you're the first person Whistler's gonna look at?" Tyler asked.

"Well, I guess," Cam said.

Cam could be thick as a plank sometimes. And one thing Tyler had made a point not to do was steal from the store. He was willing to admit he'd done some stupid shit, but he wasn't that stupid.

He actually *liked* this job. At first, when his sister said she wanted him to get a part-time gig so that he could make a contribution to the household—nothing major, the gesture more symbolic than anything—he found that Whistler's, across the river in Milford, was hiring. He went in and interviewed with the boss, who said he needed someone who could do anything and everything around the store. Unpack the deliveries and keep the shelves stocked, help customers get their bags to their cars, round up carts that were scattered all over the parking lot, maybe even start working the deli counter at some point.

Didn't sound like rocket science to Tyler.

He also liked the other people, other than Cam, who worked there. He especially liked two of the women who worked the checkouts. There was Mattie, young and heavyset, and Francine, who'd been working at the store for nearly two decades, since she was in her early forties. Francine's favorite phrase, regardless of how well the day was going, was, "What a shit show."

What really got Francine going was when shoppers put all their groceries on the rubber conveyor belt, only a couple of items left to scan, and then they'd remember the one thing they forgot and run off, disappearing down an aisle, while other people waited in line with full carts. That's when Francine would turn to Tyler, roll her eyes, and whisper, "Fuckin' loon."

Mattie's pet peeve was the little old ladies who didn't use credit cards, and not only paid in cash, but waited until they were told what they owed, and only then brought up their purse, slowly opened it, found their wallet, and, in a bid to use up spare change, counted out what they owed to the penny. So if the bill came to $40.83, they would count out those eighty-three cents in nickels, dimes, quarters, and pennies.

The other day, when this happened with Mrs. Hemsworth, a regular, Mattie said to Tyler, who had helped the woman with her bags, "I just had my entire period while she was figuring that out."

So when Whistler said he was short-staffed on Monday, Tyler said he could come in. His classes were split apart that day. One in the morning, couple late in the afternoon. He could cover just before, during, and after lunch. The truth was, even if he'd had classes in the middle of the day, he'd probably have skipped them. Tyler would rather make some money than sit in some boring classroom listening—or not—to somebody drone on about the Emancipation Proclamation, like anybody cared about that anymore. History, Tyler thought, was so *over*.

So he hopped on his ten-speed and got to Whistler's shortly before eleven, and was immediately put to work in the produce section, tidying up the romaine heads, which were supposed to be arranged neatly, but which several customers had moved all over the fucking place looking for just the right ones that didn't have any hints of brown on the outer leaves.

That was when he first saw her.

She was choosing a bunch of bananas. Didn't want any that were already ripe, but didn't want a bunch that were really green. She found a bunch that was in between and put it in her cart.

It's her, Tyler thought.

It was the woman whose face he had seen on that detective's phone. Granted, that had not been the best shot, but then Tyler had done some online research and found photos of Brie Mason, and this very picky banana shopper sure as fuck looked like her.

Tyler finished his orderly stacking of the romaine lettuce and decided to try to get a better look at this woman. Sure, it *might* be her, but it probably *wasn't* her. But he had to be sure. She moved on from the fruit section, disappeared around the end of an aisle. Tyler figured he would enter the aisle from the other end, get a better look at her face.

There she was, pushing her cart, checking out jams and spreads and peanut butter. Tyler walked halfway down the aisle, busied himself rearranging cans, moving things to the front edge of the shelf. He figured, in his Whistler uniform of white shirt and black pants, she wouldn't pay any attention to him.

She was getting so close she was going to hit him with her cart if he didn't move out of the way or she didn't swing around him.

"Sorry," he said, flashing her a smile and stepping back. "Right in the way, aren't I?"

She returned the smile. "That's okay. How are you today?"

"Oh, you know, another day livin' the dream."

That made her laugh. "I'll just bet," she said, and pushed her cart past him.

No point in stalking her any further. Tyler wasn't going to get a better look at her than he already had. It sure *could* be her. But then again, it might not. What was he supposed to do? Come out and ask her: "Could I help you with your bags, and by the way, are you the lady who went missing six years ago that everyone thinks is dead?"

That definitely did not feel like the right way to go.

Should he call his sister? Call Jayne and tell her he was pretty sure he was looking at her boyfriend's missing wife? Get her to run out of her office and drive over here in a panic, only to find out that it was a simple case of mistaken identity.

He'd need to know more before he did anything like that.

Tyler kept tabs on her from a distance, until she headed for the line of checkouts. Watched her unload her cart onto the conveyor belt. Francine grabbing each item and waving it over the scanner, hearing the distinctive *beep, beep, beep.*

When the woman had put her bagged purchases into her cart and was wheeling it toward the exit, Tyler approached Francine.

"Hey," he said.

"What's up, Ty?" she said.

"That lady, I think I know her from somewhere. Who is she?"

Francine shrugged. "She's in here every once in a while."

"Can you look at her credit card receipt or something and see what her name is?"

"She paid cash."

"Shit," Tyler said. "Shit, shit, shit."

Then again, what good would a name be? He figured, if that really was Brie Mason, and she'd been hiding out for more than half a decade, she was hardly going to have a charge card in her own name.

Duh.

And in that moment, he had a theory:

Witness relocation.

Yeah, he thought. Andrew's wife had testified against the mob and the FBI had to create a new identity for her! Andrew never knew his wife had had any connection to organized crime and didn't even know the feds had created a new life for her!

God, he was a genius.

Except. Hang on. If you were going to give Brie a new name and a new life, wouldn't you think it was a good idea to move her out of Milford?

So, maybe he *wasn't* a genius.

And maybe that wasn't Brie. He decided it was time to get back to the produce section and—

No fuckin' way.

Tyler was looking out the window to the parking lot. There was the lady, putting all her groceries into the back of a station wagon.

A black station wagon. A black *Volvo* station wagon. Just like the one in the photo on the detective's phone.

She loaded up the back of the vehicle, closed the

tailgate, and wheeled her cart into a nearby collection station. Tyler watched, openmouthed, wondering what he should do.

He needed to know who she was. He needed to talk to her.

For his sister. For Jayne. So she could sort out, once and for all, what was going on with Andrew.

Tyler started running for the door. He had to dodge around some other customers wheeling carts toward the exit, and, when he reached it himself, had to hit the brakes while he waited for the glass door to swing open.

As he ran out into the lot, the Volvo was backing out of its spot.

"Hey!" Tyler shouted. "*HEY!*"

But Tyler was a good five car lengths away, and the windows were up on the woman's car. There was no way she could hear him. The Volvo's brake lights flashed for a second as she shifted from reverse to drive. Then she put her foot on the gas, heading for the road that ran past Whistler's.

"Wait!" Tyler cried, hoping she might see him waving in her rearview mirror.

But she didn't. She steered her car onto the street and drove off.

Tyler changed direction, hand already in his pocket

looking for a key, and ran into the alley beside the store, where he kept his bike chained to a rack. He quickly used the key to remove the chain, tossed it to the ground, hopped on the bike, and shot back out of the alley, nearly colliding with a Honda Civic.

As he hit the street, he caught a glimpse of the black Volvo, stopped at the bottom of the hill at a red light.

Yes.

He pumped those bike pedals like he was the devil himself.

Thirty-Nine
Andrew

At least this Matt guy wasn't one of those assholes who tries to lose you at the same time as he wants you to follow him. I've known guys like that. They say, "I'll lead the way," then run through yellow lights and get several cars ahead and you have ask yourself, what the hell are they doing?

But Matt took it easy, always glancing in his mirror to make sure he hadn't lost me. The drive gave me more time, not that I really needed it, to continue mulling over the events of the past couple of days, and further back than that.

About a year after Brie vanished, I received a message from a Milford resident vacationing in Spain who said he was sure he had seen Brie on a street in Madrid.

This traveler was a friend of a friend of mine, which was how the message found its way to me. There was no picture, no real details of any kind. I followed the story in the news, his forwarded email read, and when I saw this person I thought it might be her. Just wanted to help.

Yeah, well, thanks for that solid tip. What the fuck was I supposed to do with that?

There was a handful of letters in the mail. One lady wrote to say she had been told by God that Brie was working as a Russian spy for Putin, and had been called back to report on her mission. Clearly, Putin had been hard at work trying to get all of Milford's darkest and deepest secrets. A detective from Washington State offered his services, saying he had a solid record of tracking down missing persons. An Internet search produced not one story to support his claim.

I'd heard from a psychic, too. Some local woman, said she'd had a vision about what had happened to Brie, and was willing to share it with me for five hundred bucks. I did some checking, learned she had run this kind of game before in Milford, then moved away to San Francisco for a while. I told her if her vision was so convincing, go sell it to Detective Hardy.

It was the last I heard of her.

Maybe the way I so quickly dismissed these so-called offers of assistance comes across as disinterest on my part, or, as Detective Hardy seemed to believe, evidence that I already knew Brie's fate and therefore couldn't be bothered to follow up on any of them.

I viewed it differently. I had what I believed was a reasonably efficient bullshit detector.

And, while I had to admit Saturday's events were not as easy to toss off as those other developments, I was skeptical. I thought back to what Greg had said to me later on Saturday, that he thought Hardy was setting some kind of a trap for me. It seemed like a wild theory at the time, but in the absence of any other explanation, I wondered whether he was on to something.

Before long, I was on Wheelers Farm Road, and Matt had put his left blinker on.

We'd passed a mix of houses, some small but others large, estate-like, most set well back from the tree-lined road. I was figuring it would be one of these, but the lane that Matt turned into led right into the forest, with no structure in sight.

The road in was not paved, but two hard-packed stone tracks with a strip of grass growing between them. Granted, some of the places along this stretch of road were secluded, with lots of trees between home and road. The trees not only offered privacy, but acted as a sound barrier. The lane widened up ahead for a short stretch, enough space for two vehicles to pass, and Matt pulled over as far to the right as he could, then stuck an arm out the window and waved me ahead.

I drove the Explorer alongside his truck, pulled ahead, and stopped. Was I supposed to turn off the engine and get out, or was I about to get more directions? I glanced back and saw Matt was getting out of his vehicle.

It seemed a strange place to stop. We were still swallowed up by trees, and if there was a house nearby, I couldn't see it.

I put the Explorer in park, undid my seat belt, and opened the door. As I was stepping out, Matt was approaching. He was holding his right arm tight to his side, and I couldn't see his hand.

"Where is it?" I asked.

"We have to walk in from here," he said, then pointed with his left hand over my shoulder. "The access is washed out just ahead. That's *another* thing I got to get sorted out before I can rent this place out again. You do that kind of work, too, or know anybody who does?"

"No, and yes," I said.

I turned to see where he was pointing. The road looked okay as far as I could see. He might have mentioned this when we first talked, that this was going to be a job site with access problems. I wasn't going to be hauling my tools and supplies all the way from here to some house I couldn't even see. I'd probably need to hire an extra guy just to lug everything around so I wasn't dead-tired before I'd even started.

I swung around to express my concerns.

"I don't think—"

That was all I managed to say before Matt whipped up this thing he had been hiding in his right hand. It looked kind of like a gun, but not like any gun I'd ever seen before. And before I could get a closer look he squeezed the trigger and a couple of wires shot out at me and suddenly the most excruciating pain I had ever felt in my entire life was surging through my body, and I hit the ground and I thought, *Holy mother of God, I am fucked.*

Forty

If it weren't for traffic, and one red light after another, Tyler would have lost the black Volvo wagon.

But he was able to keep it in sight, pedaling his bicycle as hard as he could. His heart was thumping, and there was sweat forming on his brow that actually felt cool as the wind dried it off. Tyler could never remember riding his bike this quickly, or with such a sense of urgency. He had to talk to this woman.

He had to know what was going on.

About fifty yards ahead, the Volvo made a right turn. Tyler kept pedaling.

As his legs pumped, he thought about what he would say, how he would handle this. *Don't overthink it*, he told himself. *Just fucking ask her.*

Are you Brie Mason?

That seemed simple enough. And if she said no, then the follow-up was pretty simple.

Then who the hell are you?

The Volvo, at another light, made a left turn. Tyler cut across the road, prompting a trucker to hit the horn with such a blast that Tyler thought he'd have a heart attack. He didn't really know this part of Milford, although he saw some businesses he recognized. A Ford dealership, the Carvel ice-cream place his sister and Andrew took him to the first week he was here.

Then Tyler thought, what if she wasn't heading home? What if she was heading for the turnpike? Maybe she didn't live in Milford. She could live in West Haven or Orange or New Haven. Then why the fuck did she buy her groceries at Whistler? Didn't you buy your provisions close to home? If she got on the turnpike, he'd never be able to catch her.

Then he had to get close enough to read her license plate. He hadn't thought to look at it when he was running after her in the grocery store parking lot. And now that she was on city streets he couldn't get close enough to see it clearly. If he could close the distance, at least read and memorize the plate, so what if she got on the turnpike? He could tell Jayne the plate number and let her take it from there.

Hang on.

Tyler thought he was about to catch a break. The Volvo's turn signal came on. It was heading for a residential street—the sign said Rosemont—with a DEAD END sign posted at the corner. So there was no way out. The chase was over. A dead-end street was definitely not going to lead to the turnpike.

The black Volvo made the turn, clipped along down the street, and slowed as it neared the end. The blinker went on again and it turned into the driveway of a small one-story house, the very last one on the right side.

Tyler was only half a dozen houses away. He stopped pedaling and allowed himself to coast for a few seconds. He was going to need a moment to catch his breath before he could say a single word to this lady.

He wheeled into the driveway and hopped off the bike while it was still in motion. It skittered across the asphalt on its side and the forward momentum carried Tyler a few steps on his feet. He put out his hands to brace himself, and they slapped into the Volvo's tailgate window at the moment the woman was getting out of the car.

Her eyes went wide. "Oh my!" she said.

Now Tyler was bending over, hands on his knees, struggling to catch his breath. The woman's brief expression of panic turned to something closer to wonder when she realized who it was.

"Oh my!" she said again. "You're from Whistler's! Did I forget something?"

Tyler was still panting. He couldn't get the words out.

"Did you really chase me all that way?" she asked, taking a step in his direction. She was smiling now, almost laughing. "Did I drop my wallet or something?"

Tyler, still winded, shook his head. "Not . . . wallet."

"What, then?" She glanced over at his bicycle. "I hope you haven't wrecked your bike." She went over to it, grabbed it by the handlebars, and stood it up on its two wheels. "Looks okay." She studied the underside of the bike, as though looking for something. "I guess bikes don't have kickstands anymore." So she gently set the bike back on the ground on its side.

She gave Tyler another smile and came around to the back of the car and swung open the tailgate. She scanned her groceries and said, "Everything seems to be here."

Tyler said, finally, "Who are you?" And then thought, that was going to be his *second* question.

The woman froze for half a second, then slowly turned around. "Excuse me?"

"Are you her? Are you Brie? Are you Brie Mason?"

Forty-One
Andrew

During the time that I was on the ground and incapacitated from the Taser—and I didn't have to be a weaponry expert to figure out that was what I'd been shot with—Matt rolled me onto my stomach, pulled my arms around behind me, and cinched a set of plastic handcuffs around my wrists.

The Taser shot had paralyzed me for several seconds, maybe as long as a minute, and while my mind was telling my body to fight him off, my limbs were not getting the message. While I lay there, wrists bound, Matt went back to his truck, opened the driver's door, rummaged around for something, and quickly returned.

This time, in his right hand was a real gun, not a Taser. A Glock, it looked like, although guns were not my area of expertise. Whatever it was, it scared the shit out of me. In his other hand, a roll of duct tape.

He kicked me over onto my back. My bound hands dug into me, but Matt didn't appear to be concerned about my comfort. He tucked the gun into his belt and stood over me, one leg on either side of my chest. If I'd had control over my limbs I'd have tried to kick him in the balls, but it was not to be.

He ripped off a length of duct tape, then bent over long enough to slap it over my mouth, and stepped away.

"I want you to understand something from the get-go," he said. "Give me a moment's trouble and you're dead. You get that?"

I managed a nod as I shifted to my right side to take the weight off my wrists.

Matt said, "The tape's temporary. I'm gonna explain some things and I don't want you interrupting. And don't think of shouting when it comes off."

I nodded again.

"Okay," he said, taking a step back. "Don't go away."

As he walked back toward his Suburban, I tried moving my various parts. He hadn't bound my legs, and when I tried to move them, I was successful, if you can call being able to drag them across the ground like they were logs a success. And I was now able to wiggle my fingers, although for how long was anyone's guess, given how the plastic cuffs were cutting off the blood flow.

Matt came walking back. He was holding a shovel. He pointed the blade into the ground, rested one foot on it, cupped his hands over the end of the handle, and turned it into a resting place for his chin.

"You're gonna dig a hole."

I listened. He stepped around me, leaving the shovel, deep enough in the dirt that it remained standing, and looked at my bound hands.

"You're clearly a workingman. You got the hands. There's a lot of digging, and I don't need you whining about blisters."

I made some noise behind the tape that sounded something like, "Why me?"

"This whole thing's kind of a shot in the dark," Matt said. "Hoping to confirm something for myself, and I might need help with that. That's where you come in. Even for you, might not be easy, given all the time that's gone by."

He paused, gazed out into the woods, appeared thoughtful. "I hope I can find the spot. It was right close to a rock. Long as that rock's still there, we should be okay."

Matt turned his attention back to me. "I've got a reputation to maintain, you know? Word of mouth is everything, no matter what you do. So I get a call that I botched a job, that concerns me."

I'm going to die. That's the only way this ends.

"Get on your stomach and I'll snip the cuffs off. Don't try anything funny. You can take the tape off yourself."

I rolled onto my belly, my head turned so I could catch a glimpse of him standing over me. He reached down and I heard a snip and my wrists fell apart. Matt took a quick step back as I slowly rolled onto my side, then got up onto my knees. I peeled the tape off my mouth, balled it up, and tossed it into the tall grasses by the road.

"Up you get," he said.

I stood. There was a good ten feet between us. If I tried to rush him, I wouldn't get halfway there before he pulled the trigger on the Glock. And let's say I got lucky and he missed. He was still a big guy. Wrestling the weapon away from him would not be easy.

Then I thought, what if I simply turned and ran? A moving target wasn't that easy to hit, unless Matt was a real sharpshooter. And if I ducked and weaved the whole time, I might have a chance. A slim one, but a chance.

And yet, there was a part of me that wanted to know why I was here.

"Grab the shovel," Matt said.

I pulled it out of the ground and held it, horizontal, with both hands.

"Don't hold it like that," he said.

"Like what?"

"Like you're some fucking gladiator getting ready to take a swing. Hold it with one hand."

Hanging on to it with one hand, I let the shovel swing earthward. "How's that?" I asked.

Matt fixed his eyes on me and didn't say anything. We had a little staring contest for about five seconds before I said, "You killed my wife."

Matt said, "I *thought* so."

I couldn't think of a thing to say.

He pointed his thumb at the woods. "Let's go, pardner."

Forty-Two

The woman with the black Volvo looked shaken.

"What did you say?" she asked Tyler.

"You heard me," he said. "Are you Brie Mason?"

"Why would you ask me that?" she said, her voice shaking.

That was when he knew for sure. The way she said it. The look in her eye.

"Jesus, it's not a hard question," he said, his voice cracking as well.

"No, I'm not Brie Mason. Now leave me alone."

"If you're not her, then who the fuck are you?"

"You can't talk to me that way. Who the hell are *you*? You're from the market. Why are you following me?"

"Because you look like her. Like from the news stories, and you've got the same kind of car."

"The same kind of car as what?"

"The same kind of car that came to my sister's boy-friend's place. His old place."

The woman struggled for what to say next. "If you don't leave, I'm going to call the police."

"Maybe you should," Tyler said.

She grabbed some of her bags and headed for a door at the side of the house. Tyler picked up the remaining bags.

"I'll help you," he said.

"I don't want your help," she said, her back to him. When she got to the door, she set the bags down so she could free up a hand to unlock the door. But as she inserted the key she looked at Tyler.

"I can't talk about this," she said. "I'm sorry if what happened upset anyone, but I just . . . You have to leave."

"What are you saying?" Tyler asked. "Was it you?"

She had the door open, set the groceries inside, took the other bags from Tyler, then stepped into her house and closed the door. He heard the turn of a dead bolt.

"This isn't over," he said.

He walked back to his bike, hopped on it, and started pedaling away. When he was several houses away, the side door opened again and the woman took half a step out, tears in her eyes, her jaw quivering.

Tyler **didn't** know what to do next. As he rode his bike back in the direction of Whistler's, he considered his options.

He could do nothing, pretend he never even saw her, say nothing to Jayne or Andrew. But he didn't think this was the kind of thing he could keep to himself. So maybe he could call that detective. He'd heard her name—Hardy—when he'd listened to Jayne's conversation with her and, later, with Andrew.

Yeah, he could do that.

But Tyler didn't much want to talk to the cops. He didn't actually know if the police were looking for whoever knocked over those gravestones, and slashed those tires, but you didn't exactly want to walk into a police station when you'd been doing stupid shit like that. What if someone had actually seen them? What if there were descriptions out there of him and Cam?

There. That's what he'd do. He'd call Cam.

Cam was his only real friend in Stratford or Milford, the only one he could talk to. When they'd been out last night, he'd told him all about what had been going on at his place. The visit from the cop, all the stuff about Andrew's wife going missing. So Cam knew the backstory. He'd be as good as anybody to talk to about this, even if he wasn't the brightest bulb in the marquee.

Another thing he knew for sure. He wasn't going back to Whistler's to finish his shift, and he was not going back to school.

And having made *that* decision, he made one more, which was to hop off his bike because he thought he was going to be sick. He wheeled off the road into a small park. Benches, a little creek that ran through the heart of it, even a few swans swimming about.

He let the bike fall to the grass and knelt over, hands on his knees. He didn't know whether his queasiness was from the bike-riding—he'd had no lunch yet and was feeling woozy—or plain old stress. Tyler felt his stomach roll over a couple of times, but nothing was coming up. He stood, one hand on the back of a nearby bench.

His phone dinged. He took it from his pocket, saw that it was from Mr. Whistler.

Where are you?

What should he say? Quickly he tapped a reply:

Felt sick. Went home.

Hit send.

Seconds later: OK. Take care of yourself.

Now Tyler had a text of his own he wanted to send. He brought up Cam's number and tapped out with his thumb:

Call me ASAP.

Cam was probably in class, but he'd feel the vibration in his pocket even if his phone was muted. He'd sneak a look, then tell the teacher he had to go to the bathroom.

Sure enough, three minutes later Tyler's phone rang.

"What's up?" Cam asked.

As quickly as he could, Tyler laid it out for him. That he'd seen this woman who might be Andrew's wife. That he followed her home, but she refused to talk to him.

"What should I do?" Tyler said.

"That's easy," Cam said. "You go back and bang on that door until she answers and you find out what's going on. You've got a right to know. Don't be a pussy."

Well, there you had it.

He ended the call, took another moment to prepare himself mentally for what might be an unpleasant conversation, then hopped on his bike and started pedaling back to that woman's house. He was worried she might not even be there. She could have put away her groceries and gone out to run another errand or gone to work. Almost forty minutes had passed since he'd left her house.

But as he rounded the corner on Rosemont and headed down her street, he saw that her car was still there. Tyler set his bike on the lawn and went to the side door. There wasn't a doorbell, so he rapped on it, hard.

"Hey!" he said. "I still want to talk to you!"

No response.

There were two small windows set high on the door and he peered into them, using his left hand as a visor. If he spotted her, he'd bang on the glass. He wasn't leaving here until he got some answers.

As he was pressed up against the door, his right hand resting on the handle, he decided to give it a try, see if she'd unlocked it after he'd left.

It opened.

Fuck it, he thought. *I'm going in.*

Gifford Hunt, who lived in the house next door to the woman with the black Volvo, was coming out his front door at twenty-one minutes after one when he heard the shouting.

He'd just hit the remote to pop the trunk of his Buick because he was going to head to the driving range and hit a bucket of balls. Hunt, in his late sixties and retired from his traffic-light maintenance job with the city, kept his golf clubs in the trunk and liked to practice his swing when he wasn't actually heading out to the course.

The shouting—it sounded like a male, repeating,

"Shit! Shit! Oh shit!" several times—was followed seconds later by the sight of a young man, his hands bloodied, running from the house and hopping onto a bicycle.

Hunt watched, briefly stupefied, but then quickly thought to reach for his phone. He managed to capture several images of the man before he reached the end of the street and disappeared.

Now Hunt looked at his neighbor's house. He crossed the lawn and walked down the side of the house to the door. He opened it and called inside.

"Candace?" he said. "You okay in there?"

Hunt, his hand shaking, pushed the door open farther and stepped tentatively into the house. He went up two steps and into the kitchen.

"Oh, sweet mother of God," he said.

Forty-Three
Andrew

We'd trekked far enough into the woods that when I looked back, I could no longer see my Explorer or Matt's Suburban. It wasn't that they were specks in the distance. We had walked down into a small valley, then up again to the other side, and by that point had lost sight of the road we'd driven in on.

I stayed in the lead, as per Matt's instructions. He was my guide, from behind.

"That way," he'd say, and point. "Okay, over a little to the right. That's it."

After we'd been walking about five minutes, I spotted a large boulder ahead of us. A huge rock, about the size of a refrigerator, was sitting there amid the trees, as though it had been dropped from space.

"This is the spot," Matt said. "Right around here. Go stand by the rock."

I did as I was told, turning around and propping myself up on it. I still had the shovel in my hands. Matt stood about thirty feet away, looking at the ground, then at the rock, then back at the ground, one finger up in the air, as though testing to see which way the wind was blowing. He was six years in the past, trying to remember where, exactly, he'd done it.

He ran one work boot back and forth across the ground, brushing leaves and other debris out of the way.

"Was thinking there might still be a depression or something from the hole," he said, "but I'm not seeing it. But I'm pretty sure it was right here. About ten paces from the rock, right in line with that birch tree over there."

He made an X in the leaves with his foot. "Start there," he said, then backed away to be out of range, should I decide to take a swing at him with the shovel.

I stepped forward, rested the tip of the blade on the ground, got my right foot on top, and pushed down. I turned over one small pile of dirt.

"Why'd you do it?" I asked. "Why Brie? Who are you? How did you know Brie?"

I'd spent the last ten minutes or so wracking my

brain, trying to remember where I might have met this man before. Nothing about him was familiar. Nothing jumped out at me. But that didn't mean Brie couldn't have known him. Had there been something in Brie's past, something she'd never told me about, that might have prompted someone—this man—to hunt her down and kill her? Did she have dark secrets she'd kept from me, just as I'd kept some from Jayne?

"Never met her before," he said. "Didn't know her."

When he said that, I wondered whether Matt was some crazy serial killer, picking his victims at random. Maybe he'd seen Brie at the mall, on the street somewhere, and there was something about her, the way she looked, that triggered something in this guy. And he'd decided: *She's next.*

"So you just saw her and thought, *I'm going to kill her*," I said as I drove the shovel into the ground again. I was starting to make a pile of dirt to the right of the hole.

"You think I'm a psycho?" Matt asked. "That what you're calling me?"

"I'm looking for a reason." I continued to dig.

"It's called working for a living," he said.

"You were . . . hired?" I stopped shoveling, shook my head. "Someone paid you to kill my wife?"

Matt made a fist and raised a thumb. "Way to go, Sherlock."

The enormity—the reality—of what was actually happening here didn't quite hit me until that moment.

I was digging up my wife's grave.

"You buried her here," I said.

"I buried *somebody* here," he said. "Question is, is she still there? If she's not, that's a problem. And if it's not who it was supposed to be, that's a problem, too."

This was all starting to feel like a dream, or, more accurately, a nightmare. This could not be happening. I was not here. I was not digging this hole.

"Thought she was dead when I put her in, and even if she wasn't, the dirt should have smothered her." Matt seemed to be talking more to himself than to me. "Can't imagine her digging her way out. Be like some kind of Stephen King movie." He focused on me. "You one of the ones that spotted her?"

The recent sightings of Brie. He'd clearly been informed.

"No," I said. "But I heard from others who did."

Matt's head drifted slowly from side to side. "Makes no fucking sense."

What do you know? Something we could agree on.

I had to try to keep my head clear. Inside, I was shaking, and if I hadn't been holding that shovel, my hands would have been trembling, too. My stomach was rising up into my throat, and it was taking every-thing I had not to double over and vomit.

"Who hired you to kill my wife?"

Matt shook his head.

But I persisted. "What'd she do? Why would anyone want her dead?"

He continued to shake his head. "Dig."

I tossed a few more shovelfuls of dirt before pausing to ask, "How far?"

"You should hit something about a foot down."

"You're scared she somehow dug her way out," I said.

Matt bristled at the word. "I'm not fucking scared."

"Could have fooled me," I said. "You're scared she won't be here. Who told you about the sightings?"

Another head shake.

I tried to recall all the people who had seen the woman who was, or was not, Brie. There was Max, and maybe the people who lived in the new house next to him. There was Albert and Isabel, and her husband Norman. And, finally, Elizabeth.

I forced the shovel down into the dirt, but with less force than I could have. It wasn't that I was trying to buy time, although that was part of it. I was afraid of what I might hit, and how hard I might hit it. Like driving the shovel blade into what might be left of Brie would somehow do her greater injury.

"Gotta take a piss," Matt said.

Would this be my chance? Was Matt going to disappear behind a tree long enough to empty his bladder?

Evidently not. He transferred the gun to his left hand, evidently more skilled at pulling down his zipper and digging out his dick with his right. The stream landed about four feet from where I had been digging, his piss soaking into what might be the foot of my wife's grave.

I wanted to kill him. I wanted to kill him more than I'd ever wanted anything in my entire life.

Matt shook, then zipped back up. "Did I ask you to stop?"

"So let's say we find her remains," I said. "We're done? You could have come out here alone and dug her up."

"I need you to tell me if it's her."

I almost laughed. "You can't be serious."

"Maybe there'll be something," Matt said, still training his gun on me. "Like, maybe she had a filling in one of her teeth. Something like that you'd recognize. She was your wife. Who'd know better than you?"

I had created a hole a foot and a half wide, two feet long, and more than a foot deep. I hadn't encountered anything but dirt. I took a step back so that Matt could give the hole a cursory inspection.

"Hmm," he said.

Now my mind was considering the unimaginable: that Brie really had been buried alive, and somehow escaped. But if that was really what had happened, why had she gone into hiding for six years and suddenly reappeared Saturday?

"Hmm," he said again.

I cleared my throat. "Maybe you got the wrong spot."

Matt rubbed his chin. He looked to the rock, back to where I'd dug, then back to the rock again.

He pointed at the ground about two feet over from where I'd been digging.

"Try there," he said.

Forty-Four

Yellow police tape surrounded the property at the end of Rosemont Street. Two Milford police cars, parked up by the corner, blocked access to the street. Out front of the house were two more police cars, one unmarked.

Inside the house, wearing paper booties, her hands gloved, Detective Marissa Hardy surveyed the scene.

A woman, mid-thirties, sprawled out on the kitchen floor on her back, her eyes open and staring vacantly at the ceiling, her head haloed by a pool of blood that appeared to have stopped spreading. There were no signs of a fight. No upturned chairs, no broken plates or glasses, although Hardy did notice that the edge of the counter, above where the woman's body lay, had been chipped.

The countertop was not done in quartz or granite, but covered with a cheap laminate. Something, presumably the back of this woman's skull, had hit the edge. When Hardy leaned in close, she saw some blood, and a hair. She wouldn't be surprised to find that laminate chip on the back of this woman's head once the body was sent to the forensic center.

So maybe she'd been pushed, hit her head, then went down. The blow hard enough that it killed her.

Somebody pushed her very hard.

A uniformed officer, also wearing the slip-on booties, was standing at the entrance to the kitchen.

"The neighbor who called it in is outside," she said.

"Okay," Hardy said. "What's the victim's name?"

"Candace DiCarlo," the officer said. "Works at a fitness center."

"Husband?"

"Neighbor says she and her ex split up a couple of years ago. She got the house and he moved out West to Nevada, or so the neighbor says."

"What's his name?"

"The ex?"

"The neighbor."

"Hunt. Gifford Hunt. Retired guy."

"Tell him I'll be out in a second," Hardy said.

The officer retreated. Hardy took another couple

of minutes to take in the scene before deciding to go outside. Hunt, visibly shaken, was waiting for her out front of his house.

"Mr. Hunt?" she said, removing her gloves and extending a hand. "I'm Detective Hardy." She took his trembling hand into hers for a second. "Are you okay?"

"Kind of in shock, I guess," he said.

"You live here, sir?" she asked.

"That's right. My wife, she's gone to visit our daughter for a few days in Cleveland. I'm here on my own. I called her. I hope that's okay."

"Sure. That's fine."

"I told her not to come home, but I think she's going to anyway." He took a breath, put his hand to his chest. "I hope I don't have a coronary event."

"Do you have a history of heart problems, Mr. Hunt?"

"No, no, I'm kind of a hypochondriac, is all."

"You found Ms. DiCarlo?"

"Yes. I went to the door after I heard all this shouting and saw the man ride away on his bike."

"What was the shouting about? Was it two people arguing?"

"No, it sounded like one person. Just profanities. Yelling, 'Oh shit,' several times."

"Did you recognize this man?"

"No," he said, shaking his head. "Never seen him before."

"Ms. DiCarlo lived alone?"

"Yes, that's what I told the other officer. She and her husband got a divorce and he moved away."

"Boyfriends?"

He shrugged. "I don't know. Maybe. I didn't really pay much attention. It was only by chance that I happened to step out of the house when I did. I was on my way to the driving range. I retired a couple of years ago. I worked for the city, maintaining and servicing traffic lights. If a traffic light went out, I was the guy they called."

"What do you know about Ms. DiCarlo?"

"We talked occasionally. She works at a fitness center. I think she used to be a personal trainer but now she's—she was in the office, I believe. And she was involved in various things."

"What kinds of things?"

"Theater, for one. Community theater. She told me the other day they had a play coming up. She had a juicy part in it. She loved that."

"What's the name of this theater group?"

"The Stamford Players, I think. Sometimes, my wife and I, we'd go to their shows, to be supportive, you know. Saw her a couple of days ago, she said we should get tickets because they were in rehearsals for a new show."

Hardy had taken out a small notebook and pen to scribble a few notes. Then, suddenly, as if a light bulb had come on over her head, she stopped writing and froze briefly.

She turned, slowly, and looked at the car sitting in the driveway of Candace DiCarlo's home.

A black Volvo wagon.

"Mr. Hunt," she said, "is that Ms. DiCarlo's car? I'm assuming it is, but we haven't actually checked."

"Yes," he said, nodding. "She's had that for a few years."

"Stay here," she said.

Hardy walked over to the car, slowly circling it, careful not to touch it. She peered through the windows, looking inside, then stood in front of the car, examining the hood. She dug into her pocket for her phone, opened up the photos, and found the one she'd saved of the Volvo in the driveway from Saturday morning.

The car in the picture appeared to have a dimple in the hood, about halfway between bumper and windshield, on the passenger side.

Just like this car.

Then she examined the license plates, front and back. She noticed traces of what looked like mud on the edges, as though they'd been dirty, but someone had cleaned them off recently, at least well enough to avoid getting a ticket.

She went back over to continue her questioning of Gifford Hunt.

"Can you describe this person you saw leaving Ms. DiCarlo's house?"

"Slight, and young. Just a teenager. Longish hair. And he had blood on his hands. I could see that. But he was riding his bike pretty fast."

"A motorcycle?"

"No, a regular bicycle. But like I said, he was going pretty fast, so I didn't get a long look at him. But I got a shot of him riding away."

"I'm sorry, what?"

Hunt took his phone from his pocket. "I'm not really much of a techie, and it's not like me to think fast enough to do something like this, but I guess today I was a little more on the ball than usual."

He opened the photo app and brought up the snippet of video. "It's not very good," he said apologetically. "I didn't think to try and zoom in or anything."

"May I?" Hardy asked, holding out her hand.

Hunt gave her his phone.

She tapped the triangular play button and watched the few seconds of the cyclist racing off down the street.

She replayed it several times. Then, the final time, she paused the video and used her fingers to enlarge the image.

"I know this kid," she whispered quietly to herself. "Where did I just see him?"

And then it hit her.

Forty-Five

When Jayne pulled her car into the driveway, the first thing she noticed was Tyler's bicycle, abandoned on its side, on the lawn. The second thing she noticed was that the front door had been left wide open.

Tyler usually left his bike around the back of the house, hidden from view. And he knew enough to close the door when he went into the house. Something was very wrong.

She got out of her car, and as she stepped past Tyler's bike she noticed red smudges on the handlebars. There was also blood on the handle of the front door.

"Oh God," Jayne said as she went inside and closed the door behind her. "Tyler!" she shouted.

No answer.

She quickly went through the first floor, looking in the kitchen, stepping out onto the back deck. She went back inside, stood at the bottom of the stairs, and shouted, "Tyler, are you here!"

Still nothing.

She got out her phone and opened the app that allowed her to know her brother's location. According to it, Tyler, or at least his phone, was here.

Racing up the steps to the second floor, phone still in hand, she went down the hall to Tyler's room and found the door closed. It was usually left open through the day. She rapped on it lightly.

"Tyler? You in there?"

"Go away," he said.

Jayne opened the door. Tyler was sitting on the edge of the bed, bent over, head in his hands. He looked up as his sister stepped into the room. She could see the tears on his face.

"Tyler, what's happened?"

He shook his head, unable to speak.

"Jesus, Tyler, talk to me. There's blood on the front door, you— Christ, are you hurt?"

As she took a step toward him he raised his arm, palm up. "Stay back," he said.

"Just tell me if you're hurt. Do I need to get you to a doctor? Did you have an accident with your bike?"

"I'm not hurt," he said, lowering his arm, allowing Jayne to take a step closer.

He was looking at her, but at the same time not looking at her. He seemed to be staring right through her, as though seeing something that wasn't there.

"Tyler, talk to me," Jayne said. "Are you in shock?"

Jayne was still holding her phone. She brought up Andrew's number, tapped on it, and put the phone to her ear. After five rings, it went to voice mail.

"You've reached Andrew Carville. Please leave a message after the beep."

"Andrew, it's me. Please call the second you get this. Something's happened." She hit the button to end the call, then set the phone on the bedside table. She sat down on the bed next to Tyler and tentatively put her arm around him.

"Whatever's happened, you need to tell me," she said, noticing for the first time traces of blood on his fingers. "Whatever kind of trouble you're in, we can fix this."

"No," he whispered. "No."

"Whose blood is this?" Jayne asked, lightly touching his fingers. "Is it yours . . . or someone else's?"

He put his hands to his face and started to cry. It was more than a few tears. His body went into wracking heaves as he sobbed and moaned.

"Oh shit shit shit," he said.

Jayne held him close, pulled him into her embrace. Tyler mumbled something that Jayne couldn't make out.

"What was that?" she asked.

"Screwup," he said. "Fucking screwup."

"No, no, we're going to fix this."

"All my fault," he said.

"What? What's all your fault?"

He turned his head to look at her, his eyes red from weeping. "I never should have let him shovel the driveway. It was all my fault."

Jayne blinked. "What are you . . ."

But she knew he was referring to their father, who dropped dead clearing snow while Tyler slept in.

"Tyler, what does that have to do with what's happened today?"

He sniffed. "If he hadn't died, I wouldn't have come here to live, and none of what's happened . . . what happened today isn't my fault, but they won't believe that. It's because of Dad. I'm going to be punished because of Dad."

"Tyler, I don't understand what—"

The doorbell rang.

Even before Jayne had turned her head in the direction of the door, the ring was followed by a loud, repetitive banging.

"Stay here," she said to Tyler, and grabbed her phone as she fled the room.

She was almost out of breath by the time she reached the front door and opened it wide to find Detective Marissa Hardy standing there. Hardy had already noticed the bloody door handle.

"Ms. Keeling," Hardy said. "Where is your brother?"

"Tyler?" she said, noticing that there were two uniformed officers standing behind the detective and three police cars on the street in front of the house.

Hardy already appeared to have run out of patience. "Do you have *another* brother, Ms. Keeling?"

"What do you want with Tyler?" Jayne asked.

Hardy waved an envelope in front of Jayne's face. "We have a warrant for his arrest. Is he here?"

Jayne couldn't find the words.

"Are there any weapons on the premises?" Hardy asked.

"No, of course not," Jayne said. "This is ridiculous. Tyler wouldn't hurt—"

"You believe he's hurt someone?" Hardy asked. "Is there a reason why you think we're here because Tyler hurt someone?"

Jayne was, once again, speechless.

Hardy pushed past her. The two uniformed officers followed.

"Please," Jayne said, on the edge of weeping. "Please be gentle with him."

She couldn't bear to see it happen. She stepped out the front door, held up her phone, and called Andrew again. But this time the call immediately went to voice mail.

"Andrew, please, please call me," she said. "They're taking him away. They've come for Tyler."

Even though she was outside, Jayne could hear scuffling and shouting up on the second floor. Then Tyler, screaming.

"Get your fuckin' hands off me! I didn't do anything! I only wanted to talk to her!"

Moments later, Hardy and the two officers emerged from the house with Tyler, his wrists cuffed behind him. Tears streamed down his face.

Jayne ran after him as he was bundled into the back of one of the police cars.

"It's going to be okay!" she shouted. "I'll find out what's going on! I'm going to get you out of this!"

"I didn't do it!" he kept shouting. "I didn't!"

Tyler, once seated in the back of the car, turned and pressed his face to the window. His eyes were red with tears as he looked pleadingly at his sister.

She placed her hand on the glass. "Hang in there," she said. "Just hang in there."

An officer got behind the wheel and the car pulled away, Tyler twisting around so that he could see his sister out the rear window. Jayne, overwhelmed, felt on the verge of collapse. And then it happened. Slowly she crumpled, her legs weakening. She placed a hand on the pavement to keep her upper half upright.

She looked up and saw Detective Hardy standing there.

"How could you?" Jayne said. "What on earth do you think he's done?"

"We're arresting him in connection with a homicide," the detective said.

"A homicide?" Jayne said disbelievingly. "Who?"

Hardy hesitated. "That picture I showed you on Saturday? The woman at Andrew's old address? Her."

"Brie," Jayne whispered. "Brie Mason."

Hardy extended a hand and helped Jayne get back to her feet.

"This woman's name is Candace DiCarlo," Hardy said. "Lived in a house over on Rosemont."

Jayne blinked. "But . . . I don't understand. I thought you said it was Brie."

"I said it was the woman in the picture. But that woman isn't Brie."

"Are you sure? It's not Brie, but this other woman—Candace?—with her identity?"

Hardy, stone-faced, said, "We're in the early stages of our investigation, Ms. Keeling. I'm sorry. There's not much I can tell you at this point." She paused. "Do you know a good lawyer? Because your brother is going to need one."

Jayne shook her head.

The detective sighed and gave Jayne a sympathetic look. "We can place him at the scene. He was witnessed riding away, covered in blood. He's in a lot of trouble, Ms. Keeling. If I were you, I'd hire the best."

The detective went back into the house, presumably, Jayne figured, to collect evidence.

This time, instead of phoning Andrew, she typed out a text. All caps. Two words.

BIG TROUBLE

It failed to deliver.

Forty-Six
Andrew

When my cell phone rang, the sound coming from the front pocket of my jeans, Matt perked up.

"Toss it over," he said.

I got out the phone, saw that it was Jayne calling, then threw it over to Matt. It landed in the leaves. Matt bent over, grabbed it, then circled around me to reach the huge rock. Holding the phone screen down, he slammed it onto a jagged outcropping of the rock's surface three times before he was satisfied it was dead. Then he pocketed it.

"Carry on," he said.

I'd moved to the new dig location, only a couple of steps over from where I'd made the first hole. While my idea to start digging in a new spot had been simply to buy time, Matt was considering the possibility he'd had me start in the wrong place. I was ready to shovel a hole as broad as a tennis court if there was a chance it might give me time to figure out how to keep Matt from killing me.

I dug the blade into the ground and turned over some dirt. If the blade didn't connect with bone—Jesus, the idea of whose bones it would be made my head swim— once I'd gone down twelve inches, I'd ask Matt whether he wanted to consider a third location.

"Anything?" Matt asked.

"No. You can take over anytime you want."

Then it was his turn to have a cell phone go off. He took out his phone, glanced at the screen, rejected the call. I stopped and looked at him

"Wife," he said.

If only he were closer. I'd fling some dirt in his face, try to temporarily blind him. Long enough to either tackle him and try to get the gun from him, or hit him over the head with the blade. Go in sideways, open the son of a bitch's skull like a melon.

But what I actually did was drive the shovel into the ground for what felt like the thousandth time. "What if—"

I hit something.

A sliver of something gray-white, and what looked

like nearly disintegrated fabric, could be seen through the dirt.

Matt took a step forward, still keeping his distance, but close enough to see that maybe I'd found something.

"Now we're into detail work," he said. "Hands and knees."

I crouched down, the forest floor feeling cool on my knees even through my jeans. I began the process of scooping away dirt, a handful at a time, as though I were on some archaeological dig. Slowly, what looked like a rib cage began to materialize.

"I need a minute," I said, and sat back on my butt.

"Don't get all fucking weepy on me."

That wasn't going to be easy. I was overwhelmed. I'd seen more than a few movies where someone had been forced to dig his own grave, but I couldn't recall one where a man was expected to dig up his own wife. I put my soil-smeared hands over my eyes and took a few breaths.

"Come on, let's do this," Matt said. From where he stood, he tried to get a better look at what I'd uncovered. "This is good. Means she didn't crawl out or anything like that. Now we just have to make sure I didn't grab the wrong person."

"I left my DNA kit in the truck," I said. "Wait here, I'll go get it."

"Funny," Matt said. "Keep going."

I resumed digging, shifting my attention to where I figured the head would be. Slowly, I began to uncover what appeared to be a forehead, then eye sockets. Wisps of hair. A head. I was still hoping that maybe, despite the odds, this skull, and the skeleton it was connected to, could not be Brie. That somehow this was someone else, however unlikely that seemed. That maybe that woman who'd mysteriously appeared during the weekend really *was* my wife.

But then my finger caught on something.

A chain.

As I brushed away more dirt, I uncovered a choker. A necklace that would have held close to someone's neck. It was silver, made of dozens of small loops of chain, interspersed with several links shaped like the letter *G*.

Gucci.

The choker I'd bought Brie for her birthday. The one I had seen her wearing when we had our FaceTime chat on that Saturday night six years ago, the night before she disappeared.

I let go of the chain, threw my hands out ahead of me to brace my fall, and collapsed over the grave of my darling Brie.

Forty-Seven

It was Tyler himself who gave Detective Hardy the name "Cam." As they were bringing him down the stairs, Tyler had said to her, "Ask Cam. He'll tell you. I only went there to talk to her."

So the detective went looking for him. Tyler had said he worked with Cam, and when Detective Hardy learned that the two of them were employed at Whistler's Market, she called the manager there and asked where she could find this Cam person.

"He'd be at school," Whistler said, and he told her which school that was.

She went to the school office, found the principal, who determined Cam was in a chemistry class up on the second floor.

"Let's go get him," Hardy said.

They found the classroom. The principal interrupted the teacher mid-lesson, pointed to Cam, and beckoned him with his finger.

Cam, tall and skinny and ravaged by acne, stepped out into the hall and said, "What's going on?" Then he saw Detective Hardy and said, "Who are you?"

She told him.

"Oh shit," he said. "Is this about the slashed tires because we didn't have anything to do with that."

"What slashed tires?" Hardy asked.

"Nothing," he said quickly. "So what's up?"

"You were talking to your buddy Tyler this afternoon. Tell me about it."

"Why, what's happened? What's going on?"

"Why did he go to Candace DiCarlo's house?"

"Who's that?"

"Tell me about your conversation."

"Okay, so, there's this whole thing going on with Tyler's sister's boyfriend, okay? Like, a long time ago, his wife vanished and people, like, you guys, think he killed her."

"Go on."

"But a couple of days ago she came back. And Tyler saw her at Whistler's and followed her home."

"Why did he do that?"

Cam shrugged. "He wanted to know if it was really her, because all this not knowing one way or another was really fucking things up at home. And he wanted to ask her if she was going to want to stay married to his sister's boyfriend. Like, if that happens, Tyler doesn't know what that's going to mean for him and his sister, whether she's still going to want him living with her, because he can't go back with his aunt."

Hardy blinked, not entirely following. "What about his aunt?"

"That's some shit that happened back in Providence. She didn't want to look after him anymore because of her eye."

Hardy thought following this kid's line of thought was like trying to track a firefly.

"So Tyler called you, and he'd been to see this woman and asked her all these questions."

"Not yet."

"What do you mean, not yet?"

"Okay, so he'd been there once, and this woman wouldn't talk to him. She went in the house and locked the door and Tyler left. That's when he called me."

"Why did he call you?"

"I guess because he comes to me for advice." He smiled, fancying himself as someone with great wisdom. "He was wondering what he should do. He was all agitated and mixed up and everything. I never heard him like that."

"Was he angry?"

"Not angry. He was trying to figure out what to do. This lady wouldn't answer his questions."

"So what did you tell him?"

Cam shrugged. "I said he should go back there and get her to talk to him."

"Did you, now?" Hardy said.

"Yeah. Why? That a problem?"

When Detective Hardy got back into her car she took a moment.

While solving DiCarlo's murder looked like a slam dunk—Tyler admitted being at the house and there was a witness who saw the bloodied kid leaving the scene—there were still plenty of questions. If DiCarlo was, indeed, the woman captured in the surveillance video, why did she want anyone to think she was Brie Mason returning after a six-year absence?

Why pretend to be Brie?

Was it some sort of cruel trick? To make Brie's family think that she was still alive? What was to be gained by that? Why raise a family's hopes that way?

The thought had crossed her mind earlier that

Andrew was behind this, that he'd hired someone to pretend to be Brie in the hope that it would persuade Hardy he had never killed her. The trouble with that theory was, why now? Brie's disappearance was effectively a cold case. While it was always in the back of Hardy's mind, she hadn't had a fresh lead to follow in years.

Pretend to be Brie.

What had DiCarlo's next-door neighbor said? Candace was part of a community theater group. So she'd be a natural at playing a role, assuming an identity.

She got out her notebook to see whether she'd written down the name of the theater group. She had. The Stamford Players.

Then she got out her phone, opened up a browser, and Googled the theater company's name.

Up came a website for the Stamford Players. They had a new production set to open in a couple of weeks, just like the neighbor had said. Something called *The Casual Librarian*. There was information about ticket sales, who would be appearing in the production—there was a headshot of Candace DiCarlo—and then information about the play itself, that the playwright and the director were one and the same.

Albert McBain.

"Holy shit," Hardy said under her breath.

Forty-Eight
Andrew

"Well?" Matt said with more than a hint of impatience. "Is it her?"

I needed a minute to pull myself together. I wiped my eyes with the back of my arm to clear away some dirt. My hands were black with moist soil. Slowly, I got to my feet, and used the shovel to help prop me up once I was standing.

Six years of never really knowing. Assuming the worst without confirmation. But here it was. I had no doubt that this was Brie. Admittedly, I was basing my conclusion on the necklace and a few wisps of desiccated fabric that looked like a nightgown she often wore, and someday, maybe, if Detective Hardy were to find Brie's remains and do a DNA test, we'd have one hundred percent certainty.

But I didn't need DNA test results. I knew in my heart and in my gut that this was Brie.

I also knew the odds were solidly against Hardy ever having the opportunity to find these bones and conduct any forensic tests. The more likely possibility was that I would be directed to dig a second grave and plant myself in it.

Avoiding that outcome was the current priority. I would have to grieve Brie, confront the trauma of digging up the woman I had loved, at a later date, given the opportunity. So, as I was getting to my feet, I had to consider any possible way to stall, to buy time.

Matt was starting to look annoyed that I hadn't answered his question. "It's her, right? You wouldn't get that broken up over some stranger."

"No," I said.

Matt's mouth opened. "No? What do you mean, no?"

My voice was breaking. I didn't have to fake that. "It's not her."

The lie was, obviously, an impulsive strategy. My hope was that if I could get Matt to believe this was not Brie's body, he'd have to figure out what his next step might be. And given that I was the one most qualified to identify Brie, maybe he'd need me a while longer to put the pieces of this puzzle together.

Then again, he could shoot me now and be done with it.

His skeptical expression told me he wasn't entirely persuaded I was telling him the truth. "What are you talking about? You lost it. That was fucking grief."

Still holding on to the shovel, I shook my head. "Not grief . . . relief."

"How the hell can you know it's not her?"

"You expected me to be able to tell if it *was* her, but now you're asking me how I can know that it's *not*?"

"Tell me how you know."

"The necklace," I said. "Brie didn't own a necklace like that." I was taking a chance he wouldn't recall an item of jewelry Brie'd been wearing that night.

"You sure?"

I just looked at him. He got the message and sighed.

"So who the fuck is it?" he asked.

"I've no idea. This is your fuckup, not mine."

Now Matt, in addition to looking pissed, appeared mystified. "I went to the right house. I *know* I went to the right house. I'd scoped it all out. There was nobody else there. How do you explain that?"

"I don't know."

"Thirty-six Mulberry."

"Yes." Curious, that he would remember that detail but not the necklace.

"An old house. Needed work. You were going to update it, fix it up."

"Yes."

How did he know that?

He was thinking, trying to remember other details from six years ago. He slowly raised a finger and pointed it at me. "Mice."

"What?"

"You had a mouse problem, I figured. Flour on the kitchen floor. Waiting till morning to look for tracks."

I nodded.

"I walked right through it, in the dark. Left shoe prints. First job I ever did where I had to vacuum before I took off." Matt was thinking so hard I could almost smell wood burning. "You sure about the necklace?" It was clearly a detail he was fuzzy on.

"I'm sure," I said.

"She have, like, a sister or something? A friend, who slept over? Anything like that?"

Feed him something. Mess with his head.

"A friend," I said. "Sometimes, when I was out of town, like that night, she'd have someone come stay with her. Made her feel less anxious." Then, thinking fast, I added, "A friend from her school days. Parents dead, no spouse, no kids. Sort of person, if she went missing, no one would even have noticed."

Matt was moving his head side to side slowly, not buying it. "No," he said. "No." And then, very slowly, a calmness came over him.

"What?" I said, putting both my hands atop the shovel handle and resting my chin on them. "If it's not her, you've still got a problem."

"No," he said. "I don't. It doesn't matter. The person I took from your house that night is the same person that's in that grave. Whoever she is, she's not picking me out of a lineup, not going to say, 'That's the guy.' If your wife's still out there somewhere, well, yeah, I should have got her, but it's not like she's got an ax to grind with me. You get what I'm saying?"

Sadly, I did.

I might have bought myself five minutes here, but this was turning into a no-win situation. Didn't matter who was in this grave. What mattered was that *someone* was in it. Matt's mind was put at ease.

Mine, not so much.

Matt, pointing his gun at me more directly, said, "Guess we're done here. One thing all this has taught me is, be sure. Leave no room for doubt." He cracked a smile that gave me a chill.

"Wait," I said.

"What?"

"You've got a problem."

"I think *you're* the one with the problem. But it'll be over soon."

"My car."

Matt blinked a couple of times. "Hmm," he said once again.

I didn't know whose land this was, or how Matt had come to choose this part of the woods to bury Brie, but if he drove out of here and left my car behind, it would eventually be found, and the police would eventually find Brie's remains and, presumably, mine. That discovery might end up leading to Matt. Did he own this property? Did it belong to a friend of his?

"Let me go," I said.

Flatly, Matt said, "No."

"I'm serious. You . . . you've given me hope." Stick with the charade. "I now know there's a chance my wife's alive, that the woman who showed up over the weekend, it's really her. I know you didn't kill her." I pointed to the grave. "I don't know who this is, and I can't explain how you got the wrong person, but if there's a chance my wife is out there, I have to find her."

"No," he said again.

"Come on," I said. "Why?"

"Say you find her," he said. "She tells you why she disappeared. Who would have wanted her dead. Cops find that person, it leads back to me."

It was hard to argue with his logic. There was still the matter of my SUV, though.

"I'll figure things out with your car," he said. "Get a lift back." Another smile. "Don't trouble yourself."

I had no arrows left in my quiver, unless you counted begging.

"Please," I said.

"Start another hole."

I moved my hands farther down the shovel handle, eyeing the ground, wishing Matt would take a few steps closer, get within shovel-swinging range. I was going to dig this hole like I was being paid by the fucking hour. I was about to ask him where he wanted me to start when we heard something.

"Hey!" someone called.

I looked beyond Matt, in the direction of where we'd come from, where our two vehicles were.

A man was coming our way.

"Hey!" he called out again. "What's going on?"

It was Norman.

What happened next happened very, very fast.

Forty-Nine

Albert McBain was sitting in his small office at the Devon Savings and Loan on Broad Street where he was assistant manager, staring at some mortgage documents on his computer screen. He had two clients whose house deals were closing in the next couple of days, and if these docs weren't pushed through, the deals could fall apart.

But this was his only reason for coming into the office, and he didn't plan to be here for more than an hour. His boss and the branch manager, Ms. McGillivray, had told him to take the entire week off, considering that his mother, Elizabeth, had passed away the day before. And he fully intended to do that. There was much to be done, with help from his sister Isabel. A service to be planned, extended family to notify, an appointment with the estate lawyer, and then the unpleasant business of clearing out her apartment would have to be tackled.

It couldn't have come at a worse time. The Stamford Players' latest production was due to open in a couple of weeks. The previous day's rehearsal had been cut short when Albert got the call from the hospital that his mother was close to the end. Was it realistic for Albert to think that, with all that was going on, he could really pull the play together in time? Should the opening be delayed? But tickets had already been sold. Okay, not exactly thousands of them, but at least a hundred or so. Would people demand refunds, or would they be okay with hanging on to their tickets for a later date?

Whoever had said, "The show must go on!" surely hadn't had to deal with the death of a parent two weeks before opening night.

The stress of it all had given him indigestion. He opened his desk drawer and found a half-empty container of Tums. He tapped three of them into his palm and started chewing.

His phone rang.

He was going to let it go to voice mail—he'd already changed his message to indicate he would be gone for the week due to a family emergency—but he could see from the flashing light that it was not a call from outside, but from reception.

Albert sighed and picked up. "Yes?"

A young woman said, "There's a police detective here asking for you."

"Um, oh," he said. "Did you get a name?"

There was an exchange of words at the other end, and then the receptionist said, "Detective Hardy?"

"Send—send her back."

He put the phone back on its cradle and thought, *Oh no.*

Albert really did not want to talk to Detective Marissa Hardy. Needless to say, he no longer needed to feign interest in some mysterious woman who'd shown up at Brie's old address. Nor did he need the detective to track down who had waved to him and his sister and Norman from the hospital parking lot.

Not important.

He rose from behind his desk and greeted the detective as she reached his office door.

"Mr. McBain," she said.

"Detective Hardy," Albert said. "Please come in and take a seat."

Hardy sat. "I'd like to offer my condolences. I didn't know, until just now, that your mother had passed. Your receptionist said I was lucky to catch you, that you'd only come in to the bank for a short period to clear up a few things."

"Yes," Albert said solemnly. "We knew it was coming, of course, but it's still kind of a shock. I mean, we were all talking to her on Saturday and she seemed, well, she didn't seem like someone who was going to go in the next day. But things can turn on a dime, you know."

Hardy nodded sympathetically. "Of course."

"But if you only just learned about my mother, that can't be why you've come in."

"That's correct," she said.

"You still asking around about our strange sighting on Saturday?"

"In part," Hardy said slowly.

"You know," he said, "I think we might have over-reacted, jumped to conclusions. And we were several floors up from the parking lot. I'm sorry if we got you involved in this for nothing."

"Not at all," Hardy said. "I always like to follow up on any lead."

"Well, okay," he said. "But honestly, I wouldn't worry much more about it."

"The reason I'm here is, I want to ask you about the Stamford Players."

"Oh?" He was genuinely surprised. If he'd ever

known the detective was interested in community theater, it was a nugget of information that he'd forgotten.

"You're the director, and author, of the upcoming
production?"

"That's true," he said. "Although just now I was
thinking about that, wondering whether we should
postpone. Unless I can get someone else to take over
the directing. There are a couple of members of the
company I might be able to call on."

Hardy nodded. "You have a Candace DiCarlo in the
production?"

Albert thought, *Oh-oh*.

"Yes, yes, we do. Very talented actress. Not a professional, of course. She has a regular day job. But like
pretty much all of us, we have theater in our blood. We
may not be ready for Broadway, but we like to have
fun."

Hardy nodded slowly.

"Was there some reason you brought up Candace's
name?" Albert asked.

"When was the last time you saw or spoke with Ms.
DiCarlo?"

"Uh, well, let me think," he said.

Albert knew exactly when he had last seen or spoken
with Candace DiCarlo. It had been the previous evening, at the Motel 6.

"Yesterday, at some point," he said. "We had a rehearsal yesterday morning, but I had to cut it short when I got the call about my mother."

Hardy said, "Hmm."

"I'm still wondering, why do you ask?"

"I think it's very possible, Mr. McBain, that your actress Candace DiCarlo is the woman you all thought might be Brie."

Albert feigned surprise. "You don't say."

"I do."

"She told you this? She confessed to it?"

"No," Hardy said. "She did not."

Albert felt a slight sense of relief. "Then what leads you to think this?"

"Her car, for one. Her Volvo wagon appears to be the same car from the neighbor's surveillance video. And there's a witness, of sorts."

"A witness?"

"Someone who recognized her from the surveillance image."

Albert said nothing.

After several seconds of silence, Hardy said, "Aren't you curious to know why she might do something like that? Get everyone to think she was Brie?"

"Well, yes, of course. If it's actually true that it was her. Have you asked her? Point-blank?"

"I would if that were possible."

"And why isn't it?"

"Because Candace DiCarlo is dead, Mr. McBain."

Albert's lips looked ready to form words, but nothing came out. He was stupefied, and his hands, resting atop his desk, began to shake.

"Are you okay, Mr. McBain?"

"I—uh—I don't understand. Candace is dead?"

"That's correct."

"What—what happened? An accident? Was she in a car accident?"

"No, Mr. McBain. She was murdered."

Albert looked as though he might choke. He put a hand to his throat and coughed. "How . . . That's impossible."

Hardy said, "I'm afraid it's not. I'm sorry. I'm assuming, given that she was part of your theater group, she was a friend."

"She—yes, she was a friend," he said. He scanned the top of his desk as though looking for something.

"Mr. McBain?"

"I need . . . I need a drink of water."

There was a plastic water bottle on the other side of his computer monitor. Hardy pointed and said, "There."

Albert found it, twisted off the cap, and took a swig.

"This is just . . . this is horrible. This is unbelievable. Who . . . what happened?"

"We have someone in custody. The thing is, Mr. McBain, it appears that her death and her little performances on Saturday are linked. I want to ask you again, why do you think she might have posed as Brie?"

"I . . . I . . ."

Albert was too shaken to speak.

"Mr. McBain, what was the nature of your relationship with Candace DiCarlo?"

"She . . . she was in our production."

"Was that the full extent of your relationship?"

He turned away from the detective, looked at his screen, the mortgage numbers blurring beyond his tears.

"We . . . we were . . . we were seeing each other."

"Seeing each other? Romantically? An intimate relationship?"

With considerable difficulty, as though there were an iron rod in his neck, Albert managed to nod. "Yes," he said.

"If you were involved romantically, is it possible Ms. DiCarlo confided in you as to why she was pretending to be Brie?"

Albert's nose twitched at the question, as though Hardy had asked him the wrong thing. She picked that up and asked, "Or maybe it was the other way around. It was your idea, something you talked her into doing."

"That's . . . that's a little closer."

The detective said nothing. Waited.

"You see," Albert began slowly, "when Candace first auditioned with the company—this current show was not her first with us—I found myself very attracted to her, and, well, we began to see each other. Quietly, secretly, because I'm still working through a separation with my wife, Dierdre."

Hardy, content to let Albert fill the silences, continued to remain quiet.

"It's been a very difficult time, you know. I mean, never knowing what happened to Brie has weighed so heavily on the family, first of all, and then these last few months my mother has been so ill. Candace, she's been the one port in the storm for me, who's supported me through this, and I noticed, at times, that there was something about her that reminded me of Brie. She's about the same size, holds herself the same way, and from certain angles she almost looked like her. She even did her hair almost the same way."

"Go on," Hardy said.

"And as we've been getting closer, and I've kind of opened up to her more, I told her how worried I've been about my mother, how she was going to die without ever knowing what happened to my sister. Whether Brie was alive or dead. Whether someone had killed her or she'd gone off and found a new life for herself, for whatever reason. I mean, the questions that tormented my mother are the same ones that have tormented Isabel and me, but maybe one day we'll get some kind of answer. It wasn't likely my mother was going to have one before she died."

Hardy slowly nodded, like she knew where this was headed.

"And so . . . I had this idea," Albert said. "What if . . . what if my mother could die with some hope?"

"An illusion of hope," Hardy said.

"Yes, that's fair," Albert said. "At one point, early on, I'd wondered about whether to send a fake letter to my mother, as if it were from Brie, but my mother's always been something of a skeptic. She worked in the news business, and she was always the type of person who needed convincing, evidence, you know? She probably made a lot of reporters' lives hell, demanding they nail down their sources, get more confirmation, that kind of thing. So I knew my mother would take some convincing when it came to tricking her into thinking Brie was alive."

"Okay," Hardy said.

"I told Candace there needed to be witnesses. People who could claim to have seen Brie. Maybe Isabel, or her husband. Or others Brie knew. Maybe even, if there was a way, for Elizabeth to see her in the hospital. But then Candace had this idea, a way of kind of kicking it up a notch."

"And what was that?"

"Well, like I said, I'd told her the whole story, including how the cops, like you, always thought it might be Andy who killed her, you know? I've never been as sure as my sister that he had anything to do with it, but Candace was, like, maybe there's a way to give my mother some peace of mind and shake up Andy at the same time. Get some idea of whether he was guilty or not by how he reacted."

"And how did she propose to do that?"

"She'd do one of her appearances as Brie on his turf—well, his former turf. Show up where he used to live. Get seen by people who'd alert him."

"Someone like . . . Brie's old neighbor. Max."

"Yes," Albert said. "Candace had this idea of showing up in her car with groceries, then freaking out that her house was gone. I'd told her that the house had been sold, torn down, a new one built on the site. I thought it was too risky, but she was getting so excited about the role, really thought she could pull it off. That she could show up, then take off before anyone could really figure out what was going on."

"That part worked," the detective said. "How about the plan to rattle Andy?"

Albert shrugged. "I guess we wouldn't really see how that part would play out. That'd be where you come in."

Hardy's nod was one of understanding, not approval.

"Anyway," Albert said, "we thought an extra appearance or two would really bring it home when it came to convincing my mother. So Candace appeared in the hospital parking lot, which would fool Isabel and Norman. More real witnesses. Then finish it off with something big, by appearing at the hospital in the middle of the night. By that point, I figured, even someone as hard to convince as my mother would believe Brie really was alive."

"Audacious," Hardy said.

"I suppose. How she got in and out of the hospital at night without being seen—I don't know how she did it. Oh Jesus, I can't believe it."

He clapped a hand over his mouth, stifling a cry. After a moment, he continued. "I think, in a way, that our mother passed yesterday because she'd found peace. She let herself go, because she believed Brie was alive. It didn't matter that she didn't know why Brie had disappeared, why she'd been missing for six years. It was enough to know that she wasn't dead."

Albert sighed and bowed his head. "Because that's what I've always believed, and still do, that she's dead. But if Mother could die believing something different, I thought that was a good thing."

"And you were saying your sister didn't know. Does she now?"

Albert shook his head. "No. And no. I didn't want anyone else to be in on the plan because they might have given it away, told Mother by accident."

"So you've given her some false hope, as well."

"I was going to explain it to Isabel later, hoping she'd understand I . . . I was well intentioned. But I don't understand. How could what we did end up getting Candace killed?"

"You let the genie out of the bottle," Hardy said. "The law of unintended consequences."

"I'm sorry?"

"You start out intending to do one thing, and end up causing something else to happen. Mr. McBain, creating the impression that Brie was still among us may have comforted your mother, but it clearly unsettled someone else."

"Last night," he said, "she told me she thought

maybe someone was following her. I think maybe she was being paranoid, on edge, you know? But before she came to the Mo—"

Hardy's eyebrows rose.

"But before she came to the Motel 6, she said she thought a car had been following her."

"Not a bicycle," Hardy said.

"A bicycle? No, a car. Why would you ask if it was a bicycle?"

Hardy shook her head. "Never mind."

And then, suddenly, Albert crumpled. He put his face in his hands, lowered his head, and began to weep.

"I loved her," he whispered. Hardy didn't know whether he was referring to his mother, or to Candace DiCarlo. Maybe both.

His body was wracked with sobs for a few moments, and then, struggling to compose himself, he raised his head and looked pleadingly at Hardy.

"We meant no harm," he said.

Fifty
Andrew

The mind can process a lot in half a second. Let's take the first half of that half second—a mere quarter of a second.

In that quarter, when I saw that it was Norman approaching Matt and me in the woods as I stood there, shovel in hand over Brie's grave, I thought: *You bastard.*

It was Norman who'd hired Matt to kill Brie.

It all made sense. No, wait, let me qualify that. It *didn't* make sense that you would kill your sister-in-law because you were afraid your wife was going to find out you had a one-night stand with her. In a sane world, that didn't make any sense at all. But the thing was, insane things happened in our sane world all the time, and looked at from that perspective, yeah, it all made sense.

Maybe Brie had decided that she *would* tell her sister, Isabel, how she had betrayed her, even though she'd made me promise never to say a word. Brie was going to confess to her sister she'd had sex with Norman.

Norman knew, and had to stop her. He had her killed not only while I was away fishing with Greg, but while he was in Boston with Isabel. The perfect alibi.

It seemed pretty out-there, I admit. But *someone* had hired Matt to kill Brie, and Norman now seemed the most likely suspect. How else did one explain Norman's arrival, at this moment, in these woods? The only explanation I could come up with, in that quarter of a second, was that Norman knew what was out here. Knew that Matt had buried Brie here. Knew that Matt was going to bring me here.

Knew Matt, period.

The possible reappearance of Brie—and I still had no idea what that was about—had unnerved Norman, and he'd clearly been in touch with Matt to ask what the hell might have gone wrong six years back.

All that thinking went into that first quarter second. The next quarter second was occupied with a more urgent thought.

This might be your only opportunity.

I guess it was more instinct than thought, because what I did at that moment when Matt turned to see who'd called out didn't require much in the way of planning. I just acted.

I brought that shovel up level, turned that curved blade, with its pointed tip, into a spear, and charged Matt.

He still had the gun in his hand, but it wasn't pointed in my direction, and when he heard me coming, closing that eight to ten feet between us, he turned back from looking at Norman to look at me, but not in time to aim.

He'd been standing there with his jacket open, and the only thing between his belly and my shovel was a flannel work shirt. And when the blade reached him, it cut through that shirt like it was made of gossamer.

"Fuck!" Matt screamed, stumbling backward as the blade sliced open his belly, creating a jagged, almost smile-like rip in his flesh.

He tripped over his own feet and hit the ground on his right side, the arm holding the gun slamming on the ground. But Matt managed to hold on to his weapon as he put his other hand to his stomach, blood seeping out between his fingers.

My attention was focused on that gun hand. In another half second, Matt could have it pointed at me.

Which was why I needed to pin that arm to the ground and wrestle it away from him.

The adrenaline was racing through me, and I wasn't about to temper my responses. Which explains, I suppose, why I came down so hard on Matt's arm with the shovel blade.

I don't honestly think it had been my intention to cut off his hand.

But I brought that blade down with enough force, and right on target, that when it connected with Matt's upturned right wrist it went right through and into the forest floor like a cleaver going through pork tenderloin. He'd already been in the process of aiming the weapon my way, but what came up was a forearm minus a hand. A fountain of blood poured forth.

His hand, still gripping the gun, lay there on the dirt.

The scream that Matt let loose was enough to send birds scattering from the trees.

"Jesus!" shouted Norman, who was still a good sixty feet away.

I then did something that, in retrospect, makes no sense whatsoever. Intending to kick the gun away from Matt's grasp, I booted it, and the hand looped around it, a good six feet away.

His screams persisted. Blood continued to flow from

his stomach and the end of his arm. It was the latter that looked more serious.

I heard another scream, and realized very quickly that it was coming from me. A kind of primal cry, some Neanderthal reaction buried deep within me. A cry of triumph, or release. Or maybe I was just losing my mind.

But I couldn't afford to lose it for long. I hadn't forgotten my first thoughts, from only seconds earlier, that Norman was in on this. And if that was true, the threat was not over.

I wanted more than a shovel to deal with Norman. And there was that gun right there on the ground. I tossed the shovel, dropped to my knees, and pried the gun from the fingers of the severed hand, all to a background soundtrack of Matt's incessant cries of pain. That man was going to die if I didn't make some effort to save him. A tourniquet on that arm.

But that would have to wait. I had Norman to deal with. I got to my feet and pointed the gun at him.

He stopped dead in his tracks and shouted, "Christ, Andrew, it's me!"

I must have looked like a crazy person to him. Wide-eyed, covered in dirt and now splattered with blood from Matt, and waving a gun around.

"I know who the fuck you are!" I shouted at my onetime brother-in-law. "Stay right there!"

"What the hell's going on?" he yelled. "Who's that—"

"Shut up! Just shut the fuck up!" I shouted.

Matt had stopped screaming long enough to crane his head in my direction and say, "I'm gonna fucking die. Help me."

"How did you know?" I asked Norman.

"How did I know what?"

"How did you find us? How did you know about this place? You knew he'd brought me here, didn't you?"

"I don't know *anything* about this place," he said, taking steps in my direction.

"Don't come any closer, Norman," I warned, pointing the gun at him.

"Andrew, what is it you think I've done?" He took another five steps toward me. "That man, who is he?"

"Like you don't know," I said. "Why? Why'd you do it?"

"Why'd I do what?" he asked.

"Why'd you hire him? Why'd you hire him to kill Brie?"

Norman's shocked look was Oscar-worthy. "What the hell are you talking about? Brie may be back! Isabel's told you. I know that. We saw her, from the hospital."

"No," I said. "She's right back there, in that grave. Don't tell me you don't know what I'm talking about."

A moaning, dying Matt had turned over to see who I was talking to. He mumbled, "Who the fuck is he?"

That threw me. Either they were both very good at playing their roles, or Norman and this man really did not know one another.

"Tell me," I said. "How'd you know about this place?"

"I told you, I didn't," Norman said. "I've been wanting to talk to you. I tried to call you the other night but you wouldn't answer. I was driving to your house, saw you drive off, and followed. Then you turned in here and I sat up by the road, waiting for you to come out. It got to be a long time and so I drove in, saw the two cars there. Something about it didn't look right. I heard some talking in the woods, and started walking this way."

I blinked several times, trying to get the grit and sweat out of my eyes. What Norman was telling me sounded almost believable.

"You have a phone," I said.

Norman nodded.

"Call 911," I said. "Much as I'd like to let this guy die, it might be useful to keep him alive."

Norman had his phone out, was tapping in the number.

"Get back out to the road, direct them in," I said.

Norman nodded, turned, and started running back in the direction he'd come from, the phone to his ear.

I knelt down next to Matt.

"You're losing a lot of blood," I said. "I don't know that the paramedics are gonna make it here fast enough. Although, one thing that might help, that would buy you some time, would be a tourniquet."

Matt, seething between gritted teeth, said, "Yeah, that might."

"I could take a lace out of my boot," I said, "and give it to you, but I'm thinking, with one hand, you might have some difficulty applying it yourself. But I could do it for you."

Blood was soaking into the forest floor.

"What do you want?" he asked.

"A name," I said. "And an explanation."

Matt closed his eyes.

I began to unlace my boot. "What do you say? I was thinking there, for a minute, that it was Norman, but now I'm not so sure. You want to clear that up for me?"

Matt swallowed, whispered, "Not Norman."

I had the bootlace half out of the eyelets. "That's

good to know, I guess. So if it wasn't Norman, who, then?"

Matt was weighing his options. I didn't see where he had much to lose here by giving up a name, but everything to gain. He was fucked, plain and simple. He could be fucked and die, or he could be fucked and live.

I almost had the bootlace out. The blood was draining out of Matt like oil from the *Exxon Valdez*. I didn't give him much longer without the tourniquet.

"What's it going to be, Matt?"

He nodded. "Okay," he said.

Matt gave me a name.

I shuddered. "Now a few details. Convince me."

Matt gave me a few details. I was convinced, if a little shaken.

I started lacing up my boot.

"What are you doing?" he asked. "You gotta tie it off."

I continued threading the laces through the eyelets until I had them back in place. I gave them a good tug, then knotted them.

"Wouldn't want to trip on the way back to my car," I said.

Fifty-One

Statement of Tyler Keeling,
April 4, 2022, 4:30 p.m.,
interviewed by Detective Marissa Hardy.

DETECTIVE HARDY: How are you doing now, Tyler?
TYLER: I didn't do anything. I know it might look like it, but I didn't.
DETECTIVE HARDY: We'll get to that.
TYLER: And I want my sister to be here.
DETECTIVE HARDY: She's probably waiting for you, but right now it's just the two of us. I understand you've come to live with your sister recently, but she has not applied for legal guardianship.
TYLER: Yeah, but she's my sister.

DETECTIVE HARDY: There's a process to these things, Tyler. Your rights were explained, right?

TYLER: Yeah, but I didn't do anything.

DETECTIVE HARDY: Then I guess we're good to go. Why don't we start with you telling me what you were doing at Candace DiCarlo's house?

TYLER: I don't even know who that is.

DETECTIVE HARDY: That's the woman who was murdered.

TYLER: I didn't murder anybody. And I knew her as somebody else.

DETECTIVE HARDY: Who would that be?

TYLER: You already know this.

DETECTIVE HARDY: Tell me anyway.

TYLER: I figured she was Brie Mason, that woman you were asking about when you came to the house on Saturday. Like I said, I saw her at the store and recognized her and wanted to ask her some questions.

DETECTIVE HARDY: What sort of questions?

TYLER: Like, what the hell was going on, basically. Was she going to come back and still be married to Andy, you know, my sister's boyfriend? Because then everything would go to shit.

DETECTIVE HARDY: So you followed her home. How'd you do that?

TYLER: On my bike.

DETECTIVE HARDY: You must be pretty fast.

TYLER: She hit a lot of red lights, so that's kinda how I kept up.

DETECTIVE HARDY: And you followed her into her house. What happened, Tyler? Did she get scared when you confronted her? Did she fight back? Is that what happened?

TYLER: I didn't go in her house. She told me to go away. She went inside and locked the door. And so then I left.

DETECTIVE HARDY: Okay. But you went back, didn't you?

TYLER: (*unintelligible*)

DETECTIVE HARDY: I didn't hear that.

TYLER: Like, maybe half an hour or so later. Yeah.

DETECTIVE HARDY: Why'd you do that?

TYLER: It was Cam's idea.

DETECTIVE HARDY: Your friend. So Cam told you to go back and kill Ms. DiCarlo?

TYLER: Fuck, no. He just said I should go back there and not leave until I got her to answer my questions. So that's when I went back the second time.

DETECTIVE HARDY: And what happened then?

TYLER: I knocked on the door again and she didn't answer. But her car was there, so I figured she was home and, like, ignoring me.

DETECTIVE HARDY: Then how did you get into the house, Tyler?

TYLER: I kinda . . . I tried the door to see if it was still locked, and it wasn't. So I opened it.

DETECTIVE HARDY: Go on.

TYLER: And, like, as soon as I stepped in it felt weird in there.

DETECTIVE HARDY: Weird how?

TYLER: I don't know. It was really quiet. The only noise was the fridge humming. I took another step in, to the kitchen, and then I saw her.

DETECTIVE HARDY: What did you see?

TYLER: She was on the floor, on her back, and at first I thought, shit, maybe she had a heart attack or some kind of seizure or something, and so I bent down real fast to check on her and didn't even see all the blood. It got on my hands and my knees and . . .

DETECTIVE HARDY: And?

TYLER: I just need a second.

DETECTIVE HARDY: Take your time.

TYLER: I sort of freaked out. All this blood was coming from the back of her head.

DETECTIVE HARDY: Did you say anything?

TYLER: Like what?

DETECTIVE HARDY: Did you start shouting?

TYLER: I might have. I was in shock, I guess. I was

totally freaked out. I've only ever seen one other dead person.

DETECTIVE HARDY: Who would that be?

TYLER: My dad. He had a heart attack shoveling snow.

DETECTIVE HARDY: So, is that when you called the police?

TYLER: What? I didn't call the police.

DETECTIVE HARDY: I know. Why didn't you?

TYLER: Well, I mean, she was . . . there wasn't anything anybody could do. She was pretty obviously dead.

DETECTIVE HARDY: Still, just about anybody would have called 911. Get an ambulance there, just in case there was something they could do.

TYLER: I guess I didn't think of that.

DETECTIVE HARDY: Why do you think that was?

TYLER: I don't know. I guess I should've done that. But at the time, I wasn't really thinking that straight.

DETECTIVE HARDY: I see. You know that doesn't look good, don't you, Tyler? Fleeing a crime scene like that?

TYLER: Maybe it wasn't. You know, a crime scene. Maybe she just fell.

DETECTIVE HARDY: Is that how it looked to you, when you saw all that blood?

TYLER: I wanted to get home. I needed to think about what I should do. I wanted to talk to my sister.

DETECTIVE HARDY: I see.

TYLER: I would never, ever do anything like that. I didn't hurt her. I didn't touch her or anything. You have to believe me.

DETECTIVE HARDY: You'd never lose your temper, maybe do something you really didn't mean to do?

TYLER: Never.

DETECTIVE HARDY: How's your aunt doing? Clara, isn't it?

TYLER: What?

DETECTIVE HARDY: How's her eye coming along?

TYLER: That was a totally different—who told you about her?

DETECTIVE HARDY: Before I came in here I got off the phone with some folks in Providence. Seems you had a little trouble there.

TYLER: It was an accident.

DETECTIVE HARDY: Just looking at the report here . . . Here we go. Smashed a glass and some shards went into her eye. That sound about right?

TYLER: I didn't throw it at her. I wasn't aiming at her. I didn't know that would happen. I tried to get it out. I took her to the hospital.

DETECTIVE HARDY: What would make you so angry that you would do something like that, Tyler? Did she provoke you? Had she thrown something at you? Was she abusive?

TYLER: It wasn't like that.

DETECTIVE HARDY: Help me understand. You'd gone to live with her after your father died, right? Was she mean to you? Demanding? Not understanding everything that you'd been through?

TYLER: She was always trying to be so . . . so nice.

DETECTIVE HARDY: I'm sorry?

TYLER: She was always worried about my feelings, like, how I was dealing with my dad, you know, dying and everything. It was like she wanted me to have a meltdown or something, like it would be a breakthrough, and I wanted her to just leave me alone.

DETECTIVE HARDY: So your aunt nearly loses an eye because she cared too much. That what you're saying?

TYLER: It makes it sound bad when you put it like that.

DETECTIVE HARDY: I guess what I'm sitting here wondering, Tyler, is, if you could get that angry with someone who was trying to help you, how angry might you get with someone who was threatening the very stability of your home situation?

TYLER: I don't . . . it wasn't . . .

DETECTIVE HARDY: What do you think might have happened if this woman had been Brie Mason? And if Andrew decided to leave your sister and resume married life with Brie?

TYLER: I don't know.

DETECTIVE HARDY: I imagine your sister would have been devastated. A lot for her to deal with. I wonder if she would have found looking after you more than she could deal with. Maybe she would have to find another place for you to live. Is that what you were thinking?

TYLER: I don't know what I was thinking. But it wasn't that. I panicked. That's why I ran. Maybe I figured that cops like you would find a way to blame me for it so I had to get out of there.

DETECTIVE HARDY: It doesn't look very good for you, Tyler. You were there. You had Ms. DiCarlo's blood on you. A witness saw you fleeing the scene. Got it on video, even. And you had a reason for what you did. You know what might help, Tyler? If you just got it off your chest. Unburdened yourself. Admit what you did. That you were overwhelmed. That you struck out at this woman, she fell and hit her head on the way down, and she died. I don't think you ever meant for that to happen. But that's the way it went down.

TYLER: I swear, I—

There is a knock on the interrogation room door. Questioning suspended.

Hardy exited the room. A uniformed officer was standing there.

"She's demanding to see you," he said.

"The sister?"

"That's right."

Hardy nodded. "With lawyer in tow, no doubt. Check in on him in there every once in a while. Get him a drink of water or something."

Hardy found her way to the police station entrance, where Jayne Keeling was sitting alone on a bench, looking at her phone. When she saw Hardy, she tucked the phone into her purse and stood.

"Ms. Keeling," Hardy said, approaching her.

"How is Tyler?"

"He's fine."

"I want you to release him," Jayne said.

"When I heard you were here I thought you might have brought a lawyer."

"You can't hold him. He's a kid."

"I'm afraid we *can* hold him, Ms. Keeling. He's the prime suspect in a homicide."

"He didn't do it," Jayne said.

"Ms. Keeling, if you love your brother, and it's obvious to me that you do, the best thing you can do for him is get him legal representation. Like I told you before."

"You don't understand," Jayne said. "That's not why I'm here."

"Why are you here, Ms. Keeling?"

"I'm here to confess," Jayne said. "Tyler didn't kill that woman. I did."

Fifty-Two
Andrew

I sat there, in the woods, until it was clear Matt was dead, then worked my way back to my car. The keys were in it. As I got in, I tucked Matt's gun into a pocket in the driver's door, turned the vehicle around, then drove back out to the main road, where I found Norman leaning up against his silver Nissan. I powered down the window.

"Ambulance should be here any second," he said.

I nodded, like there was still time. "They better hurry," I said.

"You're not leaving?" Norman asked.

"I am."

"You can't. You're going to have to talk to the police about whatever happened back there."

"They've always figured out how to find me," I said.

"Andrew," he said, coming close to the driver's window, "what the hell was that?"

"That man killed Brie. And that was where he buried her. After Saturday's events, he wanted to be sure she was still where he'd left her. Wanted me along to try and identify her." Another pause. "It's her."

"But then who—"

"I don't know who it was that you and Isabel and Albert, and my old neighbor, saw on Saturday. I still can't figure it out."

"But why . . . why did that man kill Brie?"

"He was hired to do it," I told him.

"Jesus," he said. "By who? Did he say?"

"No," I lied.

Did I catch something in his eye at that moment? Relief? No, I didn't think so. Unless Matt had lied to me in his final moments, Norman was in the clear.

Like I said, unless he lied. You reach a point where you don't believe anything that anyone says.

"So why'd you follow me up here?" I asked. "Why'd you call the other night?"

Norman took a breath. "Because of Elizabeth, in part."

I waited.

"I had some time alone with her and she wanted to

know if I'd ever shown any gratitude for what you did. Or, more like what you didn't do."

"I wouldn't have expected any," I said. "Your wife's had you and the whole family convinced I killed Brie."

He shook his head. "I was never sold on that. I mean, yeah, I wondered, but I felt you were as devastated by her going missing as the rest of us. You were Isabel's scapegoat. Someone to blame to make herself feel better. Anyway, Elizabeth said I owed you one, for never telling."

Norman let those last three words hang out there for a moment.

"I did tell," I said. "I told Detective Hardy. I told her about you and Brie."

"I know," he said. "And I don't fault you for that. And that didn't do any harm, because Hardy cleared me right away. Me and Isabel were out of town."

It occurred to me then that being out of town didn't absolve anyone, considering that Brie's murder had been contracted out.

Norman was still talking. "The big thing is, you never told Isabel. It would have destroyed her. Given how much energy she put into ruining your life, it's a wonder you didn't want to ruin hers. And, by extension, mine."

"I didn't do it for you," I said. "I did it for Brie."

"Anyway, it seemed like it was better late than never. That I thank you."

I didn't know what to say.

"But there's more, something else that's been eating me up since she disappeared," he said. "I saw her that day."

"What?"

"That Saturday, of the weekend she disappeared, I went to the house."

I blinked. This was news to me. "When?"

"In the afternoon. There was a van there. A pest control guy. When he left I went to the door and knocked. Wanted to talk to Brie, to tell her again how sorry I was about what we'd allowed to happen. It was such a stupid thing."

"You spoke to her?"

"For half a minute. She said she didn't need any more apologies, that there was nothing more to say, and she sent me away. And that was it." At this point, he bit into his lower lip briefly. "But I can't help but think, if I'd hung around, maybe I would have seen . . . maybe I could have done something. But Isabel and I were driving up to Boston later that day, and I . . . I've always wondered if I could have done more . . ."

I could understand why he might want to beat himself up, but what had happened to Brie occurred hours after he'd come to the house. I'd spoken to her that evening. Matt, before he died, had as much as said he had come in the middle of the night.

I said, "You saved my life, Norman, showing up when you did, so I think you've paid your debt, if there's even a debt to pay."

"Yeah, well."

"There's one thing you can do for me now," I said.

"What's that?"

"I need a phone. Matt, that guy, smashed mine pretty good. I got a few calls I need to make."

Norman got his out of his pocket, but he seemed reluctant to hand it over. "Just a second," he said, and did a few taps with his thumb. I had a feeling he was deleting something he didn't want me to see.

Finally, he handed it over. "Get it back to me soon as you can?"

"I will. Is there a code?"

"Twenty nineteen," he said. "My thumbprint will open it, too, but I'd kind of like to hang on to that."

His joke made me think of that severed hand in the woods.

The phone was already active when he handed it to me, so I didn't need to enter the security code. "Thanks for this," I said, then powered up the window and hit the gas.

My contacts weren't going to be in Norman's phone, so I had to actually recall Jayne's cell phone number and enter it digit by digit. I put the phone to my ear as I aimed the car in the direction of home.

The phone rang twice.

"Hello?"

I would imagine she was puzzled when she saw Norman's name or number pop up on her screen.

"It's me," I said. "It's Andrew."

"Oh my God, I've been trying to get you for hours!"

I couldn't recall ever hearing that level of panic in Jayne's voice before. "I'm sorry, I—"

"Where have you been? Why are you using Norman's phone? Are you okay?"

There'd be plenty of time later to bring Jayne up to speed on what had happened to me in the last several hours. What I needed to know now was why she'd been so anxious to reach me.

"What's going on?" I asked.

"Where are you?"

"Heading into town."

"Come straight to police headquarters. I'm talking to Detective Hardy right now."

That was not where I wanted to be. I had something else on my mind. "What's going on there?"

"They arrested Tyler for murder."

"They *what?*"

"They think he killed the woman who came to your old address."

"*What?*" I said again. This was turning into a day of nonstop shocking developments. Jayne's comment contained more information than maybe she realized. So we now knew who was in the picture? And she was dead? And Tyler had killed her?

I supposed what I'd planned to deal with next could wait.

"I'm on my way," I said.

Fifty-Three

"That was Andrew," Jayne told Detective Hardy.

"Let's find someplace to talk," the detective said, and steered Jayne down a hallway to another interrogation room. She directed Jayne to a chair, but before she sat down herself she asked whether there was anything she could get Jayne. Water, a coffee?

"Nothing," Jayne said.

The detective took a seat across from her, pulled the chair in, then sighed sympathetically.

"Do I have to sign something?" Jayne asked. "Do you want me to write it all down?"

"Ms. Keeling, you—"

"I did it. There's no way Tyler did it."

"Ms. Keeling, the evidence against your brother is

substantial. We have motive. We have opportunity. We have a witness seeing him leave the scene."

"But you don't understand, he just wouldn't do it."

Hardy offered a sympathetic smile. "I think we both know that's not true."

"It is true, he wouldn't—"

"Would his aunt say the same thing?"

That stopped Jayne for a second. Her eyes danced. "You know about Clara."

"I know about Clara. Made some calls to Providence. Know some people there. They pulled the file." Her expression hardened. "He nearly blinded that poor woman."

Jayne shook her head. "It wasn't as bad as it sounds, and it doesn't matter anyway. Because I did it." Jayne extended her wrists, inviting Hardy to handcuff them.

Hardy ignored the gesture. "So you want to confess."

"That's right."

"Don't you want a lawyer to advise you?"

"No, I don't need one. I don't care about that. I just want to see justice done. And I don't want to see an *injustice* done. That's why I'm telling you this. Tell me what I have to sign so that you can release Tyler."

"And why did you kill this woman?"

"Because . . . because I didn't want her to come back and take Andrew away from me."

"I see. Except this woman wasn't Brie Mason."

"I thought she was at the time. That she was using a different name."

"Her name was Candace DiCarlo. The neighbors had known her for years. It was something that Albert, Brie's brother, and Ms. DiCarlo cooked up."

"What do you mean? Cooked up what?"

"Those performances were designed to persuade Albert's dying mother that Brie was still alive."

Jayne was stunned. "Oh my God. That's . . . oh my God, that's insane."

"No argument. But let's get back to your confession. I can find you a pad of paper and a pen and you can write it all out for me. But a small matter to clear up first. Once we charge you, who will we release Tyler to?"

Jayne blinked. "To . . ."

"Not to you, of course. You'll be in jail, at least until a lawyer can arrange bail, if it's granted. And if your intention is to plead guilty, you could probably start your sentence right away. So, what about Tyler?"

Slowly, Jane said, "Well, there's Andrew . . ."

"Yes, Mr. Carville," Hardy said. "Presumably

he was good enough to take Tyler in because he was living with you. But once you're out of the picture, will he still want that responsibility? And let's say he does. There's still a cloud hanging over your Andrew. Brie remains missing. There's a strong likelihood she was murdered. Andrew remains atop the list of suspects. One day his luck may run out. If he's charged and convicted and sent to prison, and you're already there, what becomes of Tyler then?

"Stop," Jayne said.

"I simply want you to consider the consequences of this impulsive, no doubt well-intentioned confession you're determined to make," Hardy said.

Jayne said something under her breath.

"I'm sorry, what?"

"I'm going to have a baby," Jayne said.

Hardy sighed. "I see."

"I found out last week," she whispered.

"Do you want to give birth in jail, Ms. Keeling? Is confessing to a crime you didn't commit, to spare your brother, worth giving birth behind bars? There are facilities that will allow you to raise a baby, in the early months, while incarcerated. But is that what you want?"

A tear ran down Jayne's cheek.

Hardy said, "Maybe, if I were you, I'd be thinking of doing the same thing. You're terrified for Tyler.

But the smartest thing you can do is find him a good lawyer. Someone who can cut a good deal for him."

Jayne reached into her purse for a tissue.

Hardy pushed back her chair and stood. "You're welcome to stay here a moment while you pull yourself together."

Hardy left the room.

As Jayne finished drying her tears, she heard the ping of a text on her phone. She took it from her purse, saw that it was from NORMAN, which meant, of course, that it was from Andrew. The text read:

I'm here.

Fifty-Four
Andrew

Jayne appeared within a minute of my text, entering the police station lobby from an adjacent hallway. I could tell she'd been crying, and at the sight of me she ran into my arms and hugged me, but not before taking in my appearance.

She let go of me, gave me a one-second appraisal, and said, "My God, what's happened to you?"

I glanced down, having almost forgotten what a sight I was. My clothes were covered with grit, my face and hands smudged with soil, dirt under my fingernails. There was probably some blood mixed in with it if you looked hard enough. I had, after all, just killed a man.

"Your story first," I said. "But let's get out of here."

It was more than privacy that prompted me to find another place for us to talk. I didn't want to run the risk of Hardy seeing me like this, and having to explain. It wouldn't be long before she learned about what had gone down in those woods.

I led Jayne outside the headquarters building, a broad, one-story, drab red-brick structure with a foreboding, massive black entryway. There were no park benches around, so I led her over to my Explorer and got her into the passenger seat. I went around and slipped in behind the wheel, turning the key only so that I could put down the two front windows to let in some air.

"Talk to me," I said.

She told me about Tyler's arrest for the murder of a woman named Candace DiCarlo, as well as the pantomime orchestrated by Albert and the dead woman. That left me speechless. Albert's stupid stunt got a hit man to second-guess himself, and nearly got me killed in the process. I wanted to find him and smash his head up against a tree.

And now Tyler had been ensnared by the entire mess.

"I'm scared to death for him," Jayne said.

"They've got a witness, they know he was there, and

there's blood," I said. Jayne nodded. "Do *you* think he did it?"

She shook her head. "No," she said confidently. "He would never do that to anyone. Except . . ."

"Except what?"

"There's something I never told you. About why Tyler's aunt wouldn't look after him anymore." She told me the story. About Tyler's angry outburst with Clara, that Detective Hardy had found out about it. "I'm sorry I never told you. I should have. You had a right to know."

I didn't see where I had anything to complain about, given how much I had kept from Jayne. "It's okay. But, shit, it makes him look bad where this Candace woman is concerned. And he ran away from the scene?"

"Yes."

"Didn't call the police?"

"No."

"Christ, Jayne, forgive me, but it kind of looks like he did it."

Jayne nodded. "It looks that way, but . . ." She paused, sniffed. "I tried to confess."

"What?"

"I told Detective Hardy it was me. I told her I did it. She wouldn't believe me." Her voice briefly adopted an almost dreamlike quality. "Maybe I can still convince her."

"For God's sake, Jayne," I said, "there's got to be a better way to help him than doing something crazy like that."

"I love him," she said. "He's my brother. I was never there for him. It's time that I was."

"Listen, Jayne, I have to tell you what happened to me today. Why I'm such a mess."

She focused on me and said, "Tell me."

"I know what happened to Brie."

Her focus became sharper. "Oh my God."

I related the events of the afternoon. How Brie was murdered by a hit man named Matt, then buried in the woods north of town. How Norman showed up at the right time and that Matt was dead. I didn't get into the shoelace story, or that I got some significant information out of Matt before he died.

"Dear God, he made you dig up her grave," Jayne said, looking as though all that had happened, to both of us, in the last few hours was going to cause her to faint. "Andrew, how are you even putting one foot in front of the other? What are you doing sitting in the car talking to me for? You need to go in there and tell all this to Hardy."

"In time."

"Now that you know who killed Brie, maybe she can figure out who it was who hired him."

When I didn't say anything right away, Jayne whispered, "You know."

"I know."

"Tell her. Tell *me*."

I shook my head. "I want to be sure. There needs to be a conversation." It was time for a change of subject. "We need to find a lawyer for Tyler."

"I don't . . . I can't think of anyone."

"I hired a woman named Nan Sokolow a few years ago when Hardy was harassing me. See if you can get in touch with her."

"And what are you going to do?" But she knew. "Don't do this yourself."

"I have to."

"I don't think . . . I'm not sure I can drive. I'm a total wreck."

"I'll drop you."

She started looking in her purse for something. Seconds later, I heard the jangling of keys. "I'm not sure I locked my car."

Jayne was reaching for the door handle when I said, "I'll do it. Where are you parked?" She pointed to the far end of the lot. "Be right back."

I jumped out of the Explorer and strode off in the direction of her car. As I got closer, I saw that she'd most likely not only left it unlocked, but the driver's window was down.

When I got back to my car, Jayne said, "What took so long?" She was correct in thinking that I had been gone longer than it should have taken.

"The windows were down," I said. "Had to get in and turn the key to get them up. Engine didn't want to turn over at first."

"Oh," she said.

I started the Explorer. We hardly said a word to each other on the way. When we got back to our place and were in the driveway, Jayne said, "You really need to clean yourself up."

I didn't want to take the time for that, but she was right. I could take a shower and change into some fresh clothes in ten minutes, I was betting.

I did it in nine.

As I was getting ready to head back out again, Jayne met me at the door. "I'm going to drop Norman's phone back at his place," I said. "Can I have your cell?"

I figured, given that we were among the last people on the planet with a landline, she could use that to try and reach Nan Sokolow. Jayne got her phone and handed it over. I didn't have to ask her for her pass-code. We used the same one for both our phones.

"It's going to be okay," I said. "We're going to get through this."

She put her arms around me again. "Call me with any news."

"You, too."

I went to the car and got in. I put both cell phones in the center console—easy enough to tell one from the other. Norman had a drab brown leather cover on his, and Jayne's encasement was vivid with a floral design. I grabbed it, wanting to double-check that I could, in fact, get into it, and I did.

I must have sat out there for a few minutes, not re-alizing how much time had gone by, because finally I heard a rapping at my window and found Jayne stand-ing there, staring at me. Through the glass she said, "What's going on?"

After I'd set down her phone, keyed the ignition, and powered down the window, I said, "I think I'm in a bit of a daze. Overwhelmed. Shell-shocked, maybe."

"Come inside. I'll make us some coffee. Or make you something stronger."

"No, I've got to go."

She stepped away as I backed onto the street, stood and watched as I drove off. In my rearview mirror, I saw her step into the street and wave. I was halfway down the block when Jayne's phone rang. The caller ID was blocked.

I picked up.

"Hello?"

"Mr. Carville." I knew the voice.

"Detective Hardy," I said. "Sorry, you were probably wanting to speak to Jayne."

"No, in fact I was hoping to reach you. I tried your number and it went straight to voice mail."

"My phone's broken," I said.

"I need to see you right now."

"Sorry, I've got a lot on my plate at the moment. What's this about?"

"I think you know. Your name just popped up on another matter. Something that happened up on Wheelers Farm Road."

"Figured I might hear from you."

"There's a dead man in the woods and an open grave. I'm heading up there shortly. Meet me there."

"He wasn't dead when I left him, but he said his name is Matt," I offered. "He killed Brie. Her remains are in that grave. I think if you do a DNA test on them, that'll be confirmed. He lured me up there, made me dig her up on the off chance I might be able to say whose bones they were, and then he intended to kill me."

"But he didn't."

"No. I got lucky. Norman—Brie's brother-in-law—happened to be in the right place at the right time and created enough of a distraction that I came out of it alive."

"You killed this Matt person."

"Like I said, he was alive when I left." I was surprised how easy it was to lie about this. "I'd sent Norman to call for an ambulance. He went up by the road to wave them in. I stayed with Matt a few more minutes, talked some, then made my way back to my car and said goodbye to Norman."

"Why was Norman there?"

"He wanted to thank me."

"Thank you?"

"For never telling Isabel what I told you. For not ruining their lives when I had every reason to. You can ask him, if you want. He saw me driving out of town and followed."

"Meet me there. I'm not going to ask again."

"That's good," I said, "because I'd be getting tired of having to say no. I know who did it, Detective Hardy. I know who hired him to kill my wife."

"This Matt told you?"

"Yes."

"Why would he do that?"

"I guess he felt a need to unburden himself," I said.

"Tell me. I want the name."

"Soon," I said. "I've got a few questions to ask first."

"Mr. Carville—Andrew. Please, just meet me at—"

There she was, asking again within seconds of saying she wouldn't. I ended the call. And then, in case she could use Jayne's phone to track me, I powered it off.

I imagined she'd be putting out a description of my car. I hoped I could get done everything I wanted to do before I was spotted.

First stop was to drop off Norman's phone.

I wanted to have a word with Isabel. Who'd been up in Boston, with her husband. Far, far away when Brie was abducted and murdered.

Fifty-Five

Detective Hardy was almost at the scene when Andrew Carville ended their call.

"Shit," she said.

She saw a collection of vehicles up ahead, pulled over onto the shoulder of Wheelers Farm Road. Police cars, an ambulance. She parked her car and went to the first uniformed officer she saw, a man who didn't look old enough to have graduated from high school. Why, Hardy wondered, did everyone seem younger every year?

"Where's the guy who called it in?" Hardy asked.

The officer pointed to a man leaning up against a silver Nissan. Hardy recognized Norman from the times she had met, over the years, with his wife, Isabel. Hardy walked over to him.

"Norman, isn't it?" Hardy said.

Norman pushed himself off the car and extended a hand. "Yeah. The paramedics, then that cop over there, they told me to wait for you. The one who really should have waited is Andrew. But he took off."

"I know, but for now you're all I've got. Tell me what happened."

Before Norman had gotten very far into his story, Hardy said, "Show me," and Norman led her down the rutted road to where he had found Andrew's car—now gone—and the SUV that belonged to the other man. Hardy gave the vehicle a quick look, including opening the glove box and looking for the registration.

"Matthew Beekman," she said under her breath, and made a quick call with her cell. Once she was finished with that, she let Norman continue giving her the tour.

"I heard voices coming from up that way," he said, pointing deeper into the woods. They started making their way until a large rock became visible in the distance.

"That's where it happened," Norman said.

"Tell me what you saw."

Norman said Andrew, shovel in hand, was standing over a pile of dirt and two holes in the ground, a few feet ahead of the rock. The other man was pointing a gun at Andrew. When Norman called out, all hell broke loose.

When the gunman looked around, Andrew charged him with the shovel.

"He told me to call for help, and that's kind of all I know," Norman said.

"Mr. Carville says you followed him up here."

Norman looked to the ground and nodded. "Yes. I had some things I wanted to say to him."

Hardy waited. Norman told her he'd wanted to thank Andrew, and also wanted him to know he had been to the Mason house on the Saturday of the weekend Brie vanished.

"You never told me that," Hardy said.

Norman shrugged. "I know."

Hardy told him to go to his car and wait in case she needed to speak with him further, then made her way closer to the scene.

Matt's body had not been moved. The area had already been cordoned off with police tape, a few nicely placed trees used as anchor points for the corners. Hardy ducked under the tape and moved carefully around the scene. Studied the wound in Matt's belly, the severed hand, the liters of blood that had drained from his wounds into the forest floor. Then she had a look at the hole in the ground that revealed a hint of uncovered skeleton, a necklace that still looped loosely around the neck.

Her cell rang.

"Yes?" she said.

"Ran that name," said a man at the other end. "Matthew Beekman. Forty-one, lives in New Haven. Suspected in at least five contract hits since 2011, at least three related to ongoing investigations of biker gangs, but never charged. Did you hear about this Glenn Ford guy who bought it couple of nights ago?"

"Glenn Ford the actor? He died a long time ago."

"Some writer guy. Witness in a biker hit, hiding out up in Hartford. They think Beekman's involved in that one. Day job runs a laundromat, married, two kids. Regular family guy who makes money on the side killing people, making them disappear."

"Pull together everything you can on him and send it to me," she said, and ended the call.

Hardy looked at the partially uncovered grave, and then the forest around it. She wondered whether any of Beekman's other victims might be buried out here. She looked back at the dead hit man, and the hand that rested among the leaves a stone's throw away from the body.

"Where's the gun?" she said out loud to herself.

Fifty-Six
Andrew

While I'd been intending to make Isabel and Norman's house my next stop, something new was nagging at me that prompted a detour along the way.

I wanted to take a run by Candace DiCarlo's house. I wanted to see where it happened. A couple of minutes online, and I'd found the location. There were two police cars at the end of Rosemont, plus a van and a flatbed truck. I couldn't park near the house. I left my car more than three houses away.

I was doing a lot of thinking as I got out of the Explorer. About who had ordered the hit on Brie, and who might really have killed Candace DiCarlo.

It was all coming together for me. I was pretty sure

I knew what had happened, and I believed Jayne when she said that Tyler couldn't have done it.

An idea came to me. A long shot. Might not amount to anything. Something that, if I was going to try it, I had to make the decision right then and there. It'd either work, or it wouldn't. Time, and the thoroughness of Detective Hardy, would determine that.

I pulled on a pair of rubber gloves that had been sitting in the center console back from when we were going through the pandemic. I'd always slipped them on when I had to press all those buttons at the self-serve gas bar. They were tucked down there along with a couple of masks and a nearly empty bottle of hand sanitizer that I should have thrown out long ago. I snapped the gloves into place.

Hands in my pockets, I walked up to the house, saw the Volvo wagon in the driveway, and recognized it from the surveillance shots I'd gotten from the man who'd built the house on my old lot. That explained the flatbed truck. They were probably going to take the car away and subject it to a forensic examination.

The closest I could get to it, however, was the end of the driveway, because the property itself was marked off with police tape. The car was maybe ten feet away. A uniformed officer was standing at the end of the drive to make sure I wasn't going to cross the yellow tape perimeter.

At the side of the house was someone in one of those getups you see them wearing in the crime shows. A hazmat suit. Conferring with someone else in the house. That explained the van parked in the street. These were the so-called scene-of-crime tech guys. Even when a case looked like a slam dunk—they already had Tyler in custody—the authorities wanted their case to be airtight. No stone left unturned, and all that.

Confident that Tyler had not killed DiCarlo, I was willing to try something that might steer the investigation away from him. Muddy the waters, as it were.

"Wow, what happened here?" I innocently asked the cop standing guard.

She gave me a friendly smile. "Sorry, sir. I'm not really at liberty to provide any details."

I looked toward the end of the street. "Do you know if they're closing off Rosemont completely?"

She followed my gaze as I took my hands out of my pockets. "Don't know, sir." She turned her head back to look at me. By then my hands were tucked away again. "I'm going to have to ask you to go back to your vehicle."

"Sure thing," I said, nodding respectfully.

I was ready to go, anyway. I'd done what I'd come

to do. I returned to my truck and peeled off the rubber gloves.

I parked in front of Isabel and Norman's house, a bland two-story built in the seventies. Norman's Nissan was not there, so I figured he was still where I'd left him, no doubt enduring a barrage of questions from Detective Hardy. But Isabel's car was there.

With Norman's phone in my pocket, I went to the door and rang the bell. Isabel's eyes popped when she saw who was standing there. It wasn't like I'd dropped by to say hello very often in the last six years.

"What do you want?" she asked.

I held out Norman's phone. "First of all, to return this. It's Norman's."

She took the phone and, looking alarmed, asked, "Why do you have this? Is he okay? What's happened?"

"He's fine," I said. "I know this is not a good time, that you're probably making arrangements for your mother's service. But I wouldn't be here unless it was important. May I come in?"

I could have asked her to be my best friend and not received a more stunned expression. "Okay," she said slowly.

She directed me to the living room. I sat on a La-Z-Boy chair, resisted the temptation to kick it back into a reclined position, and waited for Isabel to take a spot on the couch opposite me.

"Where's Norman?" she asked.

I told her.

"What's he doing up there?" she asked.

"He happened to spot me up that way, maybe he thought my car had broken down or something, and got out to see whether I was okay." I paused. "The thing is, he saved my life."

"I don't understand," she said.

"Before I get to that, let me tell you why I'm here," I said. "You've made my life something of a living hell the last few years, and—"

"I've had every reason to—"

I raised a hand to cut her off. "Let me finish. In your position, I might have done the same. I'd have wanted justice for my sister. Believe me when I say I've wanted the same for Brie, but I didn't have a convenient sus-pect to focus my attention on. I was . . . directionless in more ways than one. I wanted to know what had happened to Brie but had no idea where to look. I knew I hadn't done it, but there was no way to convince you of that. So you went after me. I can't say that, over the years, I blamed you."

I took a breath and said, "I'm a little parched."

Isabel didn't move for a second, then, realizing I was

asking for a glass of water, went into the kitchen and returned with one.

"Thank you," I said. "Anyway, I don't know if the news has reached you yet, but the woman you saw from the hospital window, the woman who came to my old place, was definitely not Brie."

"Who was it?"

"A woman named Candace DiCarlo. An actress. Well, an amateur actress would be more accurate. If you want to know more about why she did what she did, you're going to want to talk to your brother."

"Albert?"

I nodded, and told her the few facts that I knew.

"Oh my God," she said, astonished. "What a complete fool. Didn't he understand that, in getting our mother's hopes up, he'd be getting *everyone's* hopes up?"

"I think it's fair to say he didn't think it all the way through," I said. "But his little charade ended up backfiring pretty spectacularly. It got someone killed." I told her that Candace was dead, but left out, for now, who'd been arrested for the crime.

"And there's more. The person—the people— responsible for Brie's death also became somewhat unnerved by the possibility that she might still be alive."

I let that sink in for a minute.

"I see," she said.

"Because Brie isn't alive. That was confirmed for me today. Someone was hired to kill her."

"Dear God," Isabel said.

"That way, Brie could be killed while the person who hired this hit man was out of town."

I watched Isabel closely for her reaction.

"Why are you looking at me like that?" she said. "What are you implying? Norman and I were in Boston. Andrew, what are you suggesting?"

"I'm not suggesting anything," I said. "I'm going to tell you what I know. Because you deserve to know before anyone else."

Fifty-Seven

Tyler had been brought back to the interrogation room where he'd been interviewed earlier by Detective Hardy. He sat at the table alone. A small bag of potato chips and a bottled water had been left for him. He devoured the chips. He hadn't had a proper meal since breakfast and his stomach had been growling.

Tyler had no idea what might happen next. He was scared.

The door opened.

A woman carrying a small briefcase entered. She looked to be about the same age as Tyler's sister. Dark hair and glasses. She was wearing black slacks and a white blouse with a black jacket over it, and when she looked at Tyler she smiled.

"Hello, Tyler," she said. "My name is Nan Sokolow. I'm going to be your lawyer."

"Hi," Tyler said nervously.

"Your sister, Jayne, has engaged my services on your behalf," Nan said, sitting across the table from Tyler. She took in his puzzled expression and said, "I'm here to help you. The first thing I want to know is, have they been treating you well?"

Tyler shrugged. "They got me these chips."

"I just want to be sure you haven't been mistreated in any way."

"They've got me here when I didn't do anything. Isn't that being mistreated?"

"That's what I'm here to talk about with you. From now on, I don't want you to say anything to the police or answer any of their questions unless I'm right beside you."

"I already answered a ton, but I didn't tell them anything bad."

"You admitted you were there. That you went into the house."

"Yeah, well, that."

She managed a wry smile. "We'll do what we can about that, but just so you understand, not another word."

"Okay."

"I want you to tell me everything you told them. And anything that you might have left out."

Tyler told his story.

"So when you left Ms. DiCarlo's house the first time, she was still alive."

"Yeah."

"And when you came back, she was dead."

"Yeah."

"And during this period you talked to your friend Cam." Tyler nodded. "How much time elapsed between your first and second visits to Ms. DiCarlo's house?"

"I don't know exactly."

"Half an hour?"

"Maybe a little more than that."

"Forty minutes?"

Tyler thought. "Probably. They took my phone, but my texts with Cam are probably there. They'd show when I was talking to him."

"Okay." Nan made a note on her yellow legal pad. "When you were at the scene the second time, when you found Ms. DiCarlo, did you get the sense that there might be anyone else in the house at that time?"

"Like, hiding?" Tyler asked.

"Yeah, like hiding," she said.

"I didn't hear anyone. But, I mean, I didn't exactly

go looking around. After I found her, I wanted to get out of there as fast as possible."

"You were in shock."

"Well, I don't know if I was in—"

"You were in shock," Nan said again.

"Yeah, okay, I guess I might have been."

Nan smiled. "Good, you're catching on. What I'm trying to work out here, Tyler, is a defense strategy, and one part of that defense is being able to prove that you weren't the only one with an opportunity to do Ms. DiCarlo harm. It looks to me that there's as long as three-quarters of an hour that someone else could have entered that home and killed that woman."

"You think?"

"Well, Tyler, if you didn't do it—"

"I didn't."

She smiled. "Of course. What I'm going to be arguing is that there was plenty of time for someone else to get into that house and kill Ms. DiCarlo. And anything you can think of, anything you might have noticed, that might suggest someone else had been in the house will be very helpful to us."

Tyler nodded slowly.

"Maybe . . . the sound of someone breathing, hiding in a closet. Or a squeak on the stairs. Someone clearing their throat really quietly. You get where I'm going here?"

Tyler nodded again. "I might . . . I might have heard something."

"And when you heard this noise, you realized, instinctively, that the killer might still be in the house, which is why you didn't call the police, and instead ran for your life."

"I guess . . . I guess that's what might have been what I was thinking."

Nan smiled. "There you go. Let me make some more notes."

Fifty-Eight
Andrew

I told Isabel I wanted to take her for a ride.

"I don't want to see my sister's grave," she said. I had filled her in on most of what had happened to me in the afternoon. "I'm not ready for that. I'm not sure I can handle it."

"Not there," I said. "Someplace else."

She shot me one wary look before we left. "What if this is a trick? What if I end up disappearing just like Brie?"

"Call or text anyone you want," I said, "and tell them you're with me. That should offer you some level of protection."

She agreed to go. Once we were in my car, she had questions.

"If you know who hired this hit man," Isabel said, "then why haven't you gone straight to Detective Hardy?"

Both hands on the wheel, I glanced her way and smiled. "She and I have something of a strained relationship, which you should understand better than anyone. Anyway, before she slaps the cuffs on this person, I want a little face-to-face time. And when you've heard the truth, maybe you'll finally be satisfied I didn't have anything to do with Brie's disappearance."

Isabel looked increasingly uncomfortable. She was quiet for a moment, then said, "I'm going to kill Albert." Her brother had tried to phone her twice in the last twenty minutes, and both times Isabel had declined the call. "What an idiot."

"I suppose," I said, trying to give her brother the benefit of the doubt, "that he thought he was doing the right thing."

"You know what the road to hell is paved with," she said.

"I do."

"Even though I did everything I could to get Hardy to go after you," she said, "I always held out some slim hope, you know? So when I saw that woman from the hospital window, pretending to be Brie, I wanted to believe. Didn't you?"

I had to think about that. "If there had been a way for Brie to get in touch, to let me know she was okay, she would have done it directly. So I was skeptical. But Albert's stunt accomplished more than he could have imagined. It might have given some false hope, but it also started off a panic."

"You know, I was always jealous of her," Isabel said. "Of Brie."

I glanced over at her, then eyes back to the road.

"She was always the prettier one, the more popular one. I wanted to be that pretty, that popular. And then she ended up with you, and I guess I became even more envious."

Wasn't expecting that.

"Handsome, skilled, decent," she said. "That's what you were. And I ended up with Norman."

"Norman's okay."

Isabel looked reflective. "I've treated him horribly," she said.

I didn't see any point arguing with that.

"Belittled him, mocked him. All I've ever wanted was for him to strike back, to stand up to me, to put me in my place. I felt like I was pushing him to be a man, and he just wasn't up to it. I don't know why he's put up with it."

"Maybe he believes he deserves it," I said.

Isabel gazed out the window. "Wherever it is we're going, are we almost there?" she asked.

"Almost," I said.

I'd been heading north on the Milford Parkway, and when we reached the Merritt Parkway I took the long curving ramp to get onto the westbound lanes. We kept going until we got to Trumbull, where I took the White Plains Road exit. I made a few rights and lefts until we'd reached our destination.

"I remember shopping here once or twice," Isabel said as we entered the lot of the TrumbullGate Mall. "I didn't know it had gone under."

I gave her the two-minute lesson on how Trumbull-Gate was typical of hundreds of malls across the country. Victims of online shopping, the collapse of anchor stores, and, more recently, the pandemic, which forced millions of people to alter their retail habits.

"The owners tried to make a go of it but they've thrown in the towel. Now they're letting various contractors pick over the remains. The retailers removed all their merchandise years ago, but there's plenty of other stuff to cannibalize. Shelving, railings, light fixtures, all sorts of stuff."

The massive lot was empty, save for part of the north

end that had been cordoned off and was full of those Hyundais.

"There's his truck," I said, pointing to a pickup parked by a false front that hid the loading docks.

I parked the car, grabbed Matt's gun, which I'd tucked into a compartment in the door, and got out. Awkwardly, I slipped the weapon into the back of my belt, then, like a true gentleman, went around to the other side of the truck to open the door for Isabel.

"What's with the gun?" Isabel asked, raising a worried eyebrow.

"Never know what you'll run into in an abandoned mall," I said, offering a reassuring smile, but Isabel did not look particularly reassured. "It's okay. I just don't want to leave this in the truck."

Then I made a trip over to Greg's vehicle, found it unlocked, and opened the driver's door. I leaned in, peered under the seat.

"What are you looking for?" Isabel asked.

"Nothing," I said, then slammed the door shut. I looked around to see if Greg's girlfriend Julie's car was here, and didn't see it. I was relieved about that.

I pointed to some nearby loading docks.

"This way," I said. I led her up a set of stairs that went up to the loading area, then found an unlocked door that took us into a cinder-block hallway. We went a short way down it to another door, and when we opened it, we were in the main area of the mall.

"I don't think I've ever met Greg," she said.

"Oh, he's quite charming," I said. "He's my best friend."

Fifty-Nine
Andrew

"Well, isn't this creepy," Isabel said.

The abandoned mall was making the same impression on her as it had on me when I'd come in here two days earlier.

She let out a minor shriek when a squirrel ran across her path. A pigeon flew by, but I didn't see any sign of that hawk this time. And I spotted a couple more sleeping bags than I did my first time here, but no actual homeless people. I figured they went out and about during the daylight hours.

We found more evidence of unauthorized visits. Used condoms, McDonald's wrappers. I knew from reading online articles that exploring abandoned sites was a popular pastime for some people. But so far, we seemed to have the place to ourselves.

Except for Greg. He was here somewhere.

"Let's head upstairs," I said. "That's where I saw him last."

We went to the escalator. I went first, testing to make sure the steps, while not moving, were at least secure. They seemed structurally sound, so I motioned for Isabel to follow me, pointing out the steps that were missing. I offered a hand since there was no rubber handrail to grab on to, and she took it with what seemed some reluctance.

When we got to the upper level I raised a finger, signaling Isabel to be quiet while I listened for sounds of work. Power tools, hammering. There was mostly silence.

One thing was different from last time. More of the railings that were designed to keep customers from plunging to the first level were missing.

"Last time I was here," I said, pointing, "he was working in that end."

Our steps, and our occasional words to each other, echoed throughout the empty space. We'd only taken a few steps when I heard an industrial grinding or cutting sound. Short, repetitive bursts. Too noisy for a cordless drill. Probably that reciprocating saw I'd seen Greg wielding the last time I was here.

I pointed, and we started walking in the direction of the sound.

We'd gone about a hundred feet, sidestepping trash, a rusted-out bicycle with one wheel, a couple of shopping carts, and a leaning, bird-shit-stained statue of P. T. Barnum, the long-dead founder of the Barnum & Bailey Circus. He was, according to the plaque that was hanging to the base by a single screw, a native of Connecticut. Right now he looked more like the toppled statue of Saddam Hussein.

We stopped in front of what was once a dollar store, faded banners advertising 50 PERCENT OFF! and ALL SALES FINAL! dangling from the ceiling. Inside, hacking away at some wood shelves, was my longtime buddy Greg Raymus.

He had on a pair of plastic goggles, but no helmet. Greg had always shunned extra steps to protect himself. There was an inch-long cigarette pinched between his lips.

He did like to smoke them down to nothing.

He must have sensed us standing there in the concourse watching him, because he took his finger off the saw's trigger, set it down, swept the goggles from his eyes, and looked in our direction.

"Hey!" he said, and laughed nervously. "Wasn't expecting to see you. At least, not till later."

He tossed the goggles and strolled out into the concourse, still holding the saw, pointing it toward the floor. It hung from his arm like some bizarre weapon designed to kill aliens. He took the inch of cigarette from between his lips and tossed it.

"Greg," I said evenly. "Thought I'd just drop by."

He looked at Isabel and said, "Have we met?"

She shook her head. "No."

"This is Isabel," I said. "Brie's sister."

Greg put on a concerned face. "It's nice to meet you," he said solemnly. "I really liked Brie."

I could sense Isabel's tenseness. She'd figured it out. Why I had brought her here, why we were talking to Greg. She was owed this. Her campaign to get justice for Brie had been genuine and heartfelt. The only problem was that it had been misdirected.

The true target was standing here in front of her.

"Where's Julie?" I asked, feeling the gun at my back, under my jacket.

"She was here a bit ago," he said. "Been gone most of the day. Just dropped off some donuts. Want one?"

"No, thanks," I replied. Casually, I said, "Matt's dead."

Greg blinked three times. "I'm sorry, what?"

"He died a few hours ago," I told him. "In the woods, where he'd buried Brie."

Greg laughed nervously. "I have no idea what you're talking about. Matt who? What woods?"

"You called him," I said. "When you thought Brie might have returned. Wondered whether he'd actually done what you'd hired him to do. Freaked him out, too. So he took me along, had me dig her up just to be sure."

"Honestly, Andy, nothing that you're saying makes any sense to me."

"But you can rest easy," I said. "He did what you paid him to do. That Brie who showed up this week was a fake. But I'm guessing you know that by now, too."

"What?"

"Did you see her by chance, too? Just like Tyler did? Followed her back to her place and killed her before you realized you had the wrong person?"

"Okay, now I'm really confused."

I had no doubt that he was. At least about the most recent accusation.

"It's only been a little while since I found out it was you who wanted Brie killed, so I haven't had long to try to figure out why, but I've got a couple of ideas," I said. "I'm guessing it had something to do with the business. Something Brie found out."

Greg said nothing, but his silence spoke volumes.

"You son of a bitch," Isabel said.

Greg licked his lips. "Look, Andy—"

"What always seemed weird, but I never really thought about until today, was how Brie encouraged me to take that fishing trip with you. She *wanted* me to spend time with you. That wasn't like her, you know? Because she was never your biggest fan. I remember her asking me what we'd talked about, when I chatted with her on the Saturday night. Like she was waiting for some specific topic of conversation to come up."

Greg's eyes were darting about, as though looking for an escape route.

"Remember that time when you kind of made a pass at her? Had a bit to drink, acted stupid. Brie told me about it, and I took your side." I shook my head regretfully. "I made Brie feel like it was her fault. Not that she'd brought it on, but that she was making too big a deal about it. I think, after that, Brie felt there wasn't anything to be gained by pointing out your transgressions. I wouldn't take them seriously."

I took a breath. "What I'm thinking is, maybe you did something else, something bad, certainly worse than patting Brie's backside. But instead of her telling me, she twisted your arm and told you to confess. And that if you didn't, she'd have no choice but to tell me herself."

Greg appeared to shrink before my eyes. His head dropped, his shoulders slumped. He kicked at a piece of debris with his boot.

"They were going to kill me," he said, barely loud enough for me to hear.

And to his obvious surprise, I said, "The bikers."

"What?"

"Matt told me a few things at the end. You ripped off some bikers."

Greg appeared to deflate. I didn't know everything, but I clearly knew more than Greg would have guessed.

"You know I was never one to say no to something that fell off the back of a truck," he said. "If something found its way into my hands, hey, I was happy to take it. Remember that VCR I scored back in the day?"

"Yeah."

"It's a habit I should have given up. Remember when I broke my leg? Said I'd jumped from some scaffolding?"

I nodded.

"That's not exactly what happened. You know Beaver Meadow Road?"

"Vaguely."

"South of Middletown? Nice stretch of road through the Cockaponset State Forest, east of Route 9, on the way to the Connecticut River. Remember that old MG

I used to have? The convertible? Got it for a song because it wasn't in the best of shape? And didn't keep it long because I couldn't afford the repairs?"

"Yeah," I said.

"I was taking it for a spin up that way. On my own, riding along behind this biker guy. A Harley, handlebars up in the stratosphere. A fucking deer runs into the road and he swerves and wipes out. I pull over, you know, see if he's okay, and he's out cold. So I put in a call, 911. Didn't give my name, just told them where to send an ambulance."

I wanted him to move it along, but I'd waited six years to hear this. I guessed I could wait a little longer.

"Anyway, I finish making the call and I notice this satchel the guy'd been carrying. It's kind of opened some, and there's some cash that's spilled out. A lot of cash. I mean, like a hundred grand in cash, although I didn't know it was that much until later, when I counted it."

"Jesus," I said.

"The guy's still unconscious, the ambulance hasn't arrived yet. And there hasn't been another car along that stretch for a while, but you never know when one's gonna show up. So I had a decision to make, right?" He paused. "I made the wrong one."

"Did the guy live?" I asked.

"Yeah, he made it. I guess he'd made some kind of drug delivery and was coming back with the cash when he wiped out. He'd been ripped off but it wasn't like he was going to tell the cops. But he and his buddies figured it had to be whoever made the 911 call."

"You didn't leave your name, but there was a record of your number."

Another nod. "I don't know how they got it, but they did. And once they had the number they were able to track me down. Paid me a little visit. I hadn't spent much of the money, just a few hundred. Gave it back, but my apology didn't cut it."

"That's when they broke your leg."

"Yeah. Held me down, went at it with a sledgehammer."

Isabel winced, but there was no sympathy in her eyes.

"They weren't done. They said, you rip us off, you pay us back double. They wanted another hundred grand. Or the next time, we hammer your skull, they said."

"You could have gone to the police."

Greg rolled his eyes. "Yeah, tell them I ripped off some bikers, could you help me out? And if they had someone inside who could trace my call to 911, maybe they had someone inside who'd tell them I'd tattled."

"The hundred grand," I said slowly. "Let me guess. This is around the time we started losing all those jobs."

Greg grimaced. "This is hard to talk about."

I waited, feeling the gun at my back like it was a huge stone in my shoe.

Greg moved the reciprocating saw from one hand to the other. It had to be getting heavy. "Believe me when I tell you I never wanted to do this. I felt sick about it, still do. It was a shitty thing to do. At the time, I didn't see any way out, you know?" He paused, then said, "I sold us out."

"How?"

"I went to our competitors. Leaked our bids, allowing them to undercut us, even offer more for less."

"And they paid you off," I said.

He nodded. "They were big projects. It was worth it to them, slipping me twenty or thirty thousand to get those jobs. They'd recover it all on the back end. I fucked us over on enough bids to get almost all of it, then sold the MG to get the rest. I got the hundred grand I needed to keep the bikers from bashing my head in."

"You destroyed our company. All that we'd worked for."

He broke eye contact with me, and when he did I took a second to adjust the gun at my back so it wasn't digging in quite so uncomfortably. Greg might have missed it, but Isabel didn't.

I couldn't believe he'd done this to us, sabotaged our entire enterprise, and yet I knew there was an even greater betrayal to be told about.

"You could have come to me," I said. "Told me the trouble you were in. Figured a way out of it. You didn't have to sell us out."

"And what would you have done?" he said. "Were you going to pull a hundred thousand bucks out of your ass? Huh?"

I shook my head sadly and said, "Why don't you get to the part where Brie found out."

Sixty

Jayne was in the kitchen when the phone rang.

She'd been holding one of the cordless receivers that was linked to the household landline, given that Andrew had taken her cell phone with him. She'd been hoping he'd call, tell her more about what he planned to do. He'd been vague about his intentions when he'd left. Wanted to drop by Isabel and Norman's house to return his phone, he'd said. But she knew he had much more on his mind than that.

She suspected—no, *feared*—he'd gone to confront whoever it was who'd hired that man to kill Brie.

She'd wanted to think Andrew had more sense than to take the law into his own hands. She'd wanted to think he'd go straight to Detective Hardy with whatever information he had. But what she wanted him to do, and what she believed he would do, were two entirely different things. And she understood why he wouldn't have wanted to go to Detective Hardy, who had hounded him for six years.

So when the phone in her hand rang, she thought it might be him. She hit the button and put the phone straight to her ear.

"Yes?"

"It's Nan Sokolow."

"Oh God, yes, yes, thanks for calling. Are they going to let you in to see Tyler?"

"I've been," she said.

"How is he? He must be terrified."

"He's okay. Look, they have a strong circumstantial case against him, but I'm working on a strategy. An alternative way that things could have happened. That Tyler ran because he was in shock, that he thought the killer was still in the house."

"But you believe him, right? You know he couldn't have done it."

"Ms. Keeling, it doesn't matter to me whether he did it or not. What matters is that we build a credible defense for him. It's going to take some work."

Jayne could hear it in the lawyer's voice, that she believed her brother really had killed Candace DiCarlo.

"But what if—"

Before Jayne could complete her question, the doorbell rang.

"I have to go," Jayne said. Still clutching the phone, she ran to the front door, opened it, and found Detective Hardy standing there.

"Where's Andrew?" she asked.

"I don't know," she said.

"He took your phone," the detective said.

"Yes."

"And he's turned it off," Hardy said. "I can't reach him, can't track him. You must have some idea where he was going."

"I don't. I wish I knew."

"Did he tell you he thought he knew who was responsible for Brie's death?"

Jayne hesitated before answering. "Yes."

"Did he tell you who it was?"

"No."

"Do you have a guess?"

"No."

"What was his state of mind when you last saw him?"

"Seriously?" Jayne asked. "A man took him into the woods and made him dig up his own wife. What would your state of mind be?"

Hardy sighed in frustration and turned to look at the

street. When she spun back around to face Jayne, she said, "We have to find him. If he calls you, you have to let me know where he is."

"Please, God, tell me you still don't think he killed her? Tell me you're not still after him for that."

"No, I don't think he's killed anyone. Not yet. But I want to stop him before he does. I think he's armed. I think he took the gun from that man who made him dig up his wife's grave. We have to stop him before he does something stupid."

Sixty-One
Andrew

G reg said, "You remember there was a while there when Brie was helping us out in the office."

I remembered. It wasn't the fanciest headquarters. It was an office trailer, white metal, a few windows, a basic bathroom, with all the architectural charm of a kid's playhouse made out of a refrigerator's cardboard delivery carton. We had leased it and set it up on a vacant lot in Milford's west end, hoping one day to construct something more permanent. We were really busy, putting together all those bids for several jobs— the ones I now knew we'd lost because of Greg—and Brie, who was good with numbers and putting together proposals, had come in for a week or two to get us organized.

"Go on," I said.

"We were both out at a site when a call came into the office, from one of our competitors. Dumbass called the office instead of my cell. Brie took the call. Recognized the name on the caller ID as the company we most wanted—well, that you most wanted—to beat for the Wilkins job, that auto repair shop we were going to build. Brie asked if she could take a message and the guy, flustered, hung up, but not before he'd said the meeting was all set."

"She knew something was up," I said. "We'd already lost the Frampton job."

Greg nodded. "Yeah, the condo thing." He shook his head. "Brie figured something was up, followed me. Saw me meet with the guy, saw him pass me an envelope. She, uh, she confronted me about it later. Said she wouldn't tell you, that I had to man up, tell you myself. And if I didn't, she would."

"The fishing trip," I said.

"Yeah."

"But you had no plans to confess."

"I . . . I couldn't. And hear me out, okay? I was . . . I was thinking of you."

"Really."

"If I'd confessed, you being kind of a Boy Scout and all, you'd insist on going to the police. The whole thing would unravel. They'd have killed you, too. I couldn't let that happen. That's why I'm telling you all this, so that maybe you'll understand. I did something awful, but at least they didn't kill you."

My cheeks felt hot. It felt as though my eyes were filling with blood, that I was looking at Greg through a red filter.

Just shoot the fucker now.

No, I couldn't do that. Not yet, anyway.

"I explained the situation to them. They recommended someone, this Matt guy."

"He did it while we were at the cabins," I said. "You knew it would happen. You had her killed, and then let the world think I'd done it."

"Yeah, but you were *alive*," Greg said.

"And when that fake Brie showed up this week, it freaked you out."

Greg nodded. "I called him, asked him if somehow he'd fucked it up." He looked at me pleadingly. "Would you at least give me a head start?" he asked.

"No."

"I know you're going to turn me in. I get that. Even an hour. Give me a chance to pack a bag, you know. Say goodbye to Julie. I know you won't believe this, but it's been eating me up for years." He paused. "You're the best friend I've ever had."

I had no reply for that. But I had one last question. "Tell me about Candace Di—"

Before I could get out my question, Isabel let out a cry. The homeless man who'd made an appearance my last time here was making his way toward us, and his entrance into the scene had startled not just Isabel, but all three of us.

"Hey," he said, looking at Greg.

Greg glanced nervously at him. "Not now, Neil," he said.

But Neil kept coming. "I saw your girl come in with a Dunkin's box." Neil, for the first time, focused on Isabel and me. "Some kind of meetin' going on?"

Greg raised the saw as if it were an actual weapon, using his other hand to steady it. He gave the trigger a quick squeeze. The sound it made was as intimidating as the blade that jutted back and forth at high speed.

"Fuck, fine!" Neil said, backing away.

Greg squeezed the trigger again, holding it this time, and lunged toward me. That high-speed blade, designed to cut through just about anything, would do some serious damage if it reached me. I quickly sidestepped, reaching for the gun at my back at the same time.

But I fumbled it.

The gun clattered to the floor.

"Shit!" said Neil.

Greg wasn't sure whether to go after the gun or keep coming after me with the saw. He settled on the latter, squeezing the trigger in short, menacing bursts.

There was the sound of a shot, like a cannon going off in the mall's cavernous concourse, the echo bouncing off the walls and the shattered glass ceiling.

Isabel had grabbed the gun and fired it wildly, effectively getting Greg's attention, but missing him by a mile.

"Stop it!" she screamed. "Put it down!"

She pulled the trigger again, the recoil throwing her arms upward. Greg tossed the saw and started running in the direction of the closest deactivated escalator.

He wasn't the only one running for his life. Neil, who clearly had no idea who the good guys and the bad guys were here, had figured the only thing to do was get the fuck out of there.

Isabel looked like she wanted to get off another shot, but Greg and Neil were on intersecting flight paths, and she clearly didn't want to take out the homeless guy, although with her aim I had a sense we were all safe except maybe for some pigeons roosting up near the overhead windows.

Greg was still headed for the dead escalator, but Neil had some other destination in mind, and ended up sideswiping Greg, who lost his balance and began to stagger.

toward the railing. He reached out for it to stop his fall, but instantly realized his mistake.

The bolts that held the railing to the floor were either shot or not there at all, and the railing gave way like it was made of nothing stronger than toothpicks.

Greg went over the edge and disappeared, his lungs bellowing out a loud, "Fuuuck!" as he went down.

Isabel screamed.

I was running.

I reached the escalator and descended the steps two at a time, careful to navigate the gaps where steps had been removed, and hit the lower level, my heart pounding. I had to backtrack past a few empty storefronts until I reached Greg, on his back, one leg twisted around so impossibly that it was almost up to his ear.

"Greg," I said, getting down on my knees.

He turned his head a fraction of an inch to look at me, tried to move his lips.

Isabel made it halfway down the escalator, then stopped and watched.

"Greg," I said again. "Hang in there. Just for another minute. We're not done. I've got one more thing to ask you about, and it's really, really fucking important."

I asked him my question and put an ear close to his lips to hear what he had to say.

Tuesday

Sixty-Two

Statement of Isabel McBain,
April 5, 2022, 1:10 p.m.,
interviewed by Detective Marissa Hardy.

ISABEL: Am I going to be charged with murder? Because I didn't kill him. I admit I shot at him, I admit that. But I didn't hit him. I didn't get anywhere close to him. I'm a terrible shot, evidently. It was the homeless guy. He bumped into him.

DETECTIVE HARDY: You're correct, you didn't shoot Mr. Raymus.

ISABEL: Not that I wouldn't have been happy to do it. He did it, you know. I mean, not with his bare hands. But he did it. He had Brie killed.

DETECTIVE HARDY: We know.

ISABEL: I was wrong about Andrew. I feel terrible about what I put him through. I just . . . I was so sure for so long.

DETECTIVE HARDY: I know. I thought so for a long time, too. But we've pretty much nailed down what happened and why. Your statement from our earlier interview corroborates what Mr. Carville told us. About how Mr. Raymus was sabotaging his own company. The bikers, the whole thing. And this hit man that he'd hired, we've connected him to some other homicides, including one as recent as last week. That all pans out.

ISABEL: It's over, isn't it?

DETECTIVE HARDY: Pretty much. But there's one part of what happened at TrumbullGate that I want to go over with you again.

ISABEL: Okay.

DETECTIVE HARDY: Starting with the moment that you fired the gun and Mr. Raymus started to run.

ISABEL: He was going at Andrew with this crazy-looking saw and Andrew tried to get the gun out but it fell and I grabbed it. I think I'd fired twice and then Mr. Raymus dropped the saw and ran. He bumped into this homeless man and reached for the railing and it gave way and he went over the edge.

DETECTIVE HARDY: And Mr. Carville went after him?

ISABEL: That's right. He ran down the escalator. It wasn't working, you know, because the mall's being torn apart. He got to the bottom and ran over to where Mr. Raymus fell.

DETECTIVE HARDY: You witnessed this?

ISABEL: Yes. I went partway down the escalator to get a better look.

DETECTIVE HARDY: What did you see?

ISABEL: Andrew was kneeling over Mr. Raymus and asking him questions.

DETECTIVE HARDY: Were you able to hear this conversation?

ISABEL: Some of it.

DETECTIVE HARDY: What did you hear?

ISABEL: Andrew asked about Candace DiCarlo. He said, "What about Candace? Did you kill her, too? Were you following her?"

DETECTIVE HARDY: And what did Mr. Raymus say?

ISABEL: He was mumbling. He was hurt pretty bad. Andrew had to bend over to hear him.

DETECTIVE HARDY: So what *did* you hear?

ISABEL: First I heard Andrew ask him if he'd done it. And when he heard the answer, he asked why. Like, did you spot her by chance? Did you think she was Brie when you killed her? Something like that.

DETECTIVE HARDY: And then what?

ISABEL: Andrew said something like, you son of a bitch. Like that. I didn't hear anything else because I went down the escalator to join Andrew, and by the time I got there Mr. Raymus had died.

DETECTIVE HARDY: What did Andrew say?

ISABEL: He didn't say anything. When he realized Mr. Raymus was dead, he just sat on the floor, put his head in his hands, and started to cry. He was shaking, like he was having a panic attack or something. I got down and put my arm around him and tried to calm him down. He was a wreck, you know?

DETECTIVE HARDY: He'd been through a lot. It was a hell of a day for him.

ISABEL: It really was her, wasn't it?

DETECTIVE HARDY: Sorry?

ISABEL: Not talking about Candace. Brie, I mean. In that grave.

DETECTIVE HARDY: We exhumed her remains, and yes, we did a rush on the DNA test. Compared it to samples we retrieved from her home six years ago. It was a match.

ISABEL: We can have a proper funeral now. Give my sister the send-off she deserves.

DETECTIVE HARDY: Do you think that will help at all?

ISABEL: I doubt it.

Statement of Andrew Carville,
April 5, 5 p.m.,
interviewed by Detective Marissa Hardy.

DETECTIVE HARDY: Thanks for coming in again, Mr. Carville.

ANDREW: No problem.

DETECTIVE HARDY: I spoke to Isabel earlier and thought I'd bring you in and get you up to speed on a couple of things. How's Tyler doing?

ANDREW: Glad to be home. It's going to take him a while to get over the things that happened, but I think he's going to be okay. He still has his job at Whistler's, so he's pretty happy about that.

DETECTIVE HARDY: And Jayne?

ANDREW: This has been pretty hard on all of us, but she's coming along. She's expecting, you know.

DETECTIVE HARDY: I know. Please pass on my best wishes.

ANDREW: I will.

DETECTIVE HARDY: I spoke to Isabel again about what went down in that abandoned mall.

ANDREW: It wasn't her fault, what happened to Greg.

DETECTIVE HARDY: I agree.

ANDREW: That's good.

DETECTIVE HARDY: I'd say if it's anyone's fault, it's

yours. You should never have confronted Mr. Raymus alone. He might still be around today to stand trial for what he did if you hadn't done that.

ANDREW: I . . . I'm not going to argue the point.

DETECTIVE HARDY: I wanted to get her take on the last few words you had with Mr. Raymus. I wanted to see how they matched up with what you told me in our earlier interview. That he as much as confessed to the murder of Candace DiCarlo.

ANDREW: And?

DETECTIVE HARDY: They did.

ANDREW: I had a lot more questions for him. But he died before I could get to them. Like how he got on to that woman. I'm guessing it was by chance, the way Tyler happened to see her when he was packing her groceries. In some ways, Milford's not that big of a place. You're always running into someone you know or recognize.

DETECTIVE HARDY: Albert says she thought she was being followed the night before. Maybe she was, maybe she wasn't. But if she was, maybe that was Mr. Raymus. Although his girlfriend, Julie, says she was with him that entire evening. But back to what happened at the mall. It's a wonder the fall didn't kill him instantly.

ANDREW: It didn't take long. I never really found out whether he killed Candace because he thought she was Brie, or what, but . . .

DETECTIVE HARDY: There's some things we'll never know. But we know enough to close the file on this. While there weren't any witnesses to his arrival at Ms. DiCarlo's house—pretty much everyone who lived on that street was at work, with the exception of Ms. DiCarlo's retired neighbor—we've been able to tie him to the scene.

ANDREW: You have?

DETECTIVE HARDY: I can't really get into all that right now, but we're satisfied. Let's leave it at that.

ANDREW: Okay.

DETECTIVE HARDY: So, I wish you all the best. I hope, should our paths ever cross again, it's under very different circumstances.

ANDREW: Agreed.

One Week Later

Sixty-Three
Andrew

We gave returning to a normal life our best shot.

Jayne went back to her job, Tyler still had his, and I went back to seeing those people who were hoping to hire me that I never got to that day Matt took me into the woods and made me dig up Brie.

Each of us had something to get over. Tyler's wrongful arrest and the memory of discovering that poor dead woman didn't appear to be having any long-term traumatic effects, but Jayne and I were both worried about what might be going on under the surface. In many ways, he seemed like a different kid. He wasn't getting into any more trouble, and had ended his friendship with Cam. He'd also picked up a second part-time job. Well, not a paying gig. He went to the people who maintain the nearby cemetery and said he wanted to do some volunteer work. Cutting grass, weeding, that kind of thing. Didn't want any money for it.

Jayne didn't want to smother him with concern the way his aunt had done after their father's death, but she suggested he might want to talk to a counselor about what he went through, and he seemed open to the idea.

And Jayne's pregnancy was going well. She was ever so slightly starting to show. No bleeding, and no morning sickness, at least so far. She'd been to see the doctor, who was pleased with her progress. An ultrasound was conducted, and I was in the room as the doctor rubbed that gadget across Jayne's jellied abdomen and we looked at the blurry image on the screen of the baby that would one day join our household. The doctor wasn't quite sure about the sex, and that was okay with us. We were happy to be surprised when the big day came.

And I'm coming to terms with Brie's death. After six years, I know what happened. I can now, officially, mourn her passing.

So that's the good news.

Jayne hadn't been sleeping well. At first I thought it was the pregnancy, but it was clearly more than that. It was stress, and trauma. She was, of course, relieved that Tyler'd been released, that no charges had been filed. We even had a little celebration one night. Ordered in pizza, got a cake. But her mood darkened as the days passed. She tossed and turned in the night. I'd try to engage her in conversation and she'd say nothing, as though she hadn't even heard me.

The truth was, I knew what had to be on her mind, but I didn't want to press her. But when she spent time standing at the front window, as though expecting someone to arrive, I had a pretty good idea what she was thinking.

She was waiting for Detective Hardy.

Tyler had noticed that something was off with her, too. He went up to her a couple of days ago, put his arms around her as she watched the street.

"It's not going to happen," he told her. "They're not coming back to get me."

One night, after we had both gone to bed and the lights were off, I could sense that she was awake. I rolled over, saw her lying on her back, eyes open, staring at the ceiling. I had a feeling that she was finally ready to talk about it.

"I know you're lying," she said.

"Shh," I said. "Don't worry about it."

"I know that everything you told Detective Hardy was bullshit."

"Not everything," I told her.

"I know Greg never confessed to you before he died."

"Everything he told Isabel and me turned out to be true," I said.

"Not that stuff. I'm talking about his so-called Candace DiCarlo confession."

Of course she knew it was bullshit. She knew it was bullshit because she had killed Candace DiCarlo. Her rush to confess to Hardy, to spare her brother, had been genuine. Hardy, confident that Tyler was the killer, wouldn't listen to a word she had to say.

But I knew, very soon, that Jayne's admission was the real deal.

I knew, or at least strongly suspected, as much when I got to the police station and went to lock up her car before driving her home. When I opened the door I saw the blood on the brake pedal and the accelerator. There was even a little on the steering wheel. I found a rag tucked down between the seats and did my best to wipe it all away, and took the rag with me.

Later, when I left the house to head to Isabel's, I had borrowed Jayne's phone so that I could return Norman's. But there was actually something I wanted to check.

The app that Jayne used to track Tyler worked both ways. It recorded Jayne's location history, and a quick review of the app revealed Jayne had been to the Di-Carlo house between the time Tyler first arrived and the time he went back. She'd probably been worried about him, had been checking to make sure he was really at Whistler's and wasn't just skipping school to get into mischief.

When she discovered he'd fled work and ridden his bike across town, she must have wondered where he'd gone.

So she decided to find out for herself.

And met Candace DiCarlo.

I'd thought that maybe, just maybe, there was a way to save her from this. I already knew by that time that Greg had hired a hit man to kill Brie. Was there a way to pin DiCarlo's murder on him, too? Or at least cast enough suspicion his way to have Tyler freed?

So I went to the crime scene that day.

Before I got out of my truck I donned those gloves and picked up the cigarette butt Greg had let fall down by my feet when he talked to me through the driver's-door window that morning when he came by the house to see me.

I distracted that cop who was guarding the scene long enough to flick that butt—rich with Greg's DNA—off the bottom of my thumb with my middle finger onto the driveway by the Volvo wagon. My nervous habit finally had a practical application. I prayed that the guys in the hazmat suits would find it.

Evidently, they did.

When Isabel and I arrived at the deserted mall, I tucked that bloody rag—loaded with, presumably, DiCarlo's DNA—under the seat of Greg's pickup truck.

I knew what Hardy was referring to when she said they had been able to connect my former best friend to the scene.

Sometimes, long shots pay off. There were a hundred ways it could have gone wrong, but we'd won the lottery. The thing was, when I left those woods with Matt's gun, I had in my head that I would kill Greg. As the afternoon progressed, and it became clear to me what had happened with Candace DiCarlo, a plan began to take shape that would make it even more important that Greg died. I would concoct a confession from him that he'd never be able to retract. If I ended up getting charged and going to jail, so be it. At least I'd have been able to save Jayne and Tyler.

And Greg did die. It just didn't happen the way I thought it would.

Jayne would know my story to Hardy was a total fabrication, but I was naïve enough to think maybe she'd see that things had worked out in the best possible way. That she'd relax, move on.

And so there she was, standing at the window every day, waiting for Detective Hardy to come and take her away.

In bed, staring at the ceiling, she whispered, "You made it up. Everything you told Hardy about what Greg supposedly said to you, you invented it."

I whispered, "Hardy's happy. She's satisfied. Isabel backed up my story. It worked. It's over. Case closed."

"Not for me. I have to live with this. I tried to do the right thing. I told her I'd done it. She didn't believe me, but she'd believe me now."

"You can't tell her. Not now. If you did, you could go to prison. For making up that confession, I could go to prison, too. And for planting evidence." I explained to her what I had done with the cigarette butt and the bloody rag. "And what about Tyler? And our child?"

Jayne thought about that. Weighing everything.

Her voice breaking, she said, "I didn't mean for it to happen. She came to the door, didn't know who I was, and I . . . I forced my way in. It was . . . I want to say it was an accident, but I pushed her. I thought—I believed when I got there that it really was Brie, with some new identity, and I told her I knew who she was and she was not going to ruin our lives, that she had to leave us the fuck alone, and—"

"Stop," I said, encircling her with my arms. She was shaking. "I don't need to know."

"And she started screaming at me to get out of her house, that I had no idea what I was talking about, and she came at me, and I shoved her back, even harder, and she hit her head on the counter, and then—"

I kept holding on to her, hoping that if I did it tightly enough she would stop trembling.

"I couldn't believe she was dead. I tried to wake her up, and then . . . then I guess I just panicked and I got out of there, and I had no idea Tyler was going to go back there, that someone would see *him*, but no one ever saw *me*, and—"

"Shh, shh," I said, and, slowly, her trembling eased and she turned and put her arms around me.

I wasn't going to judge her. I'd killed one man and watched him die. And I had been prepared to kill another.

But just as Tyler had been given a second chance when he came to live with us, this was our second chance.

We had to accept the things that we had done, accept that there was no way we could undo them, and accept that any attempts to set things right would only bring about greater heartache.

This was as good as it was going to get.

"We're going to be okay," I whispered into her ear. "Everything's going to be fine. We're going to have a baby."

Jayne looked at me, and, even in the midnight light, I could make out a tear running down her cheek. I wiped it away with my thumb.

Acknowledgments

I had help. Lots of help.

The folks at HarperCollins, in the United Kingdom, the United States, and Canada have had my back every step of the way.

Once again, HarperCollins editors Jennifer Brehl (New York) and Kate Mills (London) worked their magic to whip this book into shape. As always, I am in their debt.

Over in the UK, I am also supported immensely by Charlie Redmayne, Lisa Milton, Claire Brett, Joe Thomas, Alvar Jover, Georgina Green, Rebecca Fortuin, Anna Derkacz, Rebecca Jamieson, Angie Dobbs, and Halema Begum.

In the U.S., I am grateful to Liate Stehlik, Nate Lanman, Pam Barricklow, Ryan Shepherd, Bianca Flores, Jennifer Hart, David Palmer, and Dave Cole.

In Canada, a big thank-you to Leo McDonald, Lauren Morocco, Cory Beatty and Sandra Leef.

And I'd be nowhere without my terrific agent, Helen Heller.

Finally, the biggest shoutout goes to booksellers and readers. Thank you, thank you, thank you.

(Thanks also to John Aitchison, whose invaluable help with *Find You First* somehow went unrecognized.)

Until next time.

P.S. I set this book in 2022, and the storyline suggests that the COVID-19 pandemic is more or less behind us by that time. But as I was writing the novel, we were still in the thick of it. Let's hope my prognostication is on the money. I have my moments of being uncharacteristically optimistic.